The Feather
and the Stone

To Mike with Thanks

Joe St Clair

March 2022

Cover Art: Olivia Dudman

Library of Congress Cataloging-in-Publication Data
St Clair, Joe
The Feather and the Stone
1. New Age 2. Spirituality

ISBN: 978-1-8381666-6-3 (paperback)
ISBN: 978-1-8381666-8-7 (Kindle)
ISBN: 978-1-8381666-9-4 (ePub)

Pecoraro Sullivan Publishing Company
www.PSpub.Co

The Feather and the Stone

JOE ST CLAIR

PECORARO
SULLIVAN

Other Books by Joe St Clair

100 Tips for Total Life Fulfilment
The Seven Stages of the Soul
The Path to Indra

*This book is dedicated to
all those children of the Sixties
who started out on the journey and
got lost somewhere on the way.*

Author's Note to Readers

'The Feather and the Stone' was first written in 1986 and apart from one or two small editorial improvements, it remains the same today as the original. The whole book emerged from a vivid dream that I initially recorded in a notebook immediately after waking - and then fleshed out into a novel format over the following two or three weeks while the dream remained fresh in my mind. At the time, I did not attempt to analyse or rationalise the content of the dream or the manuscript. The words of the novel flowed easily onto the page as though directed from an external source and as if the words were a message not only for myself, but also for the benefit of every individual reader. I knew intuitively this book was important, but the contents were so much of a mystery to me at the time that, once completed, I simply put the manuscript into a folder and shut it away in a drawer where it has remained untouched for over thirty-six years. The novel was never written for publication, and I considered it to be a very private document that, in later years, I hoped I may come to better understand.

Fast forward to 2021 and how the world has changed since my early days as a young, aspiring trainee in a financial company! I now have a word for my 1986 'dream' that perfectly sums up and explains the phenomenon. I now believe that what I experienced was some kind of 'spiritual download'. In other words, it was not actually a dream at all. Instead, it was a unique and directed series of revelations that were imparted to me via my subconscious and designed to provide me with specific insights and learnings that I needed to fully understand. I began to realise that I had not just 'written a novel' - I had also put into words a story with a number of important and significant messages that I needed to share with others.

After sharing the manuscript with a few trusted friends - who have all actively encouraged me to publish the novel in book form - I now feel ready to share this dream-story with a wider audience. Today, thirty-six years after first writing the novel, I am better able to reflect on the messages embedded within the story and to understand why the dream I had so many years ago was effectively a sort of spiritual guidebook. These messages have served to not only determine my own life path and philosophy but have also assisted me enormously on my own life journey of discovery.

Today, my intuition tells me that the time has finally come to blow the dust off that old manuscript and convert it into a published book. When I first read my completed manuscript, back in the winter of 1986, I did not really comprehend the enormity of the messages it contained. Perhaps it was because I was too young or too naïve. Now, many years later and with the benefit of age and experience, I realise that 'The Feather and the Stone' is much more than just a novel. It is a story that needs to be shared with all souls travelling on this journey we call life.

I hope you enjoy reading it.

Joe St Clair
Autumn 2021

Prologue
Aurangabad, India, 1849

When he finally died, they mourned for weeks.

He'd known that they would of course, but it still saddened him.

It wasn't so much the professional mourners hired just for the occasion - they meant nothing to him.

It was the others - the genuine ones - the ones he had loved so much during his short life that he felt for.

He would miss them.

The funeral was beautiful and he wept. The temple had been cleaned so thoroughly that not a single cobweb remained and the numerous golden objects placed reverently on the small stone platform had been polished so brightly that it seemed each one had been fashioned from a molten teardrop fallen from a grieving sun. Fresh flowers, still moist with morning dew, lay scattered across the cold foot-worn stones, their intoxicating perfume mingled with the sweetly spiced aroma of hand-rolled 'champa' incense. It was a smell he knew well from the times he had helped his mother prepare the spices before they were bound by sandalwood resin onto short bamboo sticks in readiness for lighting as a gift to the gods.

The rough-hewn granite walls, smoothed over the years with a mixture of rice and cow dung coated in lime, were adorned with symbols and pictures written in cinnabar and ochre, each motif reminding him of a particular story that he had learned as a small child while sitting around the evening campfires. Pictures of spirals and snakes, circles, squares and triangles, stars, animals, trees, water and fire.

Most moving of all though was the music. Music that was slow, pure and solemnly expressive played on instruments almost as old as the caves themselves. A gently falling cadence played on Shehnai flutes accompanied by Mridangam drums. These were melodies that never seemed to resolve, leaving the notes lingering in the still air and yet somehow made more beautiful by their non-resolution.

The people spoke in hushed whispers, but he could hear every word.

They said, *"It was meant to be"* and *"Sometimes he chose to walk in the shadows."*

Others said, *"He watched the ripples on the water"* and *"The stone is cracked now."*

And he smiled because he was pleased that they understood everything so well.

The funeral procession moved gracefully up the smooth temple steps and between the carved stone pillars, each individual moving rhythmically in time with the music. Their bare feet took care not to crush the carpet of delicate white Yuthika and red Lotus petals that lay scattered across the floor of the temple as each mourner in turn waited patiently to gaze on the serenity of his young face.

His body had been laid carefully on the sacred wood - the one with all those faded old paintings - and they had surrounded his small body with fragrant yellow Maulsari flowers, seashells and other small devotional gifts, some that he was unfamiliar with. A golden bowl of red kumkum powder was placed beside him ready for the ceremony to follow.

The four holy men that carried the bier supporting his body lowered it from their shoulders and laid him before the altar stone. Their brown skin glistened in the soft candlelight and they shivered a little, the cold of the temple always a shock after the stifling sub-tropical heat outside.

They had dressed his body in saffron coloured silk and then finger painted his forehead and cheeks with the mark of Tilak, as was the custom. The women wept openly when they set eyes on his perfect features. The men stared in silence, tears welling in their eyes, lips quivering. Then, at last, his mother came forward, her eyes red and puffy. She delicately threaded a single white Lotus flower into his thick dark hair then kissed his cheek softly and whispered something in his ear.

The others couldn't hear anything of course. The soft weeping and the music and the chanting that echoed around the old stone walls had now merged into a single resonant drone that reverberated far beyond the confines of the cave temple and out into the verdant tumble of hills and mountains beyond.

But he could hear her clearly.

She said, *"You were the one. You are the one. You shall be the one my son..."*

Ashdown Forest, Sussex, England, 1964

The car swept over the brow of the hill, headlights arcing across black clouds that lumbered and rolled across the sky like hunchbacked trolls. The late October rain had dissolved the evening twilight into a murky, dirty night and turned the crisp late autumn leaf fall into mush. There was a damp chill in the air and the driver was glad that he'd finally got the car heater fixed and that the interior of his beloved Ford Falcon was now pleasantly warm. Pulling around a bend and straightening the wheel into a longer level stretch of road the driver glanced up into the mirror a small smile playing across his lips.

The young lad was asleep now and that was good. It had been a long day but a good one. A day for some father - son bonding without an overprotective mother around to frown at tree climbing, raft building and football on a muddy patch of grass using trees as goalposts. No wonder the lad was snoring now after all that fresh air and exercise. His mother would be mad at the state of their clothes. She had ironed their football tops and shorts, but they had been left in the cupboard in the rush to get going - and now father and son were both enjoyably mud-spattered. They were both ready to face Carol's good-natured wrath when they got home.

They'd agreed to be back by 7.30pm with the promise of one of her famous homemade shepherd's pies but he knew that it was way past 7.30 by now. Good timekeeping had never been one of his strong points. They'd been so engrossed in the game of football that an hour or two had slipped by unnoticed. The lad's tackling ability had improved over the last few weeks for sure and he had developed a sturdy right foot too. Good chance of getting a slot in the school team next term with a bit of luck.

The driver rubbed his hand across the condensation on the inside of the screen. The wipers were at full speed now as the rain had picked up momentum and settled into a relentless onslaught of water against metal and glass. The monotonous drumming on the roof was starting to get soporific and the headlights were struggling to cut through the dark looming forest bordering the road on both sides. The forest was beautiful by day of course, particularly in the late autumnal sunshine, but the ancient, gnarled branches had spent years reaching out for each other across the intrusive tarmac and finally they had met in a macabre handshake that left the road below snaking through a tunnel of grasping foliage.

The road was familiar enough to the driver. He'd driven this journey hundreds of times and it was a beautiful part of the country known as the Weald, sandwiched comfortably between the North and South Downs and still relatively unspoiled by major roads or ugly post-war new towns. Another twenty minutes and they would be home, ready for a hot bath and a good, if rather late, dinner.

The lad stirred and mumbled something in his sleep. The driver hoped it wasn't anything more than a momentary response to the movement of the car. Sometimes the poor mite suffered from nightmares and on occasions they seemed to be a little more graphic and severe than with other kids. The constant torment had worried his mother enough to consult specialists, but the outcome was inconclusive. They had no idea what caused the nightmares and put them down to a vivid imagination. Said the lad would 'grow out of it' which was hopefully true.

The driver massaged his temple and yawned. This type of driving was unpleasant and tiring. He'd rather be at home relaxing in front of a nice open fire with coffee in hand and watching one of his favourite TV shows. Ah well, not long now.

One or two cars passed on the other side of the road, their watery headlights momentarily blinding the driver and sending a wave of surface water hissing between the two passing cars. Not a night to be out walking that was for sure.

He'd always considered himself to be a good, if cautious, driver. He was certainly never one to take stupid risks or to exceed the speed limits and prided himself that he was always alert to distractions or potential hazards. Maybe that's why tonight he was a little puzzled by the feeling in his bones that something was wrong. It wasn't the atrocious weather or even the fact he was late. No, it was something else that was bothering him.

A sense of unease.

The feeling was still with him when the lad suddenly woke up from his slumber with a loud yell and pointed a finger straight at the centre of the windscreen. The driver was startled but remained composed enough to follow the line of the trembling finger and squinted at the road ahead whilst simultaneously stamping down on the brake with his right foot.

"What is it? What can you see?" he yelled loudly above the crashing of the rain on the car roof.

The lad didn't reply. Maybe it was just his eyes playing tricks or maybe he'd just awoken from a vivid nightmare. Whatever it was, it seemed to have scared him rigid and simultaneously rendered his tongue incapable of further speech. Either way the driver couldn't see anything on the road that presented any danger. The road ahead was dark and wet but that was all, just dark and wet with sodden leaves spinning and pirouetting in the wind like drunken dancers at a Halloween party.

And then, as the brakes locked and the tyres hit a patch of sodden leaf mulch, he thought he did see something, but it seemed to be no more than a fleeting black shadow that reminded him of some sort of large animal with horns.

Exactly what kind of animal it was he never surmised because a moment later his neck was broken - and his bloodied head was halfway through the windscreen as the car left the road and was swallowed by the dark engulfing mouth of the forest.

The last thing he saw were two massive trees filling his fading vision while the sickening sound of broken glass and twisted metal was still ringing in his ears.

PART ONE

'The most frightening journey
a person can ever take is the journey
into their inner self.'

Midnight.
The grand finale.

Adam Sinclair, by now pleasantly stoned, stood on tiptoe to watch the climax of the Sensational Alex Harvey Band's long-awaited set. It was a special moment. Ever since their first album he'd been totally captivated by their raw sound and wild theatrics. Now, at last, he was finally watching them play live and he wasn't disappointed. The stunning spectacle of light and sound was entrancing around twenty thousand crushed bodies pushing towards the front of the stage. The band was playing a manic Celtic jig spurred on by the gravelly Glaswegian tones of Alex Harvey himself and it was impossible to stand still. Adam threw his half empty beer can down carelessly, spilling the contents over rucksacks and blankets already jumbled under a stampede of muddy feet.

"Dance time!" someone yelled.

And then the crowd were a mass of flailing arms and legs, some parodying the Scottish sword dance, others spinning each other around so fast that the less sure-footed were hurled sprawling into the wall of bodies. A huge circle of dancers began to form that were soon whirling around haphazardly like a giant spinning amoeba, treading on toes, and knocking over anyone or anything in its path. Adam laughed out loud at the spectacle and then joined in the spontaneous linking of arms with the two strangers on either side.

Taking on a life of its own the circle dance was now turning into a blurred swirl of colours, long flowing hair and faces that started to remind him of multi-coloured gargoyles. It had only been weed that he'd been smoking he reflected momentarily, but sure as hell it felt like he'd been doing acid. He tripped over something and would have fallen but for the two revellers supporting him on either side. He continued to spin around dizzily - carried on by the momentum of the dance, the quantity of cheap gassy lager in his belly now starting to feel distinctly uncomfortable. It was too late to stop now though. The dance was in full swing and turning into an alcohol-induced barn dance encouraged by Zal Cleminson's screaming staccato electric guitar and the hypnotic driving beat.

And then his right arm was suddenly released as the reveller beside him got bored and Adam was tossed like a lifeless string puppet into the crowd. A woman puffing on a spliff in a tatty Afghan coat and headband swore at him as he fell clumsily across her feet.

He giggled and told her to relax and take it easy.

Miserable cow.

He pulled himself back to his feet and waded back into the throng. This was just brilliant. The music was brilliant, the light show was brilliant, the vibe was brilliant, and the dance must go on.

The band's set finished as expected with one of their classics - 'Anthem'. The familiar chant being taken up by the swaying crowds who now held lit matches or lighters aloft and cheered as a marching Scots band wielding bagpipes and drums, marched onto the stage in full regalia. The haunting beauty of the pipes rang out across the festival site bringing the first incredible night of the three-day music festival to an end.

Even before the last notes had faded a large contingent of revellers started to funnel through the exits heading towards the hundreds of colourful tents that filled the fields surrounding the main arena - a sea of nylon and canvas flapping noisily in the wind. As the crowds began to thin, small fires appeared, randomly dotted around the festival site. Around each fire people huddled together, warming their hands, and finding a place to sit amidst a carpet of empty beer cans. The only way to find your mates in the crowd was to locate the flag that identified your staked-out patch of grass - the flags erected just high enough to be seen over the heads of the masses. This year the American Confederate flag or the skull and crossbones seemed to predominate, each flag a clear beacon signalling a 'You can find me here' message for the stoned, the bewildered or the lost.

Every so often a cheer would go up as another 'streaker' decided to shed his or her clothes and race through the crowd naked dodging the campfires and the flying beer cans. (During the day the quality of the band on stage could be measured by the frequency of streakers during the set - each one a momentary distraction inducing good-humoured cheering and laughter).

Twenty thousand people having a bloody good time for three days. Hell's Angels, hippies, travellers, beggars, Aquarian new-agers, Jesus-freaks, visionaries, gypsies, Woodstock veterans, weirdoes and pimply kids in black T-shirts and faded jeans, acid heads, alcoholics, and other crazies. All here to immerse themselves in three solid days of music, sunshine and beer.

Three days of mud, constant rain showers, overflowing toilets and unwashed bodies, love and peace, veggie burgers and coloured beads, incense sticks and free condoms, festival T-shirt tents, Salvation Army tents, alcohol abuse 'drying out' tents and Heroin advice tents, hot dogs, poster stalls and beer cans. Millions of beer cans.

It was fun.

It was cool.

And it was psychedelic, 'groovy' and 'far out'.

Man.

Adam kicked another empty 'Party Seven' beer can into the dispersing crowd then belched loudly.

Fuckin' brilliant.

He'd been pretty much out of his skull for two solid days now and some of the guys in the next tent had been sharing some good smokes. Lebanese and Moroccan, they'd said.

No hassles. No police bastards. No aggro. No nagging Mother.

Yeah. Fuckin' brilliant!

And then the lights on the main stage were suddenly extinguished plunging most of the central arena into darkness causing the predictable chorus of cheers and whistles. Adam looked around him, wanting to savour the moment, take it all in and generally soak up the electrically charged atmosphere. For a while he just stood there watching the bobbing torches as people made their way back to their tents in the adjoining field, laughing, singing, and fooling about. There were still queues at the hot dog stalls and the Samaritans tent was still busy. Probably, mused Adam, full of sad, depressed bastards who should 'get a grip' or learn to manage their addictions better.

And talking of depression...

"Steve, you old tosser. Where's Marie?"

A pair of bloodshot eyes turned to Adam taking time to focus. Steve Lacey, eighteen, a medley of long, greasy, blond hair and patched purple flares was rocking unsteadily on his feet, still swigging from a can of insipid lager.

"Dunno mate... I think she said she was goin' back to the tent - must have been 'bout an hour ago. I 'aint seen her since."

"What? She missed the bloody finale? Stupid bitch!"

Adam kicked another empty beer can and sent it crashing into a pyramid of similar empties nearby. "Why does she always have to do that? Piss off without saying anything?"

"Cos she was mad at you" said Steve, aware that he was stating the obvious, "Y'know - when that bloke gave you those smokes earlier on and she asked you not to take 'em. You know what she's like."

Adam shrugged. "Bollocks to her then. Let her sleep and miss all the fun. Who cares?"

"Anyway" said Steve, "I'm going back to the tent to crash man. You?"

"Nah. I'll catch up with you later. I'm gonna hang around here awhile. I like the vibe."

Adam gave up trying to push his way through the crowds who were now trickling out of the small arena exit like treacle through a funnel. He sat down on the damp, flattened grass and watched the blur of bodies passing by. What's the big rush anyway?

Adam pushed a hand through the tangle of thick brown hair that tumbled down across equally brown eyes where it hung sheepdog-fashion for most of the time. At nineteen he should have been shaving but his 'baby face', as his mother called it, was still smooth and mostly free from the scourge of bristles and acne. A bit of 'bum fluff' as his grandmother put it, but not much more. It pissed him off frequently, when getting thrown out of pubs by suspicious landlords' keen to evict under-age drinkers.

In torn blue jeans, dirty off-white trainers, black T-shirt with the latest 'Yes' logo and faded blue denim jacket adorned with various rock-band badges he felt good. Around his neck were a set of small multicoloured 'love beads' he'd bought on a whim earlier from an 'Indian culture' stall and in his jacket pocket a leather wallet containing the weekend's beer money, a Durex (well shit – he was an optimist, right?) a packet of Rizla and an empty packet of 'Slim Kings'. (Yeah, the other guys laughed but what the heck? They were useful for roll-ups if nothing else.) The 'good stuff' was tucked down inside his sock, pressed up against his ankle in a small plastic bag. Just in case the pigs were bored and felt like frisking him again.

Can't be too careful these days...

His mates, who had also travelled up from the middle of Sussex on the train with him earlier in the day were now somewhere lost in the crowds. No worries. They would meet up again later. Steve Lacey and Danny Mc Connell were a good laugh most of the time. Into loud and (mostly) progressive rock music, partying, getting stoned, getting off with chicks and just hanging out. 'Difference was, that unlike Adam, this time they had left their girlfriends behind.

Wise move guys...

Marie was nothing but a hassle at the moment.

Almost wished he'd not invited her.

Almost.

Marie Cunningham sat down cross-legged in the darkness of a large, camouflaged, ex-army tent and lit a cigarette with trembling hands. The glowing match lit up her features momentarily, the hint of pink lipstick and dark curls that framed what her father called 'an elfin shaped face', probably because of the high, strong cheekbones and deep green eyes. She inhaled deeply, something she rarely did, and tried to blow out the smoke evenly to calm her anger. She was slightly built for an eighteen-year-old, but in a tight black skirt and white ski jacket - admittedly a little out of place in a sea of patched flares and psychedelic T-shirts - she had certainly turned a few heads at the festival. The wolf-whistles were embarrassing, yeah, but sort of flattering too. It made her wonder even more what the hell she was doing with a jerk like Adam Sinclair.

She leaned back onto a well-padded sleeping bag and considered the situation, watching the smoke curl up into the dark recesses of the tent. God! She must be mad to be in this place. Adam was certainly persuasive - she'd grant him that - *'Why don't you come along with me and the lads - it'll be a gas'* he had said - and at the time she had been stupid enough to believe him.

Only it wasn't a gas. It was lousy. The camp site was knee deep in mud. The loos were half a mile away and the 'Ladies' had a permanent queue outside. The facilities were so bad - and so inadequate - that most blokes were using the perimeter fence to relieve themselves - and some of the women too. Add to that, the crush of thousands of sweaty bodies, the pissheads flaked out under your feet and the junkies tripping out on acid or heroin and it was all too much. Already someone had stolen her favourite bracelet and the thought of living on greasy burgers for three days filled her with disgust. As far as passion was concerned - *sorry Adam* - it was out of the question. She was sharing some moth-eaten, borrowed tent, with a boyfriend and his two loud-mouthed so-called 'mates' and tonight she'd be sleeping in the clothes she had been wearing all day. No way was she undressing in front of those losers. She would rather, she reflected, be at home with a good book after a long shower. This was the first music festival she had ever been to. It would also, she resolved, be her last. And as for that drunken bastard, Adam Sinclair - well he could rot in hell for all she cared.

Okay, when he was sober, and away from his obnoxious mates, he could be reasonable enough, fun even. But put him with those arseholes Steve and Danny and he was instantly back to his pathetic and intolerable habits. Booze, drugs, larking about like a lunatic, showing off and mouthing off like some irritating know-it-all who really knows nothing. It made her wonder why on earth they were still together after two years. Childhood sweethearts was an old cliché that she hated but it was probably true.

She thought back to the first time she'd met him at a mutual friend's sixteenth birthday party. The attraction was instantaneous though both were too shy to admit it until a long time afterwards. So, what was it with him she wondered? He was infuriating most of the time, seemed to attract trouble like a magnet and could be cold, distant, and unfeeling when he felt like it. At other times he could be so wild and reckless that his mates seemed to have a kind of misguided awe and reverence for him - as though being a loud-mouthed yob was something to aspire to for chrissake.

She knew deep down of course that she'd put up with his irritating behaviour for one reason only. It was that tantalising hidden depth that few others could reach or penetrate; something that made him intriguingly different - special. It was a weird sort of untapped energy or potential that she had never found in a previous string of shallow boyfriends. At least that's what she had always thought until now. This time he had pushed her too far. It wasn't so much being ignored - God knows she was used to that - it was just the 'everything in excess' mentality she couldn't put up with. The 'always needing to push the boundaries a little further out' attitude and taking too many stupid risks just for a laugh. Like yesterday for example, when he'd dropped some acid and started mumbling about seeing a 'Technicolor' universe inside an empty beer can, which he'd then gone on to stare into for two solid hours and which had made those idiotic mates of his howl with laughter.

Yeah, 'really funny' Adam. Only I'm not laughing anymore.

Well, this time he could get lost for good. Her mind was made up. She'd had enough. Marie leaned out of the tent flap, glancing around at the jumble of eerily shaped dark tents, and moving black figures wondering where the hell he'd got to. She stubbed out the remains of the cigarette in the damp grass and cursed herself for smoking. Given up, hadn't she?

Yeah, right.

Soon the three lads would be back from the concert finale. Probably all stoned and still wanting to party all night. Well good luck to them. She was getting some much-needed sleep. Tomorrow, when Adam was somewhere close to sober, she would tell him that he'd finally pushed her to the limit.

She would tell him that it was all over.

For good.

Outside of the main arena Adam stopped for a moment to try and get his bearings. His eyes ached, and it was difficult to focus on the blurred image of acres of tents flapping gently in the post-midnight breeze. Most of the tents glowed with subdued inner light making shadows jump and flicker in unison with the myriad campfires burning in the small clearings between tents. There was a strong smell of freshly brewed coffee, the mellow sound of acoustic guitars and the unmistakable aroma of cannabis.

Adam stumbled over a tent peg and swore.

Where was the sodding tent?

He picked his way between two large noisy walls of canvas, fumbling around the tangle of guide ropes that were almost impossible to see in the darkness. Now, if he remembered rightly, the old ex-army tent he'd borrowed for the weekend was somewhere to his left, down towards the bank of the Thames. He shivered slightly as a cold breeze ruffled his hair. The chill of night was now seeping across the fields, ushering the last few low rainclouds eastwards leaving a clear, star filled sky in its wake.

He gazed up at the stars for a moment, like he always had done since he was a kid, always fascinated by the sheer magnitude of the universe and often awe struck by its beauty. Tonight though, his vision was blurred by alcohol and dope and he was beginning to feel a little queasy. There was a distinct dizziness in his head and a cold feeling in his stomach. It was mixing the drinks and the smokes that did it - always a bad move. He needed to crash out in the sleeping bag, get some sleep. He'd feel a lot better in the morning. Trouble was, all the tents looked the same at night and it was difficult enough to find the tent in the daylight - and that was when you were sober. It was well past midnight now and the campfires were burning lower, the soft tent lights being extinguished one by one.

"Steve! Danny! - Where are you - ya bastards?" he yelled.

"They've gone for a wank," a disembodied voice called back from somewhere in the field followed by howls of laughter from nearby tents.

Adam smiled to himself. That was what he liked about festivals, the sense of camaraderie and the humour. He retraced his steps a little, aware that his eyelids were beginning to droop and that the sick feeling in his stomach was now clawing its way up his throat. His eyes drifted to an image of a large white skull with devil's horns painted on the side of a huge wigwam from which a nauseating whiff of incense emanated. He vaguely recognised it from earlier in the day. The borrowed tent was somewhere very close, he was sure of it.

He leaned against the wigwam for a moment, a little unsteady on his feet and starting to feel even more nauseous, gradually becoming aware of two or three shadowy figures looming out of the darkness. He caught a glimpse of leather and chains.

"Lost your tent mate?"

Adam nodded.

"Er...yeah...s' around here somewhere..."

"Too bad, eh? Got any smokes?"

Adam wondered if they had noticed the oblong bulge in his jacket pocket. The packet was empty, but he wasn't in the mood for sharing anyway.

"Smokes? Nah, sorry mate."

"No fags, eh?"

Adam didn't like the sneer in the voice. Didn't like the way the three figures were closing in around him.

Another different voice, much gruffer, spoke next.

"Some tabs or acid maybe?"

"Tabs? Nah, nothing like that."

A heavy hand came to rest on Adam's shoulder. Made him jump.

"Oh dear" the sneering voice said, "The poor guy's got no smokes and no tabs to share. Now that is a shame. That is such a shame."

Steve Lacey stumbled clumsily through the open tent flap followed a few seconds later by six-foot of hair, beads, bracelets and clashing colours known as Danny McConnell. They stared for a moment at Marie who sat sullenly in the corner, back turned away from them. They exchanged nervous glances in the dim torch light.

Danny cleared his throat, "Bloody ace" he slurred jovially, "'Dat has got to be one of the best concerts 'oive ever been to."

"Absolutely fantastic" Steve concurred, still swigging from a can of lager, "Did you hear that slide guitar on Camel's 'White Rider'. Fuckin' awesome." He collapsed roughly onto a sleeping bag. It was only a 'three-man tent really. Not really room for a fourth body.

Particularly when it was female.

Danny caught Marie's eye. "So...um...Adam not back yet den?"

She didn't look up but continued to just sit there, hugging her legs to her chest.

"No."

"He won't be long" said Steve, stifling a belch, "I saw him waiting for the crowds to thin out in the main arena. Reckon he'll be back in a minute...you wanna drink?"

He held out a can in the darkness. No one had thought to remember a tent light and the single shared torch was fading fast.

"Beer? No thanks...I'm going to turn in. Look... um...tell him not to wake me up when he gets back okay? I'll be catching the train home tomorrow."

Danny and Steve exchanged another knowing look. It was Steve who spoke first.

"You're not staying for the rest of the festival then?"

"Nope."

Danny frowned. Having a woman around was awkward to be sure, but he knew how much Adam really thought of her. The offhand attitude was all just front.

"Hey c'mon now Marie - don' go being stupid" said Danny, "It's been a gas. You got into 10cc earlier didn'ya? You need to loosen up a bit - don't be givin' Adam a hard toime now - he's havin' a ball."

Marie turned, her eyes flashing angrily at the figure swaying in front of her. "Oh, don't you worry" she said through gritted teeth, "I won't cramp his style anymore. Nor yours. Next time you can all get out of your heads without me around to worry about." She turned around and pulled the sleeping bag with a broken zip up around her shoulders. Two more nights sleeping in the same clothes? No chance! She was tired, her ears were still ringing from the overpowering wall of noise in the arena, and she felt cold and dirty. If this was having a ball, then they could all shove it.

It wasn't her scene anymore.

No way.

She wanted out.

Adam's heartbeat quickened.

This sort of thing wasn't supposed to happen. Not now, not here. Not when he was having such a good time. Okay, so the fact that he felt like death was his own fault. Self-inflicted. But he was still sober enough to sense trouble when it was this close.

The nearest figure leaned forward to whisper something in his ear. He was a big heavy-set guy, long dark, greasy hair under a leather-peaked cap. Wide, staring eyes. Some teeth missing.

"So...what have we got here then boys? A lost little sheep, eh? Lost his tent and lost his mates... ah! Maybe his Mummy shouldn't have let him out alone."

"Leave it out" said Adam trying to sound chummy; casual even.

"Listen to him," grunted another voice, his features indiscernible in the thickening darkness, "Better 'elp him on his way then hadn't we boys? Now let me see...I think his tent might be this way..."

A rough pair of hands pushed Adam sideways into the arms of a third indistinct figure. He caught a whiff of whisky.

"Nah - I think it's that way" said the third voice pushing Adam roughly into another pair of leather arms that immediately pinioned him, bending his arms backwards in one swift move.

Bad news.

"C'mon guys" yelled Adam, voice cracking on the last syllable "Just leave me..."

His words were cut short by a sharp blow to his stomach that left him bent double and severely winded. Before he could catch his breath, there was an excruciating pain as a heavy boot landed between his legs.

"Aghhh...you *bastards*."

A leather glove yanked at his cheap T- shirt almost tearing it completely from his body. It left shreds of material hanging from him loosely like rotten bandages. His chest was sore - and half exposed. Felt like he was naked.

"We don't like smart arse little hippies do we boys?" said whisky-breath, "Smart arse hippies with nothing to share."

Adam focused just long enough to see a steel ringed fist hit him between the eyes. That did it. The vomit rose in his throat and exploded over the assailant's arm. *Bad move.* The guy looked down at his sleeve dripping with stomach fluid then pressed his face close to Adam's "You dirty..." Adam felt venomous spittle shower his face.

When the second kick came the pain shot through his body as though he were being disembowelled by a hot sword. Someone wrenched off his denim jacket and he could just focus long enough to see his wallet, containing his last fiver and train ticket home being removed. He couldn't see which of them took it. Not that it mattered now. He tried to call out; get someone's attention. There were thousands of tents full of people for God's sake. *Surely someone...?*

But the words wouldn't come. He'd started to spit blood instead. He could taste it thick in his mouth. Blood and vomit.

And then the figures were on him again. One of them had grabbed a handful of his long straggly hair and was wrenching it backwards. Movements became a blur and for a few terrifying moments he felt strangely detached - as though watching a movie from a distance; a movie consisting of angry fists and black leather. He felt a sharp blow to the side of his mouth followed by another heavy booted kick to the stomach.

It was the last kick that did it. The arms that had pinioned him, defenceless against the onslaught now released him like a discarded rag doll. And then he was sprawling in the wet mud between two dark tents, where at last, blackness and oblivion mercifully replaced the pain of consciousness.

It was Marie who awoke first. She was surprised to find herself shivering despite the layers of clothing and the sleeping bag and her back was hurting where the rough ground beneath the tent had made any kind of comfort virtually impossible. It must still be early. Very little light seeped through the tent drawstrings and the only sounds were of deep snoring. The smell of stale beer made her want to gag. She rubbed her eyes and pushed up her sleeve squinting at her watch. It was her favourite watch - the one Adam had bought her for her seventeenth birthday. 6.50. Jesus! Nice start to a Saturday. She could make out the dim shapes of Steve and Danny in the grey half-light. They would be sleeping off their respective hangovers for some hours yet by the sound of them. And as for...

Adam?

She frowned. His sleeping bag was empty. Maybe he had got up to take a leak. No, the bag was still laid out as it had been last night. He hadn't come back last night - and they had obviously all fallen asleep.

He must have slept in someone else's tent.

The utter bastard.

Last time she'd seen him, around midnight, he was off dancing with some woman in the arena - just to taunt her probably. If he had gone off and spent the night in another woman's tent, she would bloody kill him.

It was no good - she couldn't sleep - not now. May as well get up and find some coffee. She remembered reading in the festival programme, 'Reading Rocks', that some of the breakfast catering tents opened at 6.30. Great.

It only took a moment to slip on her shoes and run a brush through her hair. Still felt bloody dirty though and desperate for a hot bath. Adam had told her that at last years' festival loads of people had simply stripped off and jumped into the Thames as soon as the sun came up instead of queuing at the washrooms. Well, there was no chance of her following suit, skinny-dipping in a cold river. That was for sure.

There was a coffee stall not far away and fortunately few people were up and about yet so there wasn't much of a queue. Some early risers had already got their breakfast going and the enticing smell of bacon drifted on the early morning air. The sizzling smell of bacon was probably the best thing about camping; not much else appealing about sharing a tent with insects, beer cans and unwashed male bodies.

She handed over a few coins to the guy behind the coffee stall and warmed her hands around the steaming plastic cup. It tasted good. For a few moments she just stood there sipping the hot liquid and absorbing the sights, sounds and ambience of the festival site as it woke up from its collective hangover to a fresh new August morning. No sign of Adam though. He could be in any one of a thousand tents.

Something made her stop in her tracks. Yeah - *she ought to make sure* - just for peace of mind. It was about ten minutes' walk through the main camping field to reach the line of grey and white marquees set up for the festival organisers and caterers. The 'Grapevine' tent selling contraceptives was not open yet. Not that she'd be frequenting that particular facility anyway. But the 'First Aid' tent next door had already tied back its tent flap and a matronly St. John's ambulance woman was busying herself getting organised for the day. She looked up when she noticed Marie hovering outside.

"Yes love?"

"Hi. I was just wondering whether my friend has been here. He didn't come back to our tent after the show last night. I thought maybe..."

"What's your friend's name?"

"Adam. Adam Sinclair."

The woman nodded and turned to a clipboard slowly tracing her finger down a list of names.

"Sorry. No record of any Adam Sinclair" she said, then frowned. "Hold on a moment...can you remember what he was wearing?"

"Um. Blue jeans...denim jacket...black T-shirt, some beads I think..."

"Dark brown long hair? Sort of curly. Brown eyes?"

"Yeah. That's him."

The first aider touched Marie's arm. "Oh dear...I think that was the poor lad we took to hospital last night."

Marie's blood froze in her veins momentarily. "Hospital? What happened? Is he...?"

"He was found unconscious among the tents around twelve thirty" the woman continued, "We don't know what happened to him, but we think he'd been in a fight by the look of him. He'd suffered an obvious nosebleed and a black eye. Seemed to be in a lot of pain. He was taken straight to Reading General. He had nothing on him with a name or any other form of identification, so we just noted his description."

"Was he badly hurt? I mean it wasn't anything life-threatening, was it? Will he be okay?"

"He's in the best place" said the woman reassuringly, "I don't think any limbs were broken but we have no idea as to the cause of his injuries. Look...why don't you phone the hospital? I have the number here if..."

"No, that's okay. I'll go there myself, soon as I've packed my stuff. Thank you."

Marie felt sick. What the hell could have happened to him? His Mother had already lost her husband in a tragic road accident when Adam was young, and Adam was her only child. Oh no - please God...

She ran back to the tent and shook Steve and Danny awake.

Steve opened one eye; "Wossamarrer?"

"It's Adam. He's had an accident. He's been in a fight and taken to Reading General. I'm going to find him - coming?"

Steve sat up in his sleeping bag groaning.

"You sure?"

"'Course, I'm sure. For God's sake Steve - I've just come back from the first aid tent."

Marie crammed her things into a rucksack then rolled her sleeping bag under her arm. "I'm going now" she said

"So? Are either of you coming or not?"

Steve and Danny looked at each other in mutual confusion. Both heads throbbing from the night before.

"Oi' might come later" said Danny, "Oi' feel a bit rough at da moment. I'm sure Adam's okay. He probably just fell over or something."

Marie turned to Steve "You?"

"I dunno" yawned Steve, "Probably don't need us all to go. Can't be anything serious, can it? Why don't you leave us here and just go yourself? We'll maybe come along later."

Marie stared at the two of them. She wasn't usually lost for words.

"Some mates you are" she spat, "Don't bloody bother then. Just leave it all to me."

She flung open the tent flap and disappeared. The first rays of morning sunlight were starting to sneak into the tent like bony yellow fingers.

"Fock's sake what's got into her?" said Danny, "Adam's old enough to take care of himself. Oi' bet he just fell over 'cos he was too pissed to stand up. Wouldn't be the first time. He'll be foine."

"Bloody women" said Steve, "Adam said he shouldn't have brought her along. She's overreacting as usual. I'm not missin' this festival just because of her. Soddin' ticket cost enough."

"Too roight mate" said Danny reaching over for a packet of cigarettes, passing one over to his bleary-eyed tent mate, "Too fockin' roight."

In the dream, Adam was running across a field that seemed to stretch flat and uninterrupted to the horizon, but for some reason his legs felt leaden, and he didn't seem to be making much progress. The weather was grey and sullen and storm clouds were forming on the horizon like frothy grey milk boiling out of a dirty pan.

The endless field that he couldn't seem to run across - and the swirling grey storm clouds were depressing enough - but there was another feature in the dream that was even more ominous. Behind him, and to the left, some two hundred yards or so away, a large snorting creature was bearing down upon him fast. He knew instinctively that it was a bull. Because it always was. The recurring nightmare had differed only slightly in the detail for as long as he could remember. It had been with him all through his tormented childhood and now continued to haunt him through his teenage years. 'He'll grow out of it' the local doctor had assured his mother when she had taken him, five years old, kicking and shrieking to the local clinic. 'Children get nightmares. It's quite normal - nothing to worry about' the doctor had said.

Except he hadn't grown out of it.

Instead, the night horrors still came to him once or twice a week and there was nothing he, or anyone

else, could do about it. It was just 'one of those
things' you learned to live with.

Or not...

And then there was *that walk* last summer with
Marie when it was a real bull instead of a dream
bull. No way the 'clever dick' doctor could explain or
predict that was there?

Adam watched the dream-bull with mixed
emotions. He was instinctively aware that this
was only a dream and that the bull was therefore
not actually real, but he was also frustrated that he
couldn't run properly and couldn't seem to make the
dream come to an end despite trying subconsciously
to wake himself up. He could feel his heart beating
fast (that could be real or could be in the dream - he
wasn't sure) and, as per usual, he was beginning to
panic. If only he could work out what was stopping
his legs from moving, he might yet be able to sprint
to the edge of the field where there must be a gate or
at least some sort of fence or hedge to jump over, but
right now it felt like he was wading through treacle.

The other thing that was troubling him was the
weird sensation that this was not, for some reason,
quite the same as the 'usual' dream - or even the
'usual' nightmare - if there *is* such a thing as a 'usual'
nightmare. This time there was a very different and
unnatural feel to the situation which he didn't like
at all.

Somehow the usual nightmare, terrifying enough,
had taken a different turn.

Something was *wrong.*

The bull – no, not *quite* a bull, but something like
a bull, was more clearly visible now. It had gained
a hundred yards or so and was hurtling its bulk
forward with ruthless determination. Strange that
it somehow didn't look quite right. It was similar to
a bull certainly, but there was something different

about it, something vaguely familiar and at the same time rather sinister. Anyhow, in a few seconds it would make contact with him and then...

...and then he would wake up...

...sweating and hysterical.

Same as usual.

Wouldn't he?

Hold on a moment. His legs had somehow become 'unglued'. That meant it was now possible to run away, albeit in a soft-focus, slow-motion parody of real sprinting. The bull-thing continued to stampede towards him in the same slowed manner. The dream, for some reason, had now morphed into a slow black and white film. A scary unreality game in which impact was always inevitable and then it would all be over until the next time.

Adam felt damp. Had the storm clouds now broken? Was it now raining? Or was it just sweat? No - it was *sticky* damp - not wet damp.

Must be blood.

And now the bull had gone. Simply vaporised into thin air and Adam was lying on his back feeling clammy and uncomfortable. Surely the bull-thing must have collided with him by now? It always happened that way. It was a mind-movie he had subconsciously watched thousands of times and the ending was always the same. Inevitable. Steely hard bone slicing through flesh in visceral frenzy. A phantasmagoria of blood and guts erupting over his trousers and shoes and the strangely surreal thought that his mother would be furious at the mess on his clothes.

So why, this time, had the bull simply disappeared? Had it gored him already?

He couldn't remember for sure, but he certainly felt pain.

Oh God yes...

Real pain this time. Not imaginary pain.

And now the storm clouds were moving away, and brighter whiter clouds had appeared and were shifting their shapes before him. Must be waking up...

Strange...

Now he could see that the white shapes were not clouds after all, but people moving around him - and he was moving too. He was on some sort of bed. A bed in a strange unfamiliar place that smelled of bleach, sanitised alcohol and disinfectant and there were lots of wires and plastic tubes everywhere.

Something was definitely wrong. Didn't make sense. The dream wasn't supposed to end this way. He was supposed to just wake up in his bedroom at home and sigh with relief that it was all over. But for some reason on this occasion, he could feel the pain much more acutely. Lots of pain.

But then again, at least the bull had gone. He didn't *ever* want to see that bull-thing again.

No way.

Not *ever*.

Consciousness seeped back slowly.

Adam was aware that something was not quite right even before his eyes opened and he tried to focus on his surroundings. He was in a bed in a strange and unfamiliar white room - and he felt lousy. He tried to sit up then winced as a sharp pain shot through his rib cage. He relaxed back to his original position and started to look around, gradually recalling the events of...

Of when? How long had he been here?

The festival...he had been looking for his tent... that's right. Then those thugs had attacked him and stolen his wallet...yes that was it...he had felt sick and then they had punched him again and again and again. Ripped his favourite T-shirt; nicked his jacket. Beaten him half to death. *Bastards!*

It was a hospital. Yeah. Somehow, he had ended up in hospital. Either that or heaven was full of wires, peeling magnolia ceilings and paint-chipped chunky radiators.

So, they hadn't killed him after all.

Nor had the bull-thing.

Maybe God was watching over him after all?

Nah. Unlikely.

God probably had better things to do.

He breathed deeply and felt acute pain again.

Shit, I'm hurting like crazy, man.

He wondered if he was badly injured and started to mentally explore each of the painful areas. His face hurt a lot, especially around the eyes and his ribs were aching - were they broken? He could feel that they were tender and bruised and his stomach felt awful. A mixture of cramp, cold, hunger and hollowness. His limbs and eyes seemed to be intact so maybe he would live after all. It was his throat though, that felt worst of all; dry and parched as though he had been chewing on sand.

He was in a small, whitewashed ward with six beds including his own. Three beds were unoccupied and the other two contained patients. One was an older guy who was fast asleep and on the other bed a younger man was sitting up with his arm in a sling, totally absorbed with a cassette recorder and a pile of tapes. He was facing away from Adam gazing absently out of a window. The tinny drone of Pink Floyd's 'Dark side of the Moon' floated across the ward. Adam turned over and drew in his breath sharply at the discomfort. On the other side of his bed was a small cupboard with an empty green pottery vase, a jug of water and a small plastic drinking glass. Behind the cupboard was a small buzzer attached to the wall with a faded sign above it that read, 'Call Nurse'. The other bed areas were identical except the two occupied beds had a few items on their bedside units; 'get well' cards, wilting flowers and a bunch of grapes - the usual boring paraphernalia of hospitals. Although it hurt to move, he reached up and pressed the buzzer.

Might as well find out the worst.

Two minutes later the ward door creaked open and a man in a white coat and glasses appeared. He carried a clipboard which he glanced at before removing his glasses and then started to study his patient.

"How do you feel?" he asked matter-of-factly.

How do you think I bloody feel?

"Awful."

The doctor nodded. "You probably won't feel too good for a couple of days but that's only to be expected. Just woken up?"

"Yeah. So, what have they done to me then? And where am I?"

The doctor looked down at the clipboard again. He was a plumpish man - mid fifties perhaps? Balding on top and efficient looking in a dull sort of way. Adam hated doctors. He had always felt uncomfortable talking to doctors - couldn't remember why - probably those painful childhood memories or something.

"Reading General Hospital. You were brought in last night. You were found unconscious at the music festival site. Do you remember anything?"

"Too right I remember. I was beaten up by some..." Adam searched to find the right words, "...beaten up by some nutters. Sadistic bastards. There were three of them I think."

"You're lucky they didn't do too much damage. There is quite a lot of bruising around the face, stomach and chest but nothing that won't heal over time. There's a nasty cut on your neck that will probably leave a small scar though. We were more concerned that you had lost a lot of body fluid and had a degree of alcoholic poisoning. We had to use a stomach pump which revealed some narcotics usage. Fortunately, you are young, and your constitution was robust enough to cope, otherwise your condition might have been a lot more serious. An X-ray showed that fortunately no bones are broken just bad bruising. As I said - you're lucky."

Lucky?

He didn't feel lucky.

Narcotics usage. Shit. That could mean trouble.
"So...um...when can I go home then?"
"Where is home?"
"Woodsham. Sussex. Near Brighton."
The Doctor scribbled something on his notepad.
"I have recommended two full days rest before you are discharged. We need to carry out a few checks later. Just to make sure. Try and get a few hours solid sleep now and make sure you drink plenty of water. When you are ready there is some paperwork to go through. Name, date of birth, that kind of thing. It's possible the Police might want to talk to you about the assault and whether you want to press charges. They might also want to talk to you about the ingestion of drugs. That's up to them."
Adam shifted his gaze and shook his head in disbelief. Jeez - that's all he needed. Busted for drugs as well as having his head kicked in. And now he was going to miss the rest of the festival too.
Fuck it.
This wasn't his day.
"Try and get some more sleep" the doctor said, "I've given you some pain killers and some sedatives which will help you relax but you will still be feeling rough for a few days. I'll pop back later and check on your progress. Now, is there anyone we need to contact? Parents or...?"
"Nah" mumbled Adam quickly, "They're away on holiday at the moment." It was a lie. "There's no need to contact them. I'm over eighteen". The doctor nodded knowingly, turned on his heels and shut the ward door behind him. Adam turned over and shut his eyes. He already felt sick. Now he felt sicker.
What would his mother care anyway? She was far too busy with her weekly bingo or dull TV dramas to care about what he was up to. She probably couldn't even remember him mentioning the festival

anyway. And as for his father the only way he could be contacted was via a Ouija board or a medium. He didn't even want to think about things like that because that hurt him more than physical wounds ever could.

That was one wound that would never heal.

It was some indeterminate time later that Adam opened his eyes slowly. He had slept soundly for a good few hours. Must have been the sedatives. He still felt lousy though and very disorientated. His whole body was aching, and his head was sore. He'd even drunk loads of awful tasting water so things must be bad. It took a while for his foggy vision to focus on the shape standing beside his bed. He assumed it was a Nurse or Doctor until he recognised the perfume. His heart beat quickened.

"Marie?"

"Hello Adam."

He pulled himself up to a sitting position wincing as a sharp pain seared through his ribs again. He forced a smile.

"Thanks for coming."

Marie cast her eyes downward self-consciously and shrugged, "I needed to see you" she said softly.

Adam stared at her in silence for a few moments. She was a good kid. Special.

"Had some bad luck, eh?" he joked feebly, "Bumped into the wrong people or something - you know me. They nicked my wallet. I took a bit of a beating. You wanna know what they did to me?"

"I know what they've done to you. I've already spoken to the doctor. You nearly died - do you realise that? And it wasn't the fight that caused it. It was the alcohol and drugs. They had to pump your stomach."

Adam stared at her. He had no idea it was that serious. He breathed deeply.

"Yeah. Bad spliff I guess. Look, do me a favour huh? Phone Mum yeah? Just let her know I'm okay."

Marie nodded dismissively. This wasn't going to be easy.

Adam sensed the tension building. He moderated his tone a little. "Oh, and pass me a cup of water, could you? There's a jug on the cabinet. My mouth feels like the bloody Sahara. I hate water, but the doc reckons I gotta drink loads of the stuff." Marie poured some water into a plastic cup and handed it to Adam. He drank it down in one go, grimacing.

"Apparently you were hallucinating badly when they brought you in" continued Marie, "Didn't the nurses or doctors tell you?"

"Nah."

"You're a bloody fool – d'you know that? One of the nurses heard it all you know. She told me what you said…"

"Whad'ya mean 'what I said?'"

"Crying, mumbling, shouting, and ranting like an old drunk. All the signs of someone cocktailing and having a bad trip. For God's sake Adam you're old enough to know better. You could have killed yourself and you nearly did too. Screaming like that and asking for…"

"Askin' for what?"

Marie bit her lip.

"Nothing."

"Whad'ya mean 'nothing'? What was I asking for?"

"Forget it. It doesn't matter."

"Marie!"

"You were asking for your dad."

Adam stared at her. He could feel the beads of sweat forming on his forehead. An icy coldness seeped through his insides. *It always happened when…*

He wanted to reply but the words stuck in his throat. He knew, and she knew, his pathetic attempt at composure had been completely shattered. It had only happened three or four times before in his life and always at times of severe stress. He would call out for the dad he barely knew; the dad of few, but nevertheless very happy memories. The dad who had been killed instantly in a car crash, ten years ago, when Adam was just nine years old. The car crash that somehow, paradoxically, Adam had survived. They had found him nearby, thrown clear of the wreckage, physically unharmed apart from some minor cuts and bruises but severely traumatised. Mumbling about something he'd seen through the car windscreen moments before the impact. Something that he had never been able to explain coherently enough, and which had therefore been instantly ignored and dismissed as 'trauma induced imagination'. He had landed in some soft bracken and leaves, inches from an oak tree that would have split his skull open.

'A miracle' the paramedic had said at the time.

His Father had not been so lucky and was found still pinioned in his seat belt, the front of the car a tangle of twisted metal, rammed between two trees some twenty yards off the road.

'He coped with the death of his father very well considering...' his mother always told her friends and relatives.

Yeah? What did she know?

Sure, he hid it well. Hid it very well - *'considering'* - keeping it deep down inside like a bubbling volcano. Never letting it show.

Never.

And yet there in the deep recesses of his memory he kept every precious remnant of the times he so fondly remembered. Playing football in the park, making sandcastles at the seaside. Helping dad in the garden shed and laughing together as they watched silly cartoons on TV (the cartoons that for some reason his mother never found funny). Asking dad questions about life and about growing up. The things all nine-year old boys need to ask their fathers. The dad he loved so much and then hated so much for leaving him when he needed him most. Before he had finished asking all those questions that he so much needed answers for.

Adam was suddenly conscious that Marie was still staring at him. He felt raw and exposed. He also knew that Marie knew exactly what was going through his head, and he didn't want that intrusion. Not now.

"So what?" he finally managed to croak.

"Do you miss him?"

"Piss off."

Marie stared into Adam's eyes with an equal measure of contempt and compassion.

"You are lucky to be alive Adam."

"So? Who cares? What's so good about being alive anyway?"

Her eyes flashed "I care Adam. I care. Your mother cares. Do you know something? You're worse than a fool? You're...you're..."

"What? Go on, say it. I can take it."

"Just..." she clenched her fists, "Just not worth it. I've had it with you. It's over Adam. Me and you, okay? It's all over."

Adam turned his head and stared up at the ceiling and sighed deeply, a new pain now tearing at his insides.

"Is that what you came here for? To tell me that you've decided to dump me? Well, you shouldn't have bothered. You might as well just have left me here and enjoyed the rest of the festival with Steve and Danny. We were going nowhere anyhow. The whole thing was a big mistake."

Marie pretended to ignore the comment. He didn't know she'd decided to go home early. She took a deep breath.

"Do me a favour huh, Adam? Sometime, just go take a good hard look at yourself. Take a look in any mirror because all you're gonna see is a complete arsehole, right? Drugs, booze, cuts and bruises. Just look at yourself for God's sake. Bloodshot eyes, pale skin, filthy hair. You are actually destroying yourself. When I met you, I actually believed in you. D'you know that? You were something special. You had, *I dunno*, potential - whatever that means. Now take a look at you. I was obviously wrong. You're just a jerk like the rest of them. Where has your spark gone Adam? What's brought you down to this? And what about your so-called mates? Where are they now eh? Any of them come to visit you yet? The doctor told me that your guts were a lethal cocktail when they finally got you into hospital. You're a 'nothing' d'ya know that? A nobody. A shit..." Marie bit her lip as the tears she was trying to hold back flooded her eyes. Her voice softened; "I used to love you, Adam. Do you realise that you stupid, stupid man? I used to love you..."

"Marie?...I..."

Marie stamped her foot on the polished floor, "Don't say it, Adam. Just don't say anything, okay? I'm going now". She pulled a hanky from her handbag and dabbed it at the corner of her eyes "Don't ring me, don't call. Just forget it okay? Just forget it ever happened - 'us' I mean. I don't need this anymore. I've had enough. And I've had it with you. Mess up your own pathetic life if you want but I'm not going to be part of it."

Adam stared as she walked across the ward and pushed open the door into a polished corridor leading back to the main doors of the hospital. Out of his sight.

Out of his life.

Adam turned to the wall and gritted his teeth.

"Go on. Fuck off then" he yelled after her, "So who cares? Who sodding cares? I don't need you – you're just another stupid bitch. I don't need anybody. Get it? I don't need anybody..."

He looked across the room at the other two patients. They were both staring at him shaking their heads. He looked at their vases of fresh flowers, their 'get well' cards, their bunches of grapes and the chocolates. And then looked back to his own empty cabinet.

"What are you looking at?" he shouted, nostrils flaring.

He punched the pillow until the pain shot through his body and forced him to lay back wincing at the discomfort. The two other patients exchanged glances then looked away.

Adam touched the bandage on his neck. It hurt a lot. Throbbing. When he took his fingers away, they were damp and crimson.

He didn't need this. *Christ knows he really didn't need this.*

The ward had returned to silence. The old guy had pulled up his covers, turned his back on Adam and was fast asleep. The younger guy in the sling was flicking through a magazine. Adam glanced at the clock. It was half past four in the afternoon which meant he'd slept most of the day. Steve and Danny would still be in the arena drinking and partying to the music while he was stuck here with a body racked with pain and an empty sick feeling inside that he couldn't shake off. He wondered if they knew what had happened - or whether it was just Marie who had bothered to come looking for him?

And she only came to say goodbye...

Adam lay back and stared up at the peeling Victorian ceiling. Maybe he should have just died after all. Do everyone a favour. Maybe Marie was right. Maybe he was just a loser, a 'nothing' as she put it. He'd failed all his school exams, hadn't he? Couldn't find or keep a job. Drove his mother crazy every time he was in trouble for stealing or fighting or whatever.

So maybe he should just overdose now. Call it a day.

Go and join dad...

It could all be so simple.

And come to think of it, he mused with dark irony, it would also save the bull-thing from having to mess with his dreams anymore too.

Adam was still staring absently at the bare walls an hour later when a nurse appeared with a thermometer.

Nice legs.

He opened his mouth mechanically and stared directly into the woman's eyes as she inserted the cold tube between his lips. She stared back at him in a way that left him in no doubt who was in charge of the situation. Her confident yet serene look unnerved him a little. She was a looker all right. No make-up or anything - just naturally pretty. Well-scrubbed. Nice dark eyes. Enigmatic smile.

He stared, and she stared, in silence. It seemed longer than two minutes when she finally removed the thermometer and noted the reading on a chart hanging beside the bed.

"How am I doing?" he croaked.

She slipped the thermometer back into her breast pocket.

"You'll live."

"So, when can I go home then?"

"That's up to the Doctor. Tomorrow I should think. I just need to change your neck dressing. It's still bleeding a little."

"Yeah. Tell me about it. Can I get up yet?"

"Not yet. I should relax and take it easy today. You need to get lots of rest, and don't forget to drink plenty of water."

Adam shook his head in disgust.

"Is that all there is to do in this place?" he said wearily, "Just sit in bed and drink water?"

She smiled. "I could find you a book to read if you like."

He shrugged "I dunno. I don't like reading much. Is there a library here then?"

"No, I'm afraid not, but the patients often leave books behind when they leave. I can find you something if you want."

"Yeah, okay then. Anywhere I can get a fag?"

"No chance."

Adam suddenly became aware of what he must look like. He'd lost his T-shirt in the fight and had no idea where his jeans had gone. He was probably a dead ringer for Ghandi in the hospital gown they'd put him in. He wondered who had undressed him when he'd been bought in semi-conscious. He wasn't at his Saturday night chat-up best now. He was pale, bruised, aching and clammy. His black eye was half-closed, and it was still throbbing. All in all, he felt like shit and according to Marie he looked like shit too. The nurse couldn't be more different; immaculate, well groomed, clean and really rather dishy.

Adam wondered what she must think of him. Just another patient? Some jerk on dope who'd been beaten up? It was obvious that she could sense his embarrassment and was dismissing it professionally. It was hard to find his voice. A real effort.

"I suppose you must get a lot of idiots like me in here."

"A few."

"You must think I'm crazy to..." he wanted to say get stoned on weed but the words never reached his lips.

She looked back at him coolly with those haunting dark eyes again.

"That's not for me to say."

"That's the difference between you and me" Adam added, trying to be conversational, "You save lives and idiots like me try to bugger ourselves up." She tucked in his bed sheet then smiled again neither agreeing nor disagreeing. Then she said softly "To recognise that fact means that you are halfway to solving the problem."

It was an odd thing to say and took Adam by surprise. He opened his mouth to reply but a buzzer sounded further down the ward before he could think of a witty answer. Another patient needed attending to.

"I'll find you a book" the nurse said as she turned away, "I'll pop back later to see how you are."

As she left Adam mentally noted her name tag, 'T. Anderson'. A very ordinary name really. He turned over and felt a dull ache in his ribs that was bothering him.

There was something else bothering him too.

A feeling that he needed to cry.

But that was something he had forgotten how to do an awful long time ago.

"Hello...Mrs Sinclair?"

"Yes, who is it?"

"It's Marie. Marie Cunningham. I'm in a phone box in Reading."

"Marie. How nice to hear from you! Are you all enjoying the concert? I heard on the radio..."

"No. Listen. I've only got a few pence in change. It's Adam. He's been taken to hospital."

"Oh my God. What's happened?"

"He's going to be okay. Please don't worry. He'll be fine. There was a fight last night and he was beaten up a bit but it's not too serious. No long-term damage or anything. He'll most probably be discharged tomorrow and will be on his way home on the train."

"Are you sure he's okay? I can catch the train to Reading straight away..."

"No really. There's no need. He really will be fine. And you know what Adam's like. He wouldn't want you to make a fuss."

"How did it happen? Why does it always have to be him that gets involved in any sort of trouble? Are you sure he's okay? Am I able to speak to him?"

"I've just left the hospital to catch the train home. He'll be fine, honestly. I talked to the doctors and nurses, and they assured me he'll be right as rain. A few cuts and bruises that's all. If you call the ward, they'll probably let you speak to him but there's really no need to make the journey. I just thought I ought to let you know."

"That's very kind of you Marie. I'm glad you were there with him. He needs someone like you to keep him in line. God knows I can't seem to control him..."

Marie bit her lip "Yeah, well, maybe he's learned some hard lessons now."

"Oh, I do hope so Marie. Look, thanks for letting me know. You must come around to tea when you're back. I'd better let you catch your train now, hadn't I?"

"Thanks Mrs Sinclair."

"It's Carol."

"Carol. Well, I must go. And please don't worry."

"Okay. Thanks again Marie."

Marie clicked the receiver back into place and sighed deeply. No point in mentioning drugs or drink. It muddied the waters too much. She liked Carol. She was straightforward, practical and nothing like Adam made her out to be. If you believed Adam, you would have thought she was some kind of ogre or tyrant. At one time, not that long ago, Marie had wondered what Carol would have been like as a prospective Mother-in-Law. She laughed inwardly at the thought of it. Not much chance of that now. Adam could tell her *that* news. Tell her what he'd thrown away. Marie closed the door of the telephone box and shouldered her rucksack then started to walk across the road to the station.

'And now Miss Cunningham' she whispered to herself, 'It's time to get yourself a life.'

Adam lay awake staring absently at the ceiling and tried to avoid thinking about the pain in his head and stomach. He hated hospitals, the smells of cleaning fluids and polished floors, the sanitised whiteness of the sheets and the bare walls, the echoing corridors and the hushed whispers. He hated the awareness of other sick people around him, some who would probably never leave the place again. It was depressing and frightening and made him shudder. Thank God some of the nurses were alright - it was a pleasant distraction from the relentless boredom of lying in a hospital bed all day. Some of them, like 'T. Anderson', were quite gorgeous - but then he always did like women in uniform.

His gaze shifted slightly to the big Victorian sash window opposite his bed on the other side of the ward. The glass was old, thick and not very clear but he could still make out a few fields and a small copse in the distance under a very clear blue sky. He'd rather be out there somewhere, than cooped up in this gloomy forlorn place. There was something about being out in the open air that was always appealing. Something that you always take for granted until you're confined indoors. Then you realise how much you need to be free from walls, doors, and other such man-made restrictions.

His mind drifted back to days spent on Greenwood Hill, his favourite place in the world. It was nothing special to look at really - just another rise of the undulating South Downs overlooking the English Channel. An expanse of green velvet coating the pristine white chalk. From the top, the sea breezes wafted inland with an exhilarating charge of ozone, and you could see for miles in all directions.

He'd been taken up there as a kid and the place held lots of fond memories of kite flying in the summer and tobogganing in the winter. Days when mum and dad would hold hands and take a picnic hamper as they trudged up the chalky track from the valley car park. It was somewhere to escape from suburbia and fill your lungs with fresh air. Only last Summer Adam had taken Marie with him to his special place to show her the views and to sit awhile watching the boats far out at sea. They had been so much in love then.

Yeah, there had been other girlfriends, but Marie was different. She was the one that stirred him like no other woman before or since. It was up on Greenwood hill that they had laid together on the grass staring up into the bluest of skies listening to the background hum of bees or the rough hiss of grasshoppers in the foliage. It was where they had teased each other playfully and laughed at silly jokes, revelling in each other's company, hearts beating quicker every time their eyes met. And it was the place that they first kissed in a different way. Not the usual sloppy teenage kisses nervously delivered behind the local disco, or the school bike sheds, but something much deeper and sensual. On Greenwood hill, lying together and laughing together their lips had somehow met and just for a fleeting moment something had changed. Adam could still taste the softness of her mouth and the delicious flavours of femininity that had washed into him. A moment he would always treasure.

A movement outside the window broke his reverie.

Adam watched as a small flock of birds rose as one from a distant copse and curved a path across the sky as if to mock his solitary confinement, their amorphous black forms turning into small dots as they were engulfed into the all-absorbing blueness of the horizon. For a moment Adam wanted to be up there flying with them - away from all the hassle he had to put up with, day in, day out. There was something about that sort of unbridled freedom that was so bewitching and yet so unobtainable.

Adam watched until his eyes began to lose focus and started to water. Total freedom! Yeah, that would be brilliant. To be as free, literally, as a bird. And yet there was a nagging feeling somewhere in his mind that maybe even birds were not totally free. Maybe they were all following one another with the deeply embedded instincts of all migratory creatures, forced by their unique genetic instructions to go where they were destined to go, devoid of any individual willpower.

And just maybe, it was the same for people?

Most people probably thought they were free - when really, they were all just puppets in some grand cosmic theatre never getting to find out who was pulling all the strings. Living, dancing, crying, all on demand just to satisfy someone else's whims. And if that's the case then what's the point in trying to fight the inevitable? Why not just accept that fate is *what it is* because there is no way you can change it anyway?

Adam turned over in the bed and sighed deeply.

Nah. Somehow that just couldn't be right.

There had to be something more.

There *had* to be something more.

"I've brought you a few books."

The nurse's words interrupted Adams fragmented daydreams and he sat up as quickly as he could as she walked over to his bed.

"Uh...thanks. I was getting bored."

She smiled broadly which made him feel uncomfortable again. "Don't get too excited, they may not be what you had in mind, but beggars can't be choosers eh?" She placed a few books onto the bedside cabinet. "Don't forget to pass them on to the other patients", she added, nodding across the ward. "They are a bit dog-eared, but I don't think there are any pages missing. Feeling any better yet?"

"A bit...y'know...it still hurts in places. Ribs mainly. I'll get over it."

"'Course you will. You're young. Time is a great healer. So, was that your girlfriend here earlier?"

Adam reddened. "Yeah...sort of."

"Nice girl. She filled in all the paperwork for you before she left. Name, address, next of kin, date of birth - that sort of thing. She's also contacted your family to let them know what's happening. Oh, and she also left some money for your train fare home. Very thoughtful I thought."

Adam shifted uncomfortably.

"Yeah, she's always like that. Thoughtful. Anyway, thanks for the books...I'll pass them around."

"Good. Now don't forget to use the buzzer if you need me, right? Tea will be at seven."

"Great. Thanks. Um...so tell me what the 'T' stands for then."

"Sorry?"

"Your name tag, T. Anderson."

"Oh...Tina - why?"

"No reason."

She turned and walked over to the bed opposite where the older guy was reading a newspaper. Adam watched them in conversation for a few moments and then reaffirmed to himself that there was no way he could ever do a job like nursing. How could they clear up all sorts of mess, including bodily fluids, and tend fragile ill people all day for practically nothing? It was surprising that nurses smiled at all really in view of what they got paid and had to put up with.

The nurse left the ward and the monotonous silence returned. The guy with the cassette player changed a tape and put on a bulky set of headphones that made him look like one of the cyber men on Doctor Who. It sent him back into his usual trance which suited Adam. The old guy returned to his newspaper. Adam lay back on his pillow trying to ignore the pain in his ribs and the dull ache in his groin.

Can't take much more of this. Death has got to be a lot less boring.

He turned to the bedside cabinet and picked up each book in turn thumbing them through briefly. There were five books; one about the history of steam railways, a romantic novel, a tatty older book simply entitled 'Meditation', an autobiography written by a politician he had never heard of and a large gardening book full of colour pictures of roses with Latin names beneath them.

Adam sighed.

All total bollocks. A copy of the latest "Playboy" would have been good.

He slammed the books back onto the bedside unit noisily. The other patients looked up at the sudden disturbance and stared across reproachfully. The older man tutted and then returned to his newspaper. Adam waved two fingers at him then crossed his arms and started to whistle. Why not annoy the other patients as much as possible he thought, might even cheer the dull old bastards up.

There was sod all else to do in this depressing place.

It was sometime later that Adam awoke with a start and for a moment or two felt disorientated. The hospital ward was in darkness with only the sound of gentle snoring from across the room breaking the stillness and silence. The clock on the wall read 2.45 am and he must have nodded off sometime around 9.30 in the evening. Tea at seven had been a non-event. Vegetable soup and stale bread rolls. Predictable hospital fare that he had barely touched. The pain was duller now and it was slightly easier to move. He shifted position and then reached over and poured himself a glass of water. The cool liquid was refreshing and made him realise just how parched he was.

So, what had woken him up? Thankfully not a nightmare this time - and that was a bonus. No matter. He was wide awake now and falling asleep again was unlikely for a while. He let his eyes become accustomed to the darkness and took in everything around him. It was exactly the same as during the day, but now the darkness made the place even more gloomy and nondescript. He could hear heavy rain spattering on the windowpanes.

He yawned loudly and flicked on the small bedside lamp. The other patients didn't stir. He should have asked to borrow the old guy's newspaper or something. This was ridiculous. He couldn't sleep, couldn't go anywhere, and couldn't do anything. He thought about Marie for a while, but the thoughts only made him feel more solemn and dispirited. She was right about Steve and Danny though. Some mates. Where the hell were they now then?

Adam glanced over at the pile of books on the cabinet and shook his head in disbelief. He couldn't help but smile when he read the titles on the spines. What grim people must come in this place to leave such boring books? 'History of the Steam Railway' for God's sake. Must have been left by some sodding train spotter. He picked up the oldest of the books simply entitled 'Meditation' and opened it idly at the first chapter. Oh well, there was bugger all else to do - might as well read some of this drivel. He sat up and adjusted the pillows then moved the bedside lamp a little nearer until its soft glow lit up the pages. "Okay mister Sinclair" he whispered to himself, "Let's go for the 'Hare Krishna' bit then, maybe this will help me get back to sleep. It's probably no worse than counting sheep."

Shaking his head in disbelief he turned dispiritedly to the first page.

"'E's nothing but trouble you know."

"Yes well..."

"I warned you about letting 'im go to those sorts of places, didn't I? They're all the same you know. Never learn. Not like in my day. You wouldn't dream of it in my day."

"No. Well. Things have changed mother. He is nineteen after all."

"Nineteen? Nine more like it. Your father was in the Navy at eighteen. He was a man by then. Can't see your Adam joining up. Do 'im the power of good mind you."

"I don't think Adam is cut out for the forces."

"Not cut out for anything if you ask me. Where did you say it happened? One of those festivals? All drugs and nudity that's the trouble. No standards anymore. I saw it on the news."

"It's not as bad as they make out on the news. He'll be fine. I trust Marie. She phoned and told me not to worry. He should be home tomorrow."

The old lady snorted contemptuously and finished the last mouthful of tepid tea, hand shaking slightly which annoyed her.

Parkinsons. Reminded her of her age.

"Well, you tell 'im from me, I'm not surprised he got into trouble goin' to such places."

"I will Mum" Carol Sinclair sighed. She waited until her mother had finished, then carried the cups out to the kitchen.

"How's Dad?" she called, needing to change the subject.

There were a few moments silence. Could be that Patty hadn't heard, her hearing not being what it was. Or maybe she was pondering the question.

"Gramps? E's so so," the response came at last, non-committal and a touch downbeat.

Poor old Dad. Salt of the Earth. Comfortably henpecked and now more devoid of energy than Carol liked to accept. When she was young, he had seemed so indestructible, so tall and strong and so much fun. Now he just sat and watched TV all day with expressionless eyes. Not disinterested. Just a little confused that's all. Didn't like to go out anymore. Made him short of breath. Now it was just mum who came around to tea. Usually, to moan about Adam.

"You need a hand doing the dishes love?" The old lady called.

"No thanks. I'm nearly done."

"I know it's not easy for you since..."

...Since your husband died...

"No mum."

"But even so 'e should be here helping you with the housework. Not off at festivals getting drunk and starting fights."

"He didn't start it."

"Makes a change."

Carol came back into the lounge, hands on hips, trying to bite her tongue.

"He's not as bad as you make out Mum. He's just having fun with his friends. You're only young once you know."

Was Mum ever young she began to wonder?

Patty ignored the comment and picked up a beige handbag from the floor. She rifled through it for a small cosmetic mirror and pushed a veiny hand through thinning hair.

"Needs a regular job that boy. Do 'im good. Is 'e still having those nightmares? He should have grown out of all that by now."

Carol sank down into her favourite armchair with a deep sigh and glanced at the clock on the mantelpiece. Four fifteen. Mum would be on her way soon.

Thank God.

"He still gets them from time to time. He's older now. Copes with it better than he used to."

"It 'aint right at his age having those silly nightmares. Even after...well, you know...he should have got over it by now."

"Some things take a long-time mum. It's not easy for him."

"Or you dear - all this fussin' over 'im. It's probably the drinking that gives 'im the nightmares you know. You should never have let 'im start drinkin'. Makes 'em lazy. Gramps reckons it's a sign of intelligence though."

Carol frowned, "Drinking?"

"No silly" Patty cackled, "'Is nightmares. Gramps reckons it's cos he 'knows things'. Gawd knows what things mind you."

Carol looked away. She loved Dad - 'Gramps' - dearly and hated to watch the insidious creeping tentacles of senility stealing away his mind day by day. It made her feel helpless and vulnerable. All this talk of Adam reminded her that he was miles away in some hospital bed and made all her maternal instincts converge into a dull ache deep inside. For once she wanted Patty to go and leave her alone. Go back and look after confused old Gramps instead. She needed Adam to be back at home soon.

Patty sensed it was time to leave and snapped her handbag shut.

"Must be going then dear. Give me a tinkle when Adam's home again. Hope he gets better soon."

"Thanks Mum. I'll see you to the door."

After Patty had left Carol closed the door and leaned her back against it. She shut her eyes and groaned inwardly.

Why did it have to be like this? She was coping with everything wasn't she? Why did mum have to go on about Adam all the time like that?

She opened her eyes and looked at the hallway and stairs. The house was empty now. She should be pleased. Alone with just her thoughts and the empty house, moving and creaking the way all houses do.

Then something made her shiver inside.

Something not quite right about the house...

She shook her head and told herself to snap out of it. Adam would be home soon, and she needed to get some shopping done.

No time for silly notions at all.

The book didn't help Adam sleep. In fact, it kept him awake far longer than he anticipated. The first probing rays of dawn's amber glow were creeping across the ward floor by the time his eyes began to weary of the sustained concentration. Adam shut his eyes and rested them for a few moments then turned off the small bedside lamp that had now burned for four solid hours.

It had been a long time since Adam had been totally absorbed by a book. There were too many other distractions in life, and anyway, reading always reminded him of school and all the pathetic rules and regulations that he so despised. Somehow the silence, the warmth and the night had all conspired to both relax his body and energise his mind - and with no distractions Adam was able to give the book his full attention. And strangely enough he felt it had been worth it.

The book hadn't been so bad after all. Okay, it was about thirty years old and well-thumbed, but it had held his interest far longer than he expected. In fact, though he would never admit it, it was pretty damn interesting. And, come to think of it, it had made him forget about the pain for a while.

Before picking up the book all that Adam knew about meditation was that it was practised by bald-headed Tibetan monks who lived like hermits in caves and long-haired hippies from California who were partial to combining it with various psychedelic substances.

At least, that was what he had always previously thought.

The book had certainly dispelled some of those clichés. In addition, it had also awakened a sense of curiosity that had always been there since childhood but had been lying dormant for the last year or two. There was much more to this thing called meditation than he had ever realised. It wasn't just an escape mechanism from the dreariness of life after all. It was a sort of gateway into something much more enigmatic.

Come to think of it, it reminded him of something half-forgotten from his childhood.

A distant memory or some such.

Couldn't place it for sure. Anyway, mused Adam, it was something that was maybe worth a little further investigation.

Sometime.

Maybe.

A buzzer sounded in the distance and the sounds of bodies stirring disturbed his contemplation. Adam put the book back on the cabinet and yawned. It was just after 6.30, another hour or so until breakfast and then the doctor would be back to check him over. With luck the Doc would agree to let him get up and go home. Or at least walk around a bit. Then again, he could be stuck here for another day and night. Not that it mattered – the festival was as good as over and he'd missed all the bands that he'd waited all year to see. Thank God he'd been there when The Sensational Alex Harvey Band had rocked their stuff so amazingly. At least Marie had remembered to phone his mother. He knew she would of course. It was just the way she was. Reliable. Trustworthy.

He wondered if she would ever speak to him again.

The monotonous grey shades of suburbia did little to stir Adam's spirits as the train pulled out of Victoria station. It was one of those sunshine and shower days that characterised late August, but the grubby streets around Clapham still managed to radiate a dull greyness even in sunshine. At least he was out of hospital though. Wounded, but still alive.

"The Doctor says you can go now" was all Tina had said after his examination earlier this morning. He'd wanted to chat her up, ask her out, make her laugh, but the words or the bravado had deserted him. Probably both. It wasn't the same chatting up a bird when you've got a black eye and you're dressed in a baggy hospital gown.

The examination had been perfunctory and routine. Severe bruising to the stomach, ribs, face and groin area, a black eye plus some minor cuts and grazes to the neck, cheeks and lips. Nothing that wouldn't clear up after a couple of weeks; well, the physical scars maybe; the memory of the beating up would stay with him for some time yet – that was for sure. The doctor had handed him a prescription for pain killers and Tina had handed him the money Marie had left for his train fare home plus his jeans and shoes. The torn black T-shirt was unsalvageable, and blood stained, so Tina had found him an old sweater that someone had left behind in a cupboard.

"Is that it then?" enquired Adam when the examination was over, not really sure what he meant by the question. The elderly doctor had raised his eyebrows and peered over the top of half-moon specs. "Yes. You can go home now. We have decided not to report the ingestion of narcotics to the police. Had the situation been more life threatening then we would have had to file a more detailed report but fortunately for you that is not necessary – unless you want to press charges against the assailants that is. If you could ever identify them of course..." Adam had breathed out a long sigh of relief.

"No. I'm not gonna press any charges. Thanks anyway."

Tina had escorted him out of the ward and led him down the polished corridor still smiling at him sweetly.

"Goodbye then Mr Sinclair. Take good care of yourself now."

"Thanks Tina."

"Nurse Anderson to you" another smile, and then, "Good book?"

"Huh?"

"The book on meditation you were reading all night. Was it good?"

Adam had stared at her with a quizzical expression on his face. So quizzical it made his black eye throb a little. It seemed an odd thing to say. He shrugged noncommittally.

"Alright I suppose."

"I find it helps you know...well, certain people anyway."

Tina looked him squarely in the eyes.

"Those who have the courage to follow through that is..."

She'd held open the front door of the main entrance in that efficient caring way that only nurses can, and a warm August breeze made him realise how two days without fresh air made you really appreciate it again. The stuffy claustrophobic artificial warmth of hospital wards might help in the cure, but there was nothing like real fresh air.

"So" she'd added conversationally "Is it back to the festival to get drunk again or home on the train?"

Adam had pulled a face "Nah, the festival's almost over. My mates will have had a ball. There were some great bands playing today. I feel gutted. I really wanted to see 'Focus' and 'Procol Harum' but my ticket was in my wallet, so I can't get back in anyhow. Not that I feel like bumping into those thugs again. No, I feel too rough. I need to get home and get some sleep. Maybe next year."

"Sensible decision" she said, "And take my advice - stay off the drugs. There are other ways to get high you know."

"Yeah? Like what?"

"Think about it."

That was the last thing she'd said before smiling again and closing the door with a small wave, leaving him to walk to Reading rail station to catch the connection to London Victoria.

He couldn't recall the walk. His feet had moved mechanically, and each step still made his stomach hurt. Must have taken him about an hour before he finally found the right platform, still cursing about missing the festival and wondering what Nurse Anderson had meant by that last comment.

It was only when he'd boarded the two-thirty southbound that he also remembered that his rucksack and sleeping bag were still in the tent. Bugger. Hopefully Steve and Danny would bring them back and remember that the tent had been borrowed too.

The train was relatively empty at this time of day. Adam sat back and stared out of the half open window at the Surrey countryside flashing past him while pondering his situation. He hadn't had a fag or a beer in two days and he still felt like shit. He'd no money, his favourite 'Yes' T-shirt was in tatters somewhere, he'd left his rucksack behind, split up with his girlfriend, been beaten witless by a bunch of Hell's Angels, missed most of the best rock festival of the year and his 'boat race' looked like something out of the Munsters. And now he was on the train home to face his mother who would no doubt give him the usual lecture about finding a job rather than spending his meagre savings on rock concerts.

'Serves you right' would probably be the closest to sympathy he could expect from her, followed by 'If your father were alive today...'

Adam hung his head and rubbed his aching temple. Life didn't get much worse than this.

The soporific clack-clacking of the rails made him feel sleepy. It was still half an hour or so to get home, but he dare not nod off. Not because he might miss his stop, nah, that wasn't the problem. It was sleep that was the problem, or more specifically the possibility of enduring another recurring nightmare - *that* nightmare - the one that had plagued him on and off for as long as he could remember. *That* was the problem. God had sure dealt him a lousy set of cards when even the luxury of a decent night's sleep was denied to him.

And what was it about bulls and him anyway?

"Oh my God look at the state of you," Carol Sinclair exclaimed before squeezing Adam tightly and then shutting the front door before the neighbours caught sight of him.

"I'm okay Mum. No need to make a fuss."

"Nonsense. All Mothers make a fuss. Now come and sit down in the lounge while I make us a cup of tea and then you can tell me all about it."

She led Adam to the sofa and practically pushed him into it before disappearing off to the kitchen.

Carol Sinclair still looked good for forty - the birthday she had really dreaded - and shared most of Adam's features. The same thick brown hair, though hers was neatly bobbed, and wide brown eyes. Still slim enough to only have to watch her weight on occasions, she liked to keep fairly fit with the odd game of tennis and exercise classes. She also prided herself on her strong resolute disposition that was constantly tested by her wayward son (and probably her insufferable Mother too). If she had any vices, they were probably too much TV, nail biting, and coffee. She used to be very active socially, when her husband, Gordon, was alive - but had become more reclusive over the last year or two. It was only her part time job in the local Sports Centre on the reception desk that gave her a chance to meet people these days. The money wasn't that good, but it got her out of the house and that was the main thing. In many ways she and Adam were very similar. The difference being that she had studied hard at school and college and was a qualified teacher. (Not that teaching had suited her when it actually came to controlling a mob of unruly ten-year-olds as it turned out.) Adam, to her constant dismay, seemed to shrug off education as of minor importance - like everything else in his life. He'd been fine in Primary school, very bright in some subjects in fact, but the onset of his teens had seen a marked change in his interests and priorities. Teachers had said he was unruly and disinterested, a troublemaker and a ringleader. Needed more discipline at home.

Needed a 'father figure.'

Yeah. Thanks for that...

Carol worried for his future. He'd never managed to keep a single part time job whilst at school. Even simple things like paper rounds or cleaning jobs couldn't keep his interest. What hope was there now that he'd left school for good?

In a few moments she was back with a tray containing tea and biscuits which she put down in front of the sofa on a small coffee table. Adam helped himself to a biscuit.

"Marie phoned then?"

"Yes. She's such a sweet girl. Far too good for you."

"Yeah. So you keep saying. What did she actually tell you then?"

Carol perched on the arm of the sofa and took a sip of tea. "That you had been beaten up by some rough types at the festival and had been taken into hospital to be checked over. I would have caught the train then and there, but she assured me you'd be fine and would be on the way home soon enough."

Adam felt a wave of relief wash over him. No mention of drugs or anything else that might have caused a big scene.

I owe you one Marie...

"How do you feel love?" Carol asked putting a hand to his cheek, "Your eyes are so bruised, and you look so pale. Is your neck okay? I see they've put a plaster on it."

Adam picked up a newspaper from the coffee table and started to flick through it with feigned interest. Another IRA bomber had been arrested in London. More trouble in Vietnam. Same old shit.

"Are you hurting?" asked Carol.

"A bit. I probably look a lot worse than I am. The Doctor said there would be a small scar on my neck but everything else should clear up in a week or two. It's my ribs that hurt the most. They're badly bruised but luckily not broken."

"Who did it to you? Why? You know I worry when you go off to these places. Why did they do this?"

Adam shook his head and shrugged, "I dunno Mum. Wrong place, wrong time, I guess. They were just a bunch of louts outa their skulls. Most people were just there for a good time. You know what it's like. Always some idiots spoiling it for the rest. The music was good though. It was a great festival despite the fact I ended up missing most of it."

"But why is it always you though?"

Adam put the newspaper down.

"What do you mean?"

"Well, you went with Marie and Steve and Danny, didn't you? How come they're all okay? How come it's always you who seems to attract trouble? It's been the same since you were small."

"Search me. It just happens."

Carol tousled his hair for a moment and raised her eyebrows slightly while looking him straight in the eye. Adam recognised the look. Why did she always think everything was his fault? He didn't exactly ask to be beaten up, did he?

Carol tactfully changed the subject.

"So, what are you going to do with yourself now you're back? Spent all your money no doubt?"

"Yeah" said Adam "And had the rest of it nicked. I suppose it's time I started looking for a job again."

Carol had heard that line before. Many times.

"Looking for a job? You won't get an interview with your face in that mess."

"I'll apply for something in a few days" said Adam, trying hard to sound enthusiastic. "You'll see."

"More tea?"

"No thanks."

He felt her eyes burning the back of his neck. Knew she was building up to something.

"Adam..." she said at length, "You have really got to sort yourself out you know."

"Huh?"

"I said that you have really got to sort yourself out. It's a year now since you left school and apart from a series of part-time, dead-end jobs you haven't really done anything about your future. You didn't want to go to college or University, and I don't think you've got a clue about what you want to do for a living. It's time you started to think more seriously about your life."

"I suppose so."

"You owe it to yourself. Think about it. Life is very precious. For God's sake don't throw it away. Remember what that careers counsellor said when we went to talk to him at the end of term?"

Adam could remember all right. His Mother had insisted on dragging him along to some boring careers guidance meeting, so he'd deliberately worn his most outrageous clothes, made his hair look longer and more unruly than usual and chewed gum the whole time that the careers tosser had been talking. He'd severely embarrassed Carol that day and she never let him forget it. He'd shrugged in response to every question the dickhead in the suit had asked him. In the end the careers guy had simply given up trying to engender any enthusiasm and looked at Adam in disgust and contempt.

"I'm sorry" he had said to Carol whilst getting up from his seat and closing his file, "I'm not spending any more of my precious time on a lost cause."

Adam brought his mind back to the present, aware that Carol was still waiting for an answer.

"I really will find a job this time Mum. Promise."

Carol Sinclair picked up the tray and carried the teacups back to the kitchen. She wanted to say more but now was not the time.

"I hope so" she called "I really hope so. Now if I were you, I'd have a long bath."

"Yeah. I'll do that."

He shut his puffy and purple eyes for a moment and tried to relax. Relaxation was something he had always found very difficult since…

Well, since the nightmares.

Doctors had all said it was probably due to a flashback to the accident. Subliminal like. Trauma of losing his father and all that. What did they know? Fuck all. 'Fact is, the nightmares had started way before the accident. Right back to when he was a small kid snivelling in his cot. It was something the specialists couldn't actually explain but they said he would probably grow out of it.

Yeah – right. Like when?

Before or after he'd lost his mind?

Back in Reading General, Nurse Tina Anderson was just finishing her shift and was also looking forward to going home and enjoying a long hot bath. She'd finished doing the rounds and settling in all the new patients in the casualty ward. Then she'd very carefully collected the pile of books and returned them to the bookshelf by the admissions desk where she could retrieve them again tomorrow should any of the patients fancy a read.

All except one.

The tattiest and oldest of the books she took with her to the end of the corridor, the staff locker room. She reached into her pocket for the key then opened her personal locker which contained a spare uniform on a hanger and a small shelf containing a few personal trinkets and some precious family photos. Very carefully she placed the book in a small silk lined box at the back of the shelf, before locking the door again with a faint smile and turning for home.

"Adam me 'ole mate - how's it going man?"

Adam slumped into a chair next to the phone. It was three days later, and it was Steve. He had wondered when the lads would get in touch.

"So so" even toned. He didn't feel especially matey at the moment.

"Nothing broken?"

"Nope - bit fragile though - y'know how it is. So, you guys didn't bother to come and see me in hospital then?"

Steve laughed, "Hospital? I can't stand 'ospitals. Makes me think of injections and old people 'n stuff like that. No way you'd get me inside an 'ospital."

"I thought you might want to know if I was alive or not?"

Sarcasm.

Lost on Steve.

"Nah. We asked Marie...she told us all about it. Said you were okay, just beaten up a bit. Actually she 'ad a go at me about doping you up too much but what does she know? Naggin' old bitch."

Adam bit his lip. He was 'one of the boys', wasn't he?

"Yeah" he agreed wearily, "Anyway I've decided to finish with her. It's all over between us."

Steve was genuinely surprised. "Yeah? Probably a good thing though. Seems to me she was always tryin' to stop yer havin' a good time. You're probably better off wivvout 'er. So, what happened to you then? Who kicked your arse in?"

"It was after I'd left the main arena" said Adam, "I was looking for the tent and these three guys just jumped me. I couldn't really see them it was so dark. They were all out of their heads on something. I think they were from that wigwam tent with the skull painted on the side, but I can't be sure."

"The one with the big horns like a bull?"

Adam's heart missed a beat.

"Yeah."

"I saw that tent too. I think I know who you mean. Bastards. That's not what festivals are about."

"Nah. I was just unlucky I guess" said Adam, then changing the subject "So how was the rest of the festival then?"

"Brilliant mate. You don't know what you missed. Even 'George Melly' had 'em rockin'. Bet Marie was pissed off that she missed the 'Barclay James Harvest' set. She should really have stayed on."

"Yeah" agreed Adam adding mentally -

'...Instead of worrying about you being in hospital...'

"And you missed a great scene too man. There was this fish n' chip shop van tryin' to charge stupid prices, so some hippies tried to turn the van over. The owner was going mental trying to stop 'em. Anyway, this geezer managed to drive off just before the van went over, but it was full of chip oil which caught fire and this guy is driving off with flames coming out the back. It was such a laugh."

"Yeah. I'm sorry I missed it," said Adam, "Anyhow, what's doin'?"

"Friday night!" said Steve.

"Friday? What's happening?"

"Me 'n Danny are plannin' on goin' clubbin' - few beers, you know, maybe try that new disco in the High Street. You up for it?"

"I dunno..."

"C'mon man, loosen up, it'll be a gas."

Adam sighed. "You 'aint seen the state of my face."

"Ah, what the hell. No-one will see it and you were already an ugly bastard anyway. It's dark in the club. You can stay in the shadows if you want."

Something made Adam shudder inwardly.

Shadows...

"Yeah, okay then. S'pose I can always cover my black eye with some of Mum's face paint."

"Now you're talkin'. We'll be round about eight then mate. See ya."

"Yeah. See ya Steve. See you Friday." Adam put the phone back on the receiver.

Yeah, it would be good to get out with the boys again on Friday. Should be a laugh.

Shouldn't it?

Even with two black eyes and a fat lip.

Adam wondered why a night out with the boys suddenly didn't appeal to him as much as usual.

Must be the effects of that sodding medication...

G raveyards look different in summer.
　Somehow the scent of death and decay that lingers around the old weathered and lichen covered headstones in the winter months seems lifted in summer. It's almost as if the whole scenery of death, the rumbling black clouds, rain-drenched yew trees, the crumbling medieval churches and the sombre processions of pall bearers *belong* to winter and that summertime has no affinity with such things. Graveyards in late August are much more rustic and pastoral, full of ancient sun-dappled pathways and butterflies, the hum of bees and vibrant bird song, bright fragrant flowers and the exuberance of untamed foliage. Even the moss on the gravestones seems lush and green.

The churchyard of St. Cuthberts, a 13th century patchwork jumble of flint and crumbly grey stone, seemed to grow out of the hillside as naturally as if an artist had painted it there on a canvas in order to give the whole picture some indefinable romantic integrity. It *felt* right just being there.

Most of the graves contained local folk who had farmed or worked the land for centuries around the ancient parish of Hurlingfold. Nowadays of course there were newer houses in the village built for the commuters to Brighton or London. Even the local pub had acquired a juke box to the disdain of the older regulars. Hurlingfold, like everywhere else, was gradually being sucked into the twentieth century and learning to adapt to the faster pace of living.

Among the older timeworn and faded headstones that jutted unevenly from the earth like rotting teeth stood another that was comparatively new and therefore very conspicuous in its upright stature. It was also the only grave attended by a very living person whose shadow now moved across the simple engraved words on the surface of the coarse stone.

Gordon Sinclair 1925 - 1964
Beloved Husband and Father
R.I.P

Adam glanced nervously over his shoulder. Not because he was in a graveyard - no - he didn't fear the dead. It was the living he was more concerned about. He felt self-conscious and exposed standing there alone among the old stones. It was almost as if teenagers and graveyards shouldn't be seen together because it was somehow wrong; incongruous. As though the stark contrast between unmanifest potential and final dissolution was too great.

Then he berated himself for being so stupid and told himself to get a grip. What's wrong with visiting your father's grave for heaven's sake? It was a whole lot more fulfilling than last night's terminally boring disco.

He'd not bothered to tell Carol where he was going. Couldn't be bothered to explain it or to even mention it even though he knew she'd understand and be supportive and sympathetic. It was just too hard for him to talk about. It was something he found very difficult to deal with. Too personal. There were no words that could express how he felt.

No. This way was much easier.

Every couple of months it was something he had to do. Slip away with no word to anyone about where he was going. Take time just to spend a few minutes in quiet contemplation, not knowing quite why it helped or if it helped - but needing to do it anyway. It was nothing to do with religion or his beliefs about the afterlife it was just the need to be near the person who had meant so much to him. That's the only rational explanation he could give himself.

The place always brought back memories of course. He could picture himself at nine years old holding his mother's hand, the other hand clutching his favourite toys, a plastic slide viewer with dinosaur slides and a teddy bear called Benny - both hands needing something representing comfort and reassurance. He was watching the earth being shovelled onto a gleaming wooden box. He remembered how it had been a day of sunshine and showers. Remembered his grandparents standing there dressed head to toe in black and trying to comfort him when the flood of emotions had been too much for a small boy to cope with. His Grandmother and Mother had tried so hard to help him deal with those awful feelings, but it was Gramps who had managed to reassure him the most.

He remembered how dear old Gramps had squeezed his hand as they stared down at the coffin, how Gramps had knelt down beside him and whispered something in his ear which at the time had seemed so strange and yet also so comforting.

"You're Daddy's not really gone away to live with the Angels" he'd said with a wink. Then he had tapped Adam gently on the side of the head, "He's still with you in there." Then he'd put a finger to his lips to show that it was a secret that only the two of them should share.

And it was something that they still shared though always unspoken, even if Gramps was a lot older and more frequently confused these days. It was still *Adam and Gramp's secret*. Other little details about the day had stayed with him all these years. Small, insignificant things, that there was really no reason to remember. Things like the moment the rain stopped - and a shaft of sunlight had penetrated the church through a stained-glass window making fragments of dust hover and twirl like miniature spiralling galaxies before his swollen eyes. The distant sounds of the village cricket match from across the fields as the Vicar intoned a solemn eulogy while the coffin was lowered into the gaping black hole beside Adam's small feet. Sandwiches afterwards at the Black Bull Inn which he couldn't eat because his stomach felt so twisted and cold and the nice lady from the choir who had bent down to tell him that Daddy would be waiting for him in heaven and that he must be brave and look after Mummy.

And now here he was ten years on, still not come to terms with anything. Still just as confused and scared. Still unable to cry properly and release all that pent-up frustration and emotion. Still not sure why he had to keep coming back to look for answers when there was no-one to give him any answers.

It was okay for his mates. They wouldn't understand. They had never known life without their fathers' around. It wasn't something Adam wanted to talk about either. It was for him alone to deal with.

Deal with. Resolve. Come to terms with. Whatever...

It was time to catch the local bus which would be passing through Hurlingford in a few minutes time. Woodsham new town, as it was known, was less than ten miles away, but it might as well be a million miles in comparison. Adam's hometown was one of those dreary commuter towns built in the Sixties to cater for London overspill. Regimented rows of identical little boxes for people to live in, completely devoid of history and character but 'convenient for the train'. Dad had thought it was a good idea to settle there all those years ago when Adam had been a mere toddler.

Dad...

He flopped down in front of the gravestone, his knees sinking into the soft earth, eyes searching among the engraved words for some kind of subliminal message that he knew would never come.

"Love you Dad" he said softly, "And I'm sorry. I'm so sorry..."

Three Months Later

It was raining again. The cold miserable sort of rain that carries on all day and really pisses you off. Third day running. Grey, monotonous, boring, depressing and fairly typical of Sussex in late November. A few weeks ago, the crisp bright mornings and the autumnal reds and golds were refreshing and uplifting, but this?

Adam cursed as a gust of wind sprayed rainwater from an overflowing gutter on a shop front down inside his shirt collar sending icy rivulets down the length of his back. He hated winter. He pulled the collar of his coat closer, momentarily feeling the last remnant of scar tissue on his neck; another reminder of the summer festival come back to haunt him. At least it was the last scar to heal. The other scars had now faded and fortunately left no long-term physical damage. He was lucky. No doubt about it. He shivered slightly not knowing whether from the rain or the vivid memory of the assault.

The crowds were starting to disperse. Most of Woodsham's shops closed at six and the rain was sending even the most dedicated shoppers' home. The early nightfall at this time of year coupled with bad weather made even the neon lights of the shops gloomy and unappealing. The once crisp fallen leaves had now turned to mulch in the gutters and

Adam had already laughed to see one old codger slip over when trying to cross the road.

The interview had not gone well. By Adam's reckoning he'd clocked up - *or was it cocked up?* - three interviews so far but his lack of enthusiasm for any of the jobs had obviously been as evident to the interviewers as to himself. A lucky escape he had concluded; there was bound to be something better around the corner. Even this job, he had to be honest, didn't really get his juices going. It was his mother who had seen the vacancy advertised in the local paper and even phoned up to book the appointment for him; 'Accounts Clerk in a Furniture company' it read. 'Well, it's a start' she had said, 'It's offering more money than the other jobs you've applied for.' True, but now he'd blown it anyway. Okay, so it was a stupid move to go for a drink with Danny at the 'King's Head' first, but so what? He was still sober enough to answer all the stupid pointless questions - even if there was alcohol on his breath.

Why do they always ask about previous experience for heaven's sake? Don't the tossers realise that school leavers looking for their first job don't have any experience precisely because they've just left school? Accounting is terminally boring anyway. Everyone knows that. Yeah, lucky escape.

Adam stopped under a streetlight and turned out his pockets. Could've done with the money though. Not even enough left for a pint - barely enough for the bus ride home. He already owed his mother around twenty-five quid - she wouldn't be seeing much of that for a while.

Adam looked up at a crowd of giggling girls across the street. Wasn't that Emma from the College? Tasty bird.

Nah. No point. Couldn't even offer her a can of fizz.

He leaned against the lamp post and looked at his watch. 6.35. The evening was young but without promise – as usual. No money for beer, no money for chips, no money for chicks - and all he had to look forward to was the bus ride home so he could tell his nagging mother that he had messed up another interview. Nah, couldn't face another evening of nagging again. Rather walk the streets. He wished the bloody rain would stop. Should have thought to grab an umbrella.

The rain seemed to be getting more persistent though. His long-matted hair was already drenched, and streams of water fell from his chin. Maybe he could find just enough dosh for a quick half and then walk home; at least the pub would be warm and dry. Maybe he should try begging? Christ! Enough jerks had thrust out their hand to him in the past and asked for some 'spare change'.

Nah. Couldn't beg. Somehow didn't feel right. Never would.

The lights of the Odeon Cinema caught his eye. Usual crap being advertised. Mind you, if he'd found enough dosh in his pocket, he'd sit through anything. Lots of birds going in, some with blokes, some in a crowd. It was probably the only place open now the shops were closing apart from the pubs and even some of the pubs were not open yet.

Adam walked past the Cinema queue and up the hill towards the bus station. The lights of the shopping arcade were now behind him and only the old church, St Peters, and the town library lay between him and the dismal ride home. Outside the library there was a large glass fronted notice board now lashed with rain, usually a good place to check out whether any rock bands were playing the town hall this week. Although not a big town, a few good rock bands had played the Town Hall over the last few years. Adam scanned the notice board and turned his nose up. There was a poster advertising some soul band he'd never heard of. He hated soul. Oh well...

He was about to turn away when one of the other notices posted on the board caught his eye, there between the Parish notices and an advert for the W.I. Coffee Morning. It was a simple sheet of yellow A4 with black print that read:

MEDITATION
Tonight 7.00pm
Library meeting room
A free talk by Doctor David Levinson

Adam stared at the words mentally repeating them. Deep inside his gut he felt something move.

Meditation.

Now where...? Yes, of course... the book that nurse Tina had given him in hospital. That dusty old tome that he had almost flung across the ward in disgust, and then read avidly all night without sleeping.

'*Something that was maybe worth a little investigation.*'

Yeah, it all came back now. All that stuff about alternative levels of consciousness and getting attuned to your inner being etcetera. Yeah, it all sounded pretty cool. Adam checked the time again. 6.50. The talk would start in ten minutes. Should he? Nah, bound to be full of stuffy old women and middle-aged professors who'd all stare at him like he was something from Mars. Not his scene man.

Then again it was warm in the library, wasn't it? And it was still pissing down with rain and the next bus was at least another half an hour...

Sod it! Why not? What was there to lose? Might even be mildly interesting if the book was anything to go by.

And anyway, his mates need never know. They'd think he was back on acid again if he told them he'd gone to a lecture on meditation. Nah, no reason to tell 'em. Adam ran his hands through his streaming wet hair, turned his collar back down and went up the stone steps pushing open the door into the old library.

Doctor Levinson was not quite what Adam had expected. Somehow a meditation lecturer ought to be either an Asiatic robed monk type or a doddery old professor that looked similar to Einstein - right?

Wrong.

David Levinson was neither. In fact, thought Adam, he was disappointingly ordinary. Just a middle-aged regular guy in a tweed jacket that could easily pass for an Estate Agent or a Financial Consultant. Not an incense stick in sight.

Adam had only visited the library a few times and never been inside the meeting room before. It was an oak panelled Victorian affair that could sit up to around fifty people comfortably. The wooden floorboards were highly polished around the periphery of the room, but a large floral and mostly threadbare carpet covered most of the floor space in the middle where thirty or so red plastic chairs had been placed facing a single table. Only half of the seats were occupied. Adam's eyes cautiously scanned the room for any recognisable faces. If one of his mother's friends were here, then he could always mumble some apology about being in the wrong meeting before making himself scarce. No way he was gonna stay if anyone recognized him.

But it was okay. Nobody even vaguely familiar. Good.

He chose a seat a good distance from anyone else and pretended to be preoccupied with the interview letter that he'd found crumpled in his pocket. A few people were chatting softly; others sitting with arms folded looking to the front table where the speaker was shuffling his papers in preparation. One or two more people followed Adam into the room and found seats before a short, tubby woman with huge specs gently shut the door separating the meeting room from the main library.

The simple motion of shutting the door gave Adam a flicker of panic. What was he doing here for heaven's sake with all these...? He glanced around again at his fellow audience. What sort of people were they anyway? Seemed to be mostly women, with a few middle-aged and older blokes. No-one else under twenty except some studious looking chick with a briefcase and notepad a few seats in front. Too late to think about it. It was 7pm exactly and the voices had quietened down to an expectant hush.

Doctor Levinson put down his papers, walked around to the front of the table and then slowly let his eyes meet those of everyone in the room.

"Good evening, ladies and gentlemen" he began confidently, "I am delighted to have been asked to come here tonight and talk to you about something that's really rather special and also rather unique. It's called meditation..."

His eyes seemed to settle on Adam for a brief moment.

"...And it's something that changes lives."

It was only when Adam glanced at his watch that he discovered that over an hour had passed. He had only intended staying for thirty minutes or so and had no idea the time had flown by so fast. Now he'd probably missed the bloody bus. Still, he mused, all credit to Doctor Levinson that the talk had retained his interest for so long.

And, clearly, he wasn't alone in that thought. Instead of the usual shuffling and coughs symptomatic of public meetings the whole audience had been attentive and quiet. Perhaps it was because of the speaker's easy going and charismatic style. David Levinson had the sort of gentle melodic voice that stage hypnotists use to such good effect. Somnolent to a degree but with enough emphasis at the right points to keep people awake, relaxed and totally absorbed. Many of the audience had been taking notes. Others were fixated on the speaker himself.

Adam was surprised at how much of the material struck a chord with him after reading the book in hospital. At the time it felt as though he had just skimmed through the book on a superficial level and had not consciously tried to learn or retain any details. And yet, time and again, Doctor Levinson had mentioned a word or phrase that sparked all sorts of recollections.

'Meditation improves physical and mental health.'

'Meditation forms a core practice in the spiritual training of many world religions including Hinduism, Buddhism and Taoism.'

'Meditation can aid in psychotherapy.'

'Meditation is the quest for mystical consciousness.'

'Meditation provides insight into oneself.'

'Meditation opens doors into deep spiritual realms.'

'Meditation is good for you.'

Doctor Levinson had gone on to describe the various techniques that were used to attain a meditative state and how different techniques suited different types of people and cultures. He explained what meditation was - and what it was not - and a little of its long history. He covered the many misconceptions that people had about the subject and then talked of the benefits of meditation as an antidote to today's stressful lifestyle.

His talk ended with a genuinely warm smile and a shrug, "So why not give it a try? But remember - don't expect instant results, it's a gradual thing - *give it time* - believe me you won't regret it. Thank you."

There was heartfelt and genuine applause from everyone in the audience before Doctor Levinson asked if there were any questions. Two or three people raised their hands and asked for some further details on some of the points raised while others quietly left the room. Adam decided it was time that he, too, ought to start walking home when a rather obese lady on the seat immediately in front of him put up her hand. "Doctor Levinson, if I want to learn to meditate properly where can I find a good teacher?"

"That's no problem at all" he responded. "Here on the table, I have my business card and a small leaflet with contact details of local meditation tutors and recommended books. Please feel free to take a copy." A few people stood up and went to collect copies, some shaking hands with the Doctor before making their way to the door. Adam was about to follow those departing when something made him turn and pick up a copy for himself. Might as well take one, just for interest's sake. No way he wanted to actually try any of that Buddhist bullshit.

Doctor Levinson had picked up the pile of leaflets from the table and was handing them out to eager hands. As Adam held out his hand the Doctor's eyes met his own for the second time that evening.

"Hold on a moment" the Doctor said.

He reached into his inside suit pocket and withdrew a pen then quickly circled one of the names on the list of meditation tutors before thrusting the paper into Adam's hands. Adam looked questioningly as he took the leaflet, but the Doctor had turned away to talk to somebody else.

Time to go anyhow or he'd never get home.

Outside the rain had stopped and the wind had dropped too. The heavy rain clouds had disappeared, and one or two stars were appearing as Adam made his way the few yards to the bus stop. He was in luck. The last bus had been delayed. About time he had some good luck for a change.

As soon as he had boarded the bus and found a seat next to the rain spattered windows Adam took the leaflet from his pocket and studied it. There was a list of about twelve names, addresses and phone numbers and at the bottom of the page some recommended book titles and authors.

One of the twelve names was circled in blue ink.

Weird. Why should Doctor Levinson want to circle just one of the many names on Adam's leaflet? He hadn't done it for anyone else.

And who the hell was '*Jack Harland*' anyway?

Saturday night. Usual formalities.

Sift through the wardrobe for his one and only expensive shirt - *did she remember to iron it this time? God, the times he had reminded his mother about needing the smart dark blue shirt for Saturday nights.* 'Iron it yourself then' was the usual retort. She knew he was no good at ironing and so she always ended up doing it anyway - even while he waited impatient and bare chested by the front door.

Tonight though, it was there in the wardrobe, crisply ironed amongst a pile of threadbare older shirts, unwashed and screwed up T-shirts and a mound of faded blue jeans. His mother had been moaning incessantly about the state of his bedroom and particularly the pile of unkempt clothes. Lately she seemed to have given up. Resigned to his untidy ways no doubt. Kept shutting the door as though trying to seal off that part of the house '...*And this is Adam's bedroom. Best not to look in there...*'

Adam showered, washed his hair, slapped far too much Brut aftershave on his face (*okay so he wasn't actually shaving properly yet, but the first dark hairs were almost there weren't they?*) and slipped into the only decent shirt he owned. A pair of black trousers, black velvet jacket and a pair of semi-clean brown loafers and he was ready for another Saturday night.

Magic.

When Adam brushed his hair in front of the full-length mirror just inside the front door, he realised how much he actually hated dressing this way. Give him a pair of torn Levi's and a baggy sweatshirt any day. Trouble was that they only let you in 'Smokey Joe's' nightclub in smart shirt and jacket. Jeans were strictly banned. So, all over town, blokes were reluctantly ditching their comfy wear for the traditional Saturday night 'on the town' garb. No point in arguing. Adam had witnessed the same scene time and time again. Pissed blokes on the streets after pub throwing out time. Usual ritual: burger at the grub stop then queue outside Smokey Joe's until the bouncers stopped you at the entrance.

"Sorry. No jeans or T-shirts allowed."

"Aw...come on man...I won't cause any trouble."

"Sorry. Club rules. I can't let you in without a smart shirt and jacket."

"Just this once...?"

"Piss off sonny."

"Wanker."

Adam opened the door into the lounge just enough to poke his head around. Carol was sitting on the sofa with her legs up watching some noisy TV quiz show.

"See ya later."

"Where are you off to?"

"Just out with the lads - y'know - maybe Smokey Joe's nightclub later."

"Try not to wake me up when you get back. Last time you came back from there you were obviously drunk the way you barged around the house at two in the morning. Oh...and Adam don't forget that the Doctor said it would be best to lay off the drinking since your spell in hospital."

"Yeah, right"

"No - I mean it - you don't have to copy those stupid friends of yours. They might think it's 'cool' to get senseless every Saturday night but there's no need to try and keep up with them. Okay?"

"Yeah, yeah. Okay. See ya later."

Adam slammed the front door shaking his head. Mothers. All the bloody same. Steve and Danny said they would meet him at the Plough around half eight. The Plough was only ten minutes' walk. No sweat.

Adam felt quite good tonight as he walked into town. Up for it. School was a distant memory. The remaining aches and pains from Reading were almost gone, he'd got a few quid in his pocket (borrowed from Gramps admittedly) and it was Saturday night. A few drinks with the boys should be a good laugh. Then off night clubbin' - chattin' up the birds and getting into some good music. It was all a bloke wanted really. Well, that and a job too, but right now getting a job could wait.

'Tonight' - was lads' night!

It was Steve Lacey who saw her first.

He nudged Adam in the ribs and nodded in the direction of Smokey Joe's dance floor. Adam looked up through the semi-darkness and flickering disco lights and there among the dancers was a gorgeous apparition in a tight black dress. Marie Cunningham. Adam clenched his pint glass a little tighter. No doubt about it. She seemed unaware of his presence or was possibly ignoring him deliberately. No way of telling. Either way she continued to dance among the other writhing bodies moving to the incessant disco beat.

"I'll say one thing for 'ole Marie" belched Steve, "She's a good mover."

Adam put his drink down on a table, "Okay I suppose."

Danny joined them and followed their gaze. "Well, well" he said, "'Oi' feel a bit 'o fun comin' on."

Adam had spotted Danny with a small packet of coloured tablets just after they'd left The Plough on the way to Smokey Joe's. Danny had given him a sly wink at the time which meant that it would be kicking in about now. Adam had learned to accept Danny's addictions. In some ways it manifested in a swaggering over-confidence which Adam found mildly amusing.

"So" said Adam, "What did you have in mind?"

"Just been chattin' up some wenches over by the bar" said Danny nodding over his shoulder, "They're up for a dance. One of 'ems a hot-for-it blonde. What about it, Adam? Just for a laugh. Just to see Marie's face when she clocks you with the crumpet?"

"I dunno Danny. I haven't spoken to her since..."

"Aw, come on man. Just fer a laugh now. She deserves to be humbled a bit don't ya reckon?"

"Well I..."

"Yeah, let's go for it" said Steve pushing Adam's shoulder playfully.

Danny waved the three girls over from the bar area and introduced them. "'Dis is Steve and 'dis is Adam. Now boys let me introduce...er...what did ya say yer names were again?"

They giggled simultaneously. The blonde spoke first; "I'm Sue. This is Sharon and this is Rachel."

Adam looked them up and down. Sue was definitely the swan among two ugly ducklings, but he was still unsure about this. He still - sort of - missed Marie.

Sort of.

Danny seemed to get off on this sort of caper without a second thought. Adam usually needed a skin full first. Dutch courage.

"Will you fancy a dance 'den?" offered Danny, winking at Rachel.

"S'pose..."

Danny and Steve led Sharon and Rachel to the dance floor deliberately leaving Adam and Sue stood together. As he brushed past Danny whispered, "You owe me one for 'dis mate." Adam rolled his eyes. Well, it was just for a laugh after all. No big deal.

"So, we gonna dance then or what?" said Sue.

"Oh...er...yeah sure."

Adam took Sue's hand and led her to the dance floor following the others. She was a bit of alright.

Natural blonde, long hair, tall, tight short red dress and obviously knew she looked good in a languid offhand sort of way. Every so often she'd scan other blokes' eyes just to make sure they were all looking. Probably nothing much between the ears though mused Adam. Still, he wasn't exactly James fuckin' Bond, was he?

The DJ changed the record for some T. Rex and the disco lights switched from globules orange to globules purple.

Sue could dance too. More than he could do. 'Crab with a rupture' his mother had once commented. What the hell. He hated dancin' anyway. Adam manoeuvred himself so that he could see straight over Sue's shoulder to where Marie was dancing. Sue didn't even notice him stretching his neck turtle fashion. She was too absorbed in looking good for all the blokes on the dancefloor. Marie was obviously enjoying herself too and oblivious as to Adam's proximity. Then Adam saw why.

Marie was dancing with some guy who was demanding her full attention. Tall guy. Short dark hair and wide cream tie with matching jacket. She was smiling up into his eyes and laughing with genuine enjoyment. It made Adam's insides feel like ice. Shit. How the hell could he feel jealousy? He hated the cow. So, what if she had found another bloke? What did he care?

Moved on, hadn't he?

"Adam?"

"Uh?"

"Adam - you dancing wiv me or what?"

"Sorry Sue."

"You were miles away."

"Yeah...sorry."

Adam felt a surge of anger well up inside him. He smiled at Sue then put his arm around her waist and started to move more intimately with her. He shifted position so that there was no way Marie could avoid noticing him. He'd show the stupid cow a thing or two. Marie did notice. Her smile faded, and she stared at Adam groping the giggling blonde in the middle of the dance floor. Adam caught her eye, "Oh hi Marie" he waved nonchalantly before returning his gaze into Sue's eyes. Marie had stopped dancing. Her partner stopped too "Who's that?" he asked.

Marie's face hardened, "That's Adam Sinclair" she hissed through clenched teeth, just loud enough so that Adam could hear every word, "Junkie, pisshead and born loser. Someone I once had the misfortune to hang around with."

Marie resumed dancing and smiled sweetly at her partner.

Adam swore under his breath and when he looked back at Sue, she was staring at him suspiciously, making sure there was more of a distance between them. "Old girlfriend?" she said casually.

"Yeah" mumbled Adam "Something like that."

After a couple more dances Adam led Sue back to one of the tables where Steve and Danny were still chatting up the ugly ducklings. Danny was lining up a series of empty bottles in front of him as per usual and the speech was slurring. Never could handle drink. He shoved a slopping glass into Adam's hands.

"Alright mate? Did ya see the look on 'er face when she saw ya? Brill".

Adam forced a smile, aware that Sue might not be as dumb as she looked.

"Who Marie? Nah, not interested mate. She's history. 'Er loss."

"Hark at you" responded Sue catching her friends' eyes. They giggled. Sharon was sitting on Steve's lap.

Danny was no longer taking any interest in Rachel. Danny was always more interested in getting out of his skull than wasting time on chatting up ugly birds. Adam had drunk a skin full himself. They must have had a few at the Plough before setting off for Smokey Joe's. Steve was already unsteady on his feet. Funny how alcohol affects people so differently. Steve would walk into things whereas Danny would get more and more outrageous until he inevitably threw up. And as for Adam...well he tended to get moody and introspective. At least, that was his own diagnosis.

"So, don't I get offered a drink then?" said Sue, disturbing Adam's train of thought.

"Oh...yeah...sorry. So, what yer havin'?"

"White wine please."

Adam nodded and set off to the bar, checking his pockets. He'd just about enough for a wine and one more beer. After he'd left, Sue sat down in front of Steve while Rachel continued to giggle, still perched on his lap.

"Your mate always like this?" Sue asked Steve.

"Adam? Yeah - he's a good laugh. Well usually he is. Been a bit down recently - y'know, tryin' to find a job and all that".

Sue nodded sympathetically. As far as she was concerned Steve and Danny seemed so...well... typically laddish really. But not so Adam. Adam was different.

A bit Strange. Distant, Fascinating.

She opened her handbag and put on some fresh lipstick.

Adam walked back from the bar holding a glass of beer and a white wine for Sue. May as well enjoy the evening. Sue was a laugh really. She was making heads turn. *If he played his cards right...*

Then he caught sight of Marie again sitting at a table.

Alone.

He walked over. The cocky swagger was a front. He knew it and she knew it. She tried to look away, but he crouched down beside her.

"New boyfriend then Marie? Or has he left you already? I like his white suit – mus' be an Osmonds fan?"

"Get lost Adam."

"Wassamarrer? We can still be friends..."

"I don't think so. Just go away, will you? Go back to your blonde. You're drunk as usual."

"So fuckin' what? God, you think you're so...so..."

He felt someone looming over him. A deep voice said, "Is this guy bothering you Marie?"

It was the jerk from the dance floor.

"No" said Marie forcing a smile "He was just going."

Adam stood up without turning. Deliberately keeping his back to the guy.

"Aw, Marie - thought we could have a little chat..."

"Adam this is Mark. I'd prefer it if you left us alone."

"Mark, eh? Maybe we could all have a little drink together. That would be cosy."

"She said leave her alone" said Mark coolly.

Adam turned slowly to face the deep voice from behind.

"I didn't ask what you thought mate" said Adam meeting Mark's eyes "I was talking to Marie."

"Hadn't you better get back to your own crowd?" suggested Mark nodding at the drinks in Adam's hands.

"When I'm ready" hissed Adam between clenched teeth "And I 'aint ready yet - if that's all right with you..."

"*Adam please*" squealed Marie, "Why do you always have to...?"

"What's got into you?" said Adam. He knew this was upsetting her. Served her right. He waved a thumb at Mark. "And where did you find this ape?"

Mark grabbed Adam's lapels and tried to shove him away.

Bastard!

Adam flung the contents of both drinks into Mark's face then let both glasses smash to the floor. Mark wiped his eyes and snarled with rage aiming a fist at Adam's face but before it connected two burly guys in suits had intervened. One of them restrained Mark and the other frog-marched Adam to the nightclub front entrance.

"You know the rules" the bouncer said, "No fighting. No hassling. Go away and sober up if you ever want to be let in again."

"Get yer hands off me...you..."

The bouncer physically lifted Adam off his feet and flung him headlong down the three stone steps at the entrance to Smokey Joe's onto a gravelled car park. Adam's face hit the gravel and he yelped with pain. He could feel trickles of blood on his forehead and, as he struggled to his knees, he could see that the front of his best blue shirt was torn.

He could taste blood. His lips or cheek had been cut on the gravel. Memories of Reading Festival came flooding back.

Shit! He didn't need this. Scars have only just healed...

He shook his head to dislodge the small pieces of gravel from his hair then struggled to his feet. Looking up he saw a crowd had formed at the entrance. Behind the smug faced bouncer, he could make out Steve, Danny and the three girls among a few other ex-school mates. Sue stared at him for a few seconds then tossed her head and walked back inside the club. Marie was nowhere to be seen. Probably still with her precious Mark.

"And don't bother coming back till your old enough to take your drink" yelled the bouncer, "Now piss off."

Adam spat a gob of blood from his mouth. He felt like throwing up. His best blue shirt was ruined, and his face was burning. He pulled himself shakily to his feet and watched the night club door close. Everyone back inside. Back having a good time on a Saturday night.

"Fuck you all" he screamed at the closed door.

'*Fuck you all.*'

Adam picked up the phone then slammed it back on the receiver. What the hell was he doin' man?

He shook his head as if trying to shake off the clamouring thoughts that were buzzing around his long curly brown hair like a mosquito swarm. Just need some space. Need some space.

Need some *direction*. Need to know where the hell I'm going. Need to know what I'm *doing*. Need some fuckin' *answers*.

Need some *help* dammit.

Go on admit it you jerk. You need your dad.

Some chance...

Adam realised he was biting into his already swollen lower lip hard enough to draw even more blood. God, he felt rough. He had walked around three miles since being thrown out of Smokey Joe's. No way he could get a taxi in this state. Anyhow he'd spent the last of his money on the wasted drinks. Well...not totally wasted - at least he'd probably ruined smarmy Mark's evening. All he had left now was enough for one phone call. One coin left in the world and that was it. Totally skint.

He fumbled for a cigarette and lit it, noticing his hand trembling. It felt oddly different perched on a fat cut lip. He wished it was a joint instead. This was one time he needed to calm down.

He also needed a mirror. His cheek felt badly grazed, but it had stopped bleeding and the blood had started to coagulate. No lasting damage but another scar. His mother would go crazy. He must look a right mess.

Look a mess?

His *life* was a mess!

Adam leaned back against the inner wall of the red phone box and rifled through his pockets until he found the screwed-up piece of paper he was looking for.

Bollocks. It was now or never.

Adam picked up the phone, inserted the coin and waited for a dialling tone. It rang and rang. There was no answer. Then again, it was two in the morning. Not surprising really. He swore under his breath then slammed the phone down hard before kicking the phone box door in frustration.

The night was getting colder, and he was starting to shiver. He took a long drag on the cigarette and thought back to the night he'd nearly died in Reading. The physical pain from that night was now a thing of the past but the mental scars would remain for some time yet.

Like all the other scars he'd collected in his pathetic life - the recurring bull-man nightmares that no-one could explain. The failed exams. The lousy jobs. Losing the dad he barely knew, but dearly loved. Losing Marie. Losing everything that mattered.

And now this.

Things just couldn't get any worse, could they?

Could they?

Adam tore the cigarette out of his mouth and flung it into the gutter then started the long cold walk home.

The old man glanced at the antique clock on the mantelpiece for the second time in five minutes and waited for the familiar chime to sound ten. Good. Another hour and it would be time for bed - but first...

He hobbled out of the room and down a narrow hallway into a small kitchen then bent down to roll back a faded floral carpet. The hobbling was something he had never really got used to. Shrapnel wound sustained in Italy during a particularly bloody offensive in 1944. Most of the fighting was over on the day the mine had taken half his leg away. But he was one of the 'lucky ones'. Unlike thousands of others, he still had his sight. And his sanity. A lot of the other lads simply never came home, physically or mentally.

He moved the carpet aside to reveal a wooden trap door set into the floorboards and with a grunt he creaked open the hatch. A few wooden steps led down into a small wine cellar, at one time probably nothing more than a place to store coal. He was glad that he had invested in fine wines all those years ago. He had watched the bottles grow thick with dust over the years knowing that nature was magically turning the liquid into nectar within each dark bottle.

Now in his twilight years he could afford the luxury of opening a favourite vintage once or twice a week. Sadly, Ellie was no longer there to share a glass or two with him anymore (she had passed away some five years ago) but he was coming to terms with the loss now and life had been increasingly good to the old soldier.

Selecting a bottle, he brushed away a cobweb then blew dust from a yellowed label. Chateau Talbot 1955. Yes - this one would do fine. Just a glass or two before bed. The French winemakers still held all the aces when it came to this kind of quality. Italy and Spain were catching up for sure, but the stakes were still too high to match a sumptuous Bordeaux.

As he turned to ascend the wooden stairs something made him stop and incline his head to one side as though straining to listen. He frowned slightly then closed his eyes in order to concentrate. The whispers were almost imperceptible at first but gradually became clearer and more substantial. His mouth curved into a small smile, and he nodded to himself knowingly.

"So..." he whispered softly "Another one tonight then...that's good...that's very good."

He turned away from the stairs for a moment and limped over to a dark recess at the back of the cellar fumbling on a dusty shelf for a box of matches. His fingers closed around the small box, and he struck a match making shadows dance around the rough and slightly damp red Victorian brick walls.

At the back of the cellar, in a recess and on a wide wooden shelf, stood some fifty or so cream coloured tallow candles - all of them no more than an inch or so high. Many of them were partly buried within a cascade of melted wax whilst others pushed up through the wax like stunted bony fingers groping upwards in search of light.

He reached down into a cardboard box under the shelf and lifted out a smooth new candle in a brass candlestick and sat it prominently amidst its dead brothers then lit the wick with a flourish. For a moment or two the embryonic flame flickered wildly before settling naturally into its teardrop shape; a warm yellow glow reflecting hypnotically on a hundred or so dark wine bottles stacked around the room.

"Another one tonight" the old man repeated; this time to the tabby cat curling its tail around his undamaged leg. "Another candle to be lit, another star in the universe. Excellent."

He climbed the steps again and shut the trapdoor gently behind him, the soft yellow glow dissolving away as the old worn carpet was rolled back into place.

Adam winced as he dabbed disinfected cotton wool on his grazed face. It was the morning after, and he wasn't sure whether it was the hangover or the swollen tongue and face which made him feel the worse. He moved close to the bathroom mirror, sweeping his matted tangled hair to one side so he could better survey the damage. It didn't look good. The black eye sustained in Reading had long gone but his eyes were very bloodshot and dark rimmed from lack of sleep. The grazes were only superficial but the gravel outside Smokey Joe's had taken off a layer of skin and he looked a complete mess. Thank God he hadn't been tempted to drop any acid like Danny. The hangover was bad enough by itself.

Adam pulled on some jeans and a sweatshirt then staggered downstairs to face the music. He pushed open the kitchen door and then put on his best 'good morning' smile.

"Hi Mum."

"Hi Ad...oh, my God! What's happened to your face?"

"S' nothing - I fell over in some gravel last night - just a bit grazed that's all."

"You look awful. Are you sure you're alright? Your cheeks are red raw."

"I'm fine. Don't worry."

Carol Sinclair folded her arms and gave Adam that probing suspicious look that all mothers learn to cultivate. He always found it hard to deal with her when she gave him that look. She had this uncanny ability to immediately see through any attempt to disguise the truth.

"So" she said conversationally, "Let me get this right then. You went out with Steve and Danny to the Plough? Yes, I thought so. And assuming you stayed there drinking until closing time and you didn't roll in until about three o'clock this morning, I would guess you went night clubbing?" She had started to walk up and down the kitchen taking on the air of a prosecuting attorney. Adam shrugged and nodded in assent.

"And assuming you couldn't resist having another drink or two in the night club, might I be right in thinking you probably had a tad too much to drink?"

"I had a few."

"Hmm...a few drinks then out into the cold night air where the car park is strewn with gravel?"

"Yeah, well, I couldn't help it. I musta tripped over something."

She stopped speaking and looked him directly in the eyes until his head dropped.

"Sorry Mum."

"It's you who should be sorry for yourself Adam. You're the one who is getting hurt the most. And talking of getting hurt there's something else I've been meaning to ask you."

"What's that?"

"Marie" said Carol, "You've broken up with her, haven't you? You've kept it quiet, but I know it. Mothers know these things you know. It's true, isn't it?"

Adam looked away.

"Yeah, it's true. I didn't want to tell you. I know how you feel about Marie."

"Like she's the best thing that ever happened to you, you mean? So, what was it then? Did it happen at Reading or afterwards? Was it you who ended it - or did she just wake up one day and finally see sense?"

"It wasn't like that."

"No, it never is Adam. Sometimes I despair for you. You seem to have no idea of how to distinguish between good and bad or right and wrong sometimes. Marie was so good for you..."

"Yeah, I know, but..."

"But nothing. She was good for you. Fact."

Carol shook her head and sighed deeply then turned to fill a kettle with water. It was around ten now. Time for a strong coffee.

Adam sat down at the kitchen table and idly flicked through the morning paper. Another massacre in Vietnam and the ongoing saga of Watergate. Same crap as usual. He was surprised that she had not been madder with him. It seemed that she spent most of her time nagging him incessantly, which, to be fair, he deserved. But he loved her dearly - even if he rarely showed it. More so since dad had died. Must be tough for her losing a husband while she was still so young.

Carol stirred her coffee then ran her fingers through her hair pushing it back over her forehead. It meant she had something important to say.

"By the way, I've found you a job. Another job. Seeing as you screwed up the last interview."

Adam raised an eyebrow "Oh yeah? What sort of job?"

"The paint shop on the High Street. There was an advert in the window for a shop assistant. I popped in and gave them your name."

Adam sat down on the kitchen stool. "Paint shop assistant? Sounds boring. What do I have to do? Sell pots of paint all day?"

Carol's eyes flashed momentarily but she ignored the remark.

"It's a job Adam. A job. You need to do something with yourself other than hang around street corners. You need to get some money. Start saving. Do something useful with your time. For God's sake it was you that decided you didn't want to go into further education. So - get a job."

"Yeah, okay...but a paint shop for heaven's sake..."

"At least it's something. It's a start. Don't let me down this time. Give it a go."

"But..."

"No. No more 'buts' Adam. For my sake give it a go. I want you to go in the shop tomorrow and see a Mister Carson. Promise me."

Adam sighed "Yeah yeah... I promise. I'll probably hate it though."

"Better to take a job you may hate than end up as a lost cause."

'*Lost cause*'. He wondered when that phrase would be dragged up again.

Carol bit her lip. That was a bit harsh perhaps. Adam could be sensitive sometimes.

She took a sip of coffee and watched him turn on his heels without a word, climbing the stairs to the sanctuary of his bedroom.

L ost cause? Waste of space? Loser?
The various labels ascribed to him rang in his head as he sat in the bedroom staring at the wall. But he was a 'hero' wasn't he? At least that's what they all used to say - his parents, his relations, his schoolteachers - even Marie. His 'one redeeming feature', yeah, that was what they called it. There was always hope for Adam cos' he proved himself a hero once.

Once.

People would point him out after that article in the local newspaper. "That's him" they would say "The guy who saved the girl - it was in the papers."

Adam Sinclair.

Local Hero.

Yeah. Right.

Truth is that *he* was actually a total coward; but then only he knew the real truth.

He wasn't a hero - no - it just somehow turned out that way and the secret had stayed with him all this time gnawing away at his insides like a cancer so that some days he just wanted to scream the truth - let everyone know the real story.

Tell them all that Adam Sinclair was not the great hero after all. It was all a big mistake. He was really just a loser like all the rest.

And yet the reality continued to haunt him. That summer not so very long ago, a year or two at most, when school holidays seemed to last for ever and life was so much simpler. There had been other girlfriends of course but there was no way they could ever be called relationships. A few innocent fumbling kisses behind the school gym or adolescent gropes at those boring teenage parties and that was it.

But Marie was different.

There had always been something deeper with Marie. She wasn't the type to snog in school corridors and perhaps it was that aloof unobtainability that made her so intriguing and so desirable. He had pursued her with the ruthlessness of a big game hunter obsessed with the chase and she had laughed and led him on just enough to infuriate him and arouse him simultaneously. She rejected him in such a coquettish manner that he was driven to distraction until that summer afternoon not so many years ago, when he had met her walking alone and asked her if she would like to join him for a gentle walk through the fields around the town.

When she had shrugged and said 'okay' his jaw must have visibly dropped in disbelief before he managed to regain enough composure to offer her his hand which she took with a sly grin. And then he was stupid enough to pretend he knew exactly where he was going until he realized that one field looks just like any other and that somewhere he had crossed an unfamiliar stile and had lost his bearings. '*What the hell*' he had thought at the time; this was the first time he had been alone with Marie and that was all that mattered. He had used up all the feeble chat up lines that he could muster and was self-consciously rambling on about nothing in particular, which was obvious to Marie, and making her giggle.

She was the one who had suggested sitting under a shady tree and he had nodded in agreement. Whether or not she meant this to be an invitation to kiss her he never did find out, because as he moved hesitatingly towards her, she had suddenly frozen and pointed a trembling finger over his shoulder.

"Adam..."

The crack in her voice made him turn immediately and glance over his shoulder straight into the mad eyes of an enormous black bull snorting in agitation only a short distance behind him.

This time a very real bull.

For a fleeting moment he had wondered if this was the same bull that tormented him in his dreams? Haunting him. Taunting him. Never allowing him the luxury of an undisturbed night's sleep. He couldn't be sure. Real bull? Dream bull? How can you tell when reality and dreams tend to merge into a confused twilight world where nothing makes sense anymore? Maybe all the nightmares had been premonitions?

Premonitions of this very moment.

His inclination was to panic but the feelings for Marie were too strong now to be ignored. He had to take control, prove himself. Be brave...

"Take it easy" he had said, forcing a calmness into his voice that belied his own fear, "Don't move too quickly...it will be okay. I can see a gate about thirty yards away, over there near the corner of the field. If we move slowly towards it, I reckon we can get there before the..."

"Adam I'm scared of bulls" Marie was breathing heavily.

She was scared? Christ if she only but knew...

"It's okay...don't be scared...do as I do...stand up slowly and keep facing forward."

"Adam it's moving...it's lowering its horns..."

"Don't worry...it's probably scared by our presence."

Some chance!

Adam had mentally sworn at himself for his own stupidity in not taking enough notice where they were going.

"Just follow me slowly" he said, voice faltering slightly.

"What if it charges us?"

"Then just run like mad for the fence and throw yourself over it. Look...if it comes for us then I'll distract it or something, so you can get away."

'*Or something...*'

"But what about ...?"

"Don't worry about me" - *had he really said that*?

They had stood up, backs pressed up against the old oak tree. Adam felt the rough wood against his back and a mental image of being gored through and pinned against the tree flashed through his mind; an image of wet sticky redness trickling between the gnarled grooves in the brown bark, like liquid rubber being tapped. He shivered involuntarily.

What the hell should he do? What the hell *could* he do?

They backed off, moving slowly around the tree, and started to walk backwards, keeping their eyes fixed on the huge black quivering muscles of the snorting bull and glancing over their shoulders at the sanctuary of the gate only what? Fifteen yards away now?

The bull stared - the whites of its eyes clearly visible, but it wasn't moving and at first it seemed that it was a panic over nothing.

Then Marie had stumbled on an old branch or something and fallen backwards with a shriek.

Which made the bull charge.

Although everything that happened next was over in a few seconds the emotions would stay with Adam forever. A split-second decision was needed; to pull Marie to her feet so that they could both run (knowing full well that those lost precious seconds meant the bull would be upon them) or try and distract the bull so that it chased *him* instead, giving Marie a chance to get away.

But seeing the bull actually pounding towards him seemed to obliterate any further chance of rational thought. The feeling of helplessness and sheer terror had somehow rendered movement temporarily impossible - *like in that crazy hallucinogenic dream in hospital where it felt as though his knees had turned to jelly.* 'Difference was that on this occasion it was no dream.

And then mercifully adrenaline must have kicked in and next thing he knew he was running for his life swearing that he could feel the bull's hot steamy breath on the back of his neck. He had mouthed a scream, but the scream never came. The overwhelming gut-wrenching fear erupting within him had constricted his throat to such a degree that no sound could reach his lips and his heart felt like it was about to explode from his chest cavity. The ground beneath his feet shook like an earthquake as the bull gained on him, nostrils flaring, eyes malevolent and rolling wildly. With mere seconds to spare Adam flung himself over the wooden gate in the corner of the field landing badly and twisting his ankle, rolling in the dust on a farm track moaning and sobbing hysterically.

The bull ground to a halt a few yards behind, snuffling and shuffling, strangely enough not in an angry or frustrated way but almost playfully as though it was getting bored with the game of chase. By the time a sobbing Marie reached the gate the bored bull had ambled off across the field to resume grazing, taking little more notice of its intruders.

Adam fought to regain his composure lest Marie see him quivering and gasping. He cursed his selfishness and even now distinctly remembered the tears that had burned in his eyes. When it had come to the moment of truth he had failed. He had abandoned Marie to save his own worthless skin. Running away like the pathetic coward he really was and leaving her to the mercy of the bull. He was a total shit.

And then as they both stood there panting the local farmer had appeared, half angry at their stupidity in not noticing the very clear 'Beware of the Bull' sign pinned to the tree and half relieved that the outcome was not serious.

"You all right m' dear?" He had wheezed at Marie through the cigarette welded to his lower lip.

She nodded as she regained her breath and then said something that Adam would replay inside his head over and over again, like a worn vinyl record for years to come.

"I'm okay. Adam saved me. He distracted the bull when I fell over. He saved my life."

Adam had stared into her eyes whilst wincing at the pain in his ankle - what the hell was she on about? He hadn't saved her life at all - he'd bottled out - *did she really think..*?

Marie met his stare but when she spoke it was directed at the farmer.

"Adam risked his life to save me."

The scene had been replayed time and time again in Adam's mind. It still didn't make sense. None of it did.

Maybe it helped to explain the nightmares, but he wasn't even sure about that. No - the nightmares had always been there - right from early childhood. And why did Marie tell everyone, including the papers, that he was a hero? *Him* - the biggest coward on the planet? Thank God most people had forgotten about it now. That was yesterday's news.

His mind drifted back to the present.

He stretched his legs and then ran his hand over the thickened skin on his cheeks where the grazes sustained last night had turned to scabs. And then he moved his hand a little to touch the small scar on his neck. An eternal legacy from the festival. He looked out of the bedroom window at the dusky rain-filled sky stretched over suburbia like a mouldy shroud and suddenly felt very depressed. He needed some smokes. Needed to get stoned to blot it all out. Help him to forget. Steve or Danny would have something that would give him the kick he desired. He'd give Steve a call.

But there was something bothering him. Something stopping him from calling his mate to get some gear and then get stoned.

'*There are other ways to get you high you know*'.

'*Like what?*'

'*Think about it*'.

Adam closed the bedroom curtains and turned on the light. He'd got pins and needles from just sitting in the same position for so long. He looked around the room at all the glossy rock band posters of Deep Purple, Pink Floyd, Led Zeppelin and Alice Cooper and the pile of LP's strewn across the floor; the pile of dirty clothes that drove his mother to despair and the empty fag packets filling the bin. Something else was stirring in his mind. Something important. Something about last night.

And then, at last, he remembered what it was.

He walked purposefully over to the wardrobe and started to fumble in the pockets of his mud and blood-spattered jacket, looking for a very important screwed-up scrap of paper.

Carol Sinclair was engrossed in something on TV. Adam could hear the canned laughter through the closed lounge door. Good. He picked up the phone and dialled. After a few moments wait there was a click. A man's voice answered. An old man.

"Hello?"

"Hello - is that Jack Harland?"

"Yes. Who is this?"

It was a warm voice. Precise. A slight accent but not one you could place easily.

"My name's Adam Sinclair. You er...you won't know me. I was given your phone number by a Doctor David Levinson."

"Ah yes...Doctor Levinson. Lovely man and a good friend too. So, Adam, what can I do for you?"

Adam swallowed hard. Why did this all feel so unreal. So difficult. So...

Nah, had to be done.

"You ...you er...teach meditation? Doctor Levinson gave me this list you see...and I was just wondering..."

"You want to learn to meditate?"

"Well, I...yes. Yes, I do."

"I see" a pause then "Have you ever meditated before?"

"No. Never."

"That's fine. Well, Adam, we ought to arrange to meet. I'll give you my address and then we can arrange a convenient time. Now let me see...are you free at all anytime next week?"

"Er yeah...next week's fine. I've got a job interview to go to, but most of my time is free."

Jack gave Adam his address and directions. It wasn't far; maybe twenty minutes' walk from Adam's place across the other side of town.

"I look forward to meeting you then" said Jack, "And I'm delighted that Doctor Levinson thought of me. We are old friends you see. Well, thank you for ringing Adam."

Adam felt awkward. Not his usual scene.

"I er...I forgot to ask you how much you charge?"

"The first lesson is completely free. Some people find it's not for them you see. They try it once and then never bother again. Anyway, we can talk about those details later. So how about next Thursday evening then?"

"Yeah. Next Thursday. Look I...er...hope this is not going to cause you any problem? I mean taking up your time and such..."

"Not at all" Jack said warmly, "On the contrary. It will be a pleasure."

"Right. Well, that's great then. I'll be over next Thursday evening."

"I look forward to it Adam. Goodbye."

Jack Harland, 76 years of age, retired war veteran, wine connoisseur and part time meditation teacher, smiled as he put down the receiver. "It's no problem at all Adam" he said glancing into the hallway mirror, "In fact I was wondering when you'd get around to calling..."

PART TWO

"The expedition Huxley undertook into his
own brain is the last journey waiting for all of us,
whether by chemical means or through some
less hazardous door, the inward passage
to our truer and richer selves."

J.G. Ballard
Introduction to
'The Doors of Perception'
by Aldous Huxley

There is a theory, subscribed to by a few, but as yet unsubstantiated, that everything that happens in the universe is somehow preordained and part of a grand 'cosmic plan'.

There is another theory that hypothesises that not only is everything preordained but everything that exists - or has ever existed - is linked together in ways that man can barely conceive of.

And as if these two theories were not enough, there are some scholars of mysticism who even go as far as to suggest that not only is everything inextricably linked but that the linkages are able to simultaneously transcend time so that the past, the present and the future are somehow interwoven into a seamless whole.

If such theories are true then many would contend that the whole physical and spiritual history of mankind would need to be re-examined in the light of this new knowledge - and in the process some of mankind's most fundamental and cherished beliefs would be opened up to fresh scrutiny and doubtless lead to a lot of pain for some and, perhaps, enlightenment for others.

Fortunately, mused Jack Harland, this is unlikely to ever transpire due to the reassuring comfort blanket of science and rationality that the sceptics have created to keep our bodies warm at night and our minds safe, relatively speaking, from the nightmare shapes outside the door. The nightmare shapes that would otherwise dare to challenge our most hallowed and cherished concepts of reality.

For Jack, a sprightly seventy-seven next birthday, such thoughts brought a smile to wrinkled cheeks and a twinkle to blue eyes because thinking was one of the things Jack did best. Not for him the idle log fire kindled and muddled daydreams of an old age pensioner - he never had been one for time wasting introspection. Jack's thinking was focused and methodical, whether concentrating on a problem to be solved, a metaphysical concept to be analysed or bringing still-sharp memories back to mind. Old in years he may be, but a lifetime of discipline of mind and body, particularly mind, had left his mental faculties trained, honed and razor sharp.

Training the mind had been a strange pastime for a young man in the nineteen twenties and thirties. And it was frowned upon and misunderstood by the moustachioed stiff-upper-lip types that bravely flew themselves into oblivion in the blue skies of Kent in the forties. And it was equally misunderstood by the black lung'd miners that Jack had gone to school with and grew up with in a small Yorkshire town.

But then he always had been the odd one out.

Odd, because he *knew* a lot about strange things. Things that other people could never hope to understand or even conceive of. Not academically-like. More of an intuition.

'Gifted' his mother had said proudly.

'Summat strange about that boy' his father had scowled from behind newspaper and pipe. Whatever it was, it had stayed with him all these years. Jack had learned early in his life that it was something he would have to learn to live with.

Sometimes a blessing, sometimes a curse. That was true enough.

But it was rarely wrong.

And 'it' was not wrong today. Jack had felt it long before he heard the footsteps coming up the path and the ring on the doorbell. There was no need to open the door on the small chain or ask nervously 'Who's there?' like some of his equally elderly neighbours. Jack knew exactly who was on the other side of the door. And more satisfyingly Jack also knew, like some of those more radical theorists might have postulated, that this moment was destined to happen.

"Mister Harland?"

The youth looked nervous, glancing away self-consciously rather than meeting the old man's eyes. He was of average build, thought Jack, maybe on the slender side, dressed in flared blue jeans, off-white scuffed trainers, a purple T- shirt with some garish yellow logo in the middle and a tatty brown jacket with a cigarette packet sticking out of the breast pocket. Long brown hair fell in thick strands across the eyes hiding their expression as if concealed behind prison bars. His complexion was on the pale side but seemed mercifully free of acne. Seventeen maybe? Eighteen perhaps?

Jack smiled and opened the door wide, "Adam Sinclair. Come on in, make yourself at home. I'm glad you decided to come after all. Some don't you know. They phone and arrange to meet but never actually show up. Strange, isn't it? I knew you would turn up though. David Levinson is always right about these things. Come on into the front room and have a seat."

Adam wondered why old people always called a lounge the 'front room'. His own grandparents were just the same - Gramps still called the kitchen a parlour for some reason.

He followed Jack down a narrow hallway of faded green wallpaper into the front room - a little puzzled by what Jack had just said. How could Doctor Levinson have known he was going to turn up?

Weird.

Jack motioned him to take a seat on a large black leather settee which looked as though it had lost most of its leather years ago.

It was a small house, probably Victorian, and typical of what Adam called 'old people's houses'. Seemed like a turn of the century time warp in terms of decor. It was mostly antique wooden furniture - probably worth a bit - with loads of poor-quality sepia photographs in ornate silver frames cluttering every shelf or flat surface. An ancient three-piece leather suite, a late fifties television set, an open fire with some glowing coals making the room a little too warm, a lamp stand with tatty orange shade, a table covered in bric-a-brac and a large bookcase overflowing with books. Old books that gave off a musty, sweet smell that reminded Adam of museums and stuffy libraries. The whole surroundings imbued with a sense of controlled untidiness and an aura of homely tranquillity, an observation that seemed to equally describe Jack himself; an old man but not yet 'antique'. His gait was still upright and strong although Adam had detected a slight limp. He was dressed in fawn-coloured trousers, white collarless shirt and grey cardigan without sleeves - almost a waistcoat. The hair was white and thinning and the face bore all the lines and wrinkles of a well-travelled adventurer. But it was the eyes that surprised Adam most. Jack's eyes were not those of a man in his - what - Seventies? Eighties? The rheumy unfocused and flecked ovals that old people carry to their graves were not the eyes that now met Adam's. Instead, they were steel blue, jovial, twinkling and crystal clear. They radiated a confidence and intelligence that Adam had not expected. Sort of old guy that you couldn't help but take an instant liking to.

Just like Gramps.

Jack sat down in one of the matching faded leather chairs opposite Adam and let the lad take his time to get comfortable. A grandfather clock chimed eight times from another room in the house and the lounge door creaked slightly as a fat tabby cat strolled in nonchalantly with one wary eye firmly fixed on the stranger who had taken her spot on the settee.

"Allow me to introduce 'Lady'" said Jack, "Before she introduces herself that is. Fine old mouser in her day but getting on a bit now, just like me. I hope you don't mind cats." He smiled, and Adam noticed a good set of white teeth. Jack may be old, but he obviously looked after himself.

Adam felt uncomfortable. He couldn't help but feel that he was intruding into this man's life. It was difficult to know how to relate to older men since... well...since dad had died. His own grandad, on his father's side, had died when he was young and his other grandfather, 'Gramps' as he was affectionately known, had sadly grown more and more remote as the creeping tentacles of senility continued to infiltrate his mind.

He ought to try and make conversation.

"No, I don't mind cats" he replied nervously. "...Always wanted a dog but Mum was never that keen. Said I'd never take it for walks, so she'd end up walkin' it. My dad wouldn't have minded but he's... he's not around anymore..."

Change the subject...

"Are you married Mr Harland?" he asked Jack as light heartedly as he could muster.

Jack's smile flickered momentarily "I was married once" he replied softly, "And please call me Jack. No need for any formalities Adam." Jack reached over for one of the silver framed photos on a small coffee table. He looked at it fondly for a moment then handed it over to Adam. "This is Ellie, my wife. That's a photo taken when she was about twenty. She died five years ago. I miss the old girl, can't deny that. She was a rare one that's for sure."

"I'm sorry. She looks very pretty."

Adam was sincere. The faded black and white photo may well belong to a bygone age but the woman in the photo was clearly one of those stunning 1920's film star types; misty, faraway alluring eyes and tight curly dark hair that he associated with those grainy old early movies of dancing girls in feathers and beads. A dead ringer for that Josephine Baker that Gramps used to go on about.

"Yes. A real beaut' when I first met her" reminisced Jack, "I still talk to her you know, but that's maybe hard for a youngster to understand."

Adam stared at Jack for a moment then looked away feeling awkward. Not sure how to respond to the remark. Fortunately, Jack responded first by laughing heartily. "Don't worry about me" he chuckled, "I'm sure there's a lot of people think I'm quite mad, but you know I believe that a little madness paves the road to sanity don't you agree? Now...let's talk about you Adam."

The tabby, Lady, had leapt up on to the settee and sat beside Adam licking her paws, a gentle purring sound vibrating against his thigh. That was encouraging - by the look of Lady's claws he would not want to upset her.

Jack sat back into the deep armchair and bought his fingertips together, his attention focused totally on his young guest.

Adam flicked a handful of hair out of his eyes, a silly nervous habit that he knew he ought to grow out of and then cleared his throat noisily.

This was the moment he'd been dreading.

Danny Mc Connell chalked up his cue and leant over the snooker table spilling ash from the end of his cigarette onto the green baize. He smudged it away before squinting down the length of the cue and then with a deft flick of the wrist potted the pink. He stood upright again and admired his achievement, raising a pint in self-congratulation. "Ah you're a natural Danny me boy" he said to himself, "That you are."

"Jammy Irish bastard more like it" sniffed Steve Lacey, "Go on then, let's see if you can finish."

Danny put his drink down on the beer-stained table in the side room of 'The Anchor' public house and walked around the table choosing an angle of attack. He lined up for another shot and then followed through sending the last black ball into the top right pocket. Steve raised his eyes to the ceiling in disbelief.

"Dat'll be a pound I believe Mister Lacey," said Danny holding out his palm in smug satisfaction.

Steve dug into his jeans pocket and slapped a pound into Danny's palm "I'll nail you next time," he threatened good humouredly.

They put their cues back in the rack and wandered over to a table by the window overlooking a drab suburban car park.

The steady rhythm of Mud's 'Tiger Feet' pulsed from a juke box.

Steve swigged a mouthful of beer, "So where's Adam tonight?"

Danny shrugged "Dunno, I haven't seen him for a few days, but he's always been here T'ursdays. I phoned him at home, but his Mum said he wasn't in. He'd gone out earlier but didn't say where he was going. She assumed he was coming here. Means he must be chasing after some skirt."

Steve took another deep swig of beer, wiping the froth from around his mouth onto his shirt sleeve "Well it's not Marie Cunningham, that's for sure. She won't have anything more to do wiv 'im."

"Ah well he's a fool all right. No sooner do the scars heal from getting his head kicked in at Reading then he's mouthin' off in a nightclub and trying to pick a fight. S'no wonder she's keeping away from the idjit."

"Is he still working at that paint shop?" said Steve in mocking tones.

"I t'ink he is. If I remember he was getting an ear bending from his old dear about finding work. She'd spotted an ad in the local paper for a paint shop assistant. He wasn't at all interested but she practically marched him down to the shop. I reckon he hates it there."

They both laughed hysterically at the thought of Adam Sinclair behind a shop counter in a brown apron.

"Wouldn't even know which way up to hold a fuckin' paintbrush" squealed Steve, wiping a tear from his eye, "What say we go along there tomorrow and ask for some advice on painting?"

Danny slapped his thigh. "Yeah - let's do it. It'll be a great laugh - we'll ask him to explain all about undercoats and emulsions and see how long he can keep a straight face."

"About two minutes then he'll probably be sacked" said Steve "Not that he'll care mind you."

"Nah" agreed Danny "He won't give a toss about being sacked. One t'ing about Adam - he's a bloody good laugh. He don' give a shit about anything. He'll either drink it, smoke it or shag it."

"Yeah. Too true" said Steve raising his pint aloft "Here's to Adam Sinclair."

Danny raised his pint in unison.

"Adam Sinclair" he echoed, "Wherever you are tonight you old bastard."

"So...let's start from the beginning. How can I be of service to you, my friend?"

Adam had been staring absent-mindedly at the patterns on the floral carpet. This was more difficult than he expected but it was too late to go back now. There was nothing for it. He looked up and momentarily caught Jack's eye.

"I want to learn to meditate."

The old man studied Adam's expression and then nodded slowly. Adam shifted uncomfortably.

It seemed as though Jack's soft blue eyes were somehow penetrating right through his inner defences laying his soul bare, as though his brains were being spring cleaned.

...Like having a wave of fresh air blow right through your skull removing a lot of unnecessary garbage and old cobwebs...

Unnerving yeah, but strangely enough not entirely unpleasant.

He shook his head slightly trying to bring himself back to his senses. Jack was still staring at him intently which made Adam look away self-consciously. It was a while before the old man spoke and then it was only a single word that seemed to hang provocatively in the air.

"Why?"

Why? Do I really have to explain?

Adam licked his dry lips - only too aware that he did not have a well-prepared answer. "Because, well, I guess there are lots of reasons..."

"Tell me the reasons."

Adam took a deep breath. He desperately needed a cigarette but now was not the time.

"I think I need to relax more. Y'know...and...well, I...I want to understand things...why things are the way they are..."

He was fumbling, and it was obvious.

He looked to the old man to help him with the right answers, but Jack merely stared back at him patiently with a smile that seemed to say, 'carry on'.

"I guess I want to improve myself" Adam said at last, surprised at his own honesty, "I've always been impulsive...you know...selfish I suppose. I thought meditation might help me learn more about life. There's a lot of things I would like to understand...I read this book once..."

Jack nodded sympathetically. "There are a lot of things we will never understand. It depends on what it is you want to know...and why you want to know it. You have no doubt heard the phrase that 'a little knowledge is a dangerous thing'?"

"Yeah."

"Well, it is very true. Meditation is not the answer to all the world's problems you know. And it's not an escape route for the wandering mind. It is a discipline and like all disciplines it demands hard work, dedication and sometimes sacrifice."

"I realise that."

"Do you?"

The old man continued to study Adam's features closely. Adam felt uneasy again. He didn't know it was gonna turn into a bloody interview.

"Meditation is a much-misunderstood word," continued Jack, "It means many things to many people. In some ways it cannot be defined because to define something is to capture it and impose a value on it and sometimes that can lose the essence of the thing you are trying to define. You must first decide what it is you are really seeking and then once you are sure you must pursue that goal relentlessly."

"I know that this is something I really want to do."

"Is it? What makes you so sure?"

Adam was about to reply but felt tongue tied. He was not being specific enough and he knew it. Did he really know what he wanted? How could he be sure? Jack seemed to be so precise about everything.

Jack had obviously sensed his discomfort because he broke the silence with a wink. "Perhaps I'm being a little unfair and whatever else we do we must keep our sense of humour and a sense of perspective. Talking about meditation is never easy and demands a lot of concentration. So - how about a drink first?"

Adam nodded, relieved that Jack was human after all, "Yes...thanks..."

"Good. It's important that we feed our bodies as well as our minds, eh?"

Jack disappeared into the kitchen and Adam could hear him opening cupboards to find glasses. The feeling of discomfort was still with him. At first, he thought it was due to the awkwardness of intruding into an old man's privacy, but he now realised that there was something more. Jack was relaxed and approachable – and easy enough to talk to. No, the discomfort wasn't with Jack or the unfamiliarity of the surroundings. It was the subject matter. Meditation. Up until now the thoughts had all been locked inside his own head, buried in his own private world. A world he had not wanted to share with anyone else and had chosen not to. Now he was bringing all those private and personal thoughts out into the open for the first time in his life. Exposing his inner thoughts and verbalising feelings that he did not have the vocabulary for. He was acutely aware of a sense of helplessness borne of trying to explain something and then realising words alone are insufficient to get the meaning across. Then there was the vulnerability of opening himself up to possible ridicule because that sort of honesty openly revealed all his inadequacies and insecurities for all to see.

Well, Jack anyway.

He suddenly felt very small.

So - what the hell are you doing here mister know-it-all Sinclair?

Jack returned to the room and Adam's self-conscious daydreams dispersed in what he felt were almost visible clouds of soft mist.

"I've only orange juice I'm afraid" apologised Jack handing Adam a glass.

"That's fine. Thanks". He couldn't believe he'd said that. A beer would have been good.

Jack settled back into the armchair and Lady hopped across the room, winding herself around Jack's leg. The leg that seemed to move normally.

He waited until Adam had quenched his thirst before warming to his theme once again.

"You don't *really* know what you're looking for do you Adam?"

"No" sighed Adam, "You're right. I don't really know at all."

"But you *are* sincere about wanting to learn how to meditate. I can sense that."

"Yeah. Definitely. That's one thing I am certain of. I'm not sure exactly why - but I have to learn to meditate."

Jack stroked Lady's back which arched languorously in response. She started to purr softly.

"I believe you Adam" said Jack warmly, "And you have definitely come to the right place to learn one of the oldest secrets in mankind's history. I think it's time to begin, don't you?"

Adam breathed a sigh of relief.

"So, you *are* gonna teach me then?"

"Oh no" replied Jack with a mischievous wink, "We are going to teach each other."

"If you are really serious about meditation then we need to start with a few basics" said Jack matter-of-factly. "There are a number of ideas or concepts that you will need to grasp, though I'm not going to dampen your enthusiasm by complicating something that is essentially very simple. So, before we start to talk technique let's talk about why people bother to meditate in the first place. I assume I don't need to explain things in too much detail because you say you have already read a book on the subject - yes?"

"Yeah, but it was a really old book. I would still like to hear it from you. Y'know - your personal views."

Jack nodded thoughtfully. "Okay...forgive me for my lack of fluency...to be honest it's been a long time since I've shared my thoughts with someone on these types of issues...I'm a bit rusty...but let's give it a try, eh? I think we need to start with something called 'openness'...and, by that, I mean being open and receptive to new ideas however strange or unbelievable they may seem. In other words, you mustn't judge anything I say too harshly to begin with. If you are too cynical or critical of new ideas, it could severely hamper your chances of progress. Is that alright?"

"Yeah. No problem."

"Okay so let's open up our eyes and minds then. I'll start by stating some of what I call 'fundamentals' and for now I want you to suspend all disbelief and just accept what I say. We can test the logic later. Yes?"

"Yeah – fine." Adam nodded in accord.

"Good. Let's make a start then. Fundamental number one – you, Adam, are much more than your physical body...in other words your 'essence' or 'conscious awareness' does not die when your physical body dies. In effect you are immortal. No - don't interrupt yet, there's more. Fundamental number two; 'time' as you currently experience it is not as linear as it seems - the past, present and future are all inextricably linked in ways you cannot even imagine. Fundamental number three...the answers to all your deepest questions can be accessed internally - through meditation - you don't necessarily have to look for answers in the physical world. Fundamental number four...you and I and everyone else on this planet are linked together subconsciously within an overarching unity consciousness - whether we like it or not - and we therefore continuously interrelate in ways that we are rarely consciously aware of. Fundamental number five...love is the strongest force in the universe...those dreary pop songs on the radio are absolutely correct. There are lots more fundamentals of course but let's take things one by one or we can easily start getting lost. Okay so far then?"

Adam was aware that his mouth had dropped open and that his eyes had widened too.

"Those are pretty amazing statements to make so lightly."

"I know...but in this case I make no apology whatsoever. Do you want to go on?"

"Oh. Yeah. Yeah. Definitely. This is really interesting."

Jack sat forward in his armchair and once again brought his fingertips together. "Okay, as I was saying let's just accept the fundamentals for the moment and talk around them. It's part of human nature that we all want to know the answers to life's deepest mysteries – you know 'What are we here for?' 'What's the point of life?' etcetera and over the centuries thousands of theories have been put forward that are central to numerous cultures across the globe. Many cultures have come up with what they believe to be satisfactory answers and have embodied those answers into ritual, lore, traditions and customs - though the answers can equally be diverse and confusing to other alternative cultures. The 'answers' can come from science, philosophy, religion, art or poetry...in fact there is virtually no limit to our rich historical heritage when it comes to man's ability to try and rationalise his place in the great scheme of things. The really interesting thing for me though, Adam, is when widely different cultures start to come up with the same answers.

What I am driving at is that the answers and fundamental truths that you receive and experience when in deep meditation, are remarkably similar to the answers that widely divergent cultures over time and distance consistently come up with through intuition, dreams, visions, trances or whatever. Furthermore these 'answers' are not received as possibilities, likelihoods or conjectures - they are received as unquestionable certainties...facts if you will. It is one of the most extraordinary facets of meditation that when you seek an answer and then receive an insight, it is not the same as receiving a mere suggestion of an answer - it is an answer that becomes an indisputable fact. Also - and this is equally fascinating - once you are in possession of these indisputable 'facts' you seem to lose interest in trying to persuade others that you have found the truth. It is as if the acquisition of spiritual knowledge goes hand in hand with acquiring a new sense of modesty. You know you have the real answers, but you lose the inclination to try and spread the word. You don't want to become a preacher. Maybe it is nature's way of making sure that individuals find their own way to truth instead of acquiring knowledge second-hand."

Adam was aware that his brow was furrowed with concentration. He was totally captivated.

You obviously couldn't afford to let your thoughts drift when this guy was talking...

"Is that why these Indian mystic types or reclusive monks rarely share their insights with anyone unless they become a - what's the word I read in that book? Acolyte?"

"I'm sure it is. Let's be clear on one thing though - meditation can take many years to perfect. Sometimes many lifetimes."

Jack continued to develop his arguments while Adam listened attentively. There was something about Jack's voice that was hypnotic. A lilting rise and fall that carried each phrase rhythmically forward so that Adam couldn't help but want to hang onto each and every word. Hypnotic yes - but not soporific. Jack's words were keeping him wide awake and totally fascinated. Adam felt sure that Jack must have been a professional speaker at some time during his life. He was leading a verbal trail of hints and clues that compelled one to follow. He developed themes and followed them to their conclusion, occasionally taking side turnings and offering tantalising views of what might lay beyond before returning to the main trail again. His pace was measured and the logic of his arguments faultless. Adam was totally captivated. It was only when Jack paused for breath that Adam glanced at his watch and was shocked to find two hours had passed.

Jack noticed the glance. "It's all right Adam - I'm not charging."

Adam laughed aloud then felt self-conscious. Long time since he laughed so spontaneously. It felt good.

"I have to go in a moment" he apologised, "I've been so engrossed in listening to all this stuff that I didn't notice the time."

"Entirely my fault for rambling on for so long" said Jack, "And it's me that must apologise. I hope I didn't bore you."

"Bore me? No way. It's just that my brain feels exhausted trying to take in so much new information."

"...And I haven't even answered your question yet Adam. It's very remiss of me."

"How do you mean?"

"I mean you came here wanting to know how to meditate. I have not even touched on that aspect yet have I?"

"No, I suppose not. How long will it take?"

"Ten seconds to explain and then ten years to perfect."

"Are you serious? You'd better give me the ten second version then."

Jack eased himself out of his chair steadying himself on his good leg before replying. He noticed Adam staring at his dragging leg and tapped it with his walking stick. "War wound" he said dismissively, "You learn to live with it. Now here's what I want you to do - and I want you to report back in two weeks' time on your progress - is that okay with you?"

"It's a deal."

"Good. All I want you to do is find somewhere quiet where you can relax for about twenty minutes undisturbed, then I want you to sit comfortably and think about nothing."

Adam waited for Jack to continue but the old man remained silent.

"Is that it? Sit and think about nothing? That's easy - there's got to be more to it than that…"

"No. That's it. Just sit and think about nothing. Oh… I suppose there is one more thing though. If you are sitting and trying to concentrate on nothing and you find that thoughts keep interrupting your concentration, then you have to go back to the beginning and think of nothing again. Don't force it, don't fight it - just open to it. Got that? And don't expect instant results. You have to give it time."

Adam frowned "Yeah…got it. Sounds simple enough."

"A lot of things sound simple until you try them. Anyway - shall we say two weeks' time then?"

Jack opened the front door. The cool night air made Adam realise just how warm it had been inside the house.

"Thanks again Jack. Two weeks' time then." Jack held out his hand and Adam shook it surprised at how firm the grip was.

He turned and walked down the path and heard the door closing behind him.

What an amazing guy. What an incredible intellect. God - if the lads could see him now getting into all this metaphysical stuff. If *Marie* could see him now.

Adam wondered what Jack would have been like as a younger man. It was weird spending time with an older man and talking adult to adult fashion. Never got much chance of that since…

Well since…

Outside coloured lights twinkled behind the windows of suburbia. A light spattering of rain gave the road a silky black sheen like damp velvet. There was a faint smell of wood smoke lingering in the air which strangely reminded Adam it would soon be Christmas again. It was always the time he loved best when he was a kid. Not so anymore. Now it was just another excuse to get stoned. Adam turned his collar up and shivered.

'*Think of nothing*' he repeated to himself as he turned homeward, '*Think of nothing*'.

That's all there is to it!

Piece of piss...

It was three days later when she phoned.

He'd nearly missed the call completely. Carol wasn't home from the shops yet and he was already halfway out of the front door at the time. Needed some fags before the Newsagent closed. He shut the front door again and grabbed the receiver impatiently.

"'Allo?"

"Adam?"

He drew a sharp breath. Shuddered inwardly.

"Yeah. Who's that? Marie?"

"Yes, it's me. Look...um...about the other week... look, I'm sorry alright?"

Adam sat down on the stairs next to the phone table. He noticed that his hand was shaking.

"Sorry? That bastard boyfriend of yours got my face shredded."

"I know. And I'm sorry. He's not my boyfriend anyhow - he was just a guy. I didn't want you to get hurt - it was your own fault - you were mouthing off and everyone could see you were out of your head. I just wanted to phone you and say that I never meant for you to get hurt...it just happened...and I didn't want you to think it was my fault. Okay?"

"Careful now Marie. You almost sound as if you care."

"Don't be sarcastic with me Adam. You know how it is. It might have been easier to just leave things be, but I wanted to know that you were okay."

"Yeah, well I'm not okay. I'm bloody scarred thanks to that ape you were with - and the thugs on the door. Anyway, you probably wouldn't care if I was dead anyhow."

"That's not true."

"So, if you care...well...maybe we should meet up and talk about it."

"That's not what I phoned for Adam. I don't want to meet and talk about it. I just wanted to phone and say sorry. Now I've said it. That's it".

"Look Marie..."

"No. You 'look' Adam. I don't want to talk about it anymore. That's it. Listen to me. Sorry you got hurt. Take a tip from me Adam - take a tip from someone who used to care a lot about you - get a life - yeah? Get a life before you completely mess yourself up. See ya around Adam."

"Marie? MARIE..."

Too late. She'd put the phone down.

He sat there staring at the receiver for a moment then slammed it back into its cradle.

"Bitch!"

He'd put it off for three days. Not sure why. Maybe it was because it was too radical - too different - too...what was the word? - *unorthodox* - yeah, too alien from what he was used to. But then he'd made a promise to Jack, hadn't he? Promised to give it a try? Couldn't let the old chap down. No way. For once in his life, it was time to face up to things - it had to be done. He'd read that bloody book in the hospital, hadn't he? Been to the bloody lecture? Promised Jack he'd try it.

Well now was the moment of truth.

It was ten past four and Carol had just left the house for the weekly supermarket shopping trip. House was empty. As good a time as any.

Adam climbed the stairs to his bedroom and closed the door behind him. The house was silent apart from the metronome ticking of the lounge clock and it could barely be heard with the bedroom door shut.

He sat on the edge of the bed then realised the glow from the streetlights streaming through the window was too severe and distracting. He pulled the curtains until the room was in semi-darkness.

He climbed back on to the bed and leant his back flat against the bedroom wall. What now? Maybe cross his legs like in those meditation pictures you see in magazines? Yeah - that was the way to do it.

Adam sat back and tried to relax. What was it Jack had said? 'Sit comfortably and think about nothing'.

Okay - that should be easy enough.

He moved his head back slightly until it touched the wall then shut his eyes. Now what? How long are you supposed to wait for a mystical experience anyway?

'Patience Adam' he said to himself patronisingly, 'Patience.'

He'd give it fifteen minutes. That's long enough to think about sod all. The whole idea was stupid anyway. There were better things to do in fifteen minutes than to sit doing nothing. Maybe the meditation trip is a big con anyway. Maybe he was just being made a fool of.

Anyway, these were *thoughts* and Jack said he was to ignore all thoughts and just think of nothing. Think of emptiness, white, blank empty space. Think of...no - don't even think. Just let your mind be empty...let it go...all of it...just let it go...

'Go for it then' Adam whispered to himself, determined it would be his last rational thought for a full ten minutes.

'C'mon now man - go for it.'

N*othing.*
Absolutely nothing.

A waste of fucking time.

If you close your eyes, you see nothing - everyone knows that. Adam opened his eyes momentarily, blinked, then closed them again as if trying to restart a stubborn engine.

Nothing.

"*Give it time*" he said to himself mentally echoing Jack's words. "*C'mon - give it time.*"

Adam sat for a while, eyes closed, waiting. Waiting for something - *anything* - to happen.

When you are fully conscious, he mused, but sitting with your eyes shut, it is like triggering your mind to work overtime. You start to think about all sorts of trivial and unrelated things. How could it be that such insignificant things that seem to hover in the background when your eyes are open suddenly pounce eagerly into your thoughts as soon as your eyes are shut?

This was a waste of time.

Give it time...

Time. Waste of time. *Give it time...*

Time is a weird thing reflected Adam - you never have enough of it, and you're always scared of wasting it. Sometimes it drags on leaving you impatient and frustrated. Other times it goes so fast that you are annoyed or sad that it has gone. And once it has gone - well then it has gone forever.

Forever.

How long is forever? Does time really go on forever?

Adam sighed deeply and tried to flush the pointless questions from his overactive mind. This meditation lark clearly wasn't working. How the hell are you supposed to concentrate while a multitude of random thoughts were buzzing around your head like irritating wasps around a picnic?

Might as well open his eyes and forget the whole thing. It felt stupid anyway - just sitting there with his eyes tightly shut.

Tightly. Too tightly.

Adam was aware of his eyes being screwed tightly shut beneath a deep frown.

He relaxed his facial muscles and felt a sudden ease of tension.

No need to screw up your eyes and frown. What was it Jack had said?

'*Don't force it, don't fight it - just open to it*'

Okay. No effort then - just let it flow.

And wait for...

Nuthin'

Just thoughts again. Thoughts about Marie up on Greenwood hill. Thoughts about the depressingly boring job at the paint shop. Thoughts about sleepless nights and visions of angry bulls. Thoughts about his father. Hundreds of fleeting images and a deep dull noise from somewhere.

A heart beating - his own heart beating. A regular mechanical booming in the chest. In the ears. Everywhere.

And then an itch somewhere that begged to be scratched - *had to be scratched.*

Sod it!

Adam opened his eyes which were immediately blinded by the last rays of watery mid-December sunlight that streamed through the crack between the semi-closed window curtains.

He scratched his leg absently and yawned.

Meditation makes you sleepy.

Nothing else.

Just sleepy.

'Carsons Hardware and Paint Shop', on the High Street, had been in the same family for forty-three years and Leonard Carson was clearly proud of the fact. Like his father before him, who had founded the shop in the pre-war years, Leonard liked to remind everyone that it had never missed a day's trading. Even that day the Germans had kindly sent over the gift of a wayward doodlebug which had obliterated the Newsagent's next door, it had only stopped Carson's trading for a few hours.

Adam had only been working there for six weeks but he had heard the same story four times now and could imitate Len's nasal wheeze so effectively that he liked to mimic the old fool whenever the proprietor was out of earshot.

Steve and Danny had been in stitches when they'd come into the shop to tease Adam about his brown apron and Adam had retaliated by sticking a pen behind his ear, cocking his head sideways and then giving them his best impression of sad old Len. "Nah then, let me tell you young fella' abaht the time during the war when..." Even some of Len's regulars lurking among the shelves of undercoats had found it hard to keep a straight face.

Today though, Len was busying himself stocktaking while Adam manned the front desk. There had only been two customers since the doors opened, probably due to the cold, drizzly and depressingly grey January sky outside.

Adam was bored out of his skull. He never wanted the bloody job in the first place and Len Carson was one of the dullest and most irritating blokes Adam had ever had the misfortune to spend time with.

As far as Len was concerned the feeling was mutual. He'd had assistants before of course, over the years, but for one reason or another they never seemed to stay long. 'No commitment' Len had once told Adam tapping the side of his nose and winking. It was one of Len's favourite phrases.

"Well, that's abaht it then" Len said to Adam, replacing a small pencil behind his right ear where it seemed to have furrowed a permanent groove, "Time for a cuppa."

Adam glanced up at the dust encrusted wall clock with faded Roman Numerals. Eleven o'clock. You could set the time by Len's monotonous routines. Eleven o'clock was always 'time for a cuppa'. Guaranteed.

Adam boiled the kettle then carried two steaming stained and chipped china mugs back to the counter. Still no punters. Just him and tedious Len in tedious Carsons Paint Shop. Obliged by circumstances to endure each other's company until five pm.

Len slurped a few mouthfuls of tea before stopping to give Adam a quizzical look. Although never one for idle pleasantries Adam knew the old sod well enough to realise that he was about to be asked something.

"This your first job then?"

"Yup. Apart from loads of odd part time jobs when I was at school. Paper rounds, weekend window cleaning that kind of thing" (Adam had already told Len all this the day he started. Maybe the old git's memory was going).

Len reached into the pocket of his tattered brown coat and retrieved his pipe, nodding to himself as he tapped down a pinch of tobacco then lit the end.

The not unpleasant aroma of pipe tobacco wafted through the shop. The smell seemed to be ingrained into the very fabric of the building.

"Twenny years I've worked here" wheezed Len, "Twenny years gawd blimey. Can't believe it meself sometimes. Took over from my father y'know...did I tell you that?"

Adam feigned a weak smile, "Yeah, you told me."

"Twenny years" continued Len shaking his head, "Always thought I'd just help him out for a few years then move on like. Start me own business if you know what I mean. 'Course when he died, I just sort of carried on. Never planned to stay here. Always fancied doin' something different."

"So why didn't you?"

Len smoothed down the sides of his grey moustache and sucked on the old pipe. There was a sadness in his eyes that had sneaked in years ago and decided to take root.

"Dunno really. Too easy to carry on doing what's easiest I suppose. 'Course when I got married Agnes wanted security. Said I should carry on the family tradition and all that malarkey. Well, I should've put my foot down then of course but I didn't."

"You could try something different now though."

Len tried to laugh, nearly choked on the pipe, and had to remove it from the corner of his mouth to breathe again.

"Nah" he said "Too old. No point now."

"Well, I think you should always follow your dream - however old you are."

"Easily said" snorted Len, "So wha's your dream then?"

Adam sipped his tea whilst pondering the answer. Len had caught him off guard. He nearly said 'Anything but this *depressing paint shop*' but didn't want to offend the sad old paint man any more than necessary.

Instead, he said, "To follow my own destiny I guess."

Len rolled his eyes "So whas' that supposed to mean then? That's a right cop out of an answer if you ask me. Your so-called destiny might be to join the Army. Fight for your country and get some proper discipline."

"I don't think so."

"Nah. That's wishful thinking. Teenagers today - no commitment. That's what I say - no commitment. All the bloody same these days."

Adam was about to think of a witty answer, but the shop bell went. It was one of Len's regulars. Another sad old bastard who was painting his shed for the third time in two years and came in every couple of weeks for more creosote. An excuse for another chat with Len more like.

At least Adam wouldn't have to serve him. Len let Adam serve all the customers apart from a special few that Len liked to deal with himself.

"Clear the mugs away please Adam" Len said loud enough to let 'creosote man' know who was in charge, "Let's keep the counter clutter free shall we?"

Adam carried the two mugs out to the kitchen and poured the dregs into the sink.

'Got to get out of this place' he muttered to himself whilst rinsing the mugs under the creaky taps, 'This is doin' my fuckin' head in.'

It was four weeks since Adam had last seen Jack and had been given exactly what he had asked for - the 'key' to meditation.

'*Think of nothing.*'

Simple.

Or so he had thought at the time

Like before he had actually tried it...

In some ways Adam was reluctant to admit that he had been defeated by such a simple task. Did he really have to go back to the old man to tell him that he had tried to 'think of nothing' but had failed miserably because he had thought of trivia instead?

All things considered a pretty poor achievement really. Or even a non-achievement. He'd even promised Jack that he would be back in two weeks' time and now four weeks had passed. All in all, he was probably just as unreliable as Marie had always said. Then again, it wasn't entirely his fault; after all, there had been Christmas to contend with. The festive season.

Yeah, right.

Christmas used to be a magical time until dad was no longer part of it. Then it had changed and never been the same since. Now Christmas was just the drinking season; another excuse to get wasted.

Yeah – okay, there were the usual family traditions to be endured. Christmas dinner with the grandparents then the Queen's speech and the repeated old black and white films until Gramps nodded off in front of the TV and started dribbling.

Exchanging presents under the tree. Socks, after shave and some chocolates (Mum couldn't afford a lot these days) and then it was over for another year. The cold and dampness of another depressing January ushered in another year and that was that. A few days off from Carsons was a good excuse to sit around with Steve and Danny and get high but then what?

Adam stopped under a streetlamp to light a cigarette. It was only fifteen minutes' walk across town to get to Jack's place. He'd have been on time if he hadn't stopped for a pint. Okay, so it was Dutch courage, but that's exactly what he needed right now.

Wasn't as though he had to go back. Jack didn't know where he lived or anything personal. Adam could just walk away now and never see the old guy again. He could just pretend that he'd gleaned all the information he needed and that was it. Right?

Nah.

Wrong.

There was too much at stake here. It shouldn't be a pride thing - it was much more than that. Jack had gained a lifetime of experience and was an accomplished meditator. If Adam could just apply himself enough to making the effort this must surely be something worth pursuing to the end?

Or then again maybe he just wasn't cut out for that kind of thing.

Either way, he reasoned to himself, it made more sense to just be honest with Jack and cut out the bullshit. Tell him how it was. No frills. Yeah, that was exactly what he should do.

Adam quickened his pace and arrived at Jack's modest terraced house just as the first few spatters of rain started to fall from a glowering muddy grey sky. He rang the bell and waited while the inside door bolt was disengaged. A beaming Jack opened the door wide and his delight at seeing Adam again was obvious. Adam wondered how come his mother never seemed that pleased to see him?

"Hi Jack."

"Adam. Good to see you again. Come in, come in - make yourself at home. I'm just feeding Lady then I'll be right with you. I've been looking forward to hearing how things are going."

"Yeah. I'm sorry I've not been in touch Jack. You know how it is. Christmas and all that..."

"Of course. That's quite all right. I knew you'd be back."

"You did?"

Jack ushered Adam into the lounge and Adam sat down in the same leather settee as before. Jack walked down the passage to the small kitchen and started opening a tin of cat food.

"So" called Jack from the kitchen, "Did you try it?"

"Yeah."

"And?"

Adam wasn't sure how to respond. He didn't want to offend Jack or dampen the old man's irrepressible enthusiasm, but then again, he had resolved to tell the truth.

"I'm afraid it didn't work out. I tried, but nothing happened."

There was a moment's silence; then Jack called back "Nothing at all?"

"Nothing at all."

Adam heard Jack hobbling back up the hallway. He came into the lounge and sat opposite Adam on the faded armchair. He was still smiling.

"So - you found somewhere quiet, relaxed, and emptied your mind of thoughts and thought of nothing like I instructed?"

"Yep."

"And nothing happened?"

"That's right."

"Excellent" said Jack enthusiastically, "That's perfectly normal. Now you must try it again."

Adam stared. This guy was impossible.

"I dunno Jack. Maybe this meditation thing is not for me after all. Seems I just got bored. Nothing happened. I felt like a bloody idiot."

"Don't be disappointed Adam - it's the same for everyone first time. Believe me. You have to stick with it."

Adam laughed. "You're kidding. I'm beginning to think I've got better things to do then sit around on a comfy cushion just meditating on nothing. It seems such a waste of time."

Jack ignored the outburst. "Did you find you couldn't concentrate because of too many intrusive thoughts?"

"Too right I did."

"Excellent...and did you hear anything?"

"Nope."

"Not even your own heart beating?"

Adam gave him a sideways glance. "Yeah...I did actually. I heard my heart beating. What of it? I'd be bloody dead if it wasn't beating, wouldn't I? That's no big deal."

"Ah but that's where you are wrong Adam. It is a 'big deal'. In fact, I'd call it excellent progress. Now you must try it again."

"It doesn't work Jack. Look it might work for you or some other people but it's obviously not for me. I just don't have the self-discipline to focus or concentrate. I think I should forget the whole thing."

"You're wrong" Jack said again, "And you must persevere. Don't give up Adam. Try it again. It never works first time nor the second time. Not for me, not for you - not for anyone. You haven't failed at all. In fact - it sounds like you're doing fine. Unless of course you're one of those people who simply give up if you don't get instant results?"

Adam sighed and shook his head slowly, "What do you mean 'It sounds like I'm doing fine?'"

"Meditation. As I just said, the first time you try it nothing happens, nor the second. Not even the third. All you get are thoughts interfering with your concentration. If you are relaxed enough then you start to become aware of your own heart beating in the small gaps between your thoughts. That's good. That's real progress."

Adam stared back at him in silence for a few moments. "Are you kidding me?"

"No kidding" Jack said, "I promise."

Adam thought about Jack's words. Maybe he was being too impatient. If this meditation thing was all that it was cracked up to be then it deserved another chance, didn't it?

He was aware of Jack watching him as though he could read his every thought.

"Okay - if what you're saying is true then I'll give it another go. I'm not a quitter."

"That's the spirit. I knew when I first set eyes on you that you were not a quitter. I know something else too. Something that might surprise you..."

Adam cocked his head sideways.

"What do you mean?"

Jack leaned forward. His face took on a serious expression.

"I mean Adam that you have a potential that you are not even aware of. There are thousands of different types of people in this world - and each one of them is blessed with a specific gift or skill - no two individuals are alike. My gift, for better or worse, is being able to see people beneath their surface outer skin."

"Like a psychic you mean?"

"Yes. Like a psychic. It's a gift that 'can sometimes be a blessing and sometimes a curse' as my father used to say - but it's a gift, nevertheless. It allows me to see people as they really are - not necessarily what they want to portray externally."

"So, what do you see inside me then?" There was a faint crack in Adam's voice when he asked the question.

Jack looked Adam straight in the eyes.

"I see a very rare talent indeed Adam. A talent you don't even realise that you possess yet."

"Go on."

"Some people try meditation, but they will never succeed. Not because they are not earnest in their endeavours but because they simply do not have the mental aptitude to progress. Others, myself included, succeed in meditation after years of gruelling self-discipline - our determination sees us through. Then there are those people who are born 'naturals' although they do not always realise it. The keys to deep penetration into the spiritual realms are already in their hands - they just need to be shown how to find the keys to the lock. You are one of those people Adam."

"Me? You're kidding Jack. I couldn't even stop the most trivial random thoughts" blurted Adam, "I couldn't meditate to save my life."

"Ah but you will" said Jack, "Mark my words Adam. You will. You are a very fortunate person. Although you don't realise it yet, you have been blessed with a set of golden keys that others would die for. Once you have found the lock you will open a metaphysical door that will change your life forever.

You will discover things that it has taken me many years to find. I envy you."

Adam stared at Jack and shook his head in disbelief. This was too crazy for words. Somewhere deep inside himself he felt a quiver of apprehension. No, it was something more than apprehension. It was as though some deep-seated memory had been suddenly released from captivity and was now trying to free itself from bondage – trying to tear off a metaphorical blindfold and a gag to make itself heard. Adam shuddered inwardly and then felt his jaw tightening. How could Jack possibly know all this stuff? They barely knew each other for chrisssake!

But too right he wasn't a quitter!

He made a decision.

"I'm going to try it again Jack. If all this stuff is really true, then I'm going to give it my best shot."

Jack folded his arms and leaned forward, his face earnest.

"Your best shot might not be enough though Adam. Tell me something. How badly do you want to succeed?"

Adam looked away, thinking; eyes fixed on the carpet but not seeing the faded spiral patterns at all.

"I don't know why Jack, but I want it badly" he replied softly - and then surprised himself even more when he heard his own voice saying: "I want it more than anything else in the world."

Jack nodded, leaving a few deliberate moments of silence before he spoke again. "That's exactly what I hoped you would say."

Adam looked up. His features had changed. The arched eyebrows of the teenage cynic had fallen. In its place a new expression of determination and sincerity had taken root.

"So how do I do it then Jack? I want you to show me. How do I find the keys to this locked door?"

Woodsham shopping centre was typical of most country towns. Its focal point had always been the central high street that had remained much the same for centuries and around which a jumble of other houses had congregated year on year. Now that Woodsham had acquired the dubious title of 'New Town' the suburbs had steadily grown; mostly regimented streets of monotonous three bed semis and the odd corner pub or community church. It was only the high street though, that could claim any sense of 'history'. The old chemist shop, squeezed between a greengrocer and a newsagent, could trace its history back at least two hundred years and still retained its position as the main focal point in the town for people to stop and exchange pleasantries. Although Carol was never one for shopping, she considered it one of those necessary evils, particularly when she suddenly realised there were a few essentials that needed buying. Tonight, it was bingo night. Not exactly white-knuckle excitement she admitted to herself, but anything to get away from four walls for a change. There was just time to nip into the chemist before they closed and then she could rush home, take a shower then walk down to the bingo.

On the way out of the chemists and with her mind on other things she almost knocked into the person trying to enter through the same door.

"Marie!"

"Oh, hi Mrs Sinclair. Sorry, I was miles away..."

"How are you? It's been ages."

"I'm fine thanks. How's Adam?"

"Same as usual. Doesn't change. I was so sorry to hear that the two of you have fallen out. It was so kind of you to look after him following the accident at Reading."

"It was the least I could do. You know what his mates are like. Has he got a job yet?"

"Yes. Carsons paint shop. God knows how long he'll last until he gets the sack. At least he seems to be staying indoors more in the evenings though, instead of spending every night in the pub."

Marie raised her eyebrows. That didn't sound like Adam.

"Staying in more? What does he do then? He was never one for books or TV..."

"No. It is a bit strange. He's taken to spending hours alone in his room. God knows what he's up to. Sometimes I'd like to get inside that head of his."

Marie smiled and stepped inside the chemists clutching her purse.

"Now that *would* be interesting" she said, "A house of many rooms I would guess. Anyway, must go. Nice to see you again Mrs Sinclair."

"You too Marie. Take care now."

Carol stepped into the murky windswept street. A leaden January sky hung heavily over the town turning everything of colour into shades of monotonous grey.

'A house of many rooms' she repeated to herself silently. 'Mmm. Not a bad description. Probably a few dark corridors too.'

Dark corners that Adam kept very well hidden.

Carol shivered, slipped on a pair of gloves that Adam had bought her for Christmas then turned for home.

"The keys to the locked door?"

Jack stood up to stretch his good leg and walked over to the Victorian sash window. He tugged the lace curtains aside and glanced up at the rain-streaked sky and tutted. Adam was getting to know the old guy's ways. Jack was about to embark on another of his monologues.

"What you need to realise Adam is that all life is a journey. Sometimes you need to stand back for a while and take stock of exactly where you are - like stopping to read a map when you're walking in the wilderness. Every so often you need to pinpoint your position so that you can review where you have come from and more importantly where it is you want to get to. It's a fact that the majority of people in this world - millions of them - can't grasp that simple concept. There are others who are very good planners technically - they can plan something meticulously that is work orientated but in terms of planning their own lives they haven't got the first clue. They wander through life from event to event letting fate carry them along like a leaf in a stream.

But the point is this, Adam. If you don't plan your life, then you can't blame anyone if your ambitions seem to be going nowhere in particular. Take today for instance. Have you thought about what it is you need to have achieved by this time tomorrow? Do you hold a vision of where you want to be in five years' time? Ten years? Everyone needs to build their own route map for their lives."

Adam considered the question carefully. "I've never really thought about it like that. Not in the way you're describing anyway. The 'planning your life' bit I mean. Not in detail. Obviously, I plan to do things, but I suppose it's only short-term stuff really..."

"So, if I were to ask you *'where are you going in your life?'* what would you say?"

Adam frowned "I dunno really. Get a job. Get my own place. Get married someday. Have a laugh... you know...look, what exactly are you getting at Jack? - What's this about? I thought you were gonna teach me how to meditate better - find the key an' all that - not have a go at my inability to plan anything properly."

"Interesting reply" responded Jack smugly, "Do I detect a twinge of self-criticism there Adam?"

Adam stared back incredulously - Jack was too quick for him. The old codger had caught him out and perhaps he had a point after all. What was Adam Sinclair's life plan anyway?

Fuck knows...

Before Adam could respond Jack was in full flow again - changing direction instantly like the flick of a chameleon's tongue.

"We have the capacity to experience three types of consciousness during our lives Adam - and yet ninety nine percent of the worlds' population live their whole lives and experience only two - what we call 'waking' or everyday consciousness and sleep consciousness. Little do they realise that they are missing out on a vast wealth of knowledge and experience which can be gained through a third type of consciousness...the consciousness of deep meditation. Meditation is just another type of consciousness that is neither being awake nor being asleep but 'just being'. It is an awareness of self that has the capacity to enter new realms of existence with the mind tuned to full receptiveness and much more reactive than in the passive mode of sleep. It is a wonderful and magical world that can be entered through the subconscious - a world of wonder that is waiting to be explored. A world free for any man or woman to enter and learn the secrets that are rarely glimpsed in our cluttered and noisy world of waking consciousness - a world some like to call 'normality'.

The thing to remember Adam is that most people turn to meditation because they are seeking something. Usually, it is something they like to call 'enlightenment' which is a search for meaning or answers that helps them to make more sense of their lives. But what most meditators don't realise is that there is a second element to meditation and that is the ability to move around other planes of existence. You asked me how to find the doorway into this wonderful place and how to find the key. The answer is quite simple. It's perseverance. That's all you need. You already have the potential within you - now all you need is to cultivate the willpower to succeed and the perseverance to never give up."

"And if I succeed and go through this er... 'doorway' what then? Is it dangerous?"

Jack stroked his chin and considered the question thoughtfully before replying, "That depends. In itself, deep meditation is not dangerous at all. On the contrary - it is truly beneficial to mind body and spirit. Medical studies have proven the positive benefits of regular meditation and there is much documented evidence of the positive health aspects in terms of reduced blood pressure and immunity to psychosomatic disorders etcetera. The only danger, if that is the right word for it, is already inherent in the mind of the meditator...a potential if you like..."

"I don't get it Jack. Explain what you mean."

The old man walked over to the tiled Victorian mantelpiece and picked up a small dust covered bronze statue of the Buddha. He wiped the dust from it gently. Adam watched the dust motes parachute in spirals in front of the glowing fire.

"I'll try. Let's say that meditation, when it is mastered, gives you certain...how shall I put it? Certain 'powers' that can be either used beneficially for the good of all mankind or misused for personal or material gain. If used beneficially, these powers can be utilised to enormous benefit. If misused however, they can place the meditator in a potentially unpleasant situation."

"Go on."

"There are lots of things we still don't understand. Forces and energies that surround us of which we are normally totally unaware. Some are benign and can be utilised by the meditator for positive and constructive purposes. Like all things though - there is a darker side. A negative balance if you will. Should those forces be misused...for purely selfish purposes like greed or unqualified personal gain, the perpetrator opens him or herself up to the influences of evil rather than good - and that can be a dangerous thing. The mind is a very sensitive organ - the control of our impulses and motivations is fragile and open to lots of external influences. During meditation the mind is opened up and laid bare. It is vulnerable... but relatively safe if the thoughts are pure. If thoughts are less than pure, and at the same time the mind is vulnerable, then the meditator is placing himself or herself in a position where negative forces and impulses have few barriers to overcome, and they can therefore enter the meditator's field of consciousness without confrontation."

"And then what happens?"

Jack's face took on a serious expression. Once more he looked deep into Adam's eyes.

"My advice" he said gravely, "is don't let it happen."

"If I were you, I'd chuck it in mate."

Steve Lacey watched the smoke issue from his mouth in a steady stream before handing the shared roll-up over to Adam.

Adam drew on the spliff enjoying the unmistakeable warm sensation in his mouth and the buzz of the distinctive aroma. "Well maybe I will" he said, "But right now I need the dough."

"'Dat old bloke - *wossisname* - Len Carson - he's a nutter" commented Danny, "I wouldn't last five minutes wit' 'im I can tell you."

They were sitting in the garage belonging to Danny's parents on upturned crates and old car tyres, the usual refuge when the beer money ran out. Danny's folks suspected they were using the place for a crafty smoke but didn't like to interfere. '*Old enough to know better*' was all that Danny's mother had commented once.

Adam was beginning to regret mentioning how much he hated working at Carson's Paints. He was now getting the full flow of Steve Lacey's philosophy of work, which was painful enough when Steve was sober.

"If you ask me, I'd rather sign-on then work in a bloody shop with that stupid old codger. Anyroad Adam, where you bin' hiding away these last few weeks?"

"Huh?"

"Well, we haven't seen you in the Anchor or the King's Head. Don't tell me that work has left you so shagged out you've been getting an early night - or you back with Marie again or somethin'?"

Adam flicked the glowing embers of the dog-end across the garage at Steve who jumped when it hit his chest.

"Neither, you old wanker. I've been pursuing other interests."

"Other interests? Oh yeah? Like what?"

Adam opened his mouth to reply then stopped. In a way he wanted to tell them everything about Jack and his interest in meditation but how the hell do you try and broach that sort of thing? He decided it could wait until a more appropriate time. "It's hush hush" he said instead, winking.

"Hush hush is it now?" said Danny "Would dat be drinking, smoking or shagging den mister Adam Sinclair?"

Adam and Steve laughed loudly. Danny's wit was priceless. Adam could see him making it as a comedian someday - if he ever got off his arse long enough.

"Anyway," continued Adam deftly changing the subject, "I get paid tomorrow so who's up for a night out on Saturday?"

"Smokey Joe's nightclub?" suggested Steve impishly.

"Steve..." said Adam turning his head slowly to his best mate, "Piss off."

For once it had been a good dream.

That is until the shrill ringing of an alarm clock shredded it into meaningless vague fragments that he tried vainly to hold onto for a few moments.

Damn!

Okay - the dream was a little confused in parts, but hey? - wasn't that always the way? He reflected momentarily on the tinge of sadness that one always feels when an uplifting or absorbing dream is suddenly cut short in mid-flow and wondered if there was any point in trying to resurrect interrupted dreams or not. Were they just pointless flights of fancy after all? Or was there some deeper meaning that mankind hasn't yet fathomed? A message from the subconscious maybe?

Bollocks. Now he was starting to talk like Jack for heaven's sake.

He pondered the issue for a while before succumbing to the routines of harsh reality. He turned the alarm off and rolled over with a groan. What day was it? - Saturday! A small smile played across his lips. Thank God he didn't have to face another dull day at Carsons paint shop until Monday.

Saturdays were good.

He wiped the sleep from his eyes and focused on the thin strip of light beneath the bedroom curtains which this morning was more intense than usual. The last few days of January had been dull and overcast, which always seemed to manifest as a depressing grey streak of light peeking from under the equally dull, pastel curtains in his bedroom. Today it had been replaced with an amber glow that meant sunshine - and somehow that meant it was worth the effort of crawling out of bed and brewing some tea.

Adam lay there for a few moments thinking about the events of the previous day. The long hours spent at Jack's place and the deep conversations about meditation and suchlike. When he'd got home his mother had casually asked where he'd been all evening and he'd found himself unusually tongue-tied. It wasn't so much that he was embarrassed by admitting he'd been at an old man's house talking metaphysics, it was just a huge sense of awkwardness in trying to explain it. It was easier to grunt something about the lads and the pub, which is what he had said off-handedly hoping she wouldn't probe any further. She didn't - and yet she'd looked at him a little quizzically at the time. He never had been a good liar.

Then he remembered something Jack had said as he was leaving yesterday. An idea - a suggestion - that Adam should try. Keeping a diary, that was it. Recording each attempt at meditation, '*a progress journal*' he'd called it. Something that Adam had never considered before - always thought diaries were for wimps and silly schoolgirls.

He'd promised Jack that he would give it a go though. Just for a week, say. Just to see whether it made a difference or helped him to marshal his thoughts.

He wondered why he was feeling so good this morning. Energised. Could be because last night's dreams had been more enjoyable than usual which meant he'd got a better night's sleep and woke up more refreshed and relaxed. Much better than the tension that he felt after waking up following the recurring bull nightmares that usually plagued his night-time hours.

Or it could be true what Jack had said earlier in the day - that if you meditate just before going to sleep then the quality and depth of sleep is always much better. Yeah, that must be it.

He'd got back from another chat at Jack's place so fired up and enthused last night that the urge to meditate had never been stronger. Carol hadn't believed it when he'd said he wanted an early night rather than watch the football. But it was true. He'd showered quickly, shut his bedroom door, lit a candle, and relaxed like Jack had shown him. Okay - you could hardly call it a 'mystical experience', but it certainly felt good. Meditation had blurred into sleep and sleep had blurred into dreaming.

If only every night could be like that...

Adam threw back the sheets, yawned himself to his feet and sifted through a tatty chest of drawers searching for clean socks and pants.

Saturday! A night out with the boys. Have a laugh. Smoke some dope. Get stoned. Forget about all the other hassles life throws at you.

Like dreary paint shops and fickle women.

Meditation was good - yeah - but tonight it was boys' night.

Ace!

The phone rang.

"Jack?"

"Yes."

"It's David."

Jack sat down on a small stool he kept beside the phone table in the hallway and placed the telephone receiver on his lap while Lady purred as usual around his good leg.

"David! How good to hear from you. It's been a while. I hear you're getting very good audiences these days."

"Very much so - you should come and join me sometime."

Jack chuckled "It's a long time since I've been out on the lecture circuit. No-one wants to listen to an old fogey like me you know."

"That's rubbish and you know it. You are fitter than a man half your age. The audiences would love an old soldier with your credentials. Just as long as you promise not to upstage me that is."

"As if..."

"So, Jack, did he turn up?"

"We both knew he would. Yes. We have had a few sessions and there are a few more planned."

"That's great news. Progress?"

"As you would expect. Usual moves from suspicion to fascination to frustration. It's still early days."

"But this one is very special. We know that don't we? It won't be long now, will it?"

Jack smiled to himself and stroked Lady's back, running his hand through the thick silky fur.

"No, it won't be long now. You know how it is, breaking through the barriers and all that. Takes time. But I have some more work to do with him first. I'm still a little concerned about one or two areas..."

Doctor Levinson was silent for a moment.

"I picked that vibe up too Jack. Do you think he's strong enough to get through though?"

"Yes, he's definitely strong enough, but I have a feeling he might need a little help if things start to... you know..."

"We can only do so much though Jack. At the end of the day, it's up to him alone...and if he starts to falter..."

"Yes, I know. If he falters, then he will have to learn the hard way. And that will be the real test."

"Do you think he'll make it?"

"I don't know David. I really don't know. All we can do is to give him the key, the tools and the map and then..."

"...And then we pray he gets through?"

"Yes. Exactly. Then we pray he gets through."

Sunday 10th February 1975 11.05am

Dear Diary,
Bloody hell that's a corny start!
I'm starting a diary like Jack suggested. It's Sunday 10th February and the weather is cold, grey and gloomy same as every other Sunday. Mum's gone to a Church jumble sale or coffee morning or something, so she'll probably come home with some second-hand rubbish that I will be expected to wear. I'm nursing a hangover this morning (again). This is supposed to be a meditation diary, but I haven't actually started any meditation today. I'm waiting until the head clears first.

Last night I went out with Steve, Danny and a mate of Danny's called Mick who is quite a laugh. We met at the Anchor for a few pints then caught a taxi to 'Midnights' Disco and Wine bar. Danny got off with some bird called Emma, so we didn't see him for the rest of the evening. Steve had some Speed on him which he wanted Mick and I to share. I was tempted but for some reason I didn't fancy a hit. Mick and Steve went for it anyway. We had a great time until Steve threw up. He said it was just a bad trip. Mick was okay, he's usually a bit shy by all accounts but the Speed must have helped him come out of himself. He was a chattering to everyone in the club like a bloody parrot, but no-one really wanted to listen to him. He was talking shit anyway.

I just watched the two of them get smashed and laughed my head off. I stuck with drinking bitter and avoided spirits which was okay I suppose but I must have had one too many or I wouldn't feel so muggy headed today.

I'm broke now though. I bought a couple of rounds after paying to get in at 'Midnights' and I think I paid the taxi fare as well. Got to find a way to get more money. Carson's just doesn't pay enough. I can't afford to go out again tonight unless mum lends me some money, but she always reckons she's broke too.

Dad would have lent me some if he were here.

Sometimes I miss him a lot.

Maybe I'll try meditating tonight.

Sorry diary. Not a very good start, is it?

Monday 11th February 10.35 pm

Tried meditating again.

Tried to follow Jack's instructions but finding it difficult to concentrate. Too many distractions. Started with counting breaths (Jack reckons this works well for some people). Boring. Mind started to wander. Managed to get to about 300 then lost interest.

Enjoyed the stillness and the darkness but still too many things going on in my mind. Stopped around 8pm and watched TV instead. West Ham won tonight. Guess that's a good omen anyway.

Tuesday 12th February 6.30 pm

Tried meditating for about half an hour. Nothing. Feels like I'm getting nowhere.

7.50 pm

Another attempt.

Went through the relaxation exercises again that Jack had showed me. Some success. Felt quite relaxed after 15 minutes.

Tried breath counting again but still finding it difficult to hold concentration for more than a few minutes at a time. Trying to let all thoughts escape as instructed.

Not sure if this is working or not. (Amazing what trivia brain can dredge up when you try and think of nothing). Feeling very frustrated at lack of progress. If Jack's right about me having some great potential as a meditator, which I doubt, then I wish it would get bloody easier.

Will try again tomorrow.

Wednesday 13th February 9.05 pm

Late for work this morning. Len gave me a bollocking. Miserable bastard. The rest of the day wasn't bad though. Feeling relaxed tonight. Gave it a serious go. Relaxed quite easily but couldn't concentrate during meditation. Tried Jack's suggestion of lighting a candle, making the room dark and focusing on the flame. Nice atmosphere. Calming. Felt good. Think I nodded off. Came around with pins and needles in my fingers. Jack said that's a good sign. I'm not so sure.

Thursday 14th February 10.00 pm

Had a couple of pints with the lads earlier this evening.

Finding it hard to motivate myself tonight. Thoughts a bit tangled (maybe it's the beer?)

Tried to meditate for half an hour but with little success. Jack's always said that beer and meditation just don't go together. It's some kind of blocker. Kept thinking about Marie and why I was so bloody stupid to lose her. I sent her an anonymous Valentine's card yesterday. She'll probably guess it's from me and will bin it.

I guess there's part of me still can't get over her though I'm not admitting it to anybody. Well, nobody except this diary anyway. (God, I hope no-one ever reads this rubbish.)

Will try meditating again tomorrow.

Friday 15th February 8.05pm

Tried to make more of an effort tonight.

Worked on loosening up exercises. Seemed to work reasonably well. Found myself relaxing easier than previous sessions. Seemed too easy but maybe it's just laziness. I'm not sure.

Gave up on the breath counting technique. Getting nowhere. Just tried to concentrate on deep breathing.

Seemed to work a little. Difficult to tell.

Still too many random thoughts interfering and what seemed to be light patterns (like fainting sensation) Maybe eyes are shut too tightly.

Gave it 45 minutes this evening. Lights hurt eyes when I'd finished.

Still not sure if I am making any progress.

For Jack's sake I'm not giving up though. I'm going to give it half an hour or so then I'll try again.

I'm going to beat this thing.

Whatever it takes.

Adam lit the tip of the jasmine scented incense stick that Jack had given him, waited for a few moments for the flame to shrink to a soft teardrop shaped glow and then watched the first wisps of scented smoke curl upwards towards the ceiling of his bedroom.

He'd done everything Jack had told him. Stayed off the beer all day, drunk only water and made sure he'd kept himself in a very positive state of mind. Jack thought the incense stick might help induce an air of calm so Adam had agreed to give it a go. Anything was worth a try.

He was ready for another attempt at meditating in what had now become a few ritualised motions. He took a few deep breaths until he perceptibly felt a subtle relaxation of his tensed muscles, letting each out-breath slowly intoxicate him with a sense of calm.

Fine.

Next, he sat down slowly adjusting his clothing until every button or belt was moved to a comfortable and non-irritating position. Good. He closed his eyes slowly. This was the easy part.

Now I must relax.

The first few seconds were reassuringly familiar. A few more deep breaths until all the stale air was fully expelled from the lungs, then listen to the silence.

Except there never is silence...

A clock ticked faintly from somewhere in the house and the drone of an aeroplane rumbled in the distance. Somewhere outside there were voices - children playing in the street. An ice cream van playing that annoying jingle somewhere nearby.

Ignore it.

Then there were the thoughts. Ever present, ever shifting and clamouring to be acknowledged. Each thought full of its own importance and demanding that it should be heard. Each one ridiculous and petty in its own way, cluttering the brain with countless items of trivia that are sifted through day after day with tedious monotony. Each little thought demanding to be organised, categorised and scrutinised.

Let them go...

And then the waiting. Waiting for the something that is nothing and the nothing that is something.

And for what? Something indefinable, intangible, elusive and almost imperceptible. Something lurking furtively behind the screen of 'mind chatter' - a skittish ephemeral thing that likes to remain hidden in the depths of the subconscious like a nervous mole rarely daring to poke its nose through the subsoil to take a peek into the strange world beyond its natural dark domain.

Patience.

Patience.

And then sometimes, just sometimes, when and if you get it just right, there is a small ripple that permeates through your consciousness like a waft of fresh air that gently blows away the thoughts like bubbles on a breeze and inwardly cleanses leaving a vacuum.

The frightening vacuum of an empty mind.

Man's darkest fear.

Complete and utter...

...NOTHINGNESS.

When the phone rang Jack was in the cellar busily cataloguing a particularly fine Burgundy that he'd recently acquired from an old friend. It took him a full minute to drag his cumbersome leg back up the wooden stairs to answer it, but he already knew who was on the other end of the line. It was one of the peculiar side effects of many years spent meditating. A heightened sense of intuition. One of the first manifestations was the knowing that someone was trying to contact you before it actually happened.

Jack picked up the phone from the cradle and put it to his ear.

"Jack? It's Adam. I need to see you."

"I thought you had forgotten all about me. It's been two or three weeks."

"I know. I'm sorry. I've been really busy. Look... um...I need to talk to you."

"Then don't waste any more time on the phone. I'm not going anywhere. You can come around now if that suits you. So, tell me, why the sudden urgency?"

"It's the meditation thing. I think something's starting to happen."

"I see. You didn't give up then?"

"You knew I wouldn't."

"That's right" said Jack, "I knew you wouldn't. Well...see you shortly then."

"Great. I'll be there as soon as I can."

Jack put the receiver down and rubbed his hands together, a smug grin creeping over his face.

"That was Adam" he explained to Lady who was staring up at him in feline curiosity,

"We knew he could do it didn't we?"

Dear Adam,

Hope you are well. I thought it would be easier to write you this letter rather than try and phone you.

I saw Danny the other night and I asked him how you were. He told me that you had been out to some concerts and a few clubs. He also told me you were acting a bit weird lately and seemed withdrawn. Is that true?

I asked Danny if you were still smoking that stuff and he said that the last few times you had declined although Steve Lacey seems to be off his head more than ever. I hope you are not taking anything harder Adam - for your own sake!

I still regret that incident when you got hurt. I hope the scars have healed now. Like I explained on the phone I dumped the guy who tried to beat you up. I didn't really like him anyway. Thanks for the Valentine's card. It was very sweet of you. I knew it was you by the handwriting. You are supposed to disguise it dumb brain! Anyway, it made me start to think about...

Marie stopped writing and re-read the words back to herself before gazing dreamily through the window of 'Annie's Café'. She wiped a coffee stain off the scrap of paper and chewed on the end of her biro for a moment then ripped the paper into small pieces scattering them into a dirty ash tray.

She sipped a last mouthful of lukewarm coffee, took out her purse, left a few coins on the table then walked out of the door before anyone could notice the tears welling in her eyes.

"So" said Jack, almost as soon as Adam entered the front door, "You have something to tell me I believe?"

Adam had walked briskly through the damp streets barely noticing his surroundings in the rush to get to Jack's place. Now that he had arrived the warm, quiet air of domesticity almost made him blush with self-consciousness. It wasn't such a big deal really. He felt foolish.

"It's probably nothing really" Adam said, removing his jacket and hanging it over the banister rail, "I just wanted you to know that these last few days I've really been giving it my best shot...you know... meditation."

"Excellent" Jack clapped his hands together, his enthusiasm sincere and contagious. "So - come in, sit down, relax and tell me all about it."

Adam eased himself into an armchair and crossed his legs nonchalantly, aware of how warm the room felt after the cold outside. There was something about glowing coals and open fires.

"I've kept at it every night Jack - like you said. I've even started to keep a diary like you suggested. Most times I end up losing concentration...getting nowhere...but I've been persevering with your instructions to sit, relax, let go and think of nothing."

Adam looked up seeking acknowledgement. Jack's piercing blue eyes stared back at him with a look that said, 'go on.'

"Anyway" Adam continued, "The last time I tried, something different happened. I relaxed as usual, drifted into a sense of calm, just like you said - and then focused on emptying my mind. I did it exactly like you told me, letting every thought drift away rather than analysing anything. The more thoughts that appeared the more I let them go until they stopped coming altogether. My mind really did feel empty, and it seemed to stay that way for ages. It was so empty that in the end I got scared and woke up with a jolt. But the amazing thing was that when I sort of came back to reality, I felt so good! I can't explain it. I kinda felt totally relaxed and sort of refreshed and...how can I put it? More alive."

"Well, that is excellent news Adam" enthused Jack, "I'm delighted to hear it. That is a huge step forward. You are now well on the way to something more incredible than you can possibly imagine. The secret is not to stop, not to falter, but to push on and on. Remember there are no limits."

Adam considered Jack's words. He felt a warm glow inside.

"I'm gonna see it through Jack - y'know - keep meditating regularly and try to achieve all the things you've told me about. At school all my teachers said I could never stick at anything. It was probably true. But I know this is different."

"Do you know I believe you will" said Jack with sincerity, "And one day, mark my words, you will become much more proficient than I can ever be. You will be the teacher and I the pupil."

Adam gave Jack a cynical look "I don't think that's very likely."

"Then you will be pleasantly surprised my friend, but first let me ask you something."

"Go on."

Jack sat back in the armchair opposite Adam, looking him straight in the eye. When he spoke, the question took Adam by surprise.

"Have you ever thought about what it is you really want from life?"

Adam thought about the question for a moment wondering what Jack was getting at. It was something that he had hinted at once before.

"What I really want? Yes, of course I have - well sort of..."

Jack reached over to an antique looking sideboard where a half-empty bottle of red wine had been left. He gently eased the cork out, which had been reinserted as a temporary stopper, and was soon swirling the wine around in a polished crystal glass. He held it up to the window so that the light from outside passed through it like a laser and scrutinised it closely while Lady jumped onto his lap, curling up with a small purring sound.

"So, tell me then Adam Sinclair...what is your heart's desire?"

Adam stared at his feet as he considered the question.

"To be rich I suppose...well wealthy enough to..."

"To what?"

"To buy anything I want - to have no financial worries I guess."

"Fine. Let's explore that one in a bit more depth. Let's say you had more money than you could spend in a lifetime. What would you buy?"

Adam shrugged. "I dunno. A castle in the country, I guess. A luxury yacht and a fast car with white leather seats. Expensive quality clothes...I dunno... money to gamble...to spend...to enjoy myself."

"Okay…so let's carry on the supposition. What happens when you have bought all those things you wanted - and more. Now it's ten years later and there's nothing left that you want to buy…what then?"

Adam looked out of the lounge window for inspiration. At the rain spattered glass and the glow of dusk settling over the rooftops of suburbia. Where was Jack going with this?

"I dunno…I mean how can I say? Maybe I'd buy more of the same…paintings for investment or…"

"Hold on" interrupted Jack, "There's no need to invest…you are never going to run out of money remember? Okay - carry on."

"Right. Um…good food…wine…holidays…"

"Fine. But what about your health? You couldn't enjoy all those things without your health."

"Yeah, sure I'd need my health."

"And friends?"

"Yeah."

"Love?"

"Yes."

"Children?"

"Perhaps."

Jack nodded. "Now let's say we take away your health, friends, love, family, children and things like that and just leave you alone with the money - how's that?"

Adam shifted in his seat.

"Not so good."

"Why?"

"Because…" Adam began then stopped. He thought for a moment about the question. "Because you need more than just money to be happy."

"Hold on then Adam, that's a new word; 'happy' what does it mean to be happy? Is it something to do with love and friendship and being with other people?"

"Sure."

"So, give me some other words then...give me a list of what brings happiness...let's leave out money for the moment."

"Okay...well there's er...sunshine, freedom, laughter, joy, kindness..."

"Compassion?"

"Yeah."

"Wisdom, satisfaction, relaxation?"

"Yeah - all of those."

"Equality, generosity, care, beauty, sympathy..."

Adam nodded "Aha."

Jack stared out of the window in ponderous silence for a few seconds. "It seems to me that most of those things can be acquired without much, if any, money. And surely some of those qualities like compassion, generosity, equality and care don't sit too easily with limitless wealth."

"I can see what you're driving at" sighed Adam "You're trying to sell me the old line that money doesn't bring happiness."

"Maybe I am. Though, I'm not saying that's always the case. Maybe what I am saying is that there is one thing that is much more important than money... perhaps even more important than all those other qualities we have just mentioned...and that is a simple thing called contentment."

"How do you mean?"

"I'll try and explain. Hear me out. Rich people can suffer like anyone else. They can still be greedy, selfish, sad, frustrated, confused, desperate and lonely. Money does not usually bring complete contentment, indeed sometimes it is a positive barrier that inhibits contentment and yet contentment of body, soul and spirit is what brings true inner peace and happiness. Pure contentment is bliss, and it is the goal that much of mankind seeks to attain. Some do. Most do not. And the strange thing is it is often the poorest and humblest people that acquire true contentment. Maybe it is because they have less to lose and that the real key to achieving contentment is to lose things rather than gain them. Possessions can poison the soul and burden us down. Lack of possessions purifies the soul as Buddhists have always maintained. Think about it rationally Adam and you will inevitably come to the same conclusion as I have done. Examine the argument, test it against the logic of experience and watch supposition turn to certainty. Once the logic of the argument becomes obvious to you then the way forward becomes crystal clear. Now, how about a drink? This wine is really rather good you know."

Adam shook his head in disbelief "No I'm fine thanks. Look...um...why are you telling me all this stuff Jack? I don't get it."

Jack gave Adam a conspiratorial nod and looked theatrically over his shoulder before responding.

"So why am I telling you all this stuff Adam?"

'*Crafty sod!*' thought Adam - '*Turnin' the question back on me.*'

"Because..." Adam replied at length, "Because, let me guess, because this is the stuff that I'm gonna find out anyway through deep meditation?"

"And what else?"

Adam was thoughtful for a moment while he reflected on Jack's original question.

"Because I need to be sure of what I really want before I go looking for it?"

"Adam you're a lot smarter than you look!"

Adam stared at Jack like a gawping fish. Jack raised the wine glass in salute then downed his last mouthful of wine with relish.

Carol picked up the dirty clothes strewn across the bedroom floor and sighed. Didn't matter how many times she reminded him that the linen basket might just as well have been on another planet than a few yards down the hallway. He'd been quite tidy as a child but then teenagers weren't renowned for bedroom organisation. Just look at it. Not an inch of wall space left. She recognised some of the posters; Dylan, The Beatles and The Rolling Stones were familiar enough but some of the newer posters were new to her. Stuff like Bowie, Pink Floyd, Deep Purple and Black Sabbath. Some of the images made her shiver. Why did they have to be so gothic and dark? The floor was covered in LP's, some in their sleeves and some not. The desktop was a mess of papers, beer cans, an empty cigarette packet, congealing coffee mugs and, as always, a dusty picture frame with a picture of Adam at five years old sitting on his dad's shoulders.

She opened a drawer to put some papers away - but the drawer too was full of 'stuff'. And what was this? Candles, incense, matches, a diary and a dog-eared book called 'The Meaning of Consciousness'. She picked up the book and read the back cover.

Weird.

Then she picked up the diary and bit her lip. Should she? Diaries were private things, and she should respect everyone's right to privacy.

Then again, she was his mother. It was only right that mothers should care and look out for the welfare of their offspring.

She turned the cover of the diary over. Just to see. Just to read a few words that's all.

No harm done.

She read a few sentences then let her eyes drift, focusing only on her innermost thoughts.

Then she closed the diary, put it back into the drawer, shut the drawer and turned to sort out the dirty washing.

A noise behind her made her jump. Something had fallen off the cluttered desk.

It was the picture.

She bent down and picked it up wiping the dust from the glass and just for a moment looked into the eyes of her husband and her child in happier times. She caught her breath. Swallowed hard.

As she replaced the picture on the desk a gust of wind from the open window ruffled Adam's bedroom curtains and momentarily filled the room with fresh air.

"So" said Jack after returning the empty wine glass to the sideboard, "From what you tell me this is the start of a new and more serious side of young Adam Sinclair then? Meditation-wise you have broken through the first set of hurdles in remarkably quick time if I may say so. And you are now on the verge of something very, very exciting. Let me tell you what I want you to do."

"I'm listening."

"Good. This is important. From now on I want you to meditate as much as possible, for as long as possible. You must ensure that you break through the barrier of trivial thoughts into that state that you described to me earlier, the feeling of complete calm and relaxation. Okay so far?"

"Okay so far."

"Right. Next, I want you to notice your new surroundings. Don't try and force your thoughts but just take note of any sounds, colours or textures that you experience, but you must remain totally impassive. That's the most important thing. Don't try and analyse anything. Instead, just notice things. If you start to consciously think about anything that you see around you, then you will start another stream of thoughts and that will stop your progress. Do you understand?"

"Yeah, I think so. It sounds difficult though."

Jack stroked the stubble on his chin and nodded slowly.

"For most people it's so difficult it is nigh on impossible - and it can take years to get right. But as for you Adam...I think with the right amount of determination and tenacity you can not only achieve it, but my prediction is that you will sail beyond this interim stage into a much, much deeper realm of the subconscious."

Adam was touched by Jack's faith but was doubtful.

"I could never do that."

Jack shook his head purposefully and wagged a finger.

"Never say never. You can do anything you want. Anything. There are no limits. Remember that."

"Yeah, well, it's easy to say that, but come on Jack, I've got as many limitations as the next guy. Nobody's perfect."

"But we are all potentially perfect Adam and I disagree with you when you say things like 'I've got limitations' because when you say that then you are right because you have just convinced yourself of those limitations. Equally when you say 'I'm brilliant' you are conditioning your brain to make you brilliant. It's quite simple really. Don't ever underestimate your abilities. And don't get fooled by other cynics or the media either. Avoid being conditioned by other people's expectations of you. What you think is what you become."

"How do you mean?"

"In all sorts of ways. It's amazing just how much influence things like Newspapers, TV and radio can have on our lives. They try and manipulate us and make us their slaves. Some days we can wake up feeling really good and positive and then be totally knocked for six by the headlines in the paper or a TV news report. Just think about how much of the press today is full of Vietnam atrocities, IRA bombings and all this Watergate stuff. Every day, all over the world, wonderful, positive, compassionate events are happening, but the media ignores them because good news does not sell. Instead, we are subjected to a daily ration of gloom and doom to the extent that in the end we start to really believe that the world is all bad and depression is a normal and acceptable reaction to what we are bombarded with.

Now don't get me wrong, I'm not decrying the validity of the news service - as long as it is unbiased and independent that is. It is an amazing achievement and has a lot going for it. What I am saying is that if we can try and ignore the negative for a couple of days and start to search out the positive elements of life then depression and lethargy slips off the shoulders like a black cloak and leaves us feeling alive, refreshed confident and powerful. Try it. It works."

Adam fell silent while he digested Jack's words. Jack was one remarkable guy. Adam had never met anyone like him - ever.

Everything the old codger said seemed to make so much sense. More than all those dull teachers at school for starters.

"So, let me get this right. I've got to totally ignore all negative influences and instead focus totally on meditating and finding my way past all the intrusive thoughts?"

"Exactly."

Adam nodded to let Jack know he had absorbed his every word.

"Guess I'd better be going Jack. It's later than I thought. I'm back at work tomorrow."

"Keep it up Adam. You are doing better than you think. Shall we say same time next week then?"

"Same time next week" Adam confirmed, "Can't stop now can I Jack?"

Sunday afternoon.

Gloomy, boring, predictable and depressing Sunday afternoon. Sullen and turgid March skies, windows streaked with rain, endless dull sport on TV and bugger all to do. He'd spent the last two months working in Carson's, the local paint shop, and hated every minute of it. 'Until a proper job comes along' Carol had said, 'It will stop you just loafing about aimlessly'. Oh well, at least it meant having some money to go out with. So, he'd gone along and listened to old Mr Carson (the son) lecturing him about the fascinating intricacies of the paint business. It had been a real effort to sound interested. The bottom line was that Mr Carson needed an assistant and it turned out that he, Adam was the only applicant for the job. For two months he'd stood behind a shop counter in brown overalls selling tins of paint to a motley crowd of home decorating enthusiasts and chain-smoking tradesmen. Boring wasn't the word for it.

Adam lifted the stylus off the record he had been listening to and threw the vinyl on the bed, the echoes of Hawkwind's 'In Search of Space' still ringing in his ears. Something was bothering him. Something more than working at Carson's.

Something that had been bothering him for some time...

It was, Adam surmised, a sort of side effect of the increasing amount of meditation he was undertaking. Somehow the more easily he was able to relax, the more other buried or hidden thoughts that reached back into his early childhood were resurfacing. Things he'd deliberately pushed to the back of his mind.

Weird.

He went downstairs and poked his head around the lounge door. Carol was slumped on the sofa engrossed in some glossy gossip magazine. She looked up. "Make us a cuppa love."

Adam nodded and mindlessly filled a kettle with water then flicked the switch to 'on'. A few minutes later he put the tea and biscuits down on the coffee table between the sofa and the TV.

Carol Sinclair smiled. "Thanks love, so what you up to then?"

"Nothin' - just listenin' to records n' stuff."

She nodded knowingly. Words between Mothers and their teenage sons were few at this period of their lives, often strained and always merely functional. Somewhere between ages fifteen and nineteen conversation becomes a rare commodity. It returns sometime in early adulthood. That's just the way it is.

She was therefore surprised when Adam sat down in a chair, helped himself to a custard cream from the open packet, and then looked at her with a curious and slightly serious expression on his face.

"Mum?"

"Uh huh?" she looked up, laying the magazine face down on the sofa.

"Can I ask you something?"

"Of course."

Adam sighed, looked away.

"What was Dad like? *Really* I mean..."

Something gave her an icy jolt at the base of her spine. She tried not to show it but couldn't help shuffling uncomfortably in her seat. This was out of character for Adam. He never - *ever* - mentioned his dad. She looked at him over the top of her recently required reading specs. "Why do you ask?" her tone flat and even.

Adam shrugged, "I just wanted to know that's all. I've been thinking about it a lot lately. I seem to have lots of pictures in my head of when I was young and dad was here, and I like to think I remember lots about him. It's just that my memories of him get sort of jumbled. And I can't remember which bits are real - and which bits I just imagine. You know..."

Carol tried to suppress a lump in her throat.

"Well, your father was very much like you" she responded as calmly as possible, "It seems to me you grow more like him each day as you get older. He was quite a deep person but a very kind person. He loved you very much..."

She blinked quickly before the moisture in her eyes became visible to Adam. "He always wanted a son and he loved to play rough and tumble with you. He was like all dads really. You know...wanted the best for you and everything...taught you how to kick a football and make a go-kart. You always enjoyed it when he read you stories at bedtime... Rupert Bear was your favourite."

"Yeah, I remember that" said Adam with a flicker of a smile, "But what do you think he would be like if he were still alive now? Today..."

His mother removed her specs and gazed into the middle distance. She thought for a moment. "He would be just the same I expect. He'd still worry about you and try to show you how to do the sorts of things that fathers' and sons enjoy together. He certainly wouldn't tolerate some of your recent behaviour Adam, that's for sure."

Adam ignored the remark. There were so many memories stirring within him. So many questions he wanted to ask. So much he needed to understand. Why did it have to be *him* that had to be left without a dad? Why did it have to be his dad driving on that particular road, at that particular time? Why couldn't his dad still be alive now, so that Adam could ask him all those questions teenage boys so need answers to? Why did he have to die when Adam was only nine years old - before he was old enough to understand or cope with the loss? Why didn't he even get the chance to say goodbye properly? Why? Why? *Why?*

"I wish dad were still alive" he blurted out before he could stifle his tongue. He felt sick and empty inside.

His mother reached over and pulled Adam's head down onto her shoulder before he could see the tears forming in her eyes.

"So do I Adam," she sobbed softly, "So do I."

"Come on man, it'll be a laugh."

"I dunno Steve."

"What's got into you? Nothing ever happens around this dump. It's Saturday night and the Fair's in town. C'mon man."

"Okay. Why not? Look, I'll meet you at the Anchor in an hour. We can have a pint then wander over to the Fair."

"Now you're talking sense. See you later then."

Adam put the phone down and sighed. What *had* got into him? He couldn't understand it himself. Yeah, so he was getting into this meditation thing but so what? Didn't mean he had to stop having fun, did it? Sure, the guys would crease up laughing if he ever admitted he was visiting an old pensioner and his cat once a week to talk metaphysical but so what? It was his life.

Adam reached over and opened a packet of biscuits lying on the kitchen table stuffing two at once into his mouth. He'd always enjoyed going out with the boys, Jesus, he had always been the ringleader. Always the one who would take the biggest risk, push the boundaries just a bit too far, get the biggest laughs. 'Outrageous behaviour' - yeah - that was what his headmaster had called it, 'outrageous behaviour'. But the boys looked up to him for inspiration, didn't they? He set the standard and they would follow. 'Cock of the walk' his grandmother had called him once disparagingly. His Mother just called him a 'reckless idiot' who should grow up a bit and know better.

What the hell? Life was for living, wasn't it? Who wanted to be a boring old git? A night out with the lads at the Fair was starting to seem like a damn good idea.

Adam glanced at his watch: 7.32. He'd said to Steve that he'd meet him in an hour. Just enough time to enjoy another deep meditation. He thought it over for a moment.

Nah. Not tonight.

Tonight, he needed a break. The last few weeks had been very intense trying to take in the import of all Jack's ideas as well as concentrating on trying to perfect his own meditation techniques. Tonight, he deserved a night off.

A night out with the boys.

He called to his mother to say he was going to the Fair later, after a quick shower.

He heard Carol acknowledge him over the drone of the TV. (That's all she ever seemed to do these days. Watch the bloody TV) He hoped he'd never get to be that boring and the thought of it scared him.

He went upstairs and turned on the shower.

As it turned out the Anchor was too crowded with Saturday night revellers to get to the bar, so they went to the off-licence instead. Danny had just got paid so was happy to fork out for a four-pack of cheap lager. He handed the cans out ceremoniously to Adam, Steve and Mick.

Mick was a mate of Danny's that had started to hang around with them a lot. He seemed alright thought Adam - bit of a gentle giant, mostly quiet but tended to go a bit overboard when he was stoned. Getting stoned seemed to be Mick's favourite pastime. It wasn't a big deal. Adam liked to get a good buzz as much as the next guy, but Mick was starting to experiment with more exotic substances. Adam felt a bit uncomfortable with anything stronger than weed. He'd dropped some acid a couple of times but that was enough.

Mick however seemed to be up for anything.

Adam thumbed open the can of lager and took a swig.

Up ahead there were throngs of people on a patch of parkland in the middle of town. There was a dizzying array of coloured lights and a relentless disco beat. A big wheel was spinning in the middle of the maelstrom of noise and colour and bumper cars were spinning and crashing amidst raucous laughter. Candy floss was everywhere.

Some skinny young girls walked past on tottering heels, chewing gum and screeching at each other.

"Fancy comin' on the Ghost train wiv me then?" yelled Steve as they brushed past. The skinniest one turned around and poked her tongue out at him. "Get lost Lacey. You *are* a fuckin' ghost."

"And you're a fuckin' witch." he shouted back.

Adam howled with laughter. "Then you'll make a fine pair" he bellowed to them both.

At the entrance to the fair Mick nudged Adam in the ribs and pointed at a coloured marquee.

"Go on" said Mick "It'll be a gas."

"Nah" said Adam taking another swig of beer and belching loudly, "I don't believe in all that crystal ball rubbish."

Steve Lacey looked up at the garish wooden sign hanging over the entrance to the small Fairground tent sandwiched between a hot dog stall and the dodgems. 'Gypsy Rosalie - Fortune Teller' it read in fading red and blue letters.

Steve had to shout in order to be heard above the bone-jarring noise emanating from the dodgem loudspeakers, a distorted version of Desmond Dekkers 'Israelites' could be vaguely recognised if you listened carefully enough.

"Me 'n Danny went in there yesterday" he yelled into Adam's ear, "She's a batty old dear. She looks into a crystal ball and tells your fortune."

"Oh yeah?" said Adam scornfully "So what did she tell you then? That you'll probably be penniless and pissed by the end of the evening? I could've told you that for nothing and saved you the money."

Steve nearly choked on his beer from laughing. Adam was good company when he bothered to come out these days.

"Well, she told me dat I'm going on an interestin' journey soon" yelled Danny.

"Well, that was true then" yelled back Adam, "Since you were just about to queue up for the big wheel. Ever felt conned Danny me ole' mate?"

"Okay smartarse, what are you so scared of? 'Dat she moight tell you you're just a wanker?"

It was Adam's turn to laugh "No. I know that already. Nah, I'm not scared. It's just that it's a waste of money."

Steve reached in his pocket and shoved a handful of coins in Adam's hand "Then have the old gypsy on me" he said insistently, "We're going on the big wheel again. Catch you later."

Mick, Steve and Danny turned their backs and wandered over to the big wheel. Adam shook his head in disbelief and stared at the coins in his hand. "Oh, what the hell..." he mumbled to himself and pushed aside a grubby curtain to enter the dimly lit tent.

Gypsy Rosalie, a large and red-faced old woman, sat at a small table having a crafty fag between punters. In the middle of the table a small crystal ball stood on a rather ornate oriental tablecloth with gold tassels.

She motioned to Adam to sit down opposite her and removed the overfilled ash tray off the table on to the floor.

She gave a rather forced smile revealing more gaps than teeth. "Sorry love" she said in the husky tones of a long-term smoker, "I didn't see you there. That's it, sit down. What's yer name?"

"Er...Adam..."

He stared at her red and gold headscarf noting the wisps of grey hair curling around the edges and the sari style wrap around dress that one would expect a gypsy Fairground fortune teller to wear.

He smiled back weakly, feeling a tinge of sadness for the old dear as well as feeling embarrassed and self-conscious. He wondered how many lager-swilling pissheads she'd already had to put up with tonight. Just like every other night probably. He wondered if she really was a gypsy or just an old hag on the make.

"Fifty pence for your fortune" she rasped matter-of-factly, "Or a pound for a full ten minutes."

"Oh...er...just the fifty pence version thanks" said Adam, handing over the money.

She clamped a fat wrinkled hand around the coins and dropped them into a small wooden box, which appeared somewhere out of the voluminous folds of the sari-dress.

"Okay Luvvie" she coughed, "Let's 'ave a look into the crystal ball. If you watch it very carefully you might see it clouding over in the middle and then I can look into your future to see what it holds for you..."

"Yeah," said Adam feeling that this was already a big mistake, "Right..."

Gypsy Rosalie stared at the crystal ball and Adam stared too. It was a clear glass sphere some four or five inches wide that sat on a small metal tripod covered in a red silk handkerchief. Apart from his own distorted reflection there was bugger all else to see in the crystal sphere. Adam looked up at the old woman who remained transfixed by the ball.

Jeez - what a way to earn a crust...

Adam continued to sit there fidgeting while Gypsy Rosalie continued to stare into the ball. He felt an urge to whistle. Seconds later she was frowning and sitting back in her chair letting out a long slow deep breath.

"Give me your hands Adam."

"Uh?"

The old lady reached out across the table and grasped both of Adam's hands. The crystal ball lay between them almost symbolically, almost as if it was a barrier separating the streetwise teenager from the strange old gypsy. Adam noticed her numerous flamboyant rings reflecting and distorting on the crystal's smooth surface.

The gypsy held both his hands tightly and then shut her eyes. She was still frowning but this time in concentration rather than bewilderment. After about ten seconds she released her grip and opened her eyes fixing her gaze on him. He was aware of a trickle of sweat on the back of his neck.

"So...um...what did you see then?" he said a lot more nonchalantly than he felt.

Gypsy Rosalie continued to stare into his eyes searchingly for a few moments then removed the crystal ball from the table putting it somewhere under the table as though it was no longer of any interest.

"Extraordinary," she said, "The crystal ball can only tell you so much you know. Sometimes the Tarot works better. That's why I needed to feel your hands. You have a very powerful aura, Adam."

"You what...?"

"I said you have a very powerful aura. 'Tell-the-truth you are probably a better fortune teller than me. You certainly have 'the gift' there's no doubt about that. Are you psychic?"

Adam shook his head. Was she for real?

"No...at least I don't think so." Adam's heart was beginning to beat harder.

"I think that you are, whether you realise it or not. But you are more than psychic. I've never felt such an energy flow. You have a quite extraordinary level of power flowing through you. I hope you learn to use it wisely."

"Right. Thanks", said Adam, uncomfortably. "Look er...I'd better go" he got up from the chair clumsily.

"There's something else too..." said Gypsy Rosalie her eyes animated and searching Adam's own eyes as though trying to locate something.

"I see danger."

Adam felt a chill deep in his gut. He didn't need to listen to any of this...

"Sorry" he said "I really gotta go..."

"It's been nice to meet you, Adam. 'Know what'?" She started to wheeze.

"What?" Adam was nearly out of the tent.

"We've met before."

"I don't think so" said Adam, "But...thanks anyway."

Adam disappeared into the Fairground throng to look for Steve, Danny and Mick. What the fuck was he supposed to say to the lads? That he hadn't even got as far as finding out what the future held for him? That the only thing the old bat had come up with was that he had a powerful aura and some sort of psychic energy? They'd die laughing at that one! He knew it'd be a waste of time.

And what did she mean by 'danger'. Was she trying to spook him?

Gypsy Rosalie stood at the tent entrance watching Adam's back merge into the crowd. She reached for another cigarette, lighting it with a trembling hand and took a long draw.

"Oh yes we have met before Adam," she said to herself, "But not in this life."

It was two days later that Adam picked up the phone and called Jack to arrange visiting him again.

Gypsy Rosalie's words had been bothering him - intruding into his thoughts like a brooding vulture. He needed Jack's common sense and rationality to try and make sense of the whole incident. Most likely she was just a batty old dear talking nonsense but deep down something kept niggling him. A suspicion that perhaps there was a grain of truth in what she'd said. Perhaps, like Jack, she really was sensitive to something within him that he couldn't see in himself.

And if there really was something 'odd' about him then he needed to know why.

It was around 2.30 in the afternoon when Adam finally arrived at Jack's place and by then the earlier feelings of ominous portent had thankfully subsided a little. Now he felt too embarrassed to talk about the chain-smoking old gypsy and his 'powerful aura'. Instead, he decided to take a different tack. As far as Adam could tell this fortune telling lark was all about trying to foresee your own destiny or your own fate. It was about trying to gain an insight *now* into who you will be sometime in an indeterminate future. So, pondered Adam, if your destiny is already pre-written how could meditation change anything? His daily meditations were certainly starting to improve - which was a comforting thought. He was practising regularly and gaining more and more confidence. So today he could afford to talk to Jack less about his meditation progress and more about this whole destiny thing.

When he'd exchanged the usual pleasantries and felt more relaxed, he asked Jack about his view of 'fate' and predicting the future. Jack listened intently and stroked his chin before replying. Adam recognised the signs of concentration.

"Who you are, and who you will be, depends on a combination of things including your genetic make-up, your beliefs and willpower and your karma" responded Jack at last.

Adam's brow furrowed. "So, what I believe in determines what job I end up doing - is that what you're saying?"

"That's not exactly what I'm saying, but there is an element of truth in that statement. What I mean is that the sort of person you become, or develop naturally into over a period of time, depends on what you believe in at a fundamental level – and I'm not talking about religion. I'm talking about what you might call your internalised model of the world and how people relate to each other in it. Everyone has a personal viewpoint of reality though we share certain common standards, but what you might call your *core beliefs* is what creates your own individuality."

"Beliefs can change over time though."

"You bet they do, and that is one of the really beautiful things about the human condition, the freedom to choose and change our beliefs. As our beliefs change so we develop as individuals. The important thing is to understand that our beliefs can be modified for good or for ill depending on the degree of influence we are willing to let other people's beliefs have on us. Some of us are very easily influenced whilst others are so entrenched in their own views that they close up their minds to any external influences. A dangerous stubbornness that limits growth in my opinion."

"Yeah - I've met people like that - just won't listen to any point of view but their own."

"Exactly. And they are the sort of people who are cutting off the opportunity for their own spiritual growth."

"So how are we supposed to know what to believe and what not to believe then? I mean...how do we know what the real truth is?"

"That's something you will need to find out for yourself Adam. I could tell you some of the answers that I've found out for myself through my own meditations but there should be no shortcuts because that would defeat the objective of the exercise. You need to find some fundamental truths out for yourself because that is the only way you will be convinced of their integrity. Why should you believe what I tell you? Why should I impose my own beliefs on you? That's a very dangerous precedent. Unfortunately, the history of mankind bears witness to what happens when beliefs are forced upon others against their will. It usually ends in bloodshed."

"Will I know a true belief from a false one?"

"Ultimately the answer is yes - but it's only fair to warn you that there are 'others' who might want to impose false beliefs on you as a sort of test. You must learn how to distinguish between truth and falsehood. It's a skill that comes with practice, and um, right 'attitude' if you see what I mean."

Adam nodded "So who are these 'others' then?"

"They are...how can I put it...negative influences who will try to win your confidence. False friends you might call them."

"Yeah" reflected Adam, biting a lip, "I know just the sort you mean."

"We must always question everything" continued Jack, "And I don't mean by applying so called conventional wisdom. I mean throwing aside pure rationality for a while and freeing the spirit a little, bringing back a sense of childlike wonder into our appreciation of things."

"Suspending disbelief?"

"Exactly. The trouble we all have is becoming accustomed to applying the critical rules we all learned at school, the scientific method if you will, and, in the process, we have become desensitised to the real world. We are all losing our ability to feel. We know nothing Adam. Our wisdom, as we call it, is constructed on myth. It is a false safety valve - but something we all strive to keep a hold of for fear of our sanity. Take our perception of the environment we live in for example. The Earth has been around for billions of years and how many years of knowledge have we acquired personally about it? I'll tell you - the answer is just a few lifetimes - fleeting microseconds in the scheme of things. But even that is an over exaggeration because all we really experience is a tiny fraction of the Earth. We live in a small subsection of the biosphere that can support our bodily functions. We cannot survive in the upper atmosphere, and we cannot survive in the internal rock of the Earth's core. We are destined to survive naturally on a thin balloon skin that we call the Earth's surface. In our lifetimes we probably spend ninety percent of our time within a small radius of just a few miles from 'home' with the benefit of a few holiday excursions to other parts of the balloon skin.

Then think about your experiences within this very limited framework. Most of our lives we experience everything during the day and sleep at night. Okay, every so often we may reverse the process if we work nights or choose to remain awake for some purpose, but most people live their lives predominantly as day-creatures and miss all the subtleties of nature's night miracles.

It's even worse than that though Adam. People like you and me rarely leave the towns and cities to gain the wisdom that our country cousins enjoy, the farmers or forestry workers who have a much greater awareness of the changing seasons and the moods of the weather. We wear shoes, so we rarely directly feel the sensations of grass or sand between our toes. City smog blots out the stars, which is sadly quite tragic. We rarely touch the real world of trees and mountain streams and feel their energy and intelligence. That's something that people used to do much more, as little as fifty to a hundred years ago, but now few of us bother anymore because we feel nature has been mastered and is now more of a novelty or raw resource provider. We have lost our respect for nature - it has become a slave to man. So, what, you might ask, do we *really* know about our environment? Most of it is what we learned from a school textbook. When was the last time you went out and talked to the trees?"

Adam raised an eyebrow. "Come again?"

"You should. They have been around a lot longer than you or I. There is a probably a lot we could learn from them."

"Sounds like hippy shit talk to me."

"Well maybe I'm being a little provocative" smiled Jack, "Wasn't it Bob Dylan who said, 'don't criticise what you can't understand'? A very wise philosophy to live by in my opinion. Sometimes I look at pictures of those people who choose to lead an alternative lifestyle and I think maybe they have a more balanced view of reality than some of our politicians."

Adam laughed out loud. You couldn't pull any wool over this old boy's eyes. He was sharp as a razor.

"So - what do you make of all this *new age* rubbish then?" asked Adam.

"I think there are a lot of gems hidden in the 'rubbish'" replied Jack.

"Seems to me it's just a way of parting gullible die-hard hippies from their money."

Jack started to pace the room. "There's certainly a lot of truth in that fact...but even so there's a lot of stuff going on that falls under the so called 'alternative' umbrella that is quite refreshing and exciting. It's separating the wheat from the chaff, so to speak - that's the key."

"So what *gems* are you interested in then?"

"Quite a lot actually and it's nearly always a question of degree. There is usually a grain of truth in almost all wacky new ideas but very often the grains are embellished into money-spinning opportunities by bandwagon entrepreneurs. Take health for example; you can now take your pick from hundreds of these new-fangled health practitioners who can diagnose every problem you ever thought you had and then provide relief with anything from crystals to American Indian chants and drums. Things like massage, homeopathy, acupuncture, energy medicine, flower remedies etcetera are all hovering around the edges of mainstream medicine and in some cases are starting to be accepted as having a contribution to make. Other remedies are still too 'way out' to be considered. But then again who are we to judge? Anyway, you asked about which parts of the so called 'new age' or Aquarian portfolio of offerings I think are interesting. It's a good question because I find it difficult to compartmentalise some of the concepts. I don't like fixed boundaries because a lot of the ideas have fuzzy edges. They blend into each other and supplement each other. In fact, some of the ideas only make sense when they are linked to other ideas."

"Like what for instance?"

Jack stroked his stubble "Like all the 'personal growth' stuff. Take all the adverts in glossy lifestyle magazines for weekend retreats for example. They all offer much the same thing - but it's sold in different packaging. At the end of the day retreats are all about taking time out of the usual routines to focus on your own personal development. It doesn't matter whether it's an 'encounter group' or sacred chanting group or whatever. These are all just different methods to take you to the same place - finding your true inner self."

"Similar to meditation then?"

"Similar yes. But not an alternative. Meditation is about reaching a very specific state of consciousness and before you can really reap the benefits of meditation you need to be at ease with yourself. Know who you really are. These 'alternative' weekend workshops and the like are all about taking that first step - finding out who you really are. Once you have resolved that question, in other words once you really know yourself, then you are ready to take the big next step, the step into meditative consciousness."

"What about me Jack? Are you saying I need to know myself first?"

Jack stopped walking around the room and sat down in his favourite armchair with a sigh.

"That's a difficult one Adam...I'm not sure how to put it really... let's say that under normal circumstances I would advise anyone to invest time and effort into getting to know themselves very deeply before attempting any type of meditation. The reasons are very clear. The better one knows oneself the better one can cope with the whole meditative experience. But you are rather unique. As I've already told you before. You have a very rare and a very special talent; the ability to open meditative doors faster than most of us could ever dream of or aspire to. I'm not saying that one should run before they can walk. But in your case, you certainly have the ability to do so."

Adam thought Jack's words over. There was an obvious question surfacing.

'You have a very powerful aura'.

"Why Jack?"

"Why what?"

"Why do I have this ability that others don't? You've never explained that to me. Why me? Is there a reason? Is there something special or unusual about me that I'm not aware of? Something you're not telling me?"

Jack looked away as if deliberately trying to avoid eye contact. "Yes, there is a reason, Adam. I wish I could give you the answer, but I can't. It's something that you have to find out for yourself. Believe me you will find the reason soon enough - but it is imperative that you learn the answer through your own efforts. Any answer from me would only dilute the message."

"Aw, come on Jack - give me a clue - I need some understanding here."

Jack shook his head.

"No clues" he said, "But let me just say that you will be amazed when you find out the reasons for your extraordinary ability. You probably won't believe it at first. You will be sceptical and think it's all a scam. But it's not - you'll see."

"When will I see?"

A faint smile played across Jack's lips. "When you look in the mirror and look past your reflection and over your shoulder."

"What? Is that some kind of clue? What are you talking about?"

"That's enough for today then Adam. I think Lady wants feeding...oh, but there is one other thing..."

"Go on."

"When you are a more experienced meditator you will find it very easy to calm the mind and focus your thoughts much more easily. After a while you will start to slip effortlessly into what might be called the 'meditative state' and then..."

"Then what?"

"Then you have to decide where it is exactly that you want to go."

Adam shook his head and sighed inwardly. Sometimes Jack could be infuriating. The old man was clearly intimating something but not going to elaborate.

Halfway home Adam realised that he never had got around to mentioning the encounter with Gypsy Rosalie and his amazing 'aura' to Jack after all. And what was the other weird word Jack had used - 'karma' - what the hell did that mean?

The security guard looked Adam up and down with barely concealed contempt.

"Sign here" he sniffed, stabbing a finger at a grubby logbook.

Officious old fart thought Adam. Usual stereotype. Probably retired Army - loves uniform and the Services' life.

Retired early, couldn't hack it, so found a job as a security guard where he could wear a uniform again, assume a small measure of authority and then take smug delight in ordering people around. You see 'em everywhere.

Adam put on his dimmest expression and then signed the logging-in book in the wrong box just to annoy the old guy. It worked. The security guard tutted and crossed the signature out pointing to the correct spot on the paper again with a stubby finger.

It was his first day at a hardware supplies warehouse. The paint shop job hadn't worked out. He'd hated every minute, made it too obvious and been shown the door last week after turning up late for the third time and with a monster hangover. Old Mr Carson had been glad to see the back of him. His Mother had not been pleased. Natch. She'd found this warehouse job in the local rag. It sounded just as boring, but it was nearer home and paid slightly more so he hadn't argued too much.

Might be a laugh. Might be some tasty birds. Who knows?

The security guard signalled Adam to follow him and led him down a steely grey corridor into the body of the warehouse where endless racks of plastic guttering, wood, tools, and electrical components lay ready for packaging and transportation. Adam followed him taking careful note of anything worth nicking until the guard stopped outside a small office. There was a middle-aged balding guy in the office wearing blue overalls and drinking a mug of coffee. The security guard cleared his throat until the balding guy looked up and then came over to the open door.

"Adam Sinclair sir" said the guard sycophantically, "He's starting today in the warehouse."

"Thank you, Reg," said the man, "Come in Adam."

Reg turned on his heels like he was on the parade ground again and disappeared between the racking. Adam followed the man into the office, a small untidy room with one desk heaving with papers, a grey nondescript filing cabinet filling one corner and a girly pin-up calendar on the wall.

The man held out his hand. "Gordon Davis" he said matter-of-factly, "Warehouse Manager." Adam shook his limp hand and grunted.

"Any experience in Warehouse work son?"

"Nah...not really, but I'm pretty adaptable. I've been working in a paint and hardware shop for the last couple of months."

Gordon nodded dismissively "Hmm we'll see... anyway, things you need to know...overalls are over there, find some that fit. Lunch is between twelve and half past, plus a tea break for ten minutes every two hours. That's the rules and I don't like them broken. See this list? It's called a packing list. It tells you what to collect off each shelf and what forklift number they go on. There's a lad called Jim 'bin doing this for three years. He'll be back from tea break in a couple of minutes. He'll show you the ropes. Any questions?"

Adam put on his best 'deep concentration' expression for dramatic effect and furrowed his brow "No...I don't think so."

Gordon nodded "Good. I run a tight ship here. Under my supervision nothing goes missing or misfiled. That's the way I run things. Efficiently see. I don't take any nonsense. I expect everyone to pull their weight. Okay Adam, welcome to 'Lomax Brothers Merchandising'. They're a good solid family firm. You'll like it here."

Gordon, the boring, balding, middle-aged Warehouse Manager went back into his office and shuffled papers busily leaving Adam to sort through the pile of overalls until 'Jim' arrived.

'*Like it?*' thought Adam '*I already hate it mate.*'

"Hey! Marie!"

Marie Cunningham turned around in the semi-darkness of 'Crystals Night Spot', nearly spilling a vodka and orange down her black dress and squinted at the figure who'd called her name. She thought so. It was the Irish lilt in the voice that gave him away.

"Oh, it's you."

Danny McConnell emerged from the crowded bar area and pushed back long unkempt hair off his glowing forehead. She could smell stale sweat and beer.

"How do Marie. Sure, it's long time no see. So... what you up to den?"

She shrugged noncommittally. Danny never was one for deep and meaningful conversation.

"You still going out wid' dat creep 'dat tried to beat Adam up?"

"No, I'm not" she replied emphatically "It wasn't serious anyhow."

"Not loike wid' Adam den?"

Marie lowered her eyes. Nice lashes Danny thought.

"So" continued Danny "You by yourself den or wit' a bloke? Could you fancy a dance now?"

She shook her head on both counts. "No thank you Danny. I'm with a girlfriend tonight, not that I'd dance with a time waster like you anyway." She took a sip from her glass and put on her best bored voice, "So how's Adam these days? I don't see him around much anymore."

If Danny was offended by the remark it didn't show. Maybe he was just used to insults. "'Oi' see him now and den but he doesn't come out dat often. We had a beer the other night then went up the fair which was a laugh. I t'ink he's still working at Lomax Brothers in the warehouse, and he hates it. I asked him to come out tonight, but he couldn't make it. Steve reckons he's made friends wid some old bloke who talks weird shit. 'Oi don't know what he's up to, tell the truth. Anyway, see ya around Marie. You'll be missing the chance of a good time mind."

"Yeah...yeah, see ya round Danny."

Marie pushed her way through the mass of bodies and found a seat next to Rachel, an old school friend. The DJ had found another skull splitting '45 so speech was virtually inaudible.

"Wasn't that Danny McConnell?" yelled Rachel.

"Yeah."

"What's he like?"

"An arsehole". Marie swilled the vodka and orange around in her glass. "Don't waste your time, Rachel. But...he did give me some interesting information..."

"Like what?"

Marie grinned to herself smugly then downed the contents of the glass in one.

"I couldn't possibly say."

The procedure was now a simple routine. Adam felt he had come a long way since those half-hearted early attempts to meditate. What with Jack's guidance on technique and Adam's own perseverance in honing his own approach he could literally feel the progress being made each time he applied himself.

It was Tuesday evening. The day in the warehouse had been boring as hell and he had nearly lost his rag with that prat of a Manager, Gordon Davis, who had threatened him with the sack just because he'd got back five minutes late from morning tea break. Tosser!

At one time Adam would have given the guy some lip or even hit the bastard, but he was more laid back these days. It just wasn't worth the effort. Jack was right when he said that the more you meditate the more likely you are to stay relaxed in potential stressful situations. It was because you took what Jack called a 'wider world view' and realised that minor irritations, like Gordon Davis for instance, are really not worth wasting time over.

Adam pulled the curtains shut in his bedroom secure in the knowledge that his mother would be at the bingo for at least another two hours and that with the door shut he couldn't hear the phone. Perfect.

He fumbled for his cigarette lighter and then lit a red candle that he'd found in the local market two days ago. He wasn't sure it helped but Jack had suggested that candle flames help to induce relaxation, so what the hell, he'd give it a go.

Using the lighter made him momentarily crave a cigarette. Nah. Not good mixing smoking and meditation. Maybe later.

Adam placed the candle on top of his chest of drawers and watched the flickering yellow flame for a few moments. There was always something mesmerising about fire.

Makes you daydream.

He undid his trouser belt and removed it from his trousers so there was no pressure at the waist then stretched for a few moments trying to consciously release any points of tension in his body. It was the back of his neck that was usually the tightest.

When he felt relaxed enough, he pulled up a chair and placed the pillow from his bed on the seat to make it even softer then sat down and closed his eyes gently, just enough to register the flickering candle flame. He took a few deep breaths and concentrated on the ebbing and flowing of air in his abdomen with each breath.

Now he would wait for those irritating thoughts to arrive that had to be dealt with before he could progress any further. Each thought must be acknowledged, accepted, registered, and then released. Each one a separate bubble that he imagined rising from his scalp to float away through the walls of his bedroom and on up through the clouds into the upper atmosphere and then on into deepest space. Thoughts like: 'What if the lads could see me now?' 'Suppose Mum comes home early and finds me meditating? Should I tell her that I've taken up meditation? What would she make of it?' 'I wonder how long I can stick it at Lomax Brothers?' 'I wonder where Marie is now? Christ I still really miss her', 'I wish I could afford a car or a motorbike but how can I raise enough money?' 'Maybe I should give up smoking'.

The trickle of thoughts continued for a while and Adam made no effort to stop them or analyse them. That's one of the mistakes he'd made when he started meditating. Now he just let them flow until they had all dissipated into thin air like crackling wood sparks leaping from a bonfire.

After the thoughts had stopped flowing, Adam let his awareness shift in order to focus on his inner self, becoming more aware of his regular breathing and the rhythmic pulse of his heart. After a while he felt a deep sense of calm and inner stillness, which he also recognised as another danger point. This was the moment where on previous meditations he had drifted into deep sleep. The trick was to acknowledge the relaxed feeling but not to let the focus waiver.

Jack had explained that there was nothing actually wrong in drifting off to sleep, except that it was so easy to do, that maintaining the focus on meditation needed a little effort. Adam mentally congratulated himself when both the thoughts and the sleepiness passed, and he realised that he was on the verge of breaking through what he called the 'consciousness barrier' into deeper realms.

Then he concentrated on emptiness exactly the way Jack had told him, letting the sensation of floating in empty space take over completely until he was no longer consciously aware of his surroundings. The bedroom festooned with pop star posters, the dirty clothes on the floor, the candle, or the silence. He was totally absorbed into a world of white nothingness.

The goal he had been striving for all these past months.

He took care not to congratulate himself too much on reaching this point. Even a moment of self-congratulation would be enough to break the spell and bring unwanted reality flooding back.

No, he must retain the focus and...

And what?

Adam became aware of the cloudy white emptiness that filled his inner vision starting to slowly change hue. The stark whiteness was almost imperceptibly turning into the palest of eggshell blues. Then moment by moment the blueness was becoming darker and richer. Adam's only emotion was one of curiosity. This was something he had not anticipated. The blue colour was so beautiful that he felt a sudden quickening of his heartbeat that signified excitement.

Control it...

Ignore it...

The blue was now so vibrant it almost felt, well... *textured...*

The total whiteout had simply signified 'nothingness' but this was different...this was...?

Jack was right. There were simply no words in his vocabulary to describe the sensation of being totally surrounded in a womb-like sea of deepest blue and the frustration of not finding the word he wanted was enough to break the concentration.

For a brief second there was a feeling of spiralling downward as though he was a skydiver flung out of a plane into a cloudy sky and spinning helplessly in space. Then he felt himself jolt awake in the chair like one of those involuntary night spasms he used to get as a kid. His palms and forehead were damp and parts of his arms and legs were tingling. The first thing he noticed was a pool of red wax encircling the glowing candle like a viscous lava flow spreading from the lips of a steaming volcano and for a few moments he felt extremely disorientated.

He reached for a cigarette and was surprised to see his hand trembling.

Then he smiled to himself and stood up flinging the curtains open. "Yes!" he shouted to the twilit garden.

"Yes! Yes! Yes! I told you I could do it Jack."

"*I told you.*"

"That's fantastic news Adam" beamed Jack, "You have made a huge step forward and you are now standing on the verge of something truly life changing. Now it's time to talk about some other aspects of turning inward that you will almost certainly need to know about."

It was the following afternoon and Jack knew immediately from Adam's call that this was a significant moment.

Adam had turned up at Jack's place wide-eyed and breathless before giving an animated and enthused account of his last meditation experience. Jack also noted that Adam was talking differently too. The teenage cynic had inadvertently let the mask drop a little and there was a new fresh dynamism in his voice.

"It was incredible Jack" he'd said in awed tones, "I can't explain it...the blueness..."

"Sometimes there is no point in trying to explain" said Jack, "Because there are simply no words available in our vocabulary to describe other realities. That's why people who spend their lives in deep meditation like Indian Saddhu's or Buddhist monks use symbolism or allegory to try and impart the knowledge they are acquiring. The trouble with meditation is that although it is all about rationality and by that, I mean its own inherent rationality; it's not the sort of rationality we associate with day to day living. That's the dilemma we face as imperfect human beings. We live our lives believing that the only rationality worth bothering about is the one we call 'real life'. It's only when you start meditating seriously that you realise that there are other 'rationalities' out there. I personally think the most useful word that we should be mindful of throughout our lives is the word 'perspective' because everything we do, think or feel can be boiled down to that one word. But perspective on its own is not enough. In order to master our perspective, we need to add its sister word 'balance'. If you have got your perspective right, and your balance right, then everything in life falls neatly and comfortably into place. Simple enough concept, eh? But not so simple to achieve. That's why we have disputes with our neighbours. That's why we have wars."

"How do you mean Jack? What's war got to do with meditation?"

Jack stroked his chin "Meditation and wars are difficult concepts. The connections are not easy to explain. Let's keep it as simple as possible. Let's start from the obvious statement that everyone is different - c'est la vie! Each of us, as human beings, has a different view of the world which we have developed since we were young. Our individual viewpoint is organic. It changes, grows, and expands. It arises from innumerable influences; parents, school, friends, the media, direct experience, what we see and hear in the environment that surrounds us and even in our unconscious genetic make-up and karmic debt. In short, we are largely what we have seen, heard, learned and felt. Do you agree?"

That word 'karma' again!

"Yeah, I guess so."

"Good - then let's move on. One of the most important aspects of our individual growth is 'influence' by which I mean the degree to which other similar individuals can make us think that their viewpoint is further developed than our own. It's like taking a short cut - as if the other individual were saying to us 'Hey there's no need for you to wait around for this or that particular experience, I've been through it myself and it was like this...' What they are doing is transferring the idea of something to you - instead of you having to go through the particular experience yourself. Like, for instance, telling you all about a film they have seen. What they are doing is trading an idea with you - and if you choose to accept that other person's viewpoint it's as if you were saying 'Hey thanks! I'll take your view and make it my own - there's no need for me to waste any more time waiting around for the original experience myself'. That's why it is so important for you to experience the meditative state yourself, through direct personal experience, not by listening to my 'second hand' description of it.

Now, there's nothing wrong in being influenced by others to a degree, in fact it's precisely what makes all cultures tick along and engenders a valuable sense of social belonging. Where the danger lies is if you choose to trade away or 'sell' your individual sense of perspective when you agree to 'buy' the influence from others.

Let me try and give you an example. Take an extremist form of behaviour, a martyr for example. This is someone who is willing to give away his most precious gift, his life, in pursuit of a cause that he or she believes it is valid to give a life for.

Now it may well be that the particular cause is real and justified and it may well be a way of expressing dissatisfaction with a particular state of affairs or circumstances. Whatever the root of the martyrdom though, the act of sacrifice is committed because of that particular martyr's set of perspectives. The martyr has looked at the pros and cons of martyrdom and has decided that in his or her world view, *which is effectively their perspective of truth, reality, justice or whatever*, it is a valid and justified decision to sacrifice their life. Another person with a slightly different set of perspectives might concur with the feelings and viewpoint of the martyr, but come to the conclusion that, on balance, staying alive is a more worthwhile alternative."

"Aren't you just stating the obvious?"

"In many ways, yes. But the point is that we don't always see the obvious. We are weak. We succumb to the influence of others, and we often behave irrationally in the greater scheme of things. Let's take a different stance. Let's take an individual, person X, it doesn't matter what nationality, religion, or sex they are. Let's say that this person has developed something we might call 'perfect perspective'. What does that really mean? It means that surrounded by all the complexity and confusion of daily existence this person has a totally rational and balanced - *remember this other key word Adam* - understanding of life. This person is able to weigh up all the pros and cons, all the competing factors both negative and positive and all the 'influences', both good and bad, and is then able to make a one hundred per cent perfect judgement. Do you think it likely that this person would decide to become a martyr? A terrorist? A murderer or warmonger?"

"I guess not."

"Why?"

Adam frowned and tried to marshal his thoughts. He'd been put on the spot. "I'm not sure...it's not an easy question...let me think it through. I suppose that if this person had a perfectly balanced view; a totally rational view that encompassed all the issues then that person would see the senselessness in lots of things that people do and why some of our extreme actions, which always seem such a great idea at the time, are essentially pointless. Pointless because a precious life has been lost to no avail."

"Exactly Adam. I couldn't have put it better myself!"

"So - let me get this right" continued Adam thoughtfully "If I understand you correctly then what you are saying is that through meditation, we can eventually achieve something you call 'perfect perspective' which is a view of life that is totally unbiased and balanced, rather than influenced by the views of others or by our cultural background."

Jack nodded. "That's right Adam, but remember, perfect perspective doesn't come easily. It can take years to achieve and meantime social conventions, our background, our culture, and our individual experiences will all combine and interact very powerfully to try and influence us subconsciously and to provide a context within which to frame and deal with life's daily experiences. For example, let's take a moment to talk about why you are the person that you are. What I mean is, why you are Adam Sinclair. Who is it that you really are? And what image is it that you trying to project? I could argue for example, that you are the personification of the teen rebel simply trying to beat the system."

"What's that supposed to mean?" Adam said defensively, "You're sounding like my mum now Jack."

"It's nothing to be ashamed of. I did the same sort of things myself once. It's part of growing up and part of the whole revolutionary movement that manifests itself every generation. From the Mods and Rockers in the fifties through the hippie summers of the sixties and now these – what do you call them – skinheads? Of the Seventies."

"So exactly what are you trying to say Jack?"

"I'm simply making an observation. I didn't use to think things through when I was younger, but now I have more time to reflect on some of the undercurrents of our times. The other day I had to go to London. I was walking through Hyde Park and sat on a bench for a while. There were some young people there, late teens early twenties I'd guess, talking about how they were fed up with the 'system' and were opting out. Some of them had obviously 'opted out' already. They were sick of the routine of the nine to five, bored by bureaucracy, red tape, rules, and politics. They were fed up with the vagaries of our society and frustrated by all the restrictions imposed on them by twentieth century rules and conventions. In short, they craved 'freedom' and were striving to break free from the repressive culture of our times. Like the free spirits of Woodstock all they wanted was the open road, the gypsy life, the romance, and the sunshine. It sounded wonderful to me."

"And me. Sounds a bit like the spirit of Reading festival. Apart from the thugs who beat me up."

"I wouldn't disagree" continued Jack, "And yet there was so much pent-up frustration there. The frustrations born of having little money, sharing some squat and having either a dull job or no job at all. That same day I saw a middle-aged man sitting on a sun lounger in his garden sipping wine and looking as if he didn't have a care in the world. Behind him was a beautiful, detached house with roses around the door and two expensive looking cars on the drive. That sort of thing doesn't come for free Adam. It has to be worked for.

Do you know, I got to thinking about which person had really beaten the system? Is it the person who opts out of Society only to find years later that either you cannot beat the system and therefore eventually get sucked back into it whether you desire it or not? Or is it the person who says, 'If this is the system then I'm going to learn the rules, exploit them, and take the system for whatever it has to offer'. I certainly know which of the people I saw had the happiest and most contented face. Now don't get me wrong, I'm not advocating either extreme for each has its value, I am merely making the observation that we should be clear what we mean when we talk about 'beating the system'. We can beat it by truly opting out and living like a hermit in a cave in the Himalayas, which takes some true grit, believe me, or we can beat it by playing it at its own game and making those tedious repressive rules work in our favour. See what I'm driving at?"

"I think so. But I think you're suggesting that I'm some sort of victim of circumstance rather than someone with my own free will."

"Not exactly. We all have free will and it is how we use it that counts. We can use it to be a law-abiding citizen, or we can choose to ignore the law and face the consequences. In our daily lives we have to conform up to a certain level if we are to survive in the society we live in. The real point I'm making here is that it is only inside our heads that we can have total and complete freedom and that's the key point to remember. Meditation gives us this incredible unbridled freedom to follow our own internal destiny regardless of external pressures and influences. That's why some innocent prisoners can survive years inside jails in countries that suffer oppressive regimes. Alone in their cells they turn inward for solace and their internal composure then helps them to cope with the mental and physical tortures of confinement. What I am saying is that externally we can choose to conform to social norms and expectations if we so wish, and usually it's best to do so as a sensible survival strategy, but in our inner life - our meditative life - there are no barriers. We can be who we truly are and who we are really meant to be. More importantly - who we are *destined* to be."

Adam pondered Jack's words "So how do we find out who we are truly 'destined' to be' then?"

Jack got up from the armchair and started to pace the room as if movement were helping him to find the right words, the limp more emphasised after a long period sitting down.

"To learn we must first unlearn" he said enigmatically, "What I am getting at Adam is that before we can usefully learn anything at all we must first discard some of those things that we hold dearest and have taken to be true for many years. I am afraid that some of our most cherished beliefs must be brought to the surface, re-examined, dissected and if need be - discarded. Only by being brutally honest with ourselves can we hope to move forward and only by losing some of the heavy burdens of our previously acquired knowledge can we become childlike again and filled with the innocence required to start the learning process over again. Once we proclaim 'That can't be true' we have lost the opportunity of advancement and have fallen back into the blinkered and narrow world view imposed on us by the conventions of our times. Our Society is oftentimes content to wallow in its own sea of man-manufactured delusions. If we can break free from those shackles by being brave enough to start afresh with an open mind, and a question on our lips, then we can truly make progress.

Make no mistake though. It is not an easy thing to do. Even to 'unlearn' takes great courage because knowledge is a shield that we use every day to deflect transgressors who would seek to influence us.

We must stand up for our beliefs and our intrinsic truths. We must question everything the Government or the media tells us we should believe just because they say claim it's true. We should challenge the oil companies that tell us they are not causing devastation and pollution. We should stand up against the corrupt pharmaceutical companies that want to force us to compromise our precious health by selling us poisons that serve to only make them obscene profits. We must challenge the Banks that wish to rob us rather than take care of our savings. We must stand firm and, if necessary, die for our principles because when we follow our spiritual path then death no longer holds any fear for us. The spirit world welcomes back it's children who stand up for what is morally right and ethical.

To cast aside our knowledge, our shield, is to make us temporarily defenceless and vulnerable. So be it. That's why most of us are loath to even attempt it. Only the truly brave can achieve it...but believe me the rewards are great and the relearning of true knowledge provides us with a far stronger, and more resilient shield. A shield that remains with us for the rest of our lives. It is more than just a shield however...it provides us with a very special key to a fulfilling and rewarding life. It's called 'contentment' or even 'bliss' and that is the treasure at the end of the road that you have already started to follow."

Jack sat down and remained silent as though he wanted Adam to think about everything he'd said, aware that he'd been talking for nearly an hour.

Adam was staring up at the ceiling, obviously thinking hard.

"That's a lot to take in" he said softly, "I need to think about all that stuff Jack, but I sort of know instinctively that you're right."

"I'm sorry. Sometimes I tend to go on a bit" apologised Jack with a twinkle in his eye, "That's what happens when there's usually only a cat to talk to."

Adam looked around the room. He'd seen it all before but perhaps only been aware of the surface impression. At first sight the room was simply that of an old man living alone in cluttered orderliness but there was more to it than that. It was the small things that now attracted his attention. There were piles of old books that covered a multitude of diverse subjects, old photos, ornaments, pieces of pottery, curious knick-knacks and beautiful pictures on the walls. Things that were all part of Jack's life but were also something more. They somehow represented the very ambience of the house. Everything reflected a sense of optimism, purpose, hope, in a way Adam couldn't explain. It was as though the house lacked anything that might have the slightest 'negative' connotation. There was nothing garish, unsavoury, or provocative in any of the pictures, unlike the posters on Adam's bedroom wall. There were no empty cigarette packets or half-finished beer cans, no dog-eared paperbacks, or crude magazines. Everything around Jack seemed to emanate a sort of 'positive' energy, totally intangible but very real, nonetheless.

Adam glanced up at the old grandfather clock in the corner of the room. "I'd best be going Jack. Thanks for our talk today. You've given me a lot to ponder over. Am I still doing the right thing? You know...with the meditation and such?"

Jack reached over to find his walking stick so that he could ease himself to his feet and show Adam to the door.

"You are doing exactly the right thing" he replied, "And you are now quite clearly standing on the threshold."

"Threshold?" said Adam "Threshold of what?"

Jack put his hand on Adam's shoulder and winked at him.

"Why infinity of course..."

"I wouldn't if I were you."

"Bollocks" said Adam.

"No seriously" said Jim Hastings nervously and glancing over his shoulder, "Gordon won't..."

"Fuck Gordon."

It was ten a.m. in Lomax Bros Merchandising and Adam had just arrived an hour late and with a severe hangover from the night before.

According to Jim, Gordon Davis, Warehouse Manager, had said this was the last straw. He'd been unhappy with the quality of Adam's work since the day he started and found him unreliable and argumentative.

"Is that so?" is all that Adam had said when Jim explained this to him.

Adam hated the Manager as much as the obnoxious security guard. As much as he hated working for Lomax Bros. Jim was alright. Mild mannered Jim Hastings who had been Adam's work mate and instructor for these last two months. Good old Jim who had shown him how to locate things on shelves and then move them onto other shelves or wooden pallets. Which in Adam's view anyone with the brain cells of an amoeba could achieve. And nice though Jim was, brain cells seemed in short supply.

Adam had made his mind up that he couldn't hack another day at this depressing dump. Gordon's office was temporarily unoccupied giving Adam a brief opportunity to have a laugh at the sad and bald git's expense.

On the wall of the office was a cork notice board covered in photographs of all Lomax Bros senior staff. Under each photograph a name and a title. Adam removed the drawing pin from the photo of "Mr Gordon Davis, Warehouse Manager" and then with a pair of scissors carefully removed the head from the photo pinning the remains of the photo back onto the board in the correct position.

Jim stared at Adam open mouthed as Adam coolly held the circular photo of Gordon's head between finger and thumb.

"Coast still clear?" he hissed at Jim.

"Er...yeah, yeah...but what are you..?"

"Watch me" said Adam suppressing a giggle, "This'll be a laugh. I'd love to see his face when he sees this."

Adam took two paces across the room to where Gordon's girly calendar hung on the wall.

He tried the head for size. Perfect. Then he applied some glue to the back of the photographed head and carefully positioned it over the neck of the tanned, topless model.

Jim was horrified but couldn't stifle a loud chuckle "E'll go mental" Jim said.

"I hope so" said Adam, "But he looks a lot better now don't you think?"

"You'll probably get the boot," warned Jim "E's not got much of a sense of humour."

"Who cares?" responded Adam, "I can't stand this place anyhow. I'm used to getting the boot so let's make it worthwhile, eh?"

A bewildered Jim Hastings, who treasured his privileged position as king of the warehouse shelves, stared at him in utter disbelief.

Adam ground his cigarette butt into the ashtray and left the Anchor just as the landlord was calling last orders and sending the lunchtime regulars on their way. Steve had tried to persuade him to stay for another, but Adam had declined. He'd promised Jack that he would call around before three. Anyway, he'd be out with the lads again later in the evening.

Adam mumbled some excuse about needing to get some shopping for his mother, but he knew, and Steve knew, that he was a lousy liar.

It only took twenty minutes to cross town. It was a warm day, one of those magical days early May should be like. Butterflies appearing as if from nowhere and new-born lambs frolicking in the meadows, and all that bollocks.

For the first time Adam found Jack clipping some rose bushes in his front garden.

"Didn't know you were into gardening Jack."

Jack looked up and mopped his brow, "It's part of the retirement package Adam, don't ask me why, but all old fogey's start to take more of an interest in gardening once they're retired. Maybe it's something to do with all that extra time to kill. Anyway, not bad roses don't you think?"

Adam shrugged. He could barely tell a weed from a flower. Roses were something you bought for a bird if you wanted to get inside her knickers.

Jack pushed one of the rose stems towards Adam and motioned him to smell the brilliant red flower. Adam took a deep sniff and was pleasantly surprised by the aroma. It was much stronger than he expected and reminded him of something. It made him think of his grandmother for one thing. She always loved roses. But there was something else too. Something deeper.

Something about the petals…

Nah. Couldn't place it.

"Nice" he said, trying hard to sound enthusiastic.

"I'm rather fond of roses" continued Jack, "And I like to think that roses are a useful symbol to represent meditation. All that pent-up beauty and potential condensed into such a tiny bud just waiting to be released and to unfold. Anyway, come on in, I'll make a cup of tea or perhaps you'd prefer a glass of wine? That's it, take a seat. I'll be right with you after I've washed my hands."

Adam sat on the settee leaving Jack's favourite armchair free and gazed around the pleasantly cluttered room with all its history and atmosphere. Although the room was pervaded with a sense of calm and peacefulness it bizarrely also made Adam think about his own mortality. It somehow induced a realisation that someday he too would be old - and maybe alone with just a cat or dog for company. Or even bloody roses. The thought scared him silly, and he brushed it aside quickly. There were far more important things he wanted to talk to Jack about like the huge strides forward he seemed to be making with the daily meditation. It felt as though a breakthrough was imminent. By the time Jack returned with tea Adam already had his question prepared.

"Jack, you have never told me what to actually expect once I have got through the first stages of meditation. You know, past the annoying intrusive thoughts barrier and into that place where the... how can I put it? Where the whiteness starts to turn into the shimmering blue colour. Once I've controlled it and can meditate for an extended period where am I likely to end up? Standing on a fluffy cloud perhaps? Or floating in the middle of nowhere?"

'*Infinity of course...*'

Jack settled into his armchair resting his cup of tea on the wide threadbare arms. Lady curled herself around his living leg.

He took a few moments to consider his response.

"It's a good question Adam. Hmm how can I put it? Let's see now...the world inside your head is just as complex as the physical external landscape that you move within. Okay, it's not directly comparable and never can be, but I tend to think of it in terms of landscapes...because there are different places you can travel to - ranging from Tolkienesque fantasy landscapes to desert like cloudscapes and then there are places that we can't even describe because they exist nowhere else except in the depths of our subconscious."

"These er...*landscapes*...are they all safe?"

Jack stroked his stubble. "That too is a difficult one to answer...and the real answer, as I think I've mentioned before, is 'it depends'. Let me try and be more specific. The landscapes themselves are perfectly safe, but you have to be careful about the... um...entities...that live there. For the most part these 'beings' or entities, whatever you choose to call them, are friendly and co-operative but sometimes, occasionally, there are some that it is best to avoid."

'*False friends you might call them...*'

Adam nodded, remembering a previous conversation but not totally sure what Jack was getting at "So how do you know? I mean how can you tell which...er...entities are friendly - and which are not?"

"A good question again," smiled Jack, "And equally as difficult to answer. Let's say that the entities that one tends to meet whilst in deep meditation are to a large extent dependant on who the meditator is. Remember we're not dealing with a linear logic or linear time pattern here. We are dealing with the mind in all its multi-faceted glory. The mind has a way of knowing who we need to meet to grow ourselves as people. It's like an individually crafted education programme designed specifically for each unique meditator. In essence you meet who you *need* to meet whether they are good or bad. 'Goodness' and 'badness' are relative terms anyway because of something called 'karmic debt' – but that's a subject for another time. Sometimes we need to meet a diverse group of people if we are to gain an understanding of human nature. The point is that whoever you might meet on your explorations of the mindscape you can be sure that you will learn something from the experience. A word of warning though. Part of any education process has to deal with the issue of temptation and the inner realms are no different. If you succumb to temptation, then you have to live with the consequences and sometimes temptation is manifest in subtle ways during meditation. If you do meet it, then you must try to turn away from it. If there is any danger in the meditation process, then this is it. I'm sorry if this all sounds a bit far-fetched or unbelievable... I'm trying to be as honest and open as possible. It's not an easy subject. The point is that you need to possess a fair degree of inner strength to deal with the whole meditation process and the temptations and distractions that you might meet on your journey inward.

"And do you think I have the necessary inner strength?"

Jack was silent for a moment. Adam sensed that Jack was trying hard to articulate something that was very difficult to explain. "Yes, I do" he said at length, "But I also think you are still quite young and inexperienced which means you might find it difficult to avoid temptation. You need to ask yourself the question 'Who is it I see when I look in the mirror?'"

Adam frowned. "What do you mean? I see myself of course."

"Do you? If you see a reflection, it is merely a reflection without substance or dimension - is that really you? Or is the real you someone else?"

Adam's eyes narrowed "Hey, that's what you were on about the other day wasn't it? When you told me to look in the mirror or over my shoulder or something."

"Ah yes" said Jack, "I believe I did mention it come to think of it. And your answer is?"

"The answer is that I realise it's a reflection in the mirror and that it's not the real me, but I can still feel the *real* me."

Jack raised his eyebrows questioningly. "Can you really? So, if you lost all feeling, let's say you damaged all your nerve endings, but remained conscious - is that still you?"

"Of course."

"And if you were both blind and deaf?"

"I would still be me."

"Okay, so let's say you have a lifeless body with no sensory organs. Would you say that you are still you?"

"Definitely."

"Good. Then describe yourself to me...let me give you back your power of speech for a moment."

Adam opened his mouth to speak then stopped to contemplate his choice of words.

"I'm…I'm an aware entity. Aware of my existence if not my bodily form."

"Go on."

"I cannot feel external sensations, but I know that I exist because I have…consciousness…I can think about things…"

"Okay - so you can think about *things*. Now let's say you have *never* been able to see, hear, smell, feel or experience normal life…what things are you able to think about then?"

Adam repeated the question to himself mentally.

"You mean as if I were born with nothing except consciousness?"

"That's right."

"I've never thought about such things before… Christ! That's difficult…give me a clue."

"Okay, would you be aware of the concept of life? Or death even?"

Adam considered the issue. He took a while before answering.

"If you have never had any experience of death and you are a conscious energy or whatever…then no, you probably wouldn't have any idea of the concept of death…or even life for that matter."

"So, what concepts *would* you have?"

"I dunno. I just don't know…what are you getting at Jack? Where is all this leading to?"

The old man smiled then sipped from his teacup.

"What I am getting at Adam, is simply this. You need to become more aware of your true identity. Not your name and address or occupation but an awareness of who you really are deep down. It's not as easy as it sounds. The point is that you asked me what happens when you make the first breakthrough into a deeper level of meditation. My answer is that what happens to you, and what you actually experience, depends on you as an individual and no-one else. The other point I am making is that you really need to know who you are *before* you set off into the unknown. Because if you are unsure about your own identity then you may not be strong enough to ward off what one might call 'negative influences'".

"I think I know who I am though Jack. I'm not that dumb y'know".

Jack ignored the response.

"We all wear a mask, Adam. We see it every day in the mirror. We wear it at work, and we wear it at home. Unlike clothes which we take off regularly most of us leave our masks on all the time letting it stagnate and become fixed to our persona. Other people see the mask and not the real us - and that's how we like to be seen. We are scared to remove our masks Adam, very scared."

"Why?"

"Because most of us are frightened to reveal what lies beneath the mask. Scared to remove it in front of others and perhaps even more scared to remove it in front of ourselves. Perhaps we are scared of what we might find...our true selves naked, fragile and exposed. No pretence, no superficial veneer of outward presentability or respectability but the real unadorned self. The essence of our individual being. It's a very frightening experience but one that we must be prepared to undertake if we are to understand our true selves."

"So - what is it you are really trying to tell me Jack. Spit it out."

"Okay" nodded Jack "To put it simply, take off your mask Adam and find out who you really are."

"And if I can learn to do that?"

"Then you will find the inner strength to be able to go deeper into the subconscious realms than you would ever believe and there you will find all your answers, all your personal treasures, everything. You have to peel back all the layers first though Adam. It won't be easy."

Adam stood up. He felt restless. Something was bothering him.

"What about my bull nightmares Jack? The one's I told you about. Will it help me get those damn nightmares out of my head once and for all so that I can get a peaceful night's sleep?"

Jack stopped for a moment and got up from his chair. He leaned on the tiled mantelpiece and stared at his own reflection in an antique mirror. He didn't speak for a few moments and Adam knew better than disturb the old man's train of thought. When at last he spoke, the words were slow and measured.

"The nightmares are indeed in your own head Adam, but they are not there randomly. There is a reason for them, and my intuition tells me that it is probably something to do with past lives. Reincarnation. If you find the courage to track them down to their source, then you will have the opportunity to learn the reason for them. I don't believe you will ever be able to stop them until you know the reason for them and the source of them. It's like I said earlier. It's about peeling back the layers until you find the reasons for what makes you who you are."

"Do you know the reason for them?"

Jack opened his mouth to speak but shut it again then turned away avoiding eye contact. His fingers drummed on the wall.

"You *do* know, don't you?" said Adam "So why can't you tell me?"

Jack remained with his back to Adam facing the wall. His shoulders slumped a little.

"I'm sorry" he said at last, "I get carried away sometimes Adam. Forgive me. I think I've probably said too much already…".

Adam didn't bother to tell Carol he'd been sacked from Lomax Bros Merchandising for 'unacceptable behaviour'. He'd not told anyone. Plenty more jobs around without twats like Gordon Davis in charge. The only pleasure in the whole experience had been watching the guy go apoplectic with rage at Adam's artwork. Even dim-witted old Jim Hastings was crying with laughter when Gordon had discovered the re-designing to his calendar.

Some guys have no sense of humour.

He'd sat in the local park smoking hash for a couple of hours before going home, taking a long bath and then resolving to give meditation his best shot and push his own barriers as far as possible. Lomax Bros was now part of his past. Most things in life were boring these days and even going out with the lads somehow didn't give him the same buzz that it used to.

This thing called 'meditation' was the new buzz. It was, Adam realised, becoming addictive and he needed a 'fix' more and more. If Jack was right and Adam really did have some sort of natural flair for it, then he needed to go for it. He'd never been one to shy away from a challenge. Okay, so his mother was going to give him some grief when she found out he'd messed up yet another job - but what the hell? The job didn't suit him. He'd find something else. No problem. Tomorrow he'd set off for work as usual so as not to arouse suspicion, but he'd go to see Jack instead. Seeing the old guy with the gammy leg was another 'fix' he now needed regularly. Jack talked so much sense. He'd got so much real-world experience, fought in the war, travelled the physical world, and also travelled the inner worlds. And yet he lived his life with such quiet modesty that nobody would suspect that the old guy hobbling down the street to pick up his Sunday papers was such an immense personality.

As for Adam's mates, well - yeah - they were a laugh to be with, but he doubted they'd even heard of meditation. It wasn't something he was in any hurry to explain to them either.

But Marie on the other hand...

Sod it! He didn't want to think about Marie. Why did she keep creeping back into his thoughts? She was just another part of his past, wasn't she?

Ah well...no point in even dwelling on what might have been. 'Plenty more fish in the sea' as his mother would often say.

Adam waited for the downstairs door to slam signalling that Carol was off to the bingo. Great! Now he was alone at last. He adjusted the cushions on his bed until he was comfortable then reached across to open the drawer of his bedroom cabinet retrieving a slender candle. He lit the wick and melted a few drops of wax onto an ashtray then sat the candle in the small pool of liquid watching it congeal. His diary was still in the drawer, untouched for a few weeks but it had served its purpose well enough. Now the inspiration now longer needed that kind of introspection. Adam was committed to the cause.

He reached up and flicked off the bedroom light switch and the room took on a new cave like ambience lit up by the soft candle glow. It felt good. Intoxicating. He pulled the bed sheets over his legs wanting to cocoon himself both physically and mentally. He started to breathe deeper and then closed his eyes focusing on each out breath and the movement of his diaphragm. After a few minutes the stresses of the day began to seep away, and slowly and gradually a feeling of calm began to pervade his body. Now the thoughts would start to bubble up to the surface of his conscious mind and needed to be dealt with. One, two, three. Let them all go. Let them drift away.

There was a growing sense of familiarity in the meditative state now that Adam had learnt to ignore the endless stream of insidious thoughts. It seemed he'd spent countless frustrating hours trying to just get past the first step in contemplative meditation but now felt he had cracked it. It was almost, but not quite, becoming as routine as riding a bike or swimming once the basic principles had been mastered. First slip into a comfortable relaxed state, second begin to turn your focus inward, three, get rid of the infuriating thoughts that skulked ominously around your head like circling vultures then four, move beyond the 'thought field' into the peaceful quiet place where true meditative experiences are allowed to manifest. According to Jack it could take years to get from step one to step four. For Adam it had taken around six months. And now here he was once again. The same place he'd reached a few days ago, where the empty, white, cloudy cocoon like landscape within his head started to shimmer and then almost imperceptibly to start changing hue.

There was no sensation of solidity and certainly nothing firm underfoot. It was similar to the sensation of floating, only a little more rooted. The most difficult thing was to keep focused. If you didn't maintain a focused awareness, then the thoughts would flood back into your consciousness like a thousand bats emerging from a small cave at sunset. If you focused too hard then you would lose the calm detachment that allows meditation to flourish. Either way you would be instantaneously plummeted back into conscious awareness like a wrong-footed wrestler being thrown down onto the canvas with a thud.

Adam was getting used to treading that fine line between extremes. If he could just hold the focus like a tightrope walker with eyes trained on the distance, maintain the awareness, and let the experience draw him along effortlessly then the feelings generated within him were truly amazing. It was as if he had been given the keys to a new exotic fairy-tale world that he never knew existed.

And now he was back there again, savouring every subtle movement, every sound, every colour. It was a new exciting inner world that he was desperate to explore.

For the first time Adam felt confident enough to still his nervous quickened heartbeat by sheer act of will. Now he could relax and take stock of his surroundings. The first realisation was that this was neither like the experience of being wide awake nor fast asleep, it was something entirely different - inexplicable almost, just as Jack had predicted. The second realisation was that there was no real sense of 'place'. Rather it was a non-place. Adam had only managed to reach this state of focused attention once or twice before and each time his sojourn had been very brief and a little hazy. This time he was determined to try and maintain his concentration for a little longer.

He tried to move and found that his meditative 'body' immediately responded as soon as the idea of movement was considered. Good, that was easy enough. Movement meant that Adam now had the ability to visually explore this strange mindscape and to try and make sense of it.

It was a weird sort of feeling. The feather soft undulating folds of blueness were washing over him like the waves of a warm tropical sea. Very calming and not at all unpleasant.

Sensuous.

It was as Adam was visually exploring his surroundings that a new sensation began to permeate through his being like a gentle balm. It started slowly at first, like a growing sense of intuition. It was an awareness of something happening close to him. No, not something...

Someone.

Adam physically became aware of the hairs starting to rise on the back of his neck. He may be 'out' of his physical body, he reflected momentarily, but the attachment was still strong enough to send him strong physical sensations. The feeling grew stronger until it could no longer be labelled mild intuition. It became a certainty.

Someone - or *something* - was moving closer and Adam was starting to feel distinctly uncomfortable. There were no visual clues. He was still surrounded by a vista of pale blues and white frothing 'cloudlike' things which obscured anything that might be present even a few metres away. It was not unlike one of those dense autumn fogs that sometimes descend over the landscape like a white blanket reducing vision in all directions.

Adam tried to calm his growing sense of apprehension and rationalise the situation. That he was in a fairly deep level of meditation was a certainty. Objective reality for now seemed only a construct. From what Jack had told him this meant he was making good progress. Surely then, there was nothing to fear?

All he needed to do was...
Oh God...
'It' – whatever 'it' was - was getting closer.

He could sense it. Feel it. There were no sounds. No footsteps. No visual clues. Nothing in fact, that could help pinpoint the source of his growing uneasiness. And yet the sense of certainty that something or someone was moving towards him and was now lurking just a metre or so away in the swirling blue vortices was incontrovertible.

He could feel a film of sweat coating his forehead and palms. His heartbeat started to quicken. He turned slowly, peering into the dense inner fog in a desperate attempt to identify the origin of his terror. Who or what would want to do this to him? Why would anything or anyone want to intrude into his mind like this? Infiltrating his subconscious like an insidious fever?

And then he saw it.

A moving shadow. A shadow of indeterminate shape pushing through the viscous membranes of blue cloud-fog in an attempt to reach Adam's subconscious form. In a moment it would be upon him.

And then the clouds parted as the figure emerged and Adam mouthed a silent scream...

...before jerking himself upright on his bed, flinging off the bed covers and holding his head in two hands while watching his body trembling in uncontrolled spasms from his head to his feet.

"Adam!" Carol Sinclair yelled for the third time, "For heaven's sake turn that music down and come downstairs. Steve's at the door."

Adam turned the volume control down with a sigh, fading the newly purchased Deep Purple LP to what his mother would call an 'acceptable level'.

"Coming" he yelled back.

Carol ushered Steve Lacey into the hallway as Adam came crashing down the stairs.

Something must be up. Steve rarely ventured into Adam's house. Meeting at the pub was more his style.

"Wotcha, Steve."

"Wotcha, just wondered if you're doin' anything at the moment?"

"Not really. What d'ya have in mind?"

Steve glanced nervously at Mrs Sinclair who got the message and with a shrug made herself scarce.

"I'm cooking some tea around six if you are going out" she called from the kitchen.

"Yeah. Great. I'll be back for six then."

"And don't forget about that job advert I cut out of the paper for you. You know, that sub-editor's job at the Gazette. You're always moaning about the articles in the paper and reckon you could easily write something better - so do it!"

"Yeah, yeah."

"I mean it Adam."

Adam slipped on his jacket and signalled Steve to follow him out of the front door.

"And don't forget to turn your stereo off" yelled Carol after him, realising with the usual despondency that she was once again shouting to herself.

The two lads walked along the road in silence for a few minutes. Steve had turned left out of Adam's front door which meant he was heading for the park. The King's Head and the Anchor were in town in the opposite direction. It meant that Steve wanted to talk.

Dean Park was typical of almost all Sussex town parks. Not totally artificial like the Victorian suburban parks of Greater London but rather a few acres of natural forest fenced off to protect it from the ever-expanding sprawl of new town urban housing developments. At one time the great forest of the Weald stretched for thousands of acres between the chalk escarpments of the North and South Downs and was home to wolves, bears and wild boar but now little of the great forest was left, apart from the much smaller 'Ashdown Forest' with its native deer and the many lakes that filled in the hollows made by the charcoal burning industry of yesteryear.

Now a lingering corner of the great forest had been renamed 'Dean Park' after a local land-owning family and boasted a car park, café, boating lake and playground with an equal mix of deciduous woodland and open spaces for cricket or football. Steve and Adam headed past the café and down a grassy slope to the lake edge where a wooden bench provided a pleasant view across the water to the thicker clumps of trees on the far bank.

For once the bench was actually free from courting couples and old ladies feeding the waterfowl. Both lads sat down in unison staring silently across the lake. Steve reached into his inside pocket, glanced over his shoulder then produced two crudely rolled joints, passing one to Adam. He shielded his hand from the wind and flicked on his lighter. Adam took a deep breath and the tip crackled into life. He sat back on the park bench savouring the aroma and let the smoke drift out slowly into the warm late Spring air.

"How's things?" asked Steve after a while.

"Yeah. Good" replied Adam "Well...not bad. I got the boot from Lomax Bros so I'm skint again, but I couldn't stand another day at that place."

Steve laughed "You've not been out much lately. We wondered whether you were still alive or not?"

Adam took another drag on the roll-up and shrugged. "I get sick of the Anchor sometimes. Needed a bit of a change that's all. How's Danny?"

"He's okay."

"Mick?"

"Yeah. They're good. We've had a few laughs. You've been missing out."

"Maybe you're right. I could do with a few laughs after Lomax Bros. Why don't we all go out somewhere different? You know - out of town for a change. Check out some good bands or something. Get smashed."

"I'm up for it. What you got in mind?"

"I'll think of something."

Conversation stopped for a few minutes while both lads became absorbed in their own thoughts whilst gazing out over the lake. Children's laughter merged with birdsong and the distant jingle of an ice-cream van.

Adam stood up and stubbed out the joint embers then walked a few paces down to the water's edge. Steve followed. The grass sloped down gently to the edge of the lake where the gentle rhythmic lapping of the water provided a pleasant backdrop to the overall tranquillity of the scene. The lake was irregular in size but not very large. A few willow tree boughs hung over the water and there were a few visible nests in the reed beds a few yards out from shore. The boating season had not yet started in earnest and one or two fishermen sat on the opposite side of the lake like rigid garden gnomes, eyes transfixed on bobbing floats. There was a flurry of quacking and feathers from halfway around the lake where a mother with a pushchair was encouraging a toddler to throw bread to the birds. All very English really. All a bit depressing.

Steve picked up a stone from the water's edge and threw it idly out across the lake where it arced through the air before disappearing with a splash.

"I just needed to get out of the house" said Steve gazing out across the water, "Can't stand 'em arguing all the time."

Adam raised his eyebrows quizzically.

"Oh...Mum and my old man" explained Steve. "They never stop bloody arguing. Drives me nuts. Ever since my dad got laid off from his last job and has been moping around indoors. She can't stand 'im always sitting around and he can't stand her nagging him about the lack of money and suchlike. I need to get out and away from it all sometimes."

Adam nodded sympathetically, trying to remember whether or not his own parents ever used to argue like that.

"Must be tough getting used to being unemployed long term though" he said, "Is he looking for work?"

Steve shrugged "Dunno...seems to sit around moaning most of the time. Moaning at me to get a job of all things. Bloody hypocrite!"

"My old dear's the same with me" sympathised Adam, "As if getting a job is like really crucial or something. Jesus we've got the rest of our lives to think about jobs and careers and all that bollocks."

"Exactly. Anyhow I just needed to get away from it all for a few minutes. Seemed like a good time to sit in the park and enjoy a smoke. You noticed how smooth the lake is today? I've never seen it look so much like a sheet of glass."

"Yeah. The wind's died down a lot" said Adam, "It's gonna be a nice evening."

Adam picked up another pebble-like stone and threw it as high as he could towards the centre of the lake. They watched it fall with a splash sending small circular waves out symmetrically from the impact point.

"Look at that" said Steve pointing across the lake, "Amazing ripples on the water."

Something made Adam tense up. He turned to Steve slowly, staring at him with a strange expression on his face then shivered involuntarily. It felt as though someone had surgically inserted a rod of ice into his spine. His jaw dropped open.

"Whassup?" said Steve noticing the sudden change, "You all right mate? You look like you've seen a ghost…"

"I dunno…it's…" Adam's eyes focused on the middle distance. "Weird man! It was something you said. Deja vu or something. It felt for a moment like… like something I heard a long time ago…can't explain it…"

Adam flopped down onto the grass and shook his head from side to side as if trying to throw off an invisible insect. Steve frowned and sat down beside him. "Maybe it was the spliff?"

"Nah" said Adam as the icy sensation faded away, "It wasn't the spliff. It was just this weird feeling came over me. I don't know why. It was something you said. Anyway, it's gone now."

Steve shrugged "Let's go up the cafe n' see if it's still open. I could do with a drink."

"Yeah, me too."

They turned away from the lake as the sun began to sink into the branches of the far trees and the water started to reflect an amber glow.

The cafe was closed. Just. Sod's law thought Adam.

"Fancy a pint instead?" suggested Steve tentatively.

Adam thought about it for a moment.

"Yeah, why not?" he replied, "But let's make it the King's Head for a change."

They walked in silence for ten minutes. It was obvious to Steve that Adam had something on his mind. Something that was bugging him.

It was still bugging him when Steve got back from the bar holding two frothy pints of bitter.

"Ripples on the water," Adam said out loud to no-one in particular.

"Come again?" said Steve shoving the pint glass into Adam's hand.

"That's it" said Adam again, "That's what you said. Ripples on the water...ripples on the water... it means something..."

Steve shrugged and took a deep swig of beer then wiped his mouth on his sleeve. He looked sideways at Adam, his brow furrowed.

"Yeah mate" said Steve, "Of course it does. Whatever you say..."

It was a sunshine and showers Thursday morning. A day to tidy his 'pigsty bedroom' (Carol's words). Either that or go down to the shops, buy a paper, check out the 'Sits Vac' and start making some phone calls. He'd decided on the bedroom.

The desktop was the worst. Books and LP's mainly, including a tatty paperback his Mum had found in the W.I. market called 'Choosing a Career'. He hadn't even opened it yet. Still, she meant well, so he'd feigned overwhelming gratitude. Then there was the diary.

Adam turned over a few pages mentally kicking himself for failing to keep it up to date. He'd not made an entry in it since mid-March.

Which meant he'd missed all the recent stuff...

He was tempted to blame his lapse of both diary and meditation on the scare of the previous two sessions when he'd been convinced of some other 'presence' invading his space. But that was probably only half the story. Truth was he'd been genuinely busy trying to find another job, which after three disastrous interviews left him feeling distinctly pissed off. That in turn had led to him borrowing more money off his distraught mother and then drinking more than he'd done over the last few months. True, he'd had some great laughs out with the boys and all that but the feeling of 'something missing' was starting to bother him. The meditation habit was getting too strong to break and after three weeks without it, or having any communication with Jack, a kind of mental 'cold turkey' was setting in.

Now it was halfway through May and almost his twentieth birthday. Time to pick up the pieces and try again. Time to stop being an arsehole. Time to stop thinking about Marie all the time. Time to get a life and move on.

He'd meant to call Jack but just hadn't got around to it. That was something he must do today. Jack would be able to help him understand what was going on. Adam needed to tell him about the progress in dealing with those stupid annoying and distracting thoughts, about the beautiful translucent blue colour that had enveloped him and about the human-like but indefinable and vaporous shape that had loomed out of nowhere and scared him witless.

Yeah, he must call Jack as soon as possible. As soon as this mess was cleared up.

He opened his bedside drawer and cleared it of empty cigarette packets, sweet wrappers and other pieces of miscellaneous junk collected over the years then binned the lot. Into the empty drawer Adam put the meditation paperback, his diary, some candles and candle holders, matches and the packet of incense sticks, 'hippy joss sticks' as his mother called them. Yeah, that looked good. That could be his 'Meditation Drawer'.

Adam continued to stack a pile of old books back onto his bedroom shelf. Most of them had been lying under his bed for months. Old schoolbooks mostly, plus a few old comic annuals and some of his dad's books. He picked up one of his dad's old books on 'World Mythology' and started idly flicking through it.

Something caught his eye. A section entitled 'Mythology of the Bull' with a few garish pictures of mythological bulls from different cultures. It reminded Adam that since starting to meditate regularly, the bull nightmares had virtually ceased. He thought back to the years when they had constantly plagued his night-time hours, causing him screaming fits as a young child and discomfort and insomnia as a teenager. But the last month or two had been virtually nightmare-free for some reason.

Maybe it really was this meditation thing that was somehow helping to keep the nightmares at bay. He sat down on the corner of the bed and started to read.

"Great to see you again Adam" said Jack, "I was beginning to wonder about you. You mustn't feel bad about not meditating for a few weeks. Sometimes it's the same for me. We all have busy lives to lead and sometimes a break is a good thing. Anyway, you're still young. You have years and years to develop your ability - so a few missed weeks won't hurt. Now tell me how it's been going. I can sense there's something you want to tell me."

Adam was pleased to see Jack again. He'd missed the old soldier. His humour and his wisdom.

"To be honest I've been a bit lazy lately Jack. I'm never very sure about how much progress I'm really making. Sometimes I find it quite hard to distinguish meditation from...well daydreaming I suppose. I'm never sure whether I'm fully conscious or half-asleep."

Jack nodded sagely. "There are many shades of unconscious and consciousness and sometimes the boundaries are vague. It doesn't really matter, and you mustn't feel that you need to distinguish between various states. Even semi-conscious meditation can be relaxing and refreshing. You will find that the deepest levels of sleep follow any intense period of sustained meditation. Sleeplessness should never be a problem...it will always be a joy to sleep. There's something else I ought to mention too, which is actually extremely important. It's something I should have spoken of before. Sometimes, when we meditate it's easier to let the mind go blank than others. When we find it difficult to think of nothing, we need to turn that frustration into something more positive. We can do that by asking the spiritual world to help us find us find that inner quiet and at the same time we need to briefly focus on something I call the 'four key principles'."

"The four key principles? What are they Jack?"

"They are the four most important things we need to learn to devote our life to if we sincerely wish to accelerate our spiritual maturity. They are forgiveness, gratitude, compassion, and love. Whenever I get stuck trying to meditate, I merely change my focus to asking for the help of the spirit world to cultivate these four foundation principles. I mentally forgive everyone who has ever wronged me. I express gratitude for being alive and the joy of simply being part of this beautiful planet. I shed a tear of compassion for everyone who is suffering, and I radiate love to all of humanity. Usually, by the time I go through this process I find that I can then fall more easily into the meditative state."

"Wow Jack. That's pretty deep stuff..."

Jack shrugged. "It's simply what I have learned after so many years of trying to be as effective at meditation as you are becoming naturally Adam. Now, you must tell me all about your latest inner journeys. But first..."

Jack got up from his favourite armchair and reached for a bottle of red wine that was perched on a bookshelf. He poured a short measure into a glass with a gesture to Adam, who shook his head. Expensive red wines were not really his scene. A nice pint of bitter though might have hit the spot. Jack eased himself back into the armchair and took a long sip of wine while he watched Adam frown in concentration. The lad was clearly struggling to recollect the details of his endeavours.

"There's nothing to speak of really," shrugged Adam, "It still takes me a long time to relax before I get anywhere. There was something specific though that I did want to ask you about."

"Go on."

"Well, I know this might sound silly but recently I get the feeling that I'm not alone...in my mind I mean...not physically. It's a strange feeling that someone or something is standing beside me but most times when I look there's never anyone there. It's weird."

"Most times?"

"Well, I think I saw something the first time and it terrified me."

Jack leaned forward.

"What did you see?"

Adam looked at the floor, face flushed.

"I'm not sure. A blurred figure. Sort of glowing..."

Jack nodded slowly. "Does this other presence bother you at all? I mean do you feel uncomfortable or scared by the feeling?"

"No, I don't think so. At least not so much now. The first time I nearly wet my pants and completely lost all concentration. I came back with a bump so to speak. I kept going back though because although I was scared, I was also fascinated and intrigued by the experience. Now I'm not so much scared as...well I just wish I could see who it is or what it is - that's all."

"Don't worry. You will see his face soon." said Jack with conviction.

Adam looked up somewhat startled by Jack's calm and matter-of-fact diagnosis. "How do you know that?" he said rather taken aback, "And what makes you so sure it's a 'him'?"

The old man put down his half-finished glass of vintage Burgundy on a nearby bookshelf. Adam had never seen him smile so wide before. Jack knew something.

"It is a 'him' I can assure you. It can be male or female you see, but in your case, I believe with a strong degree of certainty that it is a male. It's 'my gift' to know these things."

"How can you be so sure? You've never seen this... this presence...and if you're right, then please tell me who it is."

"I'm afraid I don't know his name" confessed Jack, "But he will tell you his name if you ask him."

Adam sat forward in his seat. This was too crazy for words. How the hell could Jack possibly know about faceless shapes hovering in someone else's subconscious?

"So - who is he then?"

Jack scratched his head thoughtfully then brought his fingertips together before raising them to his lips.

"I'm not sure how to best explain this Adam without it sounding...well corny...but I'll be as honest as I can. This presence or person that you describe is, for want of better words, your next guide."

Adam stared into Jack's eyes as if searching for something more.

"What do you mean my *next* guide?"

"Well let's just say that I am guide number one," Jack continued, "I'm your guide on the conscious external level. The presence that you are starting to become aware of during meditation is guide number two...your guide to the internal world of the subconscious. When you are ready, he will take you on the next step of your journey."

"Next step? But what about you?" Adam blurted.

Jack let out a long sigh. "Shortly you will no longer need me. I will have given you all the help I can possibly give, and I will have to let guide number two take over and lead you on into the next phase of your development."

Adam looked around as though searching out words in the dark recesses of the room.

"Does it have to be that way?"

"That is the most natural way and the way you should follow. As I said, I don't know who exactly your guide is, but what I can say is that he is ready to help you and you must put your faith in him completely. He will take you to places where it is not possible for me to go - and that's the way it should be. Just to feel his presence means that you are making incredible progress. I'm genuinely delighted for you Adam."

"I don't understand. Why do I need this...this guide? And where did he come from anyway?"

"He has always been there since the day you were born. He is what some might term your 'guardian angel'. Your inner voice. Your protector and your mentor. Your alter ego. Your inner-conscience and your inner spiritual guide."

Adam turned to stare at the wall. This was a lot to take in.

When he spoke again it was slow and measured.

"So, you're telling me that this person...this *guide*... has always been there waiting for me to contact him?"

"Not exactly" replied Jack, "Everyone, including me, has an inner guide though few people even realise it. Some people hear his or her voice in times of crisis warning 'be careful' or 'take care' or suchlike. Some feel his or her presence more strongly than others. Often it is in childhood that our guide is more tangible, but that closeness soon fades as we grow up and become more cynical. Only through our contact in meditation, however, can we take advantage of our opportunity to meet him or her again. And when that moment comes our inner strength is doubled and we become a 'whole' person. 'Together' to use a rather apt sixties phrase."

"Right. So, this...my *guide*...has been there all the time but sort of hidden from my everyday thoughts?"

"Not exactly hidden" corrected Jack, "To be precise about it, your guide has been waiting for you in the gaps between your thoughts rather than in your thoughts themselves."

"The *gaps* between my thoughts?"

"Yes. Most people unconsciously shut out their guides because they never find the peace that exists between their busy thoughts. It is in the space between thoughts that we find the gateway to a deeper reality. It is what you might call the silent field of all possibilities. It's a place that exists between thoughts and it is where the guides wait for their joyful reunions with those they have always been lovingly watching over."

Adam nodded thoughtfully. Pieces of a very complex jigsaw were beginning to come together.

"So, what should I do Jack? About this guide then?"

"Talk to him" said Jack simply and directly. "Lose your fear. Let him know you are aware of him and let him communicate openly with you."

Adam let Jack's words sink in. This was too freaky for words.

"Anyway" continued Jack, "This is really excellent news Adam. But I think you have something more to tell me about your last few meditations?"

Adam wondered how Jack could be so damn intuitive. He nodded and tried to recall the events of three weeks ago.

"Well, it's hard to describe really...I started off as usual and seemed to be able to deal with the usual intrusive thoughts much better than on previous occasions. I kept the focus for what seemed to be hours. I expect it was only minutes in reality..."

"Don't bring the word 'reality' into it, Adam. It confuses the issue."

"What? Oh yeah..." continued Adam, "Anyway I started getting that tingling sensation I told you about before and found myself in a kind of white place, an empty place. It was like there was a sort of fog or cloud around me."

"Excellent...excellent" encouraged Jack.

"There was nothing to see at first" continued Adam, "And this was before the...um...'presence' started to bother me. Nothing really happened except the whiteness all around me started to change colour. The whiteness began to change into a sort of blue colour, only this time it was incredible, the blueness I mean. It seemed to expand around me in every direction until it totally enveloped me and then I was sort of floating in it with no sensation of solid ground anymore."

"This is indeed most excellent," whispered Jack clapping his hands together, "Please go on."

Adam nodded "I can't describe it Jack...it was such an amazing blueness and it somehow well... the colour became more vibrant...more intense...it was too beautiful for words...the blueness was purer than any colour I've ever seen and then it somehow seemed to darken a little and draw me into it until I was literally pulled..."

"...Into a deeper blue?"

"Yes exactly. That's exactly what happened. I was somehow moved or pulled into a deeper blue. It was like I was sort of floating in outer space. Silent and empty but also warm and relaxing. It was mind blowing."

'All I can do is give him the tools and the map and then...'

Jack sat back in his armchair with a smile spreading across his face until he couldn't help but burst into spontaneous laughter. Adam looked up, his frown turning to laughter at the sight of Jack's emotional outburst.

"What's so funny?"

Jack's eyes seemed to sparkle more than ever as if there were a hint of tears beneath the surface. Tears of genuine happiness. "Congratulations Adam," he said wiping the moisture away. "My most sincere congratulations. You have at last arrived. I knew you could do it. *I just knew it.* You have found the door into the deep blue place where your own inner guide has waited for you for so many years. Welcome to your new beginning."

"New beginning?"

"Oh yes" said Jack animatedly, "The adventure is just about to begin."

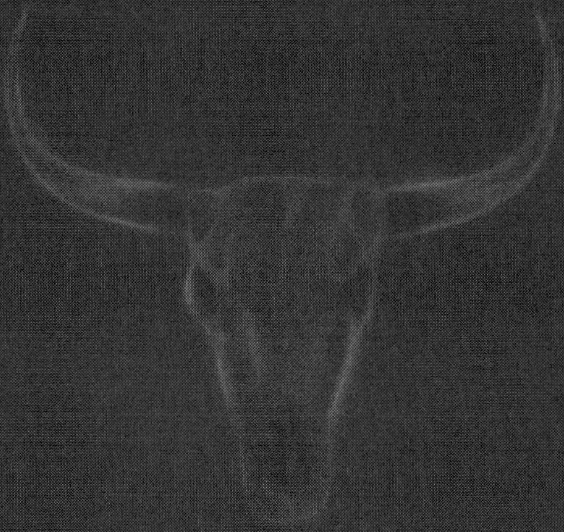

PART THREE

"Turn inward for your voyage
For all your arts
You will not find the Stone
In foreign parts."
Angelus Silesius, Alchemist

Three Months later - August 1975

The colours and the sounds were mesmerising.

Crimson spirals inter-weaved and curled around pulsating globules of purple in time with a throbbing beat that induced a spellbound trance-like state. Stunning. Beautiful.

The tableau was made even more other-wordly by the surrounding gothic arching of gnarled trees on the perimeter of the small woodland clearing and the huge log fire in the centre from which flames leapt like scorched ballerinas' illuminating the circle of enraptured faces.

Adam breathed deeply taking in the whole spectacle.

Awesome.

Danny, Mick and Steve were totally spaced out. You could see it in their eyes. Adam followed their gaze to the pure white chalk cliff face rising steeply from the other side of the clearing, beyond the fire, where a large projector with psychedelic filters had turned the stark white rock into a phantasmagoria of colour. Hidden in the dense woodland, on either side of the clearing, large speakers that had been connected to a mobile generator throbbed incessantly with distorted endless guitar solos. 'Quicksilver Messenger Service' someone had suggested.

The strange faces around the campfire, numbering anywhere between fifty and a hundred, were moving their heads rhythmically in time with the music, acres of hair swaying side to side, eyes closed, the smell of sweat, cannabis and incense overwhelming.

Everyone seemed to be sitting or kneeling apart from a guy with a glazed expression and a tatty Afghan coat working his way around the circle dispensing a liquid substance from a tiny spoon that he dipped into a bottle every now and then.

As the guy reached Steve and Danny, they poked out their tongues to receive a few drops of the free nectar followed by Mick, already out of his skull from some speed he'd dropped earlier. For a moment Adam wanted to intervene and tell him to take it easy, but it was too late. Mick's thoughts were now in some other universe.

The communal spoon was offered to Adam who shook his head. The guy shrugged and moved on. For a moment Adam had been tempted to get wasted too, but then thought better of it. Someone had to stay sober enough to find the way back through the forest to the tent and he'd already had a few pints of beer and a joint.

Adam had never been to a 'happening' before, but he'd heard about them. "C'mon man!" Steve had insisted. "It'll be a gas, we can take a four-man tent, pitch somewhere in the woods in the late afternoon, get a few beers in then find the music. Don't be an arse."

Eventually Adam had agreed. What the hell. He needed to loosen up and have some fun. The new job had been getting him down lately anyway and a weekend camping in the woods with the boys would be a laugh.

It was always Steve who 'heard' about the happenings first. Strictly word of mouth of course, no tickets or any of that shit. The venue would never be confirmed until the day before, just in case the pigs got wind of it, and to keep the numbers low and discreet.

In the early evening the woods would fill with those 'in the know', creeping ghost-like through the undergrowth looking for the clearing with the exposed chalk cliff beckoning like a blank movie screen. A natural woodland amphitheatre at the foot of the South Downs. A hidden Mecca.

Adam was glad he'd agreed to come. It was an amazing experience that was imprinting itself indelibly in his psyche. A warm summer evening in a magical setting. The colours were hypnotic and the music ethereal.

Adam moved from the kneeling position to a more comfortable cross-legged position and closed his eyes. It was nearly 2am. In a few minutes he would have to drag the lads back through the woods to find the tent and crash out, but for now he was going to close his eyes, enjoy the warm glow of the crackling fire and lose himself in the ambience of the moment.

Yeah, it was weird, but it was also wonderful. Everyone having a good time. No aggro. No hassles. No bad vibes.

Cool.

It was nearly 3am when Adam finally shifted his stiff legs and motioned the lads to follow him back to the tent.

The music was over and those wraith-like bodies that had not simply fallen asleep on the ground already were fumbling their way back through the trees, cursing as they walked into hidden branches and stumbling through the undergrowth in the darkness.

Mick needed supporting. He was only semi-conscious and mumbling incoherently. Steve and Danny weren't going to be much use either by the look of their faces in the fire glow.

"Steve man, gissa hand with Mick" hissed Adam, trying not to wake the curled bodies snoring around his feet.

"Wassat?"

"I said help me carry Mick, he's stoned, we need to get him back to the tent."

Steve and Danny made a half-hearted attempt to support Mick's puppet-like torso, but they were not far off the same comatose state themselves. Giggling and coughing, they were stumbling about in the undergrowth like senile winos.

Totally wrecked.

Mick was obviously suffering a particularly bad trip. The hallucinogenic effects of LSD were putting his senses on overdrive. Halfway back to the tent, in the depths of the trees he suddenly screamed; the high-pitched wail bouncing off the trees like ear splitting microphone feedback. Almost made Adam wet his pants.

Mick was obviously fighting some seriously nasty inner demons.

"I don't like it. It's too dark. I can't see where I am. There are shapes moving in the trees. I don't want to be in this place anymore. I can see faces everywhere. Horrible faces. Horrible faces."

Mick's voice had changed. That was scary. The words were gushing from Mick's lips not in the familiar cockney growl that Adam had grown used to but in the demented rantings of a madman.

Adam whirled Mick's body around and stepped in front of him shaking him gently by the shoulders. "Take it easy man. It's okay. You're nearly at the tent. There's nuthin' to be scared of. It's just woods and trees and stuff that's all. Relax."

Mick couldn't relax. Steve and Danny had never witnessed someone having a bad trip before. They were obviously scared witless and ran ahead to find the sanctuary of their tent. Adam watched them run off into the darkness and mouthed something under his breath about 'useless wankers'. Mick was sobbing hysterically now and waving his arms around his head as if fending off invisible assailants. His hands were lashing out at twigs and branches which were scratching his hands and wrists drawing blood. The more the branches scratched him the more he yelled.

"Monsters. Leave me alone...leave me alone...leave me..."

It took about fifteen minutes to find the tent in the oppressive darkness that hung over the thick woodland like a torn black shroud. Adam somehow managed to half-push and half-drag Mick's terrified body back to where the other guys were waiting.

Mick threw up in some bushes before collapsing in a heap onto his damp sleeping bag sobbing softly. *'At least he's rid his body of the stuff'* thought Adam, *'And it's a whole heap better than him heaving his guts up later inside the tent.'*

Steve and Danny were both snoring within seconds; but sleep was not coming so easily for Adam.

The beer fumes were overwhelming. Adam shifted himself around so that he could lie on his back, his head poking out through the tent flap, needing fresh night air.

He rested his head on his hands and looked up. Between the gnarled, groping, skeletal fingers of black branches silhouetted against the night sky he could see the pinpricks of stars. If it wasn't for the snoring of three pissheads, he reflected, this place would be even more magical. There was a smell of damp woodland that was actually very refreshing, and the night had now become much clearer, the earlier low cloud base moving on, leaving a gentle summer night breeze. It was almost perfect for meditating, almost sensual.

Except of course for the distraction of three other bodies crushed into a tent that was really far too small to sleep four.

Adam lay still awhile, just staring up at the myriad of stars burning millions of miles above him, listening to his own breathing and thinking. Reflecting.

Reflecting on life, his hopes and dreams, the messes he'd made of things, the people he'd hurt. He thought about his mum, Carol, and how she was coping with bringing him up alone. He thought about Jack and all the incredible things he'd learned from the old man. He thought about Marie which made his heart quicken. Where was she now? Would she ever speak to him again? He thought about the string of dead-end jobs that he'd taken on, one after another, hating every single one. He thought about the time he'd wasted at school larking around and not showing interest in anything. Failing exams and shrugging it off like it was cool to be a failure.

Then there was the bull. The weird snorting beast that inhabited his dreams. Lurking in his subconscious for some unfathomable reason like the grim reaper waiting for a chance to exert his presence. But why? Why?

And if Jack knew the reason – why wasn't he saying?

And then he thought about his dad and what they might have talked about now - if he were still alive.

No, don't go there. Those sorts of thoughts are too painful. Much too painful.

Adam turned over and tried to clear his mind of all the mundane and repetitive thoughts that were getting in the way of sleep. In a few hours it would be sunrise. A new day. Maybe a day to sort stuff out. Make a new start.

Maybe...

He closed his eyes and pulled a woolly hat from his rucksack shoving it down over his ears. Outside the tent something cracked a twig in the undergrowth. Small black shapes moved among the trees and bushes. The night breeze was picking up and leaves were rustling on trees that were starting to sway like billowing sails on long forgotten ghost ships. And then slowly, one by one, the moving branches began blotting out the stars.

"Your references are not very good."

Stanley T. Morgan, Chief Editor at 'The Gazette' and never one to mince his words, looked over his reading specs at the youth fidgeting nervously in the seat in front of him.

Adam cleared his throat and loosened his collar, trying not to make it too obvious he'd never worn a tie before. He had, however, anticipated the question and was well prepared. He'd been practising his best plummy accent in front of the mirror all afternoon.

"The references were from part time jobs since leaving school. Anything to earn money really. Some of the factory jobs were awful and I was never given proper training. Now I feel it's time to move on. Start a more serious career and...er...put all those pocket money jobs behind me..."

"Hmm."

"...And this is exactly the job I've been looking for. I've always wanted to work for a newspaper. I'm a hard worker Mr Morgan...I'll do anything to work my way up."

"Hmm."

Stanley T (for Thomas) Morgan re-read the letter of application and dog-eared CV again, shuffled the papers a little then leaned forward with his hands clasped in front of him over an ink-stained blotter. He hated interviewing as much as he hated the twenty-seven years he'd worked on the Gazette.

Adam couldn't help but stare at the grey hairs sprouting from his ears.

"Your qualifications are less than we would normally expect for the position of sub-editorial assistant. It clearly stated in the advertisement that grade C was the very minimum requirement in English."

"I just missed getting a C" Adam lied, "And I'm seriously thinking about going to evening classes to do a retake. I'm quite confident about achieving a much higher grade on retake. I'm actually very good with words and I read widely."

"Hmm."

"Just give me a chance to prove myself. You won't be disappointed. I'm willing to do anything to get a start in a proper job. I really feel I could be a credit to the paper." (God, he hated squirming up to smarmy old gits in crumpled suits).

World-weary Mr Morgan looked thoughtful for a moment. The lad was a typical loud-mouthed bullshitter, still wet behind the ears and poorly qualified. Not really suitable at all. Then again, no-one else had applied for the position, the starting salary was lousy, and he really did need someone to shout at to get the filing done and make tea.

"Thank you, Mr Sinclair. I will give your application serious consideration and we will write to you within the next day or two."

Adam shook the limp clammy hand that was offered to him and then left the cluttered office shutting the door gently behind him. At least it wasn't an outright 'no'.

He walked down the stone steps outside the main entrance of the Gazette, noting the sign on the front of the building that had clearly not been cleaned or changed since the mid-fifties. He pulled off his tie in a quick jerk and headed straight for the King's

Head to quench his parched throat, unaware of the flickering curtain in the room above.

'References are not very good' Stanley T. Morgan mumbled to himself again, whilst realigning the office curtains. He walked back to the desk, reached down to the second drawer, and withdrew a half-empty bottle of sherry, quickly unscrewing the cap. 'But there's something about the lad I quite like.'

His hand trembled involuntarily as he poured a short measure into the glass on the corner of his desk. He swirled the liquid for a few moments then downed it in one. 'Got a sort of spark about 'im. That's it. A sort of spark...'

"What's got into you today then?"

It was three days since the 'happening' in the woods and already a fading memory.

"Huh?"

"I couldn't help noticing you walking around grinning and whistling. I thought teenagers were supposed to slouch about looking miserable."

"Yeah...very funny mum...very funny."

"I'm serious. You're like a bear with a sore head most of the time. What's perked you up then?"

Adam shrugged, tried to think of a smug witty answer but decided against it. Nah, he'd try something different this time. Just for the hell of it. Just to test for a reaction.

"Meditation" he said.

"Meditation?"

Adam's mother put down the newspaper and rolled her eyes to the ceiling. She wondered how long it would take before Adam raised the subject. She was still feeling guilty about skimming through his private diary. "So that's what you're up to now is it? I thought you were suspiciously quiet lately. Oh well, it's better than hanging around street corners with your boozy mates I suppose. Isn't that what the Beatles were up to? Meditation? I'm sure I read it in the paper..."

"Yeah, sort of."

"I hope it doesn't involve drugs."

"No Mum."

"Well, it sounds a bit dodgy to me. Where on earth did you get this meditation idea from then? Not from Steve Lacey surely?"

"No Mum. Not Steve Lacey. I got the idea from books and stuff. Y'know."

Carol Sinclair stared at him with a bemused expression on her face.

Something not quite right here.

"I'm not sure I like the sound of it" she snorted, "Someone once told me that meditation has got something to do with black magic and the occult and can be very dangerous to meddle with..."

Adam laughed aloud, "who told you that then? No...don't tell me...let me guess. Was it one of the old dears at the church coffee morning?"

She threw the paper at him playfully, "Don't be so bloody patronising, know-it-all."

"Tea mum?"

She frowned at him.

"Go on then. A quick cuppa before I have to go the shops. And don't think I hadn't noticed you changing the subject..."

"Who me?"

Adam went off to the kitchen to fill the kettle.

His mother stared after him shaking her head and mumbling to herself 'Meditation...whatever next... little sod.'

Then she remembered something "Oh Adam..." she called through the closed door.

"Yeah."

"I forgot to tell you. Marie Cunningham phoned for you last night.

She waited for a reaction. "HELLO! did you hear me? I said..."

Adam froze, one hand holding a teaspoon over the old silver tea tin his grandmother had passed on to his mother. Sort of family heirloom.

"Yeah, I heard you" he called back.

His hand started to shake. He cleared his throat, voice just a little bit edgy. "Did she leave a message?"

"No" Carol called back, "She just said could you ring her when you get a moment."

Adam stared up at the kitchen ceiling for a moment, eyes narrowed, jaw line set hard.

He took a deep breath, steadied his hand then forcing a nonchalant, disinterested look onto his face, carried the cup of steaming tea back into the lounge.

"Tea" he said with a smile, "So don't say I never do anything for you. If she rings again tell her I'm busy but I'll try and call her sometime."

"Adam" Carol snapped back with a frown, "Ring the poor girl as soon as possible and stop being an idiot."

It was the amazing deep and vibrant blue again.
   It seemed to stretch to infinity in every direction and was subtly changing hue. Still blue, but becoming richer and deeper, gradually merging into the silver-blue of night in which a million stars burned like ice crystals in fathomless oceans.

Its beauty was indescribable and made him want to weep.

He'd become accustomed to the blue. Accustomed, but never - *ever* - indifferent. He willed it to arrive sooner so that he could wrap the sensuous folds of the silky blueness around his body. Immerse himself totally.

But this time it was different.

Different because for the first time there was the sensation of sound to accompany the vista and after so many meditation sessions experienced in silence it took time to adjust to this new sensory input. The sounds were almost music and yet not quite music. Instead, it was more like an ebbing and flowing of sound waves that reminded him of surf breaking on the shore. It seemed like there were voices singing in multi-layered harmonies and yet there were no distinct words. Behind the words that were 'not words' there was a tinkling of small bells that reminded him of something that he had heard a long time ago, something lost in the irretrievable depths of his memory.

And then he found himself swimming in a deep black-blue star-field resonating and pulsing in an endless rhythmic harmonic dance. Somehow the stars were reaching out to touch each other with gossamer-thin silken arms until every star was linked to every other star forming a glowing cobweb from which pearl like droplets of dew hung – each pearl reflected on the surface of its neighbour in an endless and infinite parade of exquisite beauty.

But what did it all mean?

Adam's mind framed the question and at the same time he realised that even if the meaning were forever hidden from him, it somehow didn't matter.

This was a place that - somehow - he *belonged* to. It was somewhere he instinctively knew he had been looking for - yet never knew where or how to start looking. Somewhere that he had needed to find.

No – that wasn't quite right. 'Find' was the wrong word.

It was somewhere that he needed to *return* to.

It was somehow like going home to a very special safe place. Warm and familiar. And that realisation sent a wave of bliss streaming through his body like an icy wind cleaning and refreshing as it passed through, leaving only purity in its wake.

It left him shaking and stunned and brought conscious awareness back in a sudden rush.

Adam caught his breath then exhaled deeply and slowly. His eyes flickered open, and he lay there in silence, his mind grappling with the misty afterimages stolen from the hazy borders of reality.

He had travelled somewhere.

Somehow, he had gone out beyond the 'blueness' into a strange and wonderful somewhere. He had no idea where that somewhere was, but he was sure of one thing.

He had returned changed.

It was then that he instinctively realised that from this day forward things could never be quite the same again.

"Jack? It's me...Adam."

"Adam! How good to hear from you. It must be weeks..."

"Yeah. Sorry I've not been in touch. Y'know how it is...work and such..."

Adam could picture the old guy sitting on the bottom stairs in the hallway. Lady curled around his feet. Smell of wood smoke from the open fire. He'd started to dial Marie's number three or four times but for some reason couldn't go through with it. Wimped out. Fingers were shaking too much. He'd dialled Jack instead.

"So - Adam, this is a wonderful surprise. Are you well? Still meditating I hope."

"You bet. It gets better and better all the time Jack. I'm finding out so much new stuff just like you said I would. I was thinking...perhaps I could pop over sometime to talk about it."

"Yes. Of course. Anytime. I'd love to. Why don't you come over next weekend? What are you doing on Sunday afternoon?"

"Nothing. Sunday afternoon's fine by me. I'll see you then Jack."

"Excellent. Sunday about three."

The receiver clicked as Adam put the phone down. He wasn't sure what made him call. Psychological probably. Couldn't face speaking to Marie, not after all these months. Needed to call someone else. Okay, so Jack had said that the new guide was all Adam needed from now on because he had taken Adam as far as he could. And yet it wasn't that simple just to break the relationship so suddenly. Not yet. And, anyway, this so called 'guide' had not appeared during the last few meditation sessions. Adam had been entirely alone. Perhaps this new guide wasn't that interested in him after all? Perhaps he'd imagined the whole thing?

He still had a nagging feeling within him that there were more things he needed to ask Jack about. Things that Jack would understand. It was one thing trying to grasp a different kind of reality during deep meditation sessions but somehow nothing could replace the comforting familiarity of chatting in Jack's living room.

Chatting to someone who would understand without judgement or ridicule. Someone who would listen and not be surprised by comments relating to strange, unfamiliar worlds beyond the everyday drudge of living. Someone who might know what lies out there in the unknown zone in that strange hidden inner world beyond the blue.

Adam took a deep breath. He'd been staring at the phone for too long and it was making him feel pathetic.

Shit. It's got to be now or never. It had to be done.

He dialled the number.

"Marie?"

A few moments silence.

"Who's that? Is that..?"

"Yeah, it's me. It's Adam. You rang me. A coupla' days ago". There, he'd done it.

Nearly bottled out again, but now he'd done it.

"Oh...yeah. Hi Adam. I...er...I didn't know whether you would ring or not. So, how are you?"

"Good...you?" It was hard to keep his voice even. Needed to sound cool. Offhand.

"Me? Yeah, I'm fine...long time no see."

"Yeah. I've been busy...you know...work and suchlike. Mum said you rang a few days ago. First chance I've had to ring back."

"That's okay. Nothing urgent. I just wanted to find out...well...how you were - that's all."

He'd missed that voice. Soft. Well spoken. He could almost smell the perfume. See into those deep green eyes.

"Yeah, I'm fine. I er..." He wasn't sure which of them was the most lost for words.

God it was embarrassing.

"I was thinking of giving you a call anyway."

"Were you?" Her voice was too quick that time. Too breathless. She must be kicking herself.

"Yeah," he continued more nonchalantly, "You know...just to see how you were. See if you were around...maybe meet up for a coffee or something."

"You hate coffee."

"Yeah. I do..."

Damn. He'd lost it. He heard her laughing at him at the other end of the phone. It made him laugh too. It was so good to hear her voice again. "Yeah, I do hate coffee. I don't know why I said that. Well...meet up for a beer then or whatever sweet sticky goo you like drinking these days."

"Only if you're buying."

He held the phone away from his ear and stared at it as if checking whether phones could simulate smug expressions.

"Yeah...I'm buying" he replied feigning a deep sigh.

"Tomorrow's Friday" she stated matter-of-factly, "So I guess that's out as you'll be drinking with your dreary mates. So how about next week. Tuesday maybe. I think I can slot you into my busy schedule then."

"Next Tuesday is fine" Adam ignored the jibe, "I could pick you up at eight."

"No. Don't do that. Mother still thinks you're an arsehole. Better meet you outside the King's Head instead."

Adam thought for a moment about how to respond to her mother's comment, but then thought better of it. He bit his lip instead.

"King's Head. Right."

"Okay. See you at eight then on Tuesday next?" Marie simpered.

"Yeah. Eight" said Adam then listened to the click at the other end of the line.

He put the phone back in its cradle and stared at it for the second time then shook his head.

"Women..." he muttered to himself, before wandering back up the stairs to his bedroom.

Behind the kitchen door, Carol Sinclair suppressed a grin then licked her finger and scored an imaginary figure one in the air.

"My God Adam," said Jack, clearly in a state of intense shock, "It's Indra's web."

"You what? What are you on about Jack?"

It was the following Sunday afternoon and Jack was in one of his energetic phases. Pacing up and down on his good leg and waving his hands in the air expressively like an eccentric scientist in one of those old black and white films. Adam knew better than to try and stop the flow.

"Indra's web. It's a concept from Hindu and Buddhist mythology. It's a kind of mythic parable. Indra is a Buddhist goddess who symbolises the natural forces that protect and nurture life. The ancient texts describe how Indra's palace is located beneath an enormous cosmic net. It's like a vast spider's web of interconnected strands with brilliant jewels attached to each of the knots of the net. Each pearl-like jewel contains and reflects the image of all the other jewels in the net which sparkle in unison. It's a metaphor that describes how everything is inextricably linked to everything else. It's a beautiful expression of total unity where every gem contains the essence of everything that exists within it."

"Yeah. It was pretty incredible,"

"Adam, it's not just incredible it's one of the most significant breakthroughs I've ever heard in forty years of meditation. Scholars have always believed that Indra's net is either a Buddhist metaphor for ultimate unity, or it is derived from a direct mystical revelation experienced by Indian holy men. No-one ever thought that it was accessible to western meditators - not alone a teenager who has only been practising meditation for less than a year. This is truly unprecedented. Ground-breaking even. I just can't emphasise enough the enormity of this experience that you've had."

Adam shrugged "It just sort of happened Jack. I can't explain it. I had no idea what it all meant."

Jack licked his lips, his eyes darting about in excitement.

"Everything is connected you see Adam. Everything. If only people realised this simple fact, then the way we live our lives would be so different. Most people don't even think about it. We talk of 'coincidence' and 'synchronicity' as though it is something mysterious or weird, something unusual or bizarre when in fact it is the norm. Things are not coincidental by chance, because everything is connected at a deeper level. It's only because the connections are so deep that we aren't consciously aware of them. Science, by definition, is reductionist rather than holistic. We seem to think we can understand the nature of reality better if we dissect it down to its lowest common denominator. And what happens if you dissect something? You kill its holistic essence that's what, or to put it another way, its life force. And its life force is the binding energy that is greater than the sum of its constituent parts. Sometimes you can only understand a 'thing' when it is complete or whole and if you see only a collection of parts then it's like studying random pieces of a jigsaw puzzle with no vision of its totality. The reality, Adam, is that every single one of us is much more than we realise. You are not only much more than skin and bone, but you are also more than your holistic spiritual presence too."

Adam's brow furrowed. For his age, Jack was remarkably animated and eloquent. Some of this stuff, though, was hard to swallow.

"Hold on a minute Jack" he said, "I can appreciate that we are much more than our purely physical bodies. I can also see that we are, as you put it, 'spiritual entities' and have a non-physical presence, but you're hinting at something more than that aren't you?"

Jack continued to shuffle around the room as if the energy of movement was firing his enthusiasm. It was a few moments before he returned warmly to his theme "Yes I am Adam. Things you have always taken for granted are not necessarily just random events. They are part of your history. Not just your current life history but part of a much deeper continuum that you are only dimly aware of, or maybe not even consciously aware of at all."

"Like what? Can you give me an example?"

"Okay...let me think a minute...there was something...now what was it? Ah yes...here's something to make you think. When is your birthday, Adam?"

"May. May 19th to be exact."

Adam thought back to that insignificant day three months ago when his twentieth birthday had come and gone with nothing to show for it except another bad hangover and a tenner from Carol.

And a card from Marie which, come to think of it, he'd never thanked her for.

"So - in astrological terms you are a Taurus."

His mind came back to the present.

"Astrology? Come on Jack, surely you don't believe in all that horoscope rubbish?"

A disembodied voice whispered something in his ear and made him shiver inwardly.

'You have a powerful aura...'

"Suspend disbelief Adam, just for a moment. Astrologically you are a Taurus, right?"

"Yeah..."

"And Taurus is, as you know only too well, the sign of the bull."

Adam stared at Jack incredulously. His mouth suddenly felt very dry "You're not suggesting..."

"...That your recurring nightmares since childhood about bulls is related to your birth sign?"

"Oh, come on Jack. How can a random configuration of stars that some old caveman happens to think looks like a bull, have any connection to my birthday or my nightmares?"

Jack smiled furtively. "I'm not saying anything Adam. I'm simply opening your eyes to certain - how should I put it? - certain synchronicities..."

"But..."

Jack held up his hand to silence Adam's interruption. He walked over to his mahogany writing desk and opened a drawer taking out a sheet of writing paper and a pen. He handed them to Adam.

"Write your name."

"What?"

"Just write your first name on the paper."

Adam shrugged and wrote A-D-A-M on the paper in block capitals.

"Who chose your name Adam?"

"My parents of course."

"And why, exactly, did they choose the name 'Adam?'"

"I'm not sure. They just liked the name, I guess. I dunno - I never asked 'em - what are you getting at Jack?"

"Turn the paper upside down."

Adam's eyes widened quizzically.

"Just do as I say. Turn the paper the other way up. That's it. Now look at the first letter of your name upside down. Focus on the inverted capital 'A'"

Adam stared at the paper "All I can see is an upside-down letter 'A'. What am I supposed to see?"

"What you are seeing Adam is more than the upside-down letter 'A'. It's one of the oldest symbols in the world that for centuries was inverted like this until a couple of centuries ago when someone decided to turn it the other way up and called it an 'A'. It's a very ancient symbol and guess what it symbolised to generations of Sumerians and Romans? Look at it closely Adam - it's the horns of the bull. Letter 'A' is the ancient symbol of the bull."

"But that's..."

"What? Coincidence? Yes maybe, but symbols are the way that man tries to make sense of the world. The bull is a very powerful symbol. There is a traditional Zen story called 'the ten bulls' that is an allegory for spiritual awakening. Zen masters tell the story to their students because stories are often a better way to explain an idea or concept than spelling things out factually. In other ancient cultures the bull symbol represents mans' so called 'astral body'. Do you see what I'm getting at Adam, or should I go on?"

Adam trawled through his mind trying to find a scrap of reason to challenge Jack with. This was too much to take in. It simply didn't make sense. Or more astonishingly, maybe some of it did make a bizarre sort of sense. Adam's natural scepticism was on shaky ground at the moment. He wasn't sure what was real and what was false anymore.

Jack was off again on another monologue.

"What I'm saying Adam is nothing is what it seems in this life. Each and every one of us is an amalgam of all of our previous lives and the sum of all the experiences and karmic lessons from those lives. Our inner self is attuned to certain influences and correspondences and not to others. We adopt certain patterns of behaviour because we are subconsciously drawn to them. Why is it that some of us like to collect specific things like stamps or coins, but not other things? Why do some of us enjoy playing tennis and not cricket? Why do some of us love Mozart but not Beethoven?

The answer is that all of us are subconsciously influenced by our inner selves. When we are born, how we are born, what we are called, who we interact with, what career we follow - all these things are not due to mere coincidence. They all happen for a reason. Once we understand the reasons behind *why* we are *who* we are and why we do what we do then we are much closer to understanding our true inner selves. But even more exciting, once we understand our true inner selves then we can also answer mankind's most enigmatic question - 'What are we here for?'"

Jack's words hung in the air, almost tangible in their portent and potency. Adam broke the silence.

"So - what are we here for then Jack? And what's all this about 'previous lives?'"

Jack tapped his nose "Ah well. That's for you to find out Adam...that's your goal..."

"Aw, c'mon Jack. At least give me a clue."

"Okay" said Jack with a smile, "Meditate."

"That's it? All I need to do is carry on meditating?"

"That's it. Just meditate."

Adam let the word's sink in.

"And the blue?" he asked.

Jack finally sat down, the old chair creaking as he did so. Lady appeared at his feet, purring.

"Ah yes the blue..." said Jack, remembering Adam's original description of the life changing meditation session he had described so vividly. "That has a very important significance. The colour blue is the veil between two worlds. Quite simply it means you have broken through the barrier Adam. It means you have successfully learned to cut through the distractions of trivial mind chatter and now you have entered the realms of deep meditation. Now the journey really begins. Now you are ready to embark on the most incredible quest of your life."

The King's Head wasn't the sort of pub you hung around outside. Unlike the Anchor, which stood proudly on the high street, surrounded by bland neon lit shops, the King's Head skulked gloomily down a badly lit side street. You walked in briskly to either the pool table or darts room, but you didn't stand around on the street because it attracted attention. Meant you were probably a pimp or a dealer or something. Sort of place to avoid eye contact.

Not that it had ever bothered Adam in the past. In fact, he'd often turned up his collar and lit cigarettes in cupped hands in dark corners just for the hell of it. 'Keep 'em guessing' he'd smirked.

Not tonight though.

Tonight, he got there early to avoid Marie having to face the embarrassment and cat calls. He'd even put on a clean denim shirt and a smattering of 'Brut' aftershave. Just hoped none of the lads were around to notice.

Marie was ten minutes late but that was cool. He'd expected it.

She turned the corner some two hundred yards down the road, but he recognised her immediately even in the twilight. It was partly the walk, languorous and sensual, but more the rather engaging habit she had of tossing her hair back from her face every so often. She stopped ten yards away from him, just outside the golden aura of the pub doorway, making

Adam feel momentarily like a gunslinger about to draw. The irony of that image made him smile. Maybe this was some kind of showdown after all. She hesitated, not sure whether she was following him inside the pub or whether he had other plans.

He had other plans.

The kiss on the cheek surprised him. Just a gentle brush of her lips but it was unexpected. Very un-Marie.

"Hi Marie. Good to see you."

"Hello Adam." She was staring him in the eyes. No smile. Just a mischievous curl of the lips. Testing him and sensing his unease. Knowing she looked damn good in a tight red dress under a short white leather jacket.

"So where are you taking me tonight then? Darts? Snooker?"

"How did you guess?"

"Hmm...it wouldn't surprise me...now where was my last special night out with Adam Sinclair...? Let me think..." She fluttered her lashes, "Was it the dog racing or the burger stand?"

He always did love her humour.

"Yeah, very funny...actually..." He linked arms, waiting to see if she pulled away, "I thought we might go to a restaurant."

She pulled away.

"Restaurant! Mister skinflint himself talking about restaurants! You never took me to a restaurant when we were going out together. A hot dog on the street is more your style Adam...won the pools or something have we?"

"Nah. Got a new job though. So, shut up or I might change my mind."

"I'm not missing this opportunity buddy. Where did you have in mind?"

Adam shrugged. "Ricardo's? Y'know that new Italian? S'posed to be good."

"Ricardo's? Bloody hell...lead on Macduff - I'll pay for the taxi."

Adam led the way down the shabby road leaving the glow of the pub behind with its tinny jukebox, pinball machine, clacking billiard balls and chink of glasses.

Halfway to the taxi rank she linked arms with him again.

The good thing about retirement, mused Jack, was that you no longer had to live life by the clock. No more shrill alarms ringing in the early hours followed by the manic rush to be in the office for 9am after negotiating the morning commuter mayhem on the roads or on the train. On the other hand, for retired soldiers, the routine of a regimented lifestyle instilled lifelong habits that were hard to break. Jack thought it was a good compromise to bin the alarm clock, but still rise fairly early each morning and tackle the day's chores quickly and efficiently.

On this particular Tuesday morning, all shopping, cleaning and gardening chores had been completed by 11.30 leaving Jack about an hour before lunch to indulge in something he had been putting off for far too long.

Research.

The house had always been a standard Victorian two-bedroom terrace and was quite adequate for Jack and Ellie's needs. Now that Jack was alone with only Lady for company the second bedroom could easily have become the proverbial storeroom, but not so. Jack's passion for books ensured that every inch of space was fully utilised and over the years his ever-expanding collection had grown to a veritable library of some thousand or so volumes covering as many and varied subjects as a conventional library. And, like a conventional library, every volume was shelved in its rightful place and meticulously catalogued.

Jack climbed the stairs, weaker leg following stronger leg in well-rehearsed synchronisation and opened the spare bedroom door, simultaneously flicking on the light switch.

The room itself was rectangular with bookshelves set against every bit of available wall space. In the middle of the room there was a small reading table with a desk lamp and an old dining chair that Jack had rescued from a junk shop many years ago; Tatty but still functional. On the corner of the table lay a small notebook and a biro. Jack reached into his shirt pocket and retrieved his spectacles placing them over his nose then traced his fingers along the top shelf on the left wall reading the titles on each of the book spines.

It had taken a lifetime to collect this number of books, but the acquisition of every single one had been a labour of love. Probably only a third of them had been purchased new from bookshops. The majority had been picked up second-hand from jumble sales, antique shops or from friends he had known over the years. Many were well thumbed, dog-eared and missing dust covers. Others were virtually untouched. Some were extremely rare.

Jack had organized the shelves by subject matter and had written out small labels which were stuck onto the lip of each shelf. Not that he really needed labels. He knew each book's whereabouts by heart. There was very little fiction among the books - less than half a shelf in fact and some subjects were not even represented. Not that it bothered Jack. As far as he was concerned libraries *should* reflect the tastes of the individual, that's what makes each library so special - so unique.

If anyone knew Jack's background, they might have expected books on military matters or even gardening to predominate but not so. If Jack's library had a 'theme' then it was a blend of history, philosophy, religion and spirituality. The books Jack had collected together over the years represented a wide-ranging wealth of material that tackled some of mankind's deepest questions. Millions of words that Jack had spent over thirty years studying and reflecting upon.

His fingers stopped at a large bound volume which he removed and laid on the desk, settling himself into the wooden chair facing the only window. The pages were yellowed with age and the words block printed with a few crudely drawn diagrams interspersed among the print. Jack adjusted his glasses and turned over the pages stopping when he came to a modern bookmark incongruously marking the passage Jack was seeking. The bedroom door creaked slightly as Lady pushed her way in. Jack leant back in his chair. He could feel the warm fur brush his left leg as he started to read the text.

"Ah, here we are. This is what we wanted" he murmured to the old tabby, "I knew I'd marked it. Yes, this is the one."

Jack started to read the ancient text, stopping only for a moment to remove his glasses and look out of the window as memories began to flood back. Jack had an extraordinary knack of remembering exactly where each of the books had been acquired and this dusty tome was no exception.

It had been in early 1944 when his army unit, the 4th Division of Montgomery's eighth army, had been involved in the offensive against the Germans in Italy. For months Jack and his comrades had been pushing forward towards Rome from the south until they came up against the almost impenetrable wall of mountains known as the Abruzzi range where the Germans had decided to make a firm stand. On top of 500 metres of solid rock stood the ancient monastery of 'Monte Cassino', one of Christianity's most sacred sites founded by Saint Benedict in AD529. An impregnable fortress protected by sheer walls of rock and the treacherous Rapido and Garigliano rivers. For months the Germans had been fortifying this last bastion of the so called 'Gustav line' whilst the Allies pushed ever forward in an almost suicidal attempt to oust the enemy, amid scenes not witnessed since the tragedy of the Somme. Jack's division were bone-weary and in shreds by the time the minefields, barbed wire, and rain-sodden mud fields had been traversed. And casualties were high. Now the bomb cratered ruins of Monte Cassino lay high above them where the last survivors of German Commander Kesselring desperately fought on, despite the relentless bombs and sustained Allied offensive. By the time Cassino was taken thousands lay dead and the old monastery was a scene of utter devastation, bloodshed, and human misery. By the time Jack attained the summit the Poles had secured the monastic buildings and captured the few remaining German conscripts; lads in their early twenties shivering and shaking amongst a wall of corpses. Wandering around the ruins Jack was not only depressed by the futility of war but also the desecration of such a beautiful place. The Monte Cassino monastery once housed one of the world's most important libraries containing over 40,000 rare manuscripts including the works of Tacitus, Ovid, Cicero and Virgil as well as priceless ancient Essene parchments relating to spiritual health and holistic vibrational healing techniques.

Although Jack was not aware of it at the time, mercifully the Germans had the foresight to move around 70,000 of these ancient books to Rome for safe keeping, but even so, many priceless treasures now lay destroyed after months of fighting. There, amongst the rubble and the dead, Jack witnessed the fruits of so much human endeavour symbolically and literally degraded to smouldering ashes. Fragments of wall frescoes, priceless works of Art, sculptures and books lay trampled in the mud, blood and dust among the fallen masonry and barbed wire. The oft-overlooked victims of war.

And it was there among the devastation of brutal conflict and burnt-out buildings that only one or two books had escaped virtually unscathed. It was there in that God-forsaken spot that Jack had had the temerity to salvage the dust covered book that now lay in his hands some thirty years later.

If the old book had once had a title, it was now indecipherable. The cover was badly damaged, and the first two or three pages blackened, but the rest of the book was reasonably intact.

And what an amazing book it was.

The majority of the book dealt with Buddhist contemplation exercises and practices and was clearly a translation of much older texts reaching back as far as the pre-Buddhist 'Bon' culture of western Tibet. Much of it was too esoteric to comprehend and other parts suffered from inadequate or poor translation.

That being said, other sections of the text were extremely poetic and intriguing, and Jack had spent many hours engrossed in the minutiae of these early Buddhist and Bon teachings.

There was one section he had referred back to time and time again. It described in detail the various levels that initiate Buddhist monks had to aspire to when in deep 'contemplation' or 'meditation'. It described how to enter into the unseen spirit realms and how each realm had its own vibrational frequency, identity and landscape as well as its own angels and demons. It described the goals that each mind-traveller must seek to attain and the pitfalls and trials that lie in wait to trap the unwary - very similar in fact, to the more famous Egyptian 'Book of the Dead'. It described both the bliss of spiritual attainment and its antithesis - the horrors manifested by attachment to the material or the temptation to fulfil selfish desires. Jack had first read the words of the sacred teachings as a young soldier, standing in the ruins of war-torn Europe when he had slipped the book into his tunic recognizing its importance even then. Now all these years later he still found it an endless source of inspiration and comfort, as it had been a few weeks after the battle when his right leg had been shattered by an unseen mortar bomb during another bloody attack on a German stronghold a little further north.

He sighed deeply then bought his mind back to the present, re-reading the words once more and nodding as he concurred with the wisdom of the unknown and probably unacclaimed author. Finally, he snapped the book shut and returned it to its allotted space on the shelf. An hour had passed, and Jack had found exactly what he had been looking for. His face was momentarily grim.

"It's just as I thought you know" he informed Lady, staring up at him while alternately licking each of her paws, "This is where the road starts to fork. I sincerely hope to God that he chooses the right path. I really do. To take the wrong turning now could be very dangerous. Very dangerous indeed."

"So" Marie leaned forward across the restaurant table, fiddling with an earring that caught the candlelight and made it glisten, "What's this new job then?"

Adam glanced up from Ricardo's menu realising he didn't know his Tagliatelle from his Cannelloni.

"The pasta's supposed to be good..."

"I'm sure it is. That's not what I asked you."

"Oh, the job..."

Adam shrugged disinterestedly. "I'm working as a cleaner on the Industrial estate. It's only temporary but the money's not bad. Working at Lomax Brothers did my head in. I've also had an interview for the Gazette - on the editorial side."

Marie sat back in her chair, visibly shocked "You?"

"What do you mean 'you?' What's that supposed to mean?"

"It means I never saw you as a hack. I thought you had to be able to spell to be an editor." Marie looked down examining the gloss on her fingernails.

"Very funny".

Their eyes met for a moment across the table. She looked bloody good by candlelight.

Made her skin sort of glow.

Made her lips seem...

Adam looked back to the menu, "So what are you ordering then?"

"You order for me" she said snapping her menu shut.

'*That's bloody typical*', he thought.'*She's not even looked at it.*'

Adam called the waiter over and ordered two pizzas', a lager and a glass of white wine then waited until the waiter was out of earshot.

"So how come you got back in touch then?" he asked seriously, "I thought you'd had it with men. Well, me anyway."

Marie licked her lips and glanced over both shoulders as if checking for eavesdroppers. Her eyes narrowed slightly.

"Actually" she whispered, "I decided I couldn't possibly live without you."

Adam sat upright.

"*Really?*"

"No."

He'd fallen for it, hook, line and sinker.

She burst out laughing while he gaped, trying to think of a witty answer to counter her little joke.

Naturally he couldn't think of one. She was too smart.

It was impossible not to laugh with her. "Ha, ha" he said, "Ha bloody ha."

The pizzas were good. The lager was bearable. The conversation was a little strained but cordial.

Marie sipped her wine slowly while browsing the sweets menu.

"Does a potential editor's salary extend to a sweet then?"

"Sub-editor. You can wash up if you carry on being cheeky."

Marie poked her tongue out at him. Such a simple gesture shouldn't have aroused him, but it did. He shifted in his chair, cleared his throat.

"Doesn't your current boyfriend mind you going out for a meal with your ex then?"

"Excuse me. My ex, ex, ex. Let's get it right Adam. I've been out with three guys since we split up."

"Pardon me for getting it wrong. Well...?"

"No - he doesn't. It was on and off anyway. Guy called Steve..."

"Not...?"

"No, you prat - not your mate Steve Lacey. Think I'd go out with that acidhead? No...another Steve..."

Adam relaxed "Oh."

"You?"

"Uh?"

"Are you going out with anyone?"

"No-one special" He hoped the lie was not too obvious.

Marie changed the subject. "I think I'll go for the cheesecake. You?"

"Nah. Hate puddings."

She laid the sweet menu down on the table. It made the candle flicker between them.

Marie fluttered her eyelashes.

"Your mates say you've made friends with some old bloke on the other side of town."

Adam froze. *How the hell...?*

"Oh yeah?"

"Yeah. They've seen you go off to his house. What's all that about then?"

Shit! Thanks for dropping me in it lads...

He caught the waiter's attention (anything to buy a few moments) then ordered a cheesecake and asked for the bill.

"There's this guy called Jack I visit sometimes."

"You didn't strike me as the 'meals on wheels' type."

"Nah. It's nothing like that. He's an amazing bloke. We talk..."

"What about?"

"Anything. Everything."

Marie played with a teaspoon.

"Including meditation apparently," she said casually.

"How the...?" Adam was visibly rattled.

"Your Mother told me. When I called to speak to you a few days ago."

Interfering old cow!

"She shouldn't have said anything. She doesn't know what she's on about. Take no notice..."

"Why? It's no big deal, is it? Why do you react like that?"

"It's none of her business. Nor yours!"

"Well pardon me for breathing."

Adam realised he was overreacting. He took a deep breath then smiled awkwardly.

"Look. It's not important. Forget it. He's just a friend that's all. We talk about loads of stuff."

"Okay. Take it easy..."

The sweet arrived and Adam glanced at the bill, added a small tip, and shoved a few notes into the waiter's hand. He waited while Marie tucked into the cheesecake in a way that only women do. She wiped the crumbs from around her mouth with a napkin.

"Look...I'm sorry" he said, face reddening.

"No problem. I'm sorry I asked."

They stared at each other for a few moments. Adam looked away first staring at the candle that had now burned down to the lip of the silver candle holder. A rivulet of red wax trickled onto the white tablecloth.

"I'll call a taxi" he said.

"Adam?"

"Yeah?"

"Thanks for a lovely meal. It was really nice to see you again." This time her voice was soft and sincere, no hint of sarcasm or mockery. It was how he remembered her voice.

"It was good to see you again too Marie" he said, "Maybe we could, you know, meet up again sometime."

"Yes. I'd like that."

He helped her into her coat, accidentally brushing her arm and catching the intoxicating scent of perfume in the process. His favourite. The one he always asked her to wear...

The waiter opened the door and Adam followed Marie onto the deserted street. It was much darker now. Large spots of rain were starting to explode onto the pavement.

"Forget the taxi" she said softly, linking arms with him, "You can walk me home."

It was the photograph that did it.

A little dog-eared and faded now where it had been inadvertently left in sunshine on a dusty windowsill, but still treasured, nonetheless. Didn't seem like it was fourteen years ago it had been taken. She could remember it as though it were yesterday. It had been one of those idyllic summer days that stayed in the memory because it represented a time when she had never felt happier. It had been a very 'English' day. The sort of day that picnics and seasides' were designed for. Innocent days full of love and laughter. Days made for children.

He was six years old when the photograph was taken. She remembered the day very distinctly. It was Gordon, her husband, who had suggested a picnic in the park followed by strawberries and ice-cream and Adam had screamed with delight and gone to find the football he'd been given for his birthday just a few days before. Funny how she still remembered things like that. It was at the time that his nightmares were keeping him awake and crying at night and she felt so helpless in not being able to comfort him. His new teddy bear, Benny, had, admittedly helped a bit, and had given him some consolation, but as a mother she was desperate to find some way to ease his suffering.

But on that particular day, the day they'd all gone to the park, and she'd photographed him sitting up on his dad's shoulders, both of them so genuinely happy in each other's company, everything in the world seemed so right, so special.

Carol put the photograph back on the shelf with a sigh.

Memories...

Now all these years later her son was twenty and her dear husband was dead. Here she was going on forty and up to her eyes in nothing but dreary housework. She sat down on the corner of Adam's bed and turned off the vacuum cleaner. It could wait. She was pleased that Adam was talking to Marie again. Marie was the only hope as far as Carol was concerned. A sensible girl, down to earth, practical - everything that Adam was not.

If only he'd listen to Marie instead of those useless friends of his whose only motives in life seemed to revolve around smoking or drinking. Well at least he'd bothered to go for that job at the local paper. Not that he was capable of sticking at any job mind you...

She looked around his room at the pop posters, science fiction books and records and wondered what went on inside that head of his sometimes. At times he could be reasonable. Well, as reasonable as testosterone fired-up young men can be - but at other times...

She knew that some people found him a little odd. Christ, she found him a little odd herself at times and she was his mother. But then again, there were times that he said weird things or looked at her in a way that made her uneasy. Nothing specific. Nothing threatening in any way. Nothing you could put your finger on. *Just something deep in his eyes...*

Something that had been there right from the start - from the time he was born that she could sense, but no-one else could.

Well apart from Gramps maybe, but then his mind was pretty befuddled most of the time these days...

Her misty eyes drifted to the bedroom window. A light September rain was starting to coat the windowpane. A sure sign that summer was virtually over, and the long depressing days of winter were looming. That thought, and the awareness of unfinished housework made Carol feel suddenly very depressed. She'd made a promise to herself after Gordon had died that she would forge her own future rather than live through their son. She'd get a job, stand on her own two feet and walk the streets with her head held high.

Oh yeah?

Easier said than done...

No. There was no time for self-pity. Adam would be okay. Deep down he was just like his father. The father he had barely known. Deep down he was a good person, and she must support him.

Whatever the future held.

Carol stood up and smoothed her skirt then turned the vacuum back on. She started to clean Adam's bedroom carpet again and tried to dismiss all the idle thoughts rattling around in her head. Most of them soon faded away as the reality of housework took over.

All except one thought.

It was something to do with Adam's room. Not the physical room itself; it was the atmosphere in the room.

It was somehow different from usual.

Nothing she could make any sense of...

...but definitely very different...

The Anchor public house seemed more crowded tonight. Adam pushed his way back from the bar through the throng of under-age drinkers and squinted through the smoke pall. Steve, Danny and Mick had somehow found a small beer-stained table to sit around on which Adam gently lowered the four pints he had barely managed to avoid spilling.

"Cheers Adam."

"Cheers mate."

"Here's to..." Steve Lacey raised his pint and racked his brains for an original thought, "Here's to the next Reading festival!"

Four pint-glasses chinked in unison "Reading!"

"I've heard they're trying to book Genesis to headline this year" said Mick, "Ace!"

"I don't care who's playing" belched Danny, "It's just a bloody great crack...well, for most of us..."

Three pairs of eyes fixed on Adam.

"Yeah. Great" said Adam stonily, "Get beaten up by some sadistic bastards, have your wallet nicked, end up in hospital, just miss getting cautioned by the pigs because you've a couple of ounces of dope in your pocket and then split up with your girlfriend. Yeah. Fucking great festival."

The other three roared with laughter. Not that Adam wanted or expected pity. He laughed with them.

"So - you up for it this year?" Steve asked Adam directly.

Adam shrugged "I dunno...maybe."

The lads put their pints down on the table.

"You're kidding me now" said Danny with genuine concern.

"No seriously" said Adam, "I'm not sure. Maybe..."

"But as the guys said, it's a gas" said Mick, nodding towards Steve and Danny, "Come on man. I couldn't make it last year. I'm not missing it this year. Nor should you. Anyway, I could do with you being around. You're pretty good at helping the stoned and bewildered."

The lads roared again as they thought back to Mick's rantings and ravings at the 'happening.'

"You were just unlucky last year" added Steve philosophically, "Could've been anybody they beat up. You were just in the wrong place at the wrong time. It won't happen again. You'll be fine."

"Yeah, I know. It's just that I'm not sure whether I'll be going yet."

"Don' be an idjit" added Danny "What's da problem wid ya?"

"There's no problem. It's just that I'm not sure whether or not I want to go this year or not, that's all. I know it would be a great laugh and all that - and I'm not worried about getting beaten up or anything - it's just...."

"Jus' what?"

Adam shrugged again. He wasn't sure what he was trying to say himself. Couldn't rationally explain why he felt so indifferent to the festival he usually loved so much.

"It's just that I'm getting into some other stuff lately...you know..." He felt his face reddening. Felt embarrassed which was crazy. Now he was wishing he hadn't said anything.

Steve raised an eyebrow "Stuff?"

"It's not important. I'm taking some time out to think that's all. Don't you guys ever think about things that are going on around you?"

Danny shrugged "Loike what f'rinstance?"

"Like stuff outside of Woodsham. You know. Other places. Other ideas. Other experiences..."

Steve took a deep mouthful of the cold amber beer and then sat looking into it. When he spoke, it was slow and emotionless. "Adam" he said, "I don't what the problem is man, but you're getting fuckin' boring lately."

Adam stared at them all individually, but they all avoided eye contact. He felt butterflies in his stomach.

Saying nothing, he lifted his pint off the table and downed it in one.

Jack was waiting at the park gates, just as he had promised, leaning on his trusty walking stick. He was obviously in a jovial mood. Adam had wanted to talk, and it was Jack's suggestion to meet in the park for a change.

"Didn't I say it was going to turn into one of those splendid Autumn afternoons? Just look at the colours of the trees. I've always said that a walk in the park does body and soul the power of good."

"Hi Jack" smiled Adam, glancing nervously around. Wouldn't do for any of his mates to see him taking a stroll in the park with an old guy. It would raise too many awkward questions.

Oh well, what the hell. Too late now. Might as well get on with it.

"Have you been here before?" enquired Jack with genuine interest. Adam thought for a moment about the time he got wasted on speed and had pranced around the park bandstand like an idiot making the lads cry with laughter, the sneaky fags behind the bushes where the park keeper couldn't see them, and the used condoms thrown irreverently among the spring flowers. Then he remembered his more recent visit with that icy feeling up his spine when he'd been skimming stones with Steve Lacey. "Yeah. Coupla times" he mumbled with a shrug.

They walked in silence for a few minutes. Jack admiring the trees and the fallen leaves as they crunched underfoot.

Adam thought about Marie.

"So" said Jack, at last "You wanted to talk about your progress with the meditation."

You had to take your hat off to Jack. Sometimes he could ramble on philosophically for hours - other times he cut to the chase.

"Yeah" said Adam, wondering where to start.

Jack pointed to a park bench with his walking stick, and they turned towards it. The bench stood on a small rise overlooking a wide expanse of parkland. Jack sat down with a sigh and made himself comfortable. Adam sat down beside him and plunged his cold hands deep into the pockets of his leather bomber jacket. He knew that Jack was waiting for him to spill the beans.

"I suppose I just needed to tell you about how I'm feeling" said Adam staring out across the Victorian landscaped gardens and lake. "It's not so much the meditation itself - that's going reasonably well at the moment...it's other stuff."

"Go on."

"It's like nobody else understands what I'm up to - apart from you that is. They think I'm some sort of weirdo...y'know - friends and family. They don't understand meditation and what it's all about...they think it's something taboo or evil or suchlike. Either that or it's just something that monks or hermits do for a living in Himalayan caves - but not ordinary people like you and me."

Adam glanced at Jack to see if there was a reaction, but Jack was still staring straight ahead admiring the view.

"So," said Adam, continuing, "I feel that there's no point in explaining what I'm doing or trying to justify it because all I get is ridicule. The trouble is I seem to be in too deep now and I'm losing some of the respect I used to have."

"Respect?" said Jack. The word seemed to hang motionless in the air between them.

"Well yeah, like with my mates and um...my girlfriend...they know that I'm into meditation and stuff, or at least suspect it, and now they look at me like I'm losing my marbles. Makes me think I should just forget the whole thing and go back to how I used to be...y'know 'jack the lad'- no offence Jack! - 'Life n' soul of the party' and all that. I'm getting too serious lately. I need to cut back on all this meditation and start going out with the boys more. Have a laugh. Get pissed. Enjoy myself like I used to."

He waited for a response. Waited for Jack to tell him to grow up and focus on what is important and not to be so frivolous and shallow. Instead, Jack just nodded sympathetically, then nudged Adam and pointed with his walking stick at some squirrels running across the grassy expanse only a few feet away. Simple creatures enjoying what they do naturally.

"So - what do you think?" said Adam after a few minutes of silence, desperately needing to know what Jack felt about the situation. Wanting some guidance.

"I think" replied Jack, "That only you can make the decision as to how you want to manage your own life. It's important to listen to other people and learn from them but at the end of the day only you can make the really important decisions that matter to you. Some people choose to spend their whole life having fun and others choose a life of meditation and seclusion. Perhaps both choices are too extreme - and a healthy balance is called for. We must all follow our own hearts Adam rather than follow the crowd. There is an old saying that I quite like: 'When ego rules, we live as fools. When ego dies, our ways are wise.'"

Adam stared at Jack, "Where did that quote come from?"

Jack smiled and tapped his head.

"From me. It's an old saying only because I first said it a long time ago!"

"You never fail to surprise me" Adam responded, "But what about *me* - what should I do Jack?"

Jack eased himself to his feet. "Let's walk through the trees awhile Adam and think as we walk. Tell me, have you ever heard the story of the five golden feathers?"

"I don't think so. What is it? A fairy story or something?"

"Yes, I suppose it is some sort of fairy tale. It's a story my mother told me when I was a child. She learned it from her grandmother. It made a big impression on me. Would you like to hear it?"

Adam shrugged, wondering where Jack was going with this.

"Yeah. Why not? Long time since someone's told me a good bedtime story."

Jack led Adam down a grassy slope into a clump of sun dappled woodland awash with fallen leaves. Slivers of watery sunlight cut through the branches. "Sometimes things are better explained through metaphor or allegory than being spelled out too rationally or scientifically" said Jack matter of factly, "If you understand what I mean."

"Yeah, I understand what you mean" said Adam, "What's the story about?"

"I suppose it's a story that answers questions," said Jack.

"What questions?"

"Mostly the one's you haven't asked yet," said Jack.

Adam stared at Jack with a mixture of incredulity and resignation.

"Hmm, why did I know you were going to say something like that?" laughed Adam; "Okay then Jack, let's hear the story of the five golden feathers…"

"Now" said Jack, stroking the stubble on his chin, "let me think. How does the story start?"

"How about 'Once upon a time'" offered Adam raising his eyebrows with mock cynicism.

"Ah yes...of course" responded Jack, with a wink. "Thank you, Adam. Once upon a time there was a wealthy merchant called Ramatha who lived in a fine house and who had made lots of money by buying goods at the lowest prices from poor traders and selling them at high prices to richer folk. He liked to keep all his money in a pouch attached to his belt so that he could always feel it next to his skin. He was very successful in all his endeavours but cared little for those from whom he made profit and always yearned for something more in life. For once he had accumulated sufficient wealth to live comfortably, he started to get bored and looked for other ways to enjoy his success.

One day he was following a path through a dense forest on his way to sell his most expensive goods at a trading fair when he heard a strange wailing sound coming from behind a large oak tree. Overcome with curiosity, he left the path and went to look behind the tree where he was shocked to find a golden bird trapped in a snare. He put down his sack of goods then bent down and forced open the snare thus releasing the bird from pain and setting it free. After a few moments the bird stopped wailing and to Ramatha's amazement started speaking to him.

'Thank you, kind sir for setting me free' the bird said, 'I must now grant you a wish that will give you your heart's desire as a way of expressing my gratitude. Tell me what it is that you desire most.'

Ramatha thought hard for a few moments and imagined to himself how good it would feel to be not just moderately wealthy, but to be the richest merchant in all the land.

After a few moments of thought he said, 'I would like you to lead me to the world's greatest treasure.'

'If that truly is your heart's desire' said the bird, 'Then I can show you the way to the world's greatest treasure, but you will need to undertake a journey to find it. Are you prepared to take that journey?'

'I am,' said the merchant.

'Then I will tell you what to do,' said the bird. 'You must follow the path you are now taking through the forest until you come to a town called Saratan. Beyond the town you will see some mountains which you must cross. You must then take a boat across the 'Sea of Dreams' to a place called the 'Land of Shifting Sands'. In the middle of the Land of Shifting Sands you will find a single steep hill. On the top of the hill is a castle. In the uppermost turret of the castle lies the world's greatest treasure'.

'I see' said Ramatha 'But how can I be sure of finding such a place?'

'Listen carefully' said the bird, 'Because in your heart I know you are a good man, I am going to give you five of my golden tail feathers to take on your journey. Whenever you are lost or in danger you must hold up one of the golden feathers until it catches the wind and then call for me. I will then come to aid you on your quest. You must take care however to use the feathers wisely. Five feathers are all I can give and not one feather more.'

Then the bird plucked five golden feathers from its own tail and held them out and Ramatha took them.

'Thank you, golden bird' he said, 'I understand, and I am now ready to undertake the journey.'

Ramatha said goodbye to the bird who flew off over the treetops. He placed the five golden feathers carefully into his sack and then continued his journey along the forest path until at dusk he finally arrived at the town called Saratan. By the time he found his way through the winding streets to the middle of Saratan it was too dark to see the mountains beyond the town, so he decided to find an inn and stop for the night.

There were some men playing cards in the town square in the middle of Saratan so Ramatha stopped to ask them if there was an inn nearby. When the men saw the merchants sack full of expensive objects, they grew envious and asked Ramatha to show them all his wares. Ramatha showed the men everything in his sack and asked them if they would like to buy anything. But the men were very poor and could not afford to pay the prices demanded. When Ramatha refused to lower the prices, the men said that if he was wealthy enough to stay at an inn then he should be prepared to sell his goods for less money to poorer folk. But Ramatha refused to lower the price and was rude to the men, so they started to chase him down a small, cobbled alleyway which led to a brick wall. When Ramatha realised he was trapped and that the crowd of men would soon be upon him he pulled one of the golden feathers from his sack and held it up above his head until it caught the wind. 'Golden bird' he called, 'please rescue me from this place for I am about to be attacked.'

In an instant, as if from nowhere, the golden bird swooped down, retrieved the golden feather in his beak and then made a gap appear in the wall for Ramatha to step through. As soon as Ramatha had stepped through the gap in the wall it closed behind him and the crowd of men that were chasing him all ran into the brick wall and wondered how Ramatha had disappeared. On the other side of the wall Ramatha found a beautiful inn with a roaring fire where he enjoyed a pleasant stay for the night.

The next day Ramatha looked out from the window of the inn and, in the distance, saw the mountains that the golden bird said he must cross. So, he set off early, carrying his sack of goods and the four remaining golden feathers.

The mountains were very high and covered in snow and for two days Ramatha climbed and climbed but the sack was so heavy it slowed him down and it began to get so cold that the silk cloak that he wore was not enough to keep him warm and he began to shiver as the cold winds tore into him. As night approached, Ramatha began to lose his way and was scared that he might freeze to death on the mountain. In desperation, he took the second of the golden feathers from the sack and held it up so that the freezing wind blew through it and then called out at the top of his voice, 'golden bird, I am lost, and I am cold, please help me.'

Just as before, the golden bird instantly swooped down from the sky and took the golden feather in his beak before disappearing again. But as he did so, the merchant saw the glow of a fire in a little hut just a little way ahead. He knocked on the door of the warm hut and a little old shepherd opened the door and beckoned Ramatha to sit by the fire then gave him some hot soup and showed him to a warm bed.

In the morning Ramatha thanked the shepherd, then looked out again at the snow-covered mountains and raging winds. 'Kind shepherd' he said, 'A golden bird led me to your door when I was lost and frozen - perhaps you can help me on my journey to find the castle on the hill that lies across the mountains and the Sea of Dreams.'

The old shepherd replied that he would give Ramatha the warmest sheepskin coat that he had ever made which would keep out the harshest weather and that he could borrow the shepherd's most faithful sheepdog to lead the merchant down from the mountains to the Sea of Dreams.

Ramatha was overwhelmed by the shepherd's kindness and asked if there was something he could do for the shepherd in return. The shepherd replied that Ramatha would not be able to complete his quest while burdened down with such a heavy sack, so he asked Ramatha to leave the sack behind and the shepherd would then distribute all the goods to the poor people of Saratan.

At first Ramatha was reluctant to part with all the expensive goods that he had hoped to sell, but he knew that without the sheepskin coat and the guide dog he would not be able to continue. He thought about it for a moment and then realised how foolish he was being. At the end of the quest, when he found the castle, he would be in possession of the world's greatest treasure so what did it matter if he was to lose a single sack of trinkets? He therefore agreed and handed over his sack of goods to the shepherd, keeping only his pouch of coins and the three remaining golden feathers.

Ramatha said goodbye to the shepherd, put on the warm sheepskin coat and followed the shepherd's dog along the many miles of mountain track which eventually led him to a beach that looked out over the Sea of Dreams. The dog led Ramatha along the beach until he came to a rowing boat with a small sail. The dog then turned away and ran back towards the mountains, his task completed. Ramatha pushed the small boat into the surf then climbed aboard and raised the sail. Soon the wind picked up, and Ramatha watched until the land disappeared from sight, and he was alone, sailing across the Sea of Dreams.

The sea was much wider than Ramatha expected and for three days he continued to sail westward, but soon the wind died down and the boat started to drift much more slowly. There was no food or drink on the boat and by the end of the third day Ramatha was starving and in desperate need of fresh water to slake his thirst. Eventually he became so hungry and thirsty he could bear it no longer. He held up the third golden feather to catch the sea breeze and called out in a parched voice for the golden bird.

'Golden bird' he cried, 'I am weak from hunger and thirst - please help me.'

No sooner had the words been uttered than the golden bird appeared from the blue sky and took the feather from the merchant's hand. Moments later a magnificent galleon appeared on the horizon and sailed towards Ramatha's small boat. It put down anchor and the captain of the ship called down to Ramatha asking him if all was well. Ramatha explained that he was trying to reach the Land of Shifting Sands and had been sailing without food or water for three days. The captain said he would tie Ramatha's small boat to the back of the galleon and tow him ashore to the Land of Shifting Sands even though the ship was originally going in the opposite direction. The captain said that although there were only enough provisions for the ship's crew, he would be prepared to give Ramatha all the food and water he needed in exchange for a purse of coins to help pay the crew and to feed their families.

'But this is all the money I possess' said Ramatha, 'It is everything I have gained from a lifetime of buying and selling my goods.'

Then Ramatha once again remembered that very soon he would be in possession of the world's greatest treasure so what did it matter if he no longer had a purse full of coins? So, he agreed, handed over all the coins from his coin purse and in return was given all the food and water he needed.

The next day he stepped ashore at the Land of Shifting Sands and thanked the captain and his crew who then turned the ship around and set off back to sea. Ramatha pulled his little boat up on to the sand and then set off to walk across a dusty flat desert where a constant breeze caused the sand to swirl around his feet.

For three long days Ramatha walked across the desert until his fine buckled shoes fell apart and his sheepskin coat became torn by the sharp thorns of cactuses and bushes. Then his food and water ran out and he was forced to eat berries and drink from pools of mud. He started to feel very tired and then very feverish. Eventually, he felt so bad that he could only crawl along the sand which turned his sheepskin coat and all his other fine clothes to rags. He felt sure he was going to die. When the pain and suffering became unbearable, he reached into his pocket for the last two golden feathers and held one of them feebly above his head. 'Golden bird' he called breathlessly, 'Help me please - I am weak and ill and about to die.'

As before, the golden bird appeared as if from nowhere and plucked the fourth feather from the merchant's trembling hand.

A few moments later Ramatha felt a hand on his shoulder and looked up at a man wearing robes and a turban standing beside a camel laden with provisions. The man put water to Ramatha's lips then helped him to his feet. The man studied Ramatha carefully then mixed some herbs in a small wooden bowl then made him swallow the mixture. At once the fever subsided and Ramatha felt much better. The man reached into a bag on the side of the camel and gave Ramatha some leather sandals to put on his sore feet and a shawl to protect him from the intensity of the sun's rays.

'How ever can I thank you?' said Ramatha when his strength returned, 'I am seeking the hill with the castle upon it, but now I have no sack of goods to sell, I have no money, I have no fine clothes, I have nothing left apart from one golden feather which is all I can give you in return for your kindness.'

'I want nothing in return' said the nomad, 'We are all brothers in this world and is our duty to help each other in every way we can and seek no reward. The hill you are searching for is over there - look carefully and you can see the castle on the top. Good luck in your quest my friend.'

The nomad climbed back onto his camel and waved goodbye. Ramatha watched him ride away across the desert then turned towards the hill that the nomad had pointed out to him.

Very soon Ramatha arrived at the foot of the hill and began to climb. It was very steep, but before long he had reached the top and stood before a magnificent towering castle. The merchant walked up to the huge wooden door and knocked but there was no answer. He tried pushing on the door and found it opened easily so he stepped inside. Once inside the castle, he expected to find lots of wonderful things and many fine rooms but all he found was a huge winding staircase that seemed to ascend into the sky. He remembered that the room with the treasure was to be found at the top of the tower, so he began to climb the stone stairs.

Up and up the stairs curved so that his legs soon became weary. There were many times when he thought he had reached the top but still the stairs continued until he could barely lift one leg in front of the other. Finally, when he was totally exhausted, the stairs came to a stop and Ramatha stood before another wooden door. At last, after all his adventures, he had finally reached the object of his heart's desire - the room that contained the world's greatest treasure. He tried to turn the handle but it would not turn so he knocked on the door but there was no answer. There was no keyhole and no key. His eyes began to fill with tears, and he began to weep because he had finally reached the end of his quest - but the door would not open. He started to beat the door with his hands and the door moved a little, so he beat the door harder and harder with his fists until his hands started to bleed and little by little the door began to yield.

Ramatha continued to beat the wooden door until he was totally exhausted and his blood, tears and sweat ran down his body. After many painful hours, the door at last fell backwards into the room with a loud crack. A cloud of dust enveloped him as he stepped forward into the gloom. As the dust settled, his eyes strained to see the piles of gold and diamonds that he had come to find, but to his horror the cold stone room seemed to be completely empty. He stared around the empty room in disbelief, falling to his knees in despair and wiping away the tears with his aching hands, crying out that he had been such a fool to have undertaken such a fruitless quest that had cost him all his worldly goods, his money, his clothes and nearly his life.

Then out of the corner of his eye he saw something moving and glittering in the darkness and out of the shadows stepped the golden bird that he had set free.

'Golden bird' he said wearily, 'I have followed all your instructions and after many hardships I have finally reached the top of the castle where you said I would find the world's greatest treasure. But there is nothing here. You have deceived me. This room is empty.'

'Do you have the last golden feather?' asked the bird.

Ramatha reached into the shawl the nomad had given him and retrieved the last of the five golden feathers.

'Yes,' said the merchant, 'But what use is a single golden feather to me? I have lost everything else that I owned on this journey.'

'The last golden feather gives you a choice' said the golden bird, 'You can choose, if you so wish, to return to your fine house and your life as a successful merchant and carry on your life as you did before, selling your goods to the poor. If you make this choice, then you will never remember me and you will never remember this journey. It will be as a dream that never really happened.'

'And my other choice?' asked Ramatha.

'Your other choice' said the bird, 'Is to keep the last golden feather close to your heart for the rest of your life which will remind you of everything you have learned during this long journey.'

'But what about the treasure?' bemoaned the merchant.

'Ah' said the bird, 'What I hope you have learned during your journey is truly the world's greatest treasure and worth more than all the gold and silver in the universe.'

The confused merchant sat down in the dust for a few moments with his head in his hands and thought very carefully about all the things that had happened to him on his journey and about the words the golden bird had said.

'Golden bird' he said at last, 'I will keep the feather.'"

Jack stopped in his tracks and smiled at Adam. "Good story?"

Adam stood for a moment savouring the scene. The autumnal colours of the woods, the carpet of leaves, the last rays of the afternoon sun filtering through the branches of the old oak trees, the soft cool breeze that carried occasional bird song and the old man with a gammy leg and a twinkle in his eye. The image now imprinted forever in his mind like a treasured photograph. It was a special moment.

"Yes" said Adam, hearing his own voice as though it came from somewhere far away, "It's a good story. Where did it come from originally?"

"Originally it was called the 'Secret of the Golden Flower' but over many years it has been adapted and refined. It purports to derive from an ancient Chinese mystic called Lu Yan, a Taoist Alchemist. At least that is what my grandmother told my mother and I have no reason to disbelieve her."

"Wow. That's amazing."

"And tell me Adam, does it answer your question? About what you should do for the best I mean."

Adam stood silent for a moment, biting on his lip. Trying to put all the pieces of a bizarre mental jigsaw into place.

A choir of discarnate whisperers were chanting something inside his head.

When ego rules, we live as fools. When ego dies, our ways are wise...

"Do you know Jack" he said at last, "I think it does. Thank you."

"Then let's get back before the park closes" said Jack turning around and leaning on his walking stick for support, "Lady will be wanting her supper."

Carol Sinclair clutched her teacup in both hands as though drawing warmth into her body via her fingertips.

It was raining again, and she had been leaning against the small kitchen work top staring out of the rain-streaked window at nothing in particular, for far too long. The garden had been largely untended since Gordon had died. Okay, so she mowed the small rectangle of grass every now and then and pulled out a few weeds, but that was about it. Lost interest really.

She sighed deeply, took a sip of sweet hot tea, and forced herself to re-examine the situation once again.

There had to be something wrong. Teenage lads don't hibernate for weeks on end, alone in their bedrooms. There must be a reason. Surely it wasn't just this meditation lark he'd briefly mentioned? His best mates, particularly Steve Lacey and Danny Mc Connell, were as puzzled as she was. Not so long ago, Adam was out most of the day and night and she had fretted like all mothers do about where he was and what he was up to. Now she had to practically force him to go outside the front door.

Could it be drugs? No, that didn't make sense. If it was drugs, he would be out trying to conceal the evidence. Anyway, he seemed to be smoking a lot less at home recently, which was good. She'd had a quiet word with Steve and Danny's parents, but they hadn't been much help. They'd told her to make the most of it as they hadn't a clue what their respective sons were up to most of the time. Alternatively, could it be girlfriend trouble? That was possible. Adam's relationship with Marie had always been something of a roller coaster but there was a bond between them that ran pretty deep from what she could see. It had taken Adam a lot of time to get around to confessing that he'd split up with Marie at Reading though he'd been back in touch a couple of times. Anyway, after bumping into Marie at the chemists Carol had a much better idea of what was going on. But girl trouble? No, that didn't make sense either. Teenage lads' hormones are on overdrive most of the time. He'd be out at the local disco sniffing around for some new dolly if there was a problem in the girl department.

She'd also noticed that he'd not mentioned the recurring bull nightmares for the last few weeks. At least that was some good news. Those nightmares had always bothered him, and she felt helpless whenever he complained about them. Maybe they had finally gone for good? Only time would tell.

And who exactly was this Jack guy that Adam seemed to have befriended? Could that have anything to do with Adam's hermit like existence? Adam had mumbled something about this old chap teaching him to meditate or such like, but surely teenage lads don't usually want to spend time with seventy-year-old pensioners?

No. Something was up – but what exactly?

She'd noticed the new 'Do Not Disturb' sign he'd drawn on a piece of cardboard and hung over the bedroom door handle. What was all that about? And why was there always that new and strange fragrant smell in his bedroom?

It used to be the stale odour of stubbed-out cigarettes in the ash tray by his bed, but this was different. Strange and spicey but pleasant enough. Must be those hippy joss sticks she'd found in his bedside cabinet drawer.

At first, she'd thought that he might be suffering from some sort of mild depression. After all he'd been asking a lot about his dad recently. But that didn't add up either. Every time he'd popped downstairs for mealtimes, or to use the phone, he'd seemed quite chirpy. Chatty even. Making jokes. He even seemed to be optimistic about the future despite the uncertainty of where he was going with his life. Carol's intuition, normally reliable and often spot on, had failed her this time. Something strange was going on, but she had to admit that this time she simply hadn't a clue what it was.

She stood up straight, finished the last dregs of tea and slipped the cup into the cold washing up water in the sink then gripped the edge of the stainless-steel work top tightly as if flexing her muscles for battle.

No - this time she'd have to tackle the issue head on. Ask him straight.

The furrowed brow was replaced with the set jaw of a woman determined to find out the truth.

"Adam" she yelled upstairs as loud as she could "Can you pop downstairs for a minute? I need to talk to you."

It was like drowning in a way.

Drowning but without the suffocation or the fear.

It was the feeling of sinking into something that was thicker than air and with the buoyancy of water but very different from either of those mediums. It was also like drowning because there was always a flurry of millions of bubbles streaming upwards while you sank downward into a whirlpool of silky blue, feeling as though you were passing through a sea of downy petals or being caressed by the hands of angels.

It took time to get to that exquisite feeling though. First you had to concentrate, lose touch with reality, quieten your inner mind-chatter then wade through the billowing clouds of white nothingness.

But if you persevered for long enough then the reward was there.

And it was always worth fighting for.

The deep blue.

Beyond the blue, if you were *really, really,* lucky, lay the gate leading to…

…to an even deeper place.

It was the 'gate' that Jack had stood in front of many times before but had never quite had the courage to go through. Thirty years of meditation in which he had learned so very much and found so much inner peace. And yet every time he reached the gate he faltered and found an excuse not to go further. On some occasions he had started pushing the metaphysical gate open in his mind so that he could take a sneaky peak beyond it. But he had never ever taken the next brave step.

He often wondered why he stopped at that point.

Fear?

Possibly. Or perhaps it was the inner strength required to move into unknown territory?

Quite likely.

Today was no different. He'd gone through the usual motions. Traversed all the usual landmarks and now, once more, stood on the threshold looking through the gate. Trying to see something - anything - that might give him a clue to help Adam on his own inner journeys.

But for some reason there was nothing but more shimmering shades of blue on the other side of the gate. Enticing, bewitching and utterly beautiful. It almost seemed to beckon and tempt you in - as if some unseen force was trying to suck your non-physical body through the gateway into a deeper hidden world where more wonders lay in wait to be revealed.

Part of Jack wanted to succumb to the temptation. To step forward into the unknown and let fate take over. He wanted to do it because he knew with complete certainty that very soon Adam would be taking the same step into the unknown and when that moment came, he, Jack, would be powerless to help or advise because this was somewhere that he had no knowledge of.

All he knew was that beyond the gate, beyond the blue, was a deeper realm where only a few enlightened souls had ever ventured. A place where, ancient Buddhist tradition maintained, one would eventually come face to face with their own destiny.

Adam slumped into the threadbare armchair that had been in the same position in the lounge for as long as he could remember. Carol had turned off the TV (always a sure sign she had something serious to say) and stood in front of the blank screen, hands on hips.

"You wanted me for something?" Adam already had a strong intuition what this was about.

Carol tried to put on a casual detached air, but it didn't convince either of them.

"Well, it's nothing really" she lied, "I was just wondering why you seem to be spending so much time hibernating in your bedroom? You used to be out all the time and now you seem to be always shutting yourself away. Is there something the matter? Is it something we should talk about?"

Adam looked away self-consciously. It was at times like these he just wanted to hug her. But hugging your mum when you are twenty is not cool. Instead, he shrugged non-commitally.

"Oh, come on Adam - don't mess me about. What's going on?"

"Nuthin'".

"Nothing? Pull the other one. You've been sitting in that room with the light off for hours and burning those...those..."

"Incense sticks."

"Incense sticks...yes. What's all that about? Is it to do with this meditation?"

"Oh that..." He was up against the ropes. Might as well come clean. "Yeah. Yeah. It's to do with meditation. It works better in darkness and with incense."

"But why are you spending so much time meditating? It's not healthy. You need to get out in the fresh air more. Get more exercise. It can't be good for you to be cooped up in the dark like that night after night."

"You'd rather I was down the Anchor with the lads?"

Carol rolled her eyes. "That's not what I meant - and you know it. So...tell me...what's all this meditation about then?"

Adam was caught wrong-footed. How the hell could he even begin to explain something that he was still trying desperately to understand himself.

Carol continued to stand there, arms folded, fingers drumming her upper arm.

"It's just something I'm into" he mumbled, "S'not like drugs or anything. It's harmless. I'll lend you a book about it if you want. It explains what it's all about."

Carol stared at him for a moment. Trying to look him square in the eyes.

"Has this old man...?"

"Jack?"

"Yes – Jack. Has he been teaching you this stuff?"

"Yeah. Sort of."

"What's that supposed to mean?"

"Yes - he's been helping to teach me to meditate. So what? S'not a crime, is it?"

"Don't be flippant with me Adam. You know what I mean. Is that really all there is to it then? Everything's really okay and you are just enjoying this new...um...hobby."

"Yeah" said Adam, "That's all there is to it."

Carol visibly relaxed and forced a smile.

"That's okay then. That's all I wanted to say. You can't blame me for wondering what this is all about can you? Oh - there is one other thing - there's a letter arrived in the post for you."

"Huh?" (He didn't get letters)

She handed over the smartly typed envelope which gave no clue, back or front, as to its origin and stood, arms folded again, waiting for him to open it. Adam slipped his finger beneath the lightly gummed flap and opened the envelope. He took out a sheet of paper and read it slowly.

"Well?"

He looked up with an expression of genuine surprise on his face.

"It's from the Gazette" he said, "They've offered me the job. Sub-Editorial Assistant."

Carol snatched the letter from his hands and read it herself. She looked up and they both stared at each other momentarily lost for words.

"That's fantastic Adam. Well done. For God's sake don't waste the opportunity this time. You seem to get sacked from every job you ever take on."

Adam ignored the remark and re-read the letter again with a smug expression on his face.

"The other jobs were rubbish" he snorted, "You wait. I'll show you that I can do this. I reckon I could definitely write better stuff than the lousy articles they write in the Gazette at the moment."

"Oh, you do, do you?"

"Yeah. No sweat. You wait."

"I'll look forward to it."

"They want me to start next week."

"Then you had better learn to iron your own shirts and buy yourself a tie then."

Adam looked at his mum and sighed deeply.

"How did I just know you were going to say something like that?" he said with a grin.

It was becoming easier and easier.

How could something that was so difficult just a few months ago now be so simple?

Find somewhere quiet where there is no chance of disturbance, relax, focus, breathe, let the thoughts go, relax, focus, breathe, go deeper, wait for the emptiness.

Then just *be*.

Enjoy the sensation of standing weightlessly within a field of silence and complete peacefulness. An ocean of tranquillity where the only reality is your own heightened sensitivity and fascination. Non-thinking, non-judgemental and open to anything and everything.

Then wait for the deepening shades of blue that draw you further and further in.

But into what?

Somehow it didn't matter anymore. It was just too beautiful for words, just as Jack had said.

Tonight, Adam felt very relaxed. Maybe it was the good news about the job at the Gazette, or the recent night out with Marie. Maybe it was because he'd told Carol the truth about his meditation and his conscience was clear.

Or maybe it was none of those things. Maybe it was just because at last he'd found the way to go deeper and deeper into a special place where angelic voices sang sweetly inside his head and where his whole being was enveloped into a comforting blanket of soft blueness that washed through his mind and body filling it with a new sense of peace and wonder.

Now, tonight, he was back in that special place again where the swirling silvery shades of blue were so real and so vibrant that the borders of body, mind, conscious and unconscious were exquisitely blurred into one.

And now, tonight, came another sensation of sinking deeper into something more.

Something new.

Something *different*.

Into...

Ohmigod.

The shadowy 'figure'.

It was there again.

'Don't be scared...Don't be scared...Hold the focus... Stay calm...Stay calm...'

It was a little blurred and indistinct around the edges - fuzzy almost - and glowing with some sort of internal natural light. Nevertheless, He? She? It? was clearly real and more tangible than a hologram. The last time Adam had sensed this presence he had been so terrified that his concentration had been completely shattered. This time he was determined to remain calm. If Jack was right, then there was nothing to fear. He must overcome all trepidation and face up to the ghost-like apparition.

Adam tried to frame some words but even as he thought them, he heard a reply deep inside his head. It was only a whisper, but it was very audible, the tone warm and precise. The shock of having someone communicate with him like this made his heart miss a beat.

'Who am I?' The figure responded unemotionally, 'I am the one who watches you. And you are the Stone. The one who walks in the shadows.'

Adam noticed that the figure's lips were not moving. The thought transference was immediate and clear. Although the experience was dream-like it was clearly not a dream. It was reality of a different sort. A reality not in the sense of full consciousness but consciousness in a new and unfamiliar context, a sensation Adam had never experienced before. Adam felt that he ought to be scared - and yet strangely enough there was no fear - only curiosity. This was a non-place. Not a dream and not real-world. It was somewhere in between.

There was something about the figure, though, that was slightly disconcerting. Not frightening or threatening in any way but disturbing because the figure was - somehow - not a total stranger. 'He' - for now Adam could see with more clarity that he was undoubtedly male, was somehow - paradoxically - familiar.

Adam thought the words 'Where am I?' and again the response was instantaneous, the words clear, precise and soft spoken.

'You are outside of your physical body, but you are quite safe. There is no need to be afraid.'

'Do you have a name?'

'My name is Shera and I have another name which is Pratihara. You may call me Shera.'

'You seem familiar to me...are you my...?' Adam felt momentarily self-conscious about using the word 'Guide?'

'That is true. You have always known me - but not as clearly as you can see me now. It is good to be once more reunited.'

'I don't understand.'

'There is no need for fear and there is no need to understand. Understanding will come in time. That you have come this far is admirable in itself.'

'Am I dreaming this - or are you real?'

'You are not dreaming. Our conversation is real - but the word 'real' is perhaps not precise enough to express this meeting or this moment. Reality is a relative term.'

'Then I am not just imagining you.'

'No. I am here.'

'Am I asleep?'

'No - you are in deep meditation. Very shortly you will have to return. That is natural. We shall meet again soon.'

'How can you be so sure?'

'I am sure.'

Adam opened his mouth to speak again but the image was blurring fast, and a swirl of grey misty material was spinning around his head and making him feel dizzy and a little nauseous. Within moments he was aware of physical reality again. Aware of the darkness of his bedroom and aware of the clammy damp sensation on his palms and forehead. His body felt suddenly unnatural and heavier than usual.

His legs had stiffened, and he shifted them a little then stretched purposefully to try and shake off the feeling of pins and needles permeating through his limbs. He shivered involuntarily and licked dry lips until the dull sensations of normality seeped back into his body.

Then he leaned back against the bedroom wall staring out of the window at the night sky dotted with stars. There was a warm feeling that started in somewhere in the region of his navel and it was now spreading outward throughout his body like the delicious sensation of immersing oneself in a warm bath. There was also a distinct feeling of smugness.

'Jack was right' he whispered to himself, 'Clever old bastard. I really do have a bloody guardian angel. Wait until I tell him he was right...'

Adam reached over to his bedside cabinet fumbling for his cigarettes and lighter. A sleek silver lighter that had caught his eye once in a local jeweller's shop. Marie had bought it for him on his seventeenth birthday.

Marie.

He flicked the lighter and watched the small teardrop of a flame flicker into life and light up the dark recesses of his bedroom. His hands were still shaking slightly as he replayed the events of his meditation. Then he frowned, took the cigarette out of his mouth and put it back into the packet, simultaneously snapping shut the lighter and snuffing the flame.

The cigarette was just habit. He didn't need it. Something was puzzling him.

What exactly had Shera meant when he'd said those enigmatic words:

'And you are the Stone. The one who walks in the shadows.'

Adam rapped on Jack's door again, harder this time. Maybe the old guy was asleep.

Come on Jack. You gotta be in.

A few moments later the sound of a creaking floorboard and a moving shadow through the frosted glass eased his concern. Adam waited for the door bolt to be disengaged and the click of the door opening.

"Jack - it's me Adam."

Jack smiled warmly and opened the door wide.

"Adam. I sensed it was you even though I wasn't expecting you. You usually..."

"Phone. Yeah, I know. This was too important. I had to come around straight away."

Jack read the earnest expression immediately.

"You'd better come in then. I was just making a cup of tea if..."

"No thanks. I'll have a glass of water though."

"Water? This must be important."

"It is."

Adam waited patiently while Jack poured himself a cup of tea then followed him into the lounge.

Jack motioned Adam to sit down, handed him a glass of water then settled himself into his favourite armchair.

"Right then," said Jack sipping the tea and looking over the top of his specs, "I'm all ears."

Adam started by telling the old man more about the amazing nights that the meditation had been so enhanced by music and choir-like chanting and the glowing net-thing that had got Jack so excited. And then Adam told him about the 'meeting' with the presence called Shera. The 'guide' that Jack had predicted would appear.

Jack listened without interruption, nodding now and then, and waiting for Adam to finish in his own time. He had never seen the lad so animated and enthusiastic as this before. It gave the old man a warm glow inside.

Adam stopped to draw breath, his eyes searching Jack's eyes for answers.

"Adam, I can't tell you how delighted I am that you have made contact with your own inner guide. Treasure this moment because it will change your life. I'll talk about the importance of this meeting in a while but first let me say that you are doubly privileged if you have managed to hear real music during your inner work. It's something I've strived for myself for many years. There is a huge difference between listening to music and experiencing music as any student of music theory will tell you. Listening to music is a passive pastime, an enjoyable one nonetheless, whereby the listener can carry on with other activities at the same time and let the sounds wash over them, ebbing and flowing in a pleasant rhythmic pulse stimulating the minute hairs of the inner ear..."

Adam wanted to interrupt. Talk about Shera. But Jack was on one of his soapboxes again. It was pointless trying to butt in.

"To *experience* music, however, is a very unique sensation. Rather than passive surrender to an external stimulus it is an active concentrated focus on an exciting and refreshing new world of sensuality. The active listener focuses in on the purity of sound, the subtleties of harmony, the satisfaction of melody and the exquisite balance of counterpoint and resonance. There are few sensations to compete with the delicious ecstasy of total immersion in the works of the great composers. Total concentration on the complexity and subtlety of dynamic and timbre becomes a unique, personal and moving experience that can lead one from darkest depression to unsurpassed joy. Music can be a healer, a motivator, a solace and a guide. It can act as a trigger for our deepest emotions eliciting both meditative reflection and ruthless determination depending on the way it energises our bodies and minds. To be receptive and at the same time focused is to embrace the total experience of music, to let it fill not just your ears but your soul too. It moves man in ways few of us are consciously aware of. To experience music whilst in deep meditation is quite incredible. It means that you are on the verge of finding your gate."

"My gate?"

"Yes indeed. The gate that marks the boundary between two worlds. There are a number of ways to enter the gate. Each person must find their own gate and not until they find the gate can they begin the journey."

"Journey? What journey?"

"To reach any destination you must be prepared to undertake a journey. Journeys can be pleasant - or they can be painful - but they are always acts of revelation. Sometimes it is necessary to experience the pain in order to appreciate the pleasure. Either way the experience is a learning process - and to learn is to grow. All of life is a journey but few people appreciate that each life is only one small step on a much bigger journey through thousands of individual incarnations. Each life is a chance to learn and grow spiritually. It is a quest that takes us from ignorance to enlightenment. Remember the story of the Golden Feather? The journey that Ramatha had to make to find the meaning of the last golden feather?"

"Of course."

"Good, because fate has bestowed you with your own golden feather Adam. You are a very privileged person. Your metaphysical feather, if you pardon the analogy, is the key that unlocks the gate."

Adam reflected on the old man's words for a few moments. He was still puzzled. All that stuff about music, gates and journeys was a lot to take in.

"You're talking in riddles again Jack. How am I supposed to find this gate?"

Jack tapped the side of his nose. "If you look you will find it. 'Seek and ye shall find'. There are clues all around you if you look carefully."

"Don't play tricks on me Jack. I don't know where to look...can't you give me a hint?"

"You could try a number of things to help in your quest. I can't tell you where to find your gate or even how to use the key to your gate...only you can do that. You could start exploring ideas yourself though. You could also try asking Shera to show you the way. If he thinks you are ready - and I think you are - he will lead you to the gate and help you on your way."

"What's on the other side of the gate Jack?"

Jack shifted in his chair as though the old war wounded leg was troubling him. He stroked his stubbled chin slowly.

When he spoke again it was soft and slow.

"I don't know Adam. I really don't know. It's taken me many years of perseverance to get as far in my meditation as you have in six months. I think that I too have now finally found my own gate and maybe all I need now is the courage to go through it. But that's for another time. Now you must trust Shera and let his wisdom take you forward. There's little more I can do. It's up to you now Adam."

Adam mulled over Jack's words. He still had so many questions that needed to be answered.

…And he still needed Jack's reassurance and guidance.

"Can I ask you something else?" he said at length.

"Of course."

"Okay" replied Adam "I want to talk about death."

Jack was unperturbed and nodded slowly. "Death, eh? That's a good one Adam…I'll give you that! The biggest mystery of all…the final frontier and all that…so…what is it you want to know?"

Adam moistened his lips and settled back into the old man's soft armchair. "Everything" he replied coolly, "I want to know what *really* happens after death…it's important if I'm to put this whole meditation thing into some kind of context and perspective."

Jack nodded again and considered the question carefully. "I suppose the most honest answer is that you will find out the exact answer to your question in due course…and that is because maybe God, or whatever life force you choose to believe in, needs death to remain a mystery for the safety and integrity of our species. It could be that man is not supposed to know the answer to the question for our own good."

"Do you really believe that?"

"To a degree yes. I've told you before that a little knowledge is a dangerous thing. And that would certainly be true about making assumptions on the true nature of death. It could be that to understand the nature of death is too dangerous to our sanity… it might undermine our most treasured beliefs and if it does that, it could lead to a breakdown of cultures and the social stability that is fundamental to those cultures."

"Are you saying that you know the answer but are not willing to tell me? Or are you saying nobody knows the answer?"

"I'm saying that I have a view, which you can choose to subscribe to or disregard, but either way the view may be too hard for you to swallow."

"Try me."

"Okay...the deal is this, Adam. First you tell me...in detail...what your own current perceptions of death are and let me quiz you a little and then I'll offer you a few of my own ideas."

"Seems fair enough."

"Good. Let's start with the basics then. Tell me what your beliefs are - and I'll try not to interrupt until you're done."

Adam looked up at the ceiling as if searching for inspiration. This was uncomfortable. But maybe essential. For some reason he needed answers

"I've not talked about my ideas to anyone before...I'm nervous even approaching the subject... maybe because it's a kind of taboo subject in our society..." he looked to Jack for support and Jack just nodded and made it clear he was giving Adam his full attention.

"I don't know the answer," confessed Adam, "But it's something that has always bothered me. In a way I'm scared of death because...well it's so final, isn't it? I suppose everyone is scared of death because it relates to pain, suffering and oblivion. It's also so unknown...I mean it could be the end of everything completely or alternatively maybe there is some truth in the heaven and hell of the Bible. Maybe if you are a sinner, whatever that means, you will roast in hell for eternity. Alternatively, you might really find yourself in heaven and attain some kind of immortality. Maybe there is some kind of 'afterlife' that we all have to experience. Either way how do you cope with those possibilities? And where do ghosts fit in? And then there are all those theories about reincarnation as you just mentioned. And what about seances and messages from the dead etcetera? It's all so confusing Jack".

"It is confusing Adam and let's face it - the mysteries of life and death are perhaps the greatest mysteries of all. Fear of death is probably the greatest of our fears because it is fear of the unknown in the most extreme sense. The final loss of control. The uncertainty. The coldness. The loneliness. The finality of it all. And yet to some…just a few…it is the ultimate goal, the new beginning, the realisation of all ambition and the most sought-after prize of all."

"Is it? I'm not sure I understand what you mean."

"Before we talk about death, we need to talk about what we understand by time, only then can the whole concept of death make sense."

"Go on."

"Time is our greatest enemy, which is a great shame because once upon a time it was mans' greatest friend."

"How so?"

"Because a long time ago time was very simple, and it stayed that way for thousands and thousands of years. There were four seasons, there was day and night, sundown and sunrise and there was the lunar month and solar year - and that was all you needed to know. There was no sense of urgency in time per se; time to our distant ancestors was a shared tribal concept, not something to be measured but something to be lived and experienced as a continuous stream of events. Time was how long it took to kill your dinner or the space between rainstorms. There was no pressure because there was no sense of time being wasted or lost and it didn't matter whether it was three o' clock or four o' clock or whatever other concept of measurement you chose to employ. When man decided to slice this experience of living into convenient chunks called 'time' he unwittingly caused a massive cultural upheaval that still sends us reeling today - thousands of years later.

When we speak of time we are usually referring to 'clock time' and everything in our world is synchronised by clock time. Clock time defines our work, our leisure, our sleeping and waking, railways and aeroplanes, televisions, washing machines, radios and even these new-fangled computers. We complain that we don't have enough time and would probably buy more of it if it were on sale. We claim it runs out on us or that we can't meet deadlines...now there's an interesting word - 'deadlines' - the greatest cause of ulcers, depression and rising blood pressure in modern man - meeting the deadlines. We are so obsessed with time that it is killing us. It is a literal deadline for some. And yet the crazy thing is that it's all totally artificial. We don't really need it - I mean not if we take it to its logical conclusion. We may need the services of 'Old Father Time' to survive in a competitive business environment, but we don't need it to survive the real trials of life.

The sad thing is that we can't rewrite history. Time is now so fundamentally embedded in our psyche that we would find it hard to adjust to a world without it. Maybe we can find some middle ground though..."

"What do you mean by middle ground?"

"Well...maybe we have to accept the fact that a regulated lifestyle is here to stay, and our wristwatch remains our master, but we do have some choice here. We have the potential to take some 'time out' if you'll pardon the pun. We can use the innate ability of our mind to still the relentless ticking of the clock and steal some 'out of time' moments back for ourselves. Time, you see, is not all that it seems... you're probably conversant with Einstein and his theory of relativity and space time?"

"A bit...yeah".

God - he wished he'd listened more in science lessons when he was at school...

"Okay. So, we know that time is not always a constant linear pattern and that it can be distorted by the laws of physics. What is not always appreciated though is that we don't have to be dependent on linear time. By stilling our mind and...how shall I put it? Defocusing a moment from the external world... we can dislocate our mind from traditional time and take a short break in the omnipresent."

"The what?"

"Yes, I know it sounds like I'm talking nonsense but hear me out Adam. What I'm getting at is that we don't have to subject ourselves to mainstream linear time if we don't want to. When you are in deep meditation it is as though time itself has been put on hold for a while. In the external world time has ticked by as normal but to the meditator an hour may have seemed to have passed in 'mental time' or the Omnipresent."

"So, what you're saying is that during deep meditation time is slowed down."

"That's right, but I do mean *deep* meditation - not superficial relaxation. I'm not saying that when you come back into waking consciousness that the bedroom clock will have stayed still. What I'm saying is that in the 'meditative realms' for want of better words - time is irrelevant. The experiences you go through whilst in a state of deep meditation might seem like hours passing - as sometimes happens when you dream - but in terms of waking consciousness or 'real time' only a few moments may have passed. You will find this out soon enough."

Adam considered Jack's words for a few moments. "Okay" he said thoughtfully, "But how does all this 'time' stuff relate to death then?"

"It relates to it Adam because if you really want to understand the concept of death you first have to disassociate it from what you know about time. Quite simply - if you try and fit the experience we call 'death' into the framework that you experience everyday - called 'time' then you will start to get very confused very quickly."

Adam smiled "I'm already bloody confused Jack" he said, "Like you wouldn't believe."

Jack laughed. "The answers to everything, life, death, time and space etcetera are all there inside your head Adam. You just need to learn how to find them. You need to go through the gate and let Shera guide you on the next step of your journey. I only wish I had the ability to go with you. Are you willing to do it though, Adam? Go through the gate and face up to whatever lies on the other side. Face up to your greatest fears?"

'I don't like it. It's too dark. I can't see where I am. There are shapes moving in the trees. I don't want to be in this place anymore. I can see faces everywhere. Horrible faces...'

Adam sat back in the old armchair and thought about the implications of what Jack was saying. Could the answers to all his deepest questions really be inside his head? Was there really some sort of spiritual gateway that he had to walk through in order to understand the true nature of things like time and death? If he understood Jack correctly it seemed there were only two choices. Stay in the relative comfort of the 'blue' zone forever or take the big step into the unknown.

"I have to do it don't I Jack?" he said at last, "I somehow know that I have to do it."

An hour later, just before walking into The Anchor for a swift pint and a fag, Adam stopped in his tracks and cursed. He'd meant to quiz Jack about Shera and all this 'inner guide' stuff, but as usual Jack had led him off down another endlessly fascinating track of thoughts and Adam had missed the moment. It would have to wait.

Right now, there were other things rattling around in his head that needed to be sorted.

It was a weird feeling.

A bit like being drunk - but without any alcohol being consumed. It was a mixture of euphoria, giddiness, light headedness and a tendency to giggle over nothing.

At first Adam had thought he must be sickening for a dose of flu or something but now he knew better. Now he knew it was symptomatic of 'overdosing' on meditation. Jack had warned him not to overdo it because there was no doubt that although regular meditation was beneficial to the body, it was like all things. Too much of a good thing can eventually be a bad thing. The light headedness - the unsteadiness on the feet were all mild side-effects of spending too much time in other streams of consciousness.

Fact is - it really was like a drug.

Totally addictive.

And now he was bloody hooked.

Adam leaned back on the bed, lit an incense stick, put out the bedroom light and started taking deep breaths. The sensations of tingling fingers and the misty swirls before the eyes were the rush.

The addict's anticipation before the hit.

'C'mon baby' Adam breathed to himself, "C'mon baby - take me there...'.

It didn't take long. Each time he went through the motions the transition between normal wakeful consciousness and the meditative state, grew less and less. Adam silently prayed that he wasn't going mad. He prayed that his 'inner guide' was not just a simple trick of the imagination, or an apparition borne of overindulgence of alcohol or weed. He prayed that he could find his way back to where his guide was waiting.

The first few moments were just as before. The sense of inner peacefulness, the blueness.

The landscape of the inner soul.

Then, to his relief, a figure stepped into his field of vision. And this time there was no fear. Just awe and fascination. The meeting of two conscious soul-beings communicating effortlessly and telepathically.

'*Hello Adam. I knew we would meet again soon.*'

'Hello Shera. I'm so glad you're here. I was afraid you might have been an illusion after all. I needed to make sure.'

'*You can be sure. I will always be here if you need me.*'

'Have you always been here?'

Shera was silent for a few moments as if he were thinking.

'*No, not always. Some things are hard to explain.*'

'And where are we exactly? We seem to be floating in a vacuum. I can't see anything else, and I can't feel solid ground under my feet. What is this place?'

'*That too is hard for me to explain. Everything will become clearer as your meditation becomes stronger. It takes a little while, but all your questions will be answered if you persevere. This place has no name. Call it what you will.*'

Adam tried to focus on his surroundings, but only grey swirling cloud-like things were visible in every direction.

'I'd call it the empty place' he said.

'*So be it. 'The empty place'. That is a good name for it.*'

'Is there anyone else here or just you and me?'

'There are thousands of others around.'

The answer surprised Adam. 'I can't see anyone else.'

'You will in time. They are all around us.'

'But who are they? Real people? Spirits? Ghosts? I need to understand Shera. Tell me more about this place.'

'If you want to understand more then you must keep your mind open to all possibilities. Labelling things as 'real' or 'dead' will only limit your understanding. When you meet others then call them only by their name - labelling anyone with anything other than their name is not necessary.'

'But where do they all live? Not in this grey, cloudy, empty place surely?'

'No not here. There are other places. You will find the other places soon enough, but you must not be impatient. It is important to move slowly at first. If you try and learn too much, too soon, it will tire you quickly. It will put a strain on your physical body which is not a good thing to do.'

'Yes, I understand that. I think I'm starting to feel tired now.'

'Then return to your physical body and relax. I will be here when you need to talk again.'

'Before I go, I need to ask you something.'

'You want to ask me how to move beyond the Empty Place into the deeper realms. You want me to help you find the way to the gate and help you through it'.

'Yes. I forgot. You can read my thoughts.'

'I will help you to find the gate then you must decide whether or not to enter. Prepare yourself well before your next meditation. Be well rested and drink only water. Then I will show you the gate. Rest now.'

'Thank you, Shera. I will rest now.'

Within moments Adam was fully conscious and aware of his heart beating fast. He slowed it down deliberately with a few deep breaths and then moistened his dry lips.

It was true what Jack had said. He had made contact with another entity whilst in deep meditation.

It was an entity that exuded an intoxicating charisma, unique, approachable and non-threatening. There had been no fear and the experience had been both exhilarating and awe-inspiring. It had been no dream, no drunken nightmare, no glitzy stage-managed illusion, but instead, an introduction to a very different type of reality. It was a reality that left Adam tingling all over with a sensation of mild shock and excitement simultaneously.

And somehow, for no explicable or obvious reason, the name, Shera, was as familiar as the person himself (if indeed 'person' was the correct description for a non-tangible entity.) And what was meant by the words Shera had said when he had first manifested - 'You have always known me.' That surely couldn't be true? Adam couldn't recollect any specific physical memory - just a vague recognition - like when you meet someone you had met a long time ago and had forgotten about. That bit didn't make sense.

At least, not at the moment.

He still felt giddy, disorientated and now there was a ringing in his ears.

No, not ringing - words!

Words?

With a sudden awakening of normality Adam realised it was his mother calling him from downstairs. He flicked on the bedroom light and kicked open the bedroom door.

"All right, all right" he yelled back, "I can hear you - I'm on my way down."

As he climbed off the bed and extinguished the embers of the incense stick, he smiled wryly at the irony of that last remark.

The blonde at the reception desk was more interested in filing down her crimson nails than in the gangly youth who stood fidgeting in front of her. She wondered if he realised that a white shirt and loud red tie clashed terribly with the crumpled blue suit. But he was a guy - so he probably didn't realise it, or even care.

She knew instinctively though, that he was staring at her breasts.

"What was yer name again?" she said through a mouth full of chewing gum.

"Adam. Adam Sinclair. I start today. I'm the new sub-editorial assistant."

If she was impressed, she didn't show it.

"Oh yeah," she said after running the crimson nail down a list of names. "Take the stairs up to the first floor. You want Gavin Carter. He should be expecting you."

"Thanks."

He waited for a moment in case she looked up again - so he could flash her one of his well-rehearsed smiles - but she seemed to be too engrossed in getting back to the nail file. He glanced down at the silver name plaque on the top of the Gazette's reception desk and made a mental note of the name - 'Debbie Riley'. Suited her he thought.

At the top of the stairs, he recognised the door through which he'd been led at interview. Solid wood at the bottom and frosted glass at the top with the words 'The Gazette' painted in a very faded gothic English. Adam turned the handle and let himself into the room. He'd not really taken much notice of the place first time around. Hadn't even noticed gum-chewing Debbie he'd been so nervous. Now he took a few moments to absorb a little of the atmosphere he'd just signed up to in his first 'career' job. It was a large room of fifteen or so desks; all of them overflowing with paper. Around three of the walls grey or black filing cabinets sprouted even more paper and the other wall, facing out over the high street, boasted four large sash windows. There was obviously a long window ledge at waist height too, but like the rest of the office, it had now become another temporary filing tray. The clack of typewriters competed with a noisy air-conditioning unit and there was a general hustle and bustle of people moving or shuffling even more scraps of paper. At the far end of the office Adam recognised Stanley T. Morgan's office. There was another door too, on the back wall, from where the aroma of freshly brewed coffee emanated.

A plump woman in a white blouse and tartan skirt caught his attention.

"Can I help?" she offered.

"Adam cleared his throat. "Er...thanks. I'm after someone called Gavin Carter. It's my first day. I'm the new sub-editorial assistant."

The woman smiled warmly, obviously more impressed than Debbie on reception. She offered her hand.

"You must be Adam Sinclair."

"That's right."

"I'm Joan. We were told to expect you. You'll be working for Gavin. Follow me and I'll introduce you."

Joan led Adam around a few desks, careful not to knock over the teetering piles of files on each desk and stopped when she arrived at the desk of Gavin Carter. Gavin was on the phone but caught Adam's eye. He motioned Adam to take a seat on a spare chair.

Adam made himself comfortable and tried not to stare too hard at his new boss. Gavin seemed to be in his late twenties maybe early thirties - difficult to tell. Smart suit, wide tie, and shiny shoes. Thick black hair, well over the collar with side parting and currently chewing on a pen while still managing to hold a conversation. He was leaning back on the chair and talking loudly in a thick confident Welsh accent. He winked at Adam.

"And you say the court case is tomorrow?" Gavin removed the pen and scribbled a few notes on his desk pad.

"Good. Good. Now don't forget to call me mind. As soon as it's over. I'll want all the spicy details of course..."

Adam waited patiently until Gavin finished and put the phone down, offering Adam his hand. The grip was firmer than Joan's limp offering.

"Bloody court clerks" Gavin said, shaking his head, "They're all bloody useless. If you don't keep pestering them, you never get a call back from them you know. Bloody useless."

He grinned widely. "You must be Adam Sinclair then?"

"Yes."

"Welcome to the Gazette. The thriving heart of all the town gossip. The hotbed of breaking news..."

Another woman nearby rolled her eyes and shook her head.

Gavin leaned back putting his hands behind his head and feet up on the desk with the air of a man totally in control, or at least, believing or giving the impression that he was.

"First job then Adam?"

"First proper job. Y'know, lots of fill-in jobs up to now."

"Ah yes. I remember starting out on all those tedious jobs you do as a teenager when I was in Swansea. Well, we'd better get you started then, hadn't we? 'Fraid it's filing to start with boyo. Same for us all. Before that though - do you know how to make tea?"

Adam nodded. He liked the breezy tongue-in-cheek style. Felt like this was someone he could get on with.

"Excellent. Excellent" said Gavin, "Then follow me to the tearoom. We'll start with the really important things first - like making a good strong cup of tea - and then we can introduce you to the dizzy heights of cutting-edge journalism. Sound good to you?"

"Definitely."

"Then onward to the tearoom."

Adam followed Gavin to the small tearoom at the back of the main office, well aware that many eyes, mostly middle-aged and mostly female, were all staring at him and Gavin with a sort of bemused resignation.

The place had a buzz about it that Adam liked.

(Unlike Lomax Bros or Carson's paint shop which were equally depressingly dull and soulless).

'Yeah', he thought, 'I could get to like it here...'

Friday night.

No doubt Mum would be fretting because he was locked away again in his bedroom. But then she didn't understand how much he needed this...this... *fix*? Tomorrow he'd take a break. Maybe phone up Steve and Danny. Go out for a few beers.

Chill out.

But not tonight.

Tonight, he had an appointment with Shera.

It seemed to take less and less time now to break through into the meditative state. Something that initially had been so insanely difficult to do was now a breeze. But it had taken a lot of time and perseverance. A lot of people simply wouldn't have the stamina to keep at it. Being stubborn and pig-headed, as Carol and Marie had often reminded him, gave him the mentality to keep at it.

'*Motivation*' Adam preferred to call it.

Jack had said that laying off the smoking would help and that seemed to be true. The craving for a fag had eased off considerably over the last few weeks. He might even be able to give up completely with a bit more effort.

Be harder to give up the spliffs though...

Back to the routine. Eyes shut, deep breaths, focused relaxation. A brief sojourn in the white nothingness of initial relaxation then he was there again - the 'empty place'. More deep breaths, relaxed concentration and then passive attention on the moment.

Adam didn't have to wait long.

Shera appeared through the translucent wisps of what seemed like clouds of gossamer and stood there in silence for a few moments. Gradually the white cloudiness developed a blue tinge and then the deep intoxicating blue began to seep in from every direction until both Adam and Shera were totally immersed in its soft folds. After a while the blue itself began to almost imperceptibly transmute into shimmering silver. The beauty of the transition made it hard for Adam to find words. It was some time before he finally managed to 'speak'.

'Hello Shera. It's good to see you again. Can I ask you something? I'd like to know where we are now. This amazing silvery blue place.'

The calm, slow, reassuring and soothing voice of Adam's inner guide entered his mind as effortlessly as on previous occasions. It made him feel good.

'It is not important to know where you are. In fact, the question is irrelevant. There is no name for this and trying to think of this as being some sort of 'place' in geographical terms will only confuse you. You have to learn not to think in spatial or temporal terms anymore.'

'That's gonna be difficult'

'At first it will be. Then it becomes natural, and you will realise that there is no need to label things. In your material life you need to label things in order to bound their reality - because that reality is indeed so subjective that you need some kind of sanity anchor to hold your world together. It's not like that here. You are now free from the need for any sanity anchors because you are now in a state of consciousness that is pure and unencumbered from any delusions. If you like, this is reality in its purest form. You do not need to be suspicious about the reliability of your own perceptions anymore. This is somewhere you

can believe in without fear or doubt. Just experience it - there is no longer any need to question it.'

'I guess I want to label this place because you said there were different layers of consciousness that I might pass through, and I was looking for some kind of reference point.'

'That's understandable - and I appreciate that you are still thinking in what you might call 'physical limitation mode', so wanting to know where you are is only natural. There are no labels here but there are layers and being able to recognise layers will help you navigate during your personal voyages of discovery.'

'Tell me about these layers.'

'Some will be too incomprehensible for you to relate to or understand at the moment. It's all about different levels of energy and vibration. I will try and explain the most relevant layers. I will start with your body - it exists in a state you would call the physical or material layer.'

'Does everything in my physical life belong to the material layer?'

'Yes - including your body and everything else you perceive as being solid - but you don't need to understand those distinctions yet. These things will become clearer soon. For the moment it is best to think of everything in your normal life as being physical.'

'Okay - so what's next after the physical layer then?'

'I think you already know the answer to that. Think back to your first experiments in meditation. Your first feelings of strangeness tinged with a little fear - and then disassociation from your body. Do you recall the uncomfortable tingling sensations, the feeling of being surrounded by emptiness and nothingness?'

'Yeah. The empty place.'

'That was the layer that everyone experiences when they are semi-conscious or meditating for the first time.

It has no name - but you might want to think of it as the layer between your own life reality and the reality of the inner worlds. It's a thin layer that is easily traversed and yet few people ever bother to try and penetrate it. It's the veil between two worlds that are both inextricably linked and yet simultaneously separated.'

'I seem to have spent nearly all of my meditation time in that empty, misty sort of emptiness. But it's the next layer that I'm really interested in - is that where I am now? Is that where you...we...are now?'

'The layer after what you call the empty place is the stepping-stone between what might be termed surface reality and deeper reality and that needs some explanation. It's a confusing place and can also be a dangerous place if you are not careful.

Imagine two worlds if you will - the perceived reality of your physical presence on Earth - let's call that the 'material' and then the inner reality discovered through deep meditation - let's call that place 'home' for want of a better name. Between those two extremes are a few thin layers that need to be navigated through. The first layer which you have called 'the empty place' is the first step that is gained through gentle contemplative meditation, and it is a safe enough place - if a little like being immersed in clouds or fog. Beyond the emptiness is a thin veil that separates the empty place from a much more profound layer which again has no name but which you recognise as the colour blue.'

'This beautiful, peaceful, blue place? Oh yeah - I love this place. The different shades of blue kind of swirl around you and gradually darken and turn into a sort of silvery black. It's amazing...'

'The deeper blue is the true border between the world of the physical and the inner worlds. The 'empty place' is just the space between the two extremes. Many who are experienced in meditation spend a lifetime accessing the empty place but sadly do not have the ability to traverse the veil. It is a rare gift to be able to traverse the veil and enter into the 'blue layer'. That you have achieved the *traverse in little over one physical year is remarkable indeed - even for someone with your abilities. You truly have been granted an exceptional gift.'*

'Yeah - Jack said the same thing. But why Shera? Why should I have this gift? What's so special about me that I should have this ability? I don't get it...'

'You will soon understand the reason and, when you are ready, the explanations for your abilities will become apparent to you. I must not tell you the answer. There are certain natural laws at work in both the inner and the outer worlds that cannot be broken.'

'Yeah, Jack said he couldn't tell me either. Guess I'll just have to be patient. So, what's beyond this blue layer then?'

'Beyond the deeper blue is another layer which is certainly not empty - on the contrary - it is a mass of activity and confusion. It is not somewhere to linger but to get through as quickly as possible and out the other side.'

'What should I call that layer? The 'chaos' or something?'

'That would not really be an accurate term because it's not strictly chaos. It is more like an overcrowded waiting area. Think of it like the outer atmosphere of the Earth which is getting increasingly populated by orbiting satellites and space debris. If a rocket wants to go the moon, then its flight path needs to pick a way through the layer of space debris before it emerges into open space.'

'So - what exactly is the debris in this layer?'

'That's the bit that is hard to explain. It takes time to get acquainted with the spiritual realms and understand the way they work. It's best to experience it yourself rather than try and relate to it in an intellectual sense. But let me put it this way - every person who has ever lived is on a spiritual pathway and moving at their own pace. Some make swift progress and some barely get off the starting line. There are others, however, who get to a certain

point and then hit a kind of spiritual block - usually a self-created block if that makes sense to you. They can't or won't move forwards or backwards and so they tend to congregate together in a kind of spiritual 'waiting room' which can get overcrowded and noisy. Like a large crowd of people all talking and shouting together in a confined space. In the end, all the voices mesh into one continuous cacophony not unlike radio interference. It's best to just wade through the crowd until you are clear of it.'

'Is that the place you said could be dangerous?'

'Yes. It is not dangerous in the life-threatening sense because we are not talking about the physical anymore. It is more a case of staying away from bad influences. Some of the residents in this layer are very confused and have lost their direction or focus. The trouble is that they often try to influence anyone who crosses their path, sometimes in a negative way.'

'Like some drunk who tries to accost you on a street corner.'

'Yes. Exactly. That is a good analogy. If you are strong enough, you'll just ignore all the noise going on around you and keep focused. But if you stop to listen then it's easy to get led astray. I'm not saying that everyone you meet in this layer is a bad influence, but it is wise to keep your wits about you.'

'How about calling it the 'Interference layer' then, seeing as the noise is like radio static and the danger is from interfering er...residents.'

'That label would be perfect.'

'And that leaves the question - where is this? Where am I now?'

'As I said before thinking in terms of location is not really very appropriate. Let's say you have learned to penetrate the veil with some success thanks to your perseverance and sheer willpower. You have found a way through the clouds into the tranquillity of the colour you know as blue, and you are now standing at the threshold

of the Interference layer. Your challenge now is to get through the Interference layer - and that is why I need to help guide you on your way.'

'You're going to help me negotiate my way through the Interference layer?'

'No. I can't do that. That's something you must achieve yourself. All I can do is give a little guidance. Progress can only be made by you and you, alone. Nothing comes for free.'

'Okay. I understand...I think.'

'Then rest now. Go back to the material. Wait until you are resolute enough and relaxed enough to attempt penetration of the Interference layer. It will not be difficult if you remain focused and avoid distractions. On the other side of the Interference layer, you will find what you are looking for. The 'gate' that leads to that which your heart truly seeks.'

('That which your heart truly seeks' - what the hell was that supposed to mean? Best come clean about it. Adam felt awkward. A fraud almost).

'Shera, I'm...er...not sure what it is that I truly seek. To be honest I'm just not sure what it is I'm really looking for.'

'You may not know what you are looking for in terms of your conscious self - but believe me - your sub-conscious knows exactly what it is that you seek.'

'Do you know what it is my sub-conscious seeks?'

'Of course. It is the same thing that everyone's sub-conscious seeks. It wants to find its way home.'

As Adam pondered Shera's enigmatic answer the surroundings began to shimmer, and Shera's image began to fade. An awareness of heavy limbs and tiredness seeped into his body and an almost unwelcome reality began to manifest itself around him, not unlike awakening from a post-operative anaesthetic.

One thing was certain. There could be no going back now. The journey had begun. Adam mentally resolved to attempt the next necessary step sometime within the next few days. Something strange had stirred within him. Something that would not rest until it had been brought to its natural conclusion. The next meditation would be more than a pleasant meander into the sub-conscious. It would be a pilgrimage through the empty place, through the veil and into the blue and beyond. Adam would make sure that the next meditation would be the special one. He needed to be fully prepared and mentally strong enough to attempt the tough part - the traverse of the Interference layer in order to find the 'gate' and then breakthrough into...

Into what?

Some kind of hidden 'truth'?

His destiny perhaps?

And what exactly did Shera mean by '*home*' anyway?

He desperately wanted to ring Jack. Tell him everything. Ask him to explain more stuff that was just too difficult to comprehend. But then hadn't Jack told him to go it alone for a while? It was Saturday morning and Adam had set aside some time to catch up with some chores he'd been putting off for too long. Tidying up his bedroom. Returning some overdue library books. Sending some belated Birthday cards.

And phoning Marie.

Adam picked up the phone cradle and sat down at the bottom of the stairs. He had been pacing up and down waiting for his mother to go shopping so that he could call Marie. Didn't want to his mother to know he was phoning her. Best to keep that quiet. He dialled the number, aware that his heart was pounding. He willed for her to answer. Needed to hear her voice. After a few moments he heard the receiver click.

"Marie? - It's Adam".

"Adam? Well...this is a surprise."

"So how are you then?"

"So-so, and you?"

"Yeah. Good. Look - I...er...really enjoyed our meal together. I thought maybe we could meet up again. You know...once in a while".

"Yes. That would be nice. I wondered if you'd ring again after I went and put my foot in it and upset you."

Adam frowned. "How so?"

"Oh, you know - I started talking about that old guy that you are friends with – Jack, wasn't it? You got a bit touchy when I bought up the subject of meditation. Guess I touched a raw nerve."

Adam laughed "Forget it" he said, "It wasn't your fault. I was more annoyed about my Mum interfering. She has a habit of doing that sort of thing. So - what are you up to then?"

Marie sighed. "The usual, out with friends, looking for a new job. Nothing very exciting. How about you?"

"I'm working at the Gazette. I got the job - y'know sub-editorial assistant and all that."

"You're kidding me."

"No. It's true. Suit and tie man now Marie. It's going well. Better than some of the other crummy places I've worked in".

"Now I've heard everything. Adam Sinclair in a suit. Excuse me while I faint."

"Thought you'd be surprised."

"And how are the lads?"

"Yeah - we still hang out. We might go to Reading Festi..."

Shit! - hadn't wanted to mention Reading.

"...That is, we might go to see some concerts...there are some good bands touring at the moment. Hey... how do you fancy coming to see Deep Purple in a couple of weeks with me and Danny?"

If she'd picked up on the reference to Reading festival she didn't react. Her voice was still warm and even.

"No thanks - I don't want to go deaf before I'm twenty. Now...if you had said 'Barclay James Harvest' or the 'Moody Blues'..."

Adam could picture her giving him that sly smile which he was powerless to resist.

"See what I can do..." he said, "So, anyway, perhaps I can ring you again soon and we can maybe meet up again. Yeah?"

"Okay. Call me in a week or two...oh...and Adam?"

"Yeah?"

"Try and keep your job this time. Don't be an arse and throw a good opportunity away. See ya then. Bye..."

The receiver clicked leaving Adam staring at the earpiece. The woman was unbelievable. Nagging him just the way his mother did. She was a cheeky bitch. Which is exactly, he reflected, why he couldn't help but love her.

Adam arrived at The Anchor public house early. He'd arranged to meet the lads at eight and it was only seven thirty-five but God he needed a pint. A 'well deserved' pint, even though he said it himself. He ordered a pint of Young's Best Bitter and carefully counted out the pennies on the damp Guinness bar mat while the landlord waited patiently. Okay - he'd been at the Gazette for a week but pay day was two weeks away and he'd had to scrounge a sub off Mum as usual. This time though, she'd be repaid in full.

The landlord walked off to the till with both hands cupped around the loose change that an hour ago had been weighing down Carol Sinclair's purse, while Adam turned around leaning his back on the bar and taking a deep mouthful of the amber liquid. He'd been feeling parched, and it slipped down his throat like a dream.

All in all, he was feeling pretty good. The new job was going reasonably well, although still early days. Gavin seemed a decent bloke to work for (even if he did tell lousy jokes and generate piles of filing) and the money would be more than he'd ever earned at the other dross jobs he'd had to put up with. Things were also improving on the women front with Marie potentially back in the frame. If he didn't screw things up, then he might even be in with a chance of asking her out again.

Best of all the meditation was going better than he could ever have expected. Looking back, it was probably one of the best decisions he had ever made - to persevere with it under Jack's guidance. To keep pushing the barriers even if, for some reason, it seemed to be causing Carol some bewilderment.

Adam took another swig and looked around at his surroundings. He found the ambience of the Anchor both familiar and unfamiliar, something he had not really pondered before.

The familiar was no surprise at all. The fading Fifties décor, the tatty juke box that only worked if you kicked it hard enough. The same old regulars playing pool or darts. The intermittent laughter and the ever-present drone of the incumbent bar stool philosopher predicting the football results to whoever might listen. The pin-striped pisshead talking to the barmaid's cleavage at the end of the bar and the crowd of yellow-jacketed workmen from the building site over the road crowded around a single table drinking and smoking as if their lives depended on it. All that was missing was the teenage contingent and they'd be here soon enough. The landlord at The Anchor had never seemed to care about under-age drinking unless it was some spotty, nervous juvenile trying it on. Maybe that's why the lads had always come here. The landlord at the King's Head always scrutinised everyone and it was often a gamble whether you could get served or not. Adam had already pissed the guy off by play fighting in the bar with some mates a year ago and been banned for six months.

No worries – he'd be twenty-one next year.

Might even be shaving properly by then.

The *unfamiliar* though - well that was something new - almost like an undercurrent that swirled beneath the surface of the normal daily ceremonies and routines of pub life. Something Adam had never noticed before or even thought about. It was almost as if he was detached from the reality of it all and was hovering invisibly over the whole scene. Watching everything but part of none of it. An invisible observer soaking up the atmosphere but unable to influence it in any way. It was a weird feeling.

It was as though the Anchor seemed to be existing in two dimensions of reality. The first was the humdrum normality that one would expect in any public house - and the other? Adam wasn't sure how to explain the other reality except that it had an air of melancholy about it. A sort of sadness that emanated from the very walls of the place and permeated everything and everyone in the building. The sensation was one of superficial pointlessness, futility even, as though nothing that happened within the four walls had any underlying purpose or direction but just 'was'. Even the beer which a moment ago had tasted like nectar had taken on a bland cardboard taste.

The murmur of voices began to blend into a meaningless drone that irritated the ear. No individual words could be heard on which to pin a specific meaning. It was akin to a disturbed wasps' nest. A blended mixture of apathy, anger, resentment, frustration and white noise.

It made Adam feel dizzy and he had to put one hand on the bar to steady himself. He felt drunk but knew that was preposterous. He'd only had a few mouthfuls. Maybe he was sickening for something. It was someone calling his name that finally snapped him back to reality.

"Adam - you auld tosser. You alright mate?"

"Huh? - Oh Danny. Hi mate. Sorry I was miles away."

"It's a bit early in da evening for getting pissed."

"Nah. I wish. Can't get pissed on this stuff."

Danny laughed out loud. "So how are you den? Long-time no see."

"Fine. Yeah. Good to see you...so what are you drinking?"

"Lager. Pint. T'anks."

Adam motioned to the bartender and ordered a lager.

"So" said Danny "how's t'ings?"

"Not bad. I've just started a new job at the Gazette. Sub-editorial assistant. It's been a laugh. Miles better than Lomax Brothers or Carsons paints."

"Yeah? Don't you have to wear a suit and tie and all dat?"

"'Fraid so."

"God I'd hate dat. Can't stand suits."

"You get used to it."

The lager arrived, and Adam counted out some more pennies while the landlord sighed deeply.

"Never t'ought oi'd see the day" said Danny over the top of the beer glass.

"Wassat?"

"You - in a fockin' suit".

Adam laughed, "Marie said the same thing. Never thought I'd see the day myself. It's not so bad. The money's reasonable and it's better than some of the places I've worked in."

"You back wid Marie den?"

"Sort of."

"What do you do den...at the Gazette?"

"This n' that. You know - filing, makin' tea, checking out stuff. I might even write some articles."

Danny looked up, pint held midway between bar and mouth.

"Bloody 'ell. That's a bit serious. What ya gonna write about? You don't know fuck all about anyt'ing."

It was said good humouredly and Adam laughed loudly wiping a tear from his eye.

"Oh, I dunno. Wait and see."

The pub door swung wide, and Steve appeared with Mick following a few steps behind.

"Whose round is it then?" Steve yelled.

"Mine" said Adam raising his pint in greeting "Hi boys. What you havin'?"

When the drinks arrived, they found a table. Mick put a beer mat under one of the table legs to stop it from rocking. Steve and Mick both laughed when Danny told them that they had to be careful not to spread any rumours because the new editor of 'The Sun' was listening in.

Adam nearly choked on his pint "Bollocks" he retaliated.

It was good to be out with the lads again. It had been a while. There were some new jokes going around and some plans for upcoming concerts. Adam listened to the old, hackneyed banter. Mick and Danny were both on the dole. Danny through choice and Mick through another recent redundancy. Steve had just got himself a new job at the shoe shop in the high street and was planning to do some office cleaning weekends to earn some more money.

Adam started to join in the conversation but gradually began to feel strange again. Sort of disassociated from everything - as though he was suddenly being sucked into the entrance of a long tunnel, further and further away from the lads at the table until they became merely a scene played out at the end of a long telescope. The dizziness returned and then the words he had been listening to became muffled, fading into the monotonous wasp-drone of meaningless noise. The last thing he remembered was Steve turning to look down the neck of the telescope with a worried frown and mouthing something about someone looking ill...

Adam had tried meditating the day before, but it never worked well after he'd been out drinking. He'd started the usual techniques around midnight but within seconds he'd fallen into a deep sleep and nearly missed getting up for work in the morning. It was not as though he'd actually been drunk on Saturday night. He'd only had two pints for God's sake.

Even so it had obviously been a bad pint. The way he'd come over all faint and lightheaded like that. Steve had only just managed to grab him before he fell off the chair. That would have been embarrassing. Instead, the lads had taken him outside and poured some water down his throat which seemed to have done the trick.

Sunday had been rather strange too. He'd slept in late, probably sleeping off that bad pint. Carol had cooked a nice roast chicken dinner, but he'd only toyed with it. Very unlike him to be off his food. Then he'd spent the whole afternoon curled up on the couch watching those interminable old black and white westerns on TV. Watching but not really watching. It was just a distraction.

Still - by the time he'd got to work on Monday he felt fine - and now he was feeling fresh and ready to go meet Shera. It was time to start exploring the hidden worlds Jack had hinted at and that Shera would hopefully lead him to. Maybe even find this mysterious 'gate' that Jack was on about.

Adam went through the usual motions and within a few minutes found himself back in that warm special place that he only wished he'd discovered years ago. There was no question that this was the place where he had last met Shera, but this time, strangely, there was no sign of him. He waited patiently, enjoying the serenity of the moment. The swirling clouds seemed a little thicker and denser than he remembered them from last time. Made it more difficult to see clearly.

Then a voice made him jump; but he managed - just - to keep the focus maintained.

'Hey now - who are you?'

A figure stepped out of nowhere and stood a few feet in front of him. Adam squinted to see who it was.

'It's...Adam...Adam Sinclair. Is that you Shera?'

It wasn't Shera.

The blurred image came into focus slowly. It was a guy. Similar age to Adam. Big smile. Hands on hips.

'How do Adam. Don't think we've met?'

Adam stared. He felt momentarily disorientated and a little scared. This wasn't exactly a teenage party. How the hell are you supposed to greet people in a metaphysical multi-dimensional environment?

The figure spoke again, relaxed, friendly. Dark haired guy - maybe five-foot six, square jawed, handsome type wearing a rugby shirt and jeans. American accent. Adam wasn't sure who he was expecting to meet in this place. Angels with wings maybe? A regular guy in jeans seemed too...well...

Normal?

'First time?'

'Sorry?'

'*First time? I mean you look a bit shocked - is this the first time you've visited here? Hey, it's okay - I don't bite or anything*'.

Adam's features relaxed into a smile. 'No, not quite the first time. Sorry I'm a bit confused at the moment. Y'know finding out who's who and what's what. Sorry, who are...?'

'*Tom. Tom Stevens. Pleased to meet you Adam*'.

Tom extended his hand and Adam responded cautiously. Unsure if his hand would meet empty air or something fleshy and substantial. It surprised him how strange it felt. Tangible alright, but somehow different. Lacking warmth and lacking something else that was more difficult to define. He shivered slightly. Tom seemed to notice his discomfort but ignored it.

'*So, tell me Adam...how did you end up here then?*'

Adam thought it was a bit of a stupid question. But then again normality was not the yardstick anymore.

'I...I'm not too sure. I've been learning to meditate. It's all very new and a bit strange. You?'

Tom nodded knowingly.

'*Meditation huh? You must be a natural then. Anyway, allow me to be your host. Anyone offered to show you around yet?*'

'No. Not really. I was expecting to find Shera. Do you know him? He's always been here waiting for me - well the last couple of times anyway.'

Tom smiled.

'*Oh yeah. I know him. Nice guy. But he hasn't shown you around yet though?*'

'No. We just talked.'

'*Great. Then you are in for a real treat. Follow me - I'll give you a tour around the place*'.

'Um...Thanks.'

'*No problem. Glad to be of service. You'll like it here.*'

'I'm not sure I know how to move around much yet.'

'No problem. Once you've got the hang of it, it's easy. Try not to move your body too consciously. Instead, just sort of think 'I want to go there' and it will happen automatically. Like for instance if you are going to follow me just think to yourself 'follow Tom' and it will happen. Trust me'.

'I'll give it a go.'

'Great. Just follow me then'.

Following Tom through the series of wispy colours and textures, the landscape of the inner world, was, as Tom had said, easy and effortless. There was hardly a sense of motion, not like the turgid pulls and pushes of gravitation and resistance that defined motion in the physical world. It was almost too easy. In a matter of moments, to his complete and utter amazement, Adam found himself in some kind of town. 'Some kind' because it was not made up of buildings he recognised, but they were definitely buildings. Buildings in all different shapes and sizes but without any doors. Tom motioned to Adam to follow him as he walked through an opening into the interior of one of the larger edifices.

Once inside, the building opened out into a vast auditorium with a high domed ceiling. There was muted music coming from somewhere and although the whole room was brightly lit there was no sign of any artificial lighting or windows. The thing that surprised Adam most of all though, was the large mass of people that filled the room from wall to wall, the buzz of conversation stopping only momentarily as many eyes fell on him before looking away again. Something was definitely very weird about the place. Adam momentarily thought he might be asleep and not meditating at all. Asleep and in the middle of some confused dream which blended the familiarity of 'The Anchor' with the weirdness of the metaphysical. It took some concentration to remain focused on the situation. One or two people had got up from their seats, leaving drinks on tables, and now strolled over towards Adam and Tom their hands outstretched.

'Hi Tom - who's your friend?'

'Allow me to introduce Mr Adam Sinclair'.

Adam shook hands with two strangers. Lads about the same age as himself. One introduced himself as Garry and the other as Mike. Garry was tall, skinny with long hair with a cigarette glued to his lip. Mike was short, bespectacled and studious looking. For a moment Adam felt that the whole situation had become bizarre, surreal even. But then again this wasn't supposed to be like 'normality' was it?

(Whatever normality means).

'Fancy a beer?'

'Uh?'

'I said fancy a beer?' Tom repeated whilst signalling a waiter to come over.

'You get beer here?' Adam heard himself say.

'Sure' said Garry, *'You can get anything here man'.*

Tom led the way to an empty table, and they all sat down. Adam realised that he had to remain calm, unaffected and aloof almost in order to stay with this situation. The slightest break in concentration could send him hurtling back into his heavy, leaden physical body. He wanted to stay a bit longer. Figure this one out.

'So - where are we?' He asked of no-one in particular.

'Just a club' replied Mike with a sniff, *'There's loads of clubs around - not been before then?'*

'No.'

'It's Adam's first time' explained Tom, *'I found him wandering around the outer limits'.*

'*Oh*' Garry and Mike both nodded knowingly.

Adam was about to ask what was meant by 'the outer limits', but a girl caught his eye at the next table. She gave him a cute smile while sipping a long drink through a straw. He felt his face redden.

A guy with a smart waistcoat and a tray appeared and raised an eyebrow at Tom.

'*Four beers*' Tom ordered. The waiter nodded and turned on his heels.

Tom noticed Adam looking at the girl on the next table.

'*That's Lamia*' he said with a smile, '*Or 'Lammy' as we call her. I'll introduce you if you like. It's great here. You can talk to anyone. Do whatever you want. You'll be really glad I brought you here*'.

Adam gave Tom a look. Something in the tone of voice.

Or maybe he was just imagining it.

The beers arrived, as normal and as commonplace as if he were sitting in The Anchor with the lads.

Real lads.

Real?

Garry took a deep swig. '*So*' he belched, wiping his mouth on his sleeve, '*I guess you'll not be staying long. No disrespect like - but I guess this is just a short er...visit?*'

Adam assumed Garry was referring to the fact that the meditative state cannot be sustained indefinitely.

What else could he mean?

'Yeah. Just a short visit. I need to get back soon.'

Garry nodded. '*Yeah. Know what you mean. Well - now you know where we are you can always come again*'.

'Yeah. I guess. Thanks.'

Adam took a mouthful of beer. It was a bit tasteless. Bland. A tingling deep inside reminded him of the need to return soon. He glanced at Lamia again. She was still staring at him. She fluttered her eyelashes.

'*Before you go back can I tell you something?*' said Tom.

'Sure. What is it?' said Adam.

'*It's a kind of gift*' said Tom with a wink. '*A sort of secret that I'd like to share with you*'.

'Go on.'

'*Just tell me something that you'd like. You know - REALLY like*'.

'What sort of something?'

'*Hey. Whatever you want*', shrugged Tom.

Adam frowned while he wondered what Tom was getting at.

What the hell...

'Well, I'm short of cash at the moment,' said Adam '...Got a few debts to pay. Is that the sort of thing you meant? And I'm keen for my new job to go well. I'm not looking for charity though....'

'*No. No. 'Course not. That's not what I meant*' said Tom '*You'll see*'.

The internal tingling feeling was growing in intensity 'I need to get back. How do I get back from here?'

'*Easy*' said Tom putting a friendly hand on Adam's shoulder, '*Just shut your eyes and say, 'I want to go back'. Simple as that*'.

'You sure?'

'*Trust me*'.

Adam closed his eyes, mentally asked to return and heard a whooshing sound in his ears. A sense of movement. A slight dizzy feeling. The image of Lamia's face swirled before him.

'*See ya then*' he heard Mike say.

'Nice guy', said Garry.

'Yeah' agreed Tom, 'Nice guy'.

The voices began to fade. A sensation of movement. A moment of nausea. Dislocation.

Then the sights and smells of a teenage bedroom.

Home.

His heart was thumping a lot more than usual. And he needed the loo.

That whole episode had been seriously weird. Unfathomable. Dreamlike - yeah. But not a dream. Exhilarating too.

He wondered what Shera would make of it. Or Jack.

He also wondered if he would ever see the gorgeous Lamia again.

Adam walked over to his favourite bench in the local park - the one overlooking the lake - and lit a cigarette noticing that his hand was shaking a little. He hadn't bothered to tell anyone where he was going - didn't want company right now.

Ideally, he would have preferred to be sitting atop the South Downs, up on Greenwood hill, staring out to sea and watching the sun going down. Laughing and daydreaming just like he had done with Marie all those years ago.

Or was it really only last year? Hard to be sure these days. There was something rather special about Greenwood hill. Not just because of the memories it invoked about his dad or Marie. It was something more than that. It was the place itself - it had some kind of atmosphere that certain places just do. A kind of inexplicable aura that was something more than just the physical landscape itself. It seemed to be imbued with the memories of all the people who had been there long before and who had also enjoyed the serenity and tranquillity of such a beautiful spot. It was as though every fold of the land, every rock, every stream and every hollow exuded positive vibrations, like Avebury or Glastonbury were reputed to do. Vibrations that you could only pick up at certain times when you were attuned to the very soul of the land itself. Like when you are in love or something.

Adam's mind drifted back to the present.

He was annoyed with himself for smoking again. Christ - he'd almost given up for good and to be honest he wasn't actually enjoying it - but hey - it might help him relax a little. He needed some space right now. Some time to reflect.

Looking out over the lake and watching small children playing and feeding the ducks made him smile. Normality.

'Yeah, I remember normality. I tried it once.'

This was the place Jack had bought him to tell him the story of the Golden Feather. Jack's way of using parable and metaphor to convey the inexplicable. What an amazing guy. Adam had wanted to call him up on the phone so many times recently and ask for help - guidance - support - anything. But he was too bloody stubborn to do it. Jack had set him the challenge to go it alone for a while and Adam had picked up the gauntlet. There was no way he was going to fail now. No way. He'd wanted to call Marie too. Tell her that despite everything, he still loved her and missed her and all that shit. Wanted to tell her all about this crazy double world he was trying to muddle through and cope with because she might - she just *might* - be able to help him through it.

But hey – *get real* - he was too bloody stubborn to do that either.

Then there were his best mates - what the fuck did they make of him these days? What did he make of *himself* these days?

He thought back to that walk in the park with Steve - the day he'd got shivers down his spine because his mate had said something really quite innocuous that had freaked him out. What was all that about? Then there was poor old long-suffering mum who worried over him like mothers do. Trying hard to be both mother and father to him. Trying to plug the gaping wound in his life that he had never come to terms with.

It was all a bloody mess really.

He thought about the Gazette. At least the new job was going reasonably well. Somewhere he could prove himself if he tried hard enough.

If...

At least it was somewhere safe, boring, routine and most of all, reassuringly normal.

Yeah - he needed normality like a medicine. A way of keeping him sane because he needed meditation too. Another medicine. He needed it badly.

Adam stubbed out his cigarette on the grass and sat back on the bench watching the children throwing sticks into the lake. Watching the ripples ebb and flow. Reminding him once more of some words he had heard a long time ago.

After a while he got up and wandered back to the park gates then up the road towards home. There was a good film on TV tonight, and it had been a long time since he'd seen a good film.

"Are you sure this is all your own work?"
"Yeah. Why?"

"Because" said Gavin Carter, sub-editor of the Gazette for the last five years and Chairman of the local Rotary Club, "It's good. Not brilliant, mind. But it's good."

Gavin was waving a piece of paper in his hand containing Adam's first try at writing a newspaper report. Though he was reluctant to admit it, he actually liked it.

Okay, realistically there was little chance of Mr Stanley T Morgan actually printing it, but what the hell. Adam had only been working for Gavin for three weeks but the two of them had hit it off immediately. Sure, Gavin was a lot older at thirty-five, had a degree in English Literature and was infuriatingly Welsh, but he'd taken Adam under his wing and taught him all the basics in his new role as sub-editorial assistant. He was also a bit of a laugh.

Adam had quickly learned the archaic filing system, how to make tea the way Stanley (and Gavin) liked it and how to sort and distribute the morning post. He'd even read some of Gavin's work and had the balls to criticize it.

"File this away will you Adam."

"Yeah, sure. What is it?"

"Oh, just my report on the local fete last week - it goes under Community Events."

"It's crap Gavin."

"Come again?"

"It's crap. I just read it. It's boring."

"Life's boring boyo. It's the local fete - 'course it's boring. It was organised by the Women's Institute. What d'you expect - a Roman orgy?"

"No. But I bet I could write it to make it sound more interesting and exciting."

"Tenner you couldn't."

"Deal. Pass me a pen would you Gavin?"

"You're a cocky little sod Adam Sinclair. Here, borrow mine - don't lose it, mind."

"So" challenged Adam later "Is it, or is it not, better than your report on the fete?"

Gavin raised his hand in mock aggression.

"Look here smartarse...I'm the sub-editor and you're the tea boy, right?"

"Right."

"Good. I'm glad we've agreed on that one. Okay your report is not bad. I'd even go so far as to say it's marginally more entertaining than my version. So, I'll grudgingly give you the tenner as hush money if you make me a cup of tea and get back to the filing. Deal?"

"Deal".

Gavin opened his wallet and took out a crisp ten-pound note. He planted a kiss goodbye on it before handing it over to Adam with a ceremonial flourish.

"Thanks Gavin. So d'ya think I've got what it takes to be an editor then?"

Gavin swept his hand back through his thick black hair putting on a thoughtful expression. Then his face relaxed.

"No boyo. I just think you're a cocky bastard who's got a weird fetish for boring village fetes. Now...tea was it you were brewing?

Adam 'arrived' in the empty place with ease. Sometimes it took a great deal of concentration just to break through the empty place into the beautiful blue vista and at other times the shifting, whirling gossamer blue veils themselves parted silently, and, according to Shera, it meant he should now be able to walk through them into the Interference layer as easily as walking through an archway between one room and another.

The empty place was not particularly welcoming; rather it was somewhere you just got used to. Now that Adam was more conversant with this environment, he began to notice subtleties that had not been apparent before. In the empty place, it was perceptibly colder, gloomier and slightly disturbing. It was like standing in the middle of a dense fog that might be full of people or might be completely empty - and you never knew which, until someone - or something - stumbled or appeared out of the gloom.

Scary...

The deep blue, in contrast, was intoxicatingly beautiful visually and radiated warmth and security in an almost womb-like way. Beyond the blue the intriguing mysteries of the Interference layer were waiting, somewhere Adam had not yet ventured but according to Shera somewhere probably best avoided or traversed as quickly as possible.

No - the 'empty place' was not particularly appealing Adam decided.

But then again this was the place where Shera always waited.

Or used to wait.

Today the clouds frothed and steamed like mud pools in volcanic hot spots, moving, changing shape and reforming in endless activity. A boiling, seething white fog where vague shapes appeared and disappeared at random like those new and fashionable lava-lamps that Adam had noticed on sale in some of the bigger stores.

A figure emerged from the fog.

It wasn't Shera.

'Howdy Adam'

'Tom'

'Hey man - don't sound so surprised. Who did you expect? I knew you were here. Thought I'd drop by. See how your doin'.'

'Fine. Yeah good. So how did you know I was here?'

Tom stared at Adam as though he didn't understand the question. He shrugged.

'I just knew. Everyone knows. It's too obvious to explain. Anyshakes - don't worry about it. What's important is having a good time - yeah? So come on pardner let's go have a good time'.

'I was waiting for Shera'.

'No problem. He's around. Let's go meet up with the other guys - y'know Mike, Garry and er...Lamia...maybe Shera is there too?'

Adam thought about it for a moment. It would be good to find Shera but how long would he have to wait? Maybe Tom was right. Maybe Shera was somewhere close, and they could look for him.

'Okay Tom. Lead on.'

'Yes Siree...'

Tom led Adam back to the same domed 'pub' which was buzzing with noise and activity just like last time. Adam wondered whether or not a bartender ever shouted 'time'. Mike and Garry were at the same table as last time with full pints of beer in front of them. They stood up when Adam got to the table, and both shook his hand.

'Adam. Hey! - good to see you again. How's it goin' man?'

'Yeah. Good thanks.'

'Adam mate - fancy a beer? Glad you made it back so soon...'

Adam couldn't help but smile. In many ways this was too bizarre for words. Hell - if Marie could see him now. These guys were friendly enough but somehow there was something not quite right. They were almost *too* friendly - cheesy friendly - acting like they'd known him for years although they'd only met once before. And acting so casually, even though he was very much alive and they...*they were...?*

The girl at the next table caught his eye again. Lamia - that was it. She'd given him the eye once before. She was even more stunning than he remembered her. She was wearing a light blue gingham shoulder-less dress like girls did in those old American movies of country dancing. He could picture her in cowboy hat and boots.

Tom pushed a glass of beer into Adam's hand.

'Cheers!'

'Thanks Tom.'

Tom followed Adam's gaze and smiled.

'Hey Lammy - over here - come and meet a mate of mine. Adam...um...'

'Sinclair.'

'Yeah. Sinclair. Lammy this is Adam Sinclair'.

She beamed at him.

'Nice to meet you Adam'.

God. She was gorgeous. Adam knew he was staring but he couldn't help it. She was about nineteen. Fair golden hair, creamy tanned skin, full sensuous lips and a stunning figure that glided as she walked over from a nearby table. If this was heaven, then there was no doubt she was the Angel. All she needed was the wings. He felt his heart quicken. He tried to say something but 'Hi' was all he managed to croak.

Lammy sat down beside him facing Tom, Mike and Garry across the table.

She sipped a long drink through a straw then turned to look Adam in the eyes. He melted.

'Didn't I see you here once before Adam?'

'Er...yeah...a few days ago.'

She giggled *'days!'* she repeated, eyes sparkling. The other guys laughed too.

Adam frowned, 'What's so funny?'

'Hey, don't worry about us' said Tom stifling his laughter, *'It's just - y'know - certain words...no-one around here talks about 'days' anymore. It's kinda old-fashioned. Days don't mean much to us guys. Time is different here. Different from what you're used to...'*

Adam recalled Jack's soliloquy on all matters temporal. 'I understand" he said sympathetically 'Sometimes it's hard to adjust...you know...'

"*Sure*".

Lammy beamed at him again.

'Take no notice of them Adam. They're just teasing. This must all be very strange for you - and you must be a very special person'.

He felt his face redden a little. Wondered if she'd noticed.

'Not really' he replied modestly, 'I've had to work hard to get this far. I learn more every time about so many things...and I'm still learning.'

'Well, there's plenty to learn if you want to learn' said Lammy looking at the others who all nodded in

accord, *'And here you can pretty much do as you please too'.*

Adam tried not to keep staring into Lammy's eyes. It was too obvious. He averted his gaze and turned to Tom instead.

'I've got so many questions I don't even know where to start' he confessed. 'Questions about this place, about who you all are and where you all come from. What you do here and how you live...'

The word 'live' hung in the air momentarily. Adam wondered if the word was somehow inappropriate. If it was, no-one reacted.

'Hey - there's no need to worry about all that stuff' said Tom congenially, laying a hand on Adam's shoulder. *'Where you have just come, from those kinds of things are important. But here they are irrelevant. This is a great place to relax, do as you please, have fun, hang out - we left all that time and space shit behind a long time ago'.*

Adam took a swig of beer inwardly philosophising at the irony of his situation. 'Unbelievable' was far too mild a term to explain the surreal. If there was a word for it, he couldn't think of it.

'So' said Adam trying to be as sociable, 'What do you guys do around here? Do you always hang out here?'

'Hey - no way man' laughed Tom, *'We can go anywhere we want. Anywhere. Well...except like, where you have come from. We can sort of go there too if we really want but it's...well it's a lot of hassle'.*

Adam caught Tom and Garry exchanging glances. Now was obviously not the time to pursue that line of questions. It could wait.

'Anyhow' continued Tom, *'Lammy can show you round can't you Lammy?'*

'Sure. Love to'.

'Really?' said Adam 'I'd like that.'

"There's something wrong".

Jack put down the newspaper on the settee, removed his specs and turned down the volume control knob on his wireless (he still couldn't get used to calling the thing a 'radio.') A frown briefly crossed his features. Not one to normally talk to himself, even when engrossed in his favourite radio programme, he was distinctly ill at ease. The feeling had come over him slowly at first but now washed over him like a rekindled memory of something sad. Lady sensed Jack's unease too, looking up at him inquisitively from her curled position on the carpet, head cocked to one side.

Jack had learned to always trust his intuition and instincts. Feelings that others might brush aside with indifference; Jack treated with respect. If Jack felt that there was something wrong - then there was something wrong.

It had been a beautiful day and Jack had spent most of it pottering in the back garden. Not that there was much to do other than a little weeding and grass mowing as he liked to keep it regularly tended.

When Ellie was alive, Autumn evenings were times for walks in the country or even the occasional meal out at the local pub. Some friends and acquaintances had tentatively hinted that he might like to re-marry but somehow that wouldn't have felt right. Now he generally enjoyed his own company and the pleasures of solitude. If he was ever lonely it was in the sense of missing Ellie rather than wanting to replace her.

Jack stroked the stubble on his chin. It was something to do with Adam. That's what was wrong.

His mind drifted back to their last meeting. All that talk about time, space, death and inner meditative journeys was enough to confuse anybody's mind. Then there was the discussion about inner guides and finding the unique keys that would open people's individual spiritual gateways to deeper unknown realms.

Jack shook his head when he thought about it, amused at the irony that these very topics would be ridiculed by most people as either avant-garde science fiction at best, or lunatic fringe fantasy at worst. And yet if those same people could just break free of their own scepticism and prejudices for just a moment, then what wonders they might behold. What treasures they might find.

He sighed deeply knowing it was unlikely to happen. It would remain as it always had been, the preserve of the few enlightened souls willing to believe in their own innate abilities and potentials, hiding away their inner knowledge from the ridicule of the masses. To be different, particularly in the not too distant past, was to invite distrust, prejudice, persecution and even death.

He envied Adam's incredible capacity to move effortlessly between the twilight worlds that the scientists choose to label 'the unconscious'. It was not an ability granted lightly. And one day, probably very soon, Adam would learn the truth about why he was 'chosen'.

If 'chosen' was the right word for it.

Tonight though, there was something wrong.

Jack's intuition was enough to warn him that somewhere 'out there' in the unseen, but very real spiritual world, there was something amiss. But intuition alone wasn't enough to pinpoint exactly what it was.

All he could be sure of is that somehow it involved Adam.

And then it came to him.

The lad was somehow in danger...

Lammy waited until Adam had finished his drink and then led him by the hand through the crowd of socialisers and out of the main doorway. Adam had been aware of a few eyes following him across the room with a sort of amused curiosity but there was nothing threatening or antagonistic in their demeanour.

Outside of the large domed 'pub' Lammy looked even more tanned and radiant. She smiled at him warmly.

'Where would you like to go?'

Adam shrugged. His face felt flushed. 'Oh anywhere...up to you.'

For the first time he started to take more notice of his surroundings. The sun looked the same as always and it was a glorious day. The landscape reminded him of Alfred Bestall's drawings in the Rupert books he had so loved as a child. Sort of a rural, rustic green and pastoral. Nothing industrial or ugly anywhere. Quite idyllic really. Sylvian almost.

Lammy watched him taking it all in.

'You like it here, don't you?' she said sweetly.

'Oh yeah. It's amazing.'

'Then let me show you where we live'.

Adam nodded and walked along beside her as she tugged him by the hand.

He wondered what she meant by 'we'.

Lammy led him around the base of a small hillock and followed a path through a few stunted oak trees. After only a few yards a small cottage appeared that seemed to almost grow out of the ground itself. There was nothing unusual about it at all. But then what was he expecting? It was a picture postcard thatched cottage made of honey coloured stone. Reminded him of pictures he'd seen of the Cotswolds.

'Come on in'.

He followed Lammy through the low doorway ducking slightly and then let his eyes adjust to the darker and cooler interior. She led him through another door on the right.

'It's only a small place but it's cosy. That's the sitting room and this is my bedroom. It's nice, isn't it?'

'It's...er...lovely. So...do you own...?"

Lammy giggled and put her hand over his mouth playfully.

'You are so funny Adam'.

'I am?'

'Yes. I think so. What do you think of me then?' She did a twirl so that her gingham dress flared.

Adam was taken aback by the forthrightness of the question. He smiled nervously and cleared his throat. He never got this tongue-tied with the birds at 'The Anchor'.

'Oh, I think you're great Lammy. A really nice pers...'

She stepped upon tiptoe and kissed him full on the mouth.

He'd expected to feel very little in the circumstances and was surprised to find the opposite was true. It was as though all external stimuli and distractions had been turned off so that every sensory nerve in his body had been tuned to maximum sensitivity. The kiss was like nothing he had ever experienced before. It was sheer intensity.

Her lips, soft, warm and sensuous melted against his own lips as her hair brushed his cheeks. She was wearing an intoxicating musky perfume which was so overwhelming it seemed to flood into his body making his heart quicken again. He felt his arms move to hold her tight against him, relishing every quiver of her body.

For a moment his memory recalled the other kisses he had known in his life. Until now the only ones that mattered were Marie's but...

...but this was something very very different.

Not even Marie's kisses could compete with this.

Lamia was manoeuvring him backwards until the back of his knees collided with the edge of the bed and he fell backwards onto it. With a giggle she launched herself on top of him clamping her lips tightly and sensuously against Adam's his.

He could feel her soft breasts pressed hard against his chest through the flimsy material she was wearing; it started a tingling sensation somewhere deep within him. She was starting to move against him, and a slow moan came from her lips as her kissing became more frenzied, her tongue pushing into his mouth exploring and probing.

Adam ran his hand through her hair until it fell over her eyes making her look even wilder and more desirable.

It crossed his mind that normally the slightest lapse of concentration would immediately start tugging him back into his physical body – but, somehow, he was managing, despite the circumstances, to hold on to this moment.

Lammy was getting more excited and demanding. She lifted her body slightly and then in one swift jerk tugged the gingham dress over her head in a single movement. Adam was momentarily surprised that she wore no underwear but the sight of her writhing, naked flesh pinning him to the bed was making him crazy with passion. Lammy gripped the two sides of his shirt in her hands then in one blur of movement tore the shirt open vigorously sending buttons in all directions across the room. The strength with which she did it surprised him, but it was also a huge turn-on.

Adam felt his face flush and became aware of his breath quickening. He kicked off his shoes and started to fumble at his leather trouser belt with one hand. Lammy's tongue was now tracing a warm wet line down his neck and shoulder. Her hand moved down to his belt and helped him push the jeans down over his thighs, her hand caressing and pulling gently, driving him mad with passion.

The burning deep within him began to intensify. It was as though long buried emotions were being drawn out from the depths of his being and seeping throughout his body making him shudder. Lammy flung herself sideways simultaneously pulling him effortlessly on top of her, reversing their positions. Her legs were splayed wide, and her eyes searched the depths of his eyes, her mouth slightly parted, her long blond hair spread out like a halo across the pillow, perfect breasts rising and falling with exertion. Up until this moment Lammy had been in total control. Now she was signalling to him that she was ready. She was naked, defenceless and wanting him desperately. Adam knew this was the moment - *his moment* - to fulfil a deep uncontrollable desire.

Except that this was also the same moment that the whole world suddenly turned crazy.

Someone – *or some 'thing'* - wrenched Adam's shoulders backwards pulling him violently off Lammy's body and off of the bed too. Adam whirled around trying to find the assailant but whoever or whatever it was, it remained completely invisible.

Even more bizarre, the very walls of the bedroom were no longer solid and smooth but had started to ripple and buckle as though caught in a silent earthquake. In one or two places, cracks appeared in the walls through which trickles of foul-smelling black liquid started to seep and then to pour.

Adam instinctively pulled his trousers back up with one hand, simultaneously reaching out to steady himself with the other but stumbling when his hand went clean through the rippling wall as easily as a rock through water.

Everything else in the room was changing too. The bedside cabinet, table lamp and wardrobe were starting to melt like heated plastic or wax although there was no heat. And then the walls and the furniture started to melt into each other until they became a mass of 'goo' bound together by the noxious black liquid. The foul concoction swirled soup-like around the floor as though the room itself were a vast mixing bowl and everything in it were mere ingredients to be bonded together into a seething cauldron of indeterminate substances.

It was at this point that Adam felt the familiar tug of his 'physical self' pulling him away from the swirling mass of chaos. He lifted a foot which came up from the floor through the thickening treacle of congealing matter and was relieved that he could just about free himself from the rising tide of melted walls and furnishings. Another tug pulled him free, and he found himself floating in the centre of what was once a room.

Lammy was still lying naked on the bed but her rapturous expression had given way to something much more sinister. She heaved herself upright with a sudden angry snarl that made Adam's blood turn to ice. Her eyes had narrowed to yellow slits and her soft, blond hair had turned into a wriggling mass of bloated maggots and spitting venomous snakes like the Gorgon from Greek mythology. Saliva dripped from sharp wolf - like fangs and her arms had turned into long leathery talons that now flicked out across the room and were tightening around his throat and windpipe.

He tried to scream, but her grip was too tight.

My God. She was trying to physically kill him - and he was powerless to defend himself against her unbelievable strength.

The last thing he remembered was his own desperate coughing and choking, unsure if it was the intensifying pressure on his neck or the acrid smell of Lammy's breath that was causing him to lose consciousness.

Carol Sinclair had always been a light sleeper. Even in those happier days when she'd shared a bed with her late husband the slightest noise would awaken her. In those days, though, she would simply reach out to touch his warm body, feeling the gentle ebb and flow of his breath with each rise and fall of his chest, and that simple reassuring touch would be enough to send her slipping back into the tranquillity of sleep. Even when Adam was young, she'd hear every small cough or whimper from his bed, the way that mothers do. And she could tell from each sound how well, or not, he was sleeping. Even in Adam's teenage years that mother's natural instinct remained. She could tell - almost through the wall that separated their bedrooms - whether or not he was sleeping soundly. Tonight, was no different. She glanced at the luminous bedroom clock noting that it was 2.33 in the morning and wondered why Adam was tossing and turning so much and mumbling in his sleep. She could recognise the heavy breathing that normally followed a night of too much drinking, but this was different. Something was bothering him.

He couldn't settle. She thought about getting up and pouring him a glass of water so she could shake him awake like she did when he was a child, reassure him and watch over him until he was sleeping soundly again. Must be that those bull nightmares were back - those awful inexplicable nightmares that no doctor or child psychologist could help with. Strangely he'd seemed to have got over them recently for the first time in his life. He'd actually told her that for the last few months they had almost completely ceased. But tonight...?

Then again it was late, and Adam was legally a man himself now and would probably resent her interference.

She turned over, pulled the bedclothes tight around her and shut her eyes. Before she drifted back into sleep something made her reach out across the bed and pat the empty space next to her as she had done so many times before. It was a fruitless gesture. As always. What did she expect after ten years sleeping alone? Some sort of miracle that would re-manifest her one and only true love back where he belonged? She knew better than to expect anything like that of course. Things like that only happen in fairy tales.

She drew her hand back and sighed deeply hoping that peaceful sleep would come quickly for both her and her son.

Adam's eyes snapped open.

He could feel his heart and his pulse racing and the cold film of sweat on his forehead.

Thank God it was over.

Thank God.

Why had he been so bloody stupid? Jack and Shera had both warned him about the 'Interference Layer.'

They had warned him about 'negative influences', and 'temptation' and suchlike. But then he'd walked straight into it like a complete idiot, hadn't he? Not thinking about the consequences - as usual.

Why did he have to be such a hero?

Pig-headed arsehole more like.

Why hadn't he just waited for Shera instead of going off to God only knows where.

If that really was the place that he had nominated the 'Interference Layer' then boy, had he learned a lesson! That was the last time he was going to that hell hole.

Who were those fucking people?

He swallowed hard and then took a deep breath noticing how dark it had grown in the room since he had started to meditate.

He was puzzled. It surely couldn't have been more than an hour at most?

He stood up shakily, feeling some cramp in his legs and then limped over to the curtains drawing them slowly.

Thick black clouds stretched to the horizon. They were rolling past the face of the moon causing moonbeams to sliver off at tangents across the landscape.

He shivered slightly. A storm was brewing - that was why it had got dark so quickly.

Strange...it had been a bright and sunny evening only a short time ago...what time was it anyway?

Adam glanced sideways at the small travelling alarm clock on the bookshelf and frowned. 8.05 pm.

He rolled up his sleeve to check his watch against the clock. 8.05 again.

For some reason the second hand on his watch was not moving. He shook his hand to try and restart it.

Must be those damn cheap batteries from Hong Kong again.

But that wouldn't explain the alarm clock. How come that had stopped at precisely the same moment?

None of this made sense. He had started meditating a few minutes before eight in bright evening sunshine and had been meditating for at least half an hour - or so it seemed.

...Could have been hours.

Now it was just after eight - dark windy and cold.
But how could that be?

Adam yawned, rubbed his eyes then turned to the window again. The wind was whipping up now and some of the trees were beginning to arch. One or two large spots of rain spattered onto the windowpane.

A flash of silver momentarily lit up the surrounding houses before another black cloud plunged the world back into a funereal darkness again. Weird.

...Something wrong here.

Perhaps it was because he felt disorientated, he reasoned with himself, yeah - that was it – disorientated because of that godawful bad experience with Lamia. That evil *'thing'* called Lammy that must have crawled out of some stinking, metaphysical, underground crypt.

Experience? Dream? Hallucination?

Somehow the time that should have passed was lost...and it made the world seem...well, *different*.

He felt distinctly uncomfortable. Couldn't put his finger on it but things were definitely not as they should be. He put his hands on the front of his denim shirt and felt for the buttons. They were all there. Intact.

He shook his head to try and lose the fuzzy feeling in his brain. Maybe a cold drink would help calm his nerves a little. There was some orange squash in the kitchen fridge downstairs. Maybe he was just tired and dazed.

Adam stumbled rather than walked out of his bedroom and onto the landing. He could hear the sound of gentle breathing from Carol's room. At least she seemed to be sleeping soundly. But even that didn't make sense. Carol usually turned in around 11pm. Why was she in bed at 8.05pm?

The landing was even darker and colder than the bedroom and felt unusually repressive. Every few seconds a break in the clouds sent a flash of silver light scudding around the walls like a searchlight briefly illuminating random images - the awful painting of a juggling clown on the wall that Mum had bought in a junk shop because she thought it looked cute; the dusty thimble collection on a shelf and the old grandfather clock that had stopped working years ago. Why had he never bothered to fix it?

There was a rumble of distant thunder as Adam reached the top of the stairs.

Then there was a different sound which caused him to stop and listen. The hairs on the back of his neck started to rise. It was not the sound of Carol's gentle breathing. It came from somewhere else. The sound of a faster and deeper heavy breathing.

...And then the smell of something he identified as 'animal'.

Animal?

Lammy?

Nah - she couldn't have followed him here. She wasn't part of physical reality. She belonged to that twilight world inside his head. Christ - why was he getting so jittery?

This wasn't happening he told himself - this was part of a dream - the dream - but a dream that was all over - in the imagination. In the meditative world. Not real life. Things like this don't happen in real life. They can't.

Can they?

He stood motionless. One sweaty palm clamped to the top of the banister rail.

His nostrils twitched involuntarily at the acrid stench of hot animal, his ears straining to catch the slightest sound.

For a few seconds there was silence and then without warning a blast of hot foul breath from behind sent him flying headlong down the stairs.

Dreams aren't real - this can't be happening.

...Ohmygod Jack. Where are you? I need some help here...

Adam reached the foot of the stairs without turning to look, stabbing at the light switch hoping that the sanity of an electric light would dissipate the creature at his heels.

Nothing happened.

Shit! There was no electricity.

Within seconds he was at the front door, fumbling at the door lock, sensing that some sort of creature was following him with a slow almost casual deliberation, each stair creaking in turn as it moved purposefully forwards.

The lock wouldn't turn. It was jammed.

Adam swore at the door - screamed at it - hit it in desperation until his fingers bled.

It didn't budge.

Just like in some fairy story...

He turned and braced his back against the door as another flash of intense moonlight briefly illuminated the hallway.

The thing was still there. Moving slowly and heavily down the last few stairs - its shape vague and indiscernible in the shifting patterns of darkness. At the bottom of the stairs, it stopped - some ten yards or so away from Adam - seeming to rock gently from foot to foot as though involved in some sort of macabre dance while continuing to snuffle and snort.

...And then slowly, very slowly, it started to shuffle forward.

When sheer terror takes over from rational thought it's funny how time seems to be suspended...

The door was somehow jammed and there was no other means of escape as the creature was blocking the route to the back door via the kitchen. He thought for a moment about shouting out to Carol. Crying for his Mum. Tell her he was having a bad nightmare. She'd come out of her room wondering what was going on like she did when he was a small child and then...

But he couldn't speak. Couldn't shout. For some reason his vocal cords were not responding.

There was nothing within reach with which to defend himself. No way out. No escape.

For a fleeting second Adam convinced himself he had not really woken up - yes! - that must be it - he was still having the same nightmare as before and any moment now he would wake up. It would be morning and there would be warm sunshine and...

The creature was less than six feet away now and its original dark amorphous shape had taken on a more solid form. Its hot breath was suffocating, and its eyes glinted in the moonlight. Saliva dripped noisily onto the hallway carpet with a *plishing sound.*

Now he could see it more clearly.

It was a huge black bull, standing unnaturally upright on its hindquarters, smooth white horns tipped forward in poised readiness.

With a gasp Adam realised that the bull was moving the same way that they move in the bullrings of Spain adjusting the angle of their heads before charging the red flags of the Matadors.

...Except that this bull was weirdly standing fully upright. Upright on two legs.

Like a man.

Why did it have to be a bull? Why God? Anything else - but please not a bull....

Please?

And then there was an ear shattering bellow as the beast lunged forward driving its enormous horns clean through the denim shirt and into the soft flesh of Adam's torso. Blood spattered the bull's face and wood splintered as the razor-sharp horns emerged through the torn flesh of Adam's back with a snap of bone and embedded themselves into the door.

Adam screamed audibly as he felt the gut-wrenching pain of impact. The door hinges were torn from the wall as the whole door collapsed backwards into the teeth of the storm.

And now Adam was crushed between the bull and the door which was still firmly attached to the bull's horns and the bull was running powerfully and frantically on all four legs - headlong into the night.

Adam was pinioned to the door through the chest, his feet unable to touch the ground, aware of the pace, stench and movement of the charging creature and desperate for death to take the pain away.

Before mercifully losing consciousness, he noticed with a sort of detached bewilderment that the bull was no longer running on solid ground anymore but instead running through a field of stars in the awesome void of the Universe.

Blackness.
   Cold, silent, vile, blackness.
   So, this was the end then?
   Just nothing but darkness and...
   Death?
   The end of everything. Dissolution. Ice cold emptiness. Finality.
   Darkness and...
   ...voices.
   Voices?
   "Come on Adam wake up. You're going to miss the bus to work".
   Carol's voice.
   "Huh?"
   "I said it's time to get up. What's the matter with you this morning?"
   Adam groaned and turned over. He was curled in a foetal position on the bed. There were no bedclothes over him. He was shaking uncontrollably. Shaking and cold. Stomach convulsing.
   Scared to open his eyes.
   Scared. But she mustn't know that.
   "Bad dream," he mumbled.
   "Yes well, we all have bad dreams from time to time. But that's no excuse for missing work, is it? If you ate your meals at the proper times and cut down on the beer you would probably get a better night's

sleep. You kept me awake half the night with your groaning, tossing and turning."

"I'm sorry..."

"You've not been taking drugs again, have you?'

"No. 'course not. I'm fine. S'nothing."

"Was it your bull nightmare again?"

Adam shuddered inwardly.

"Yeah. It was. Look I'm okay...really"

He yawned, rubbed sleep from his eyes and fumbled for his alarm clock. He frowned.

"It's working. It says 8.30 am."

"What's working? Are you sickening for something?"

"Shit."

"And that's enough bad language from you, my lad. Now get up and get your skates on."

His head was still throbbing. Thank God it was all over. Thank God for normality. Thin filaments of sunshine were filtering through his bedroom window which seemed to be coated in a thin crust of frost. He opened the curtains wider and stood staring out across suburbia for a few moments savouring the familiarity of the gardens and houses. There had been nightmares before of course, but not like last night. No way. He could still feel a dull ache in his ribs where the bull's horns had gored him, and he couldn't help but move his hands over his skin just to make sure there were no scars. It was smooth and intact. Did this mean he was going mad? Never before had a nightmare been so real - so painful - so terrifyingly vivid. The bull had always been there of course, as far back as he could remember, but not like this. Not bone-splitting real. Perhaps it was something to do with all this meditation? Maybe the depth of concentration that he was attaining over recent months was also awakening his subconscious to new levels and making even dreams take on a new almost tangible realism? Or maybe it was because he'd been a complete idiot and walked headlong into temptation despite all the warnings.

He washed and dressed quickly. There was no time for breakfast, so he grabbed a packet of crisps and an apple from the kitchen cupboard of as he ran out of the front door slamming it behind him.

"Have you cleaned your shoes?" he heard his mother yelling after him. It was something that she reminded him each morning. He glanced down at the scuffed loafers which obviously needed a good clean and sighed. Another tedious chore that he had forgotten as usual. Oh well, what the heck, nobody in the office seemed to mind the scuffed shoes - there were far more important things to worry about in the scheme of things.

Adam was halfway to the bus stop when he realised that the events of last night were still affecting him deeply. He still had that strange feeling in the pit of the stomach and an occasional sensation of nausea. Perhaps it was not such a good idea to try and face a busy day's work in the office. Maybe he should take the day off sick and try to recover. Then again there was no way that his mother would have any sympathy for someone taking a day off because they had experienced a bad dream.

Shera would understand though. Not only that - but he would probably understand the reason and the meaning behind the horrific nightmares.

Adam put out his hand to signal the bus to stop. He climbed aboard, paid the fare, then sat back gazing idly out of the window at the uniformly grey Victorian terraced houses passing him by.

Tonight, he must concentrate all his efforts on meditating so that he could contact Shera and ask him what the hell was going on. And if Tom dared to turn up first, he'd tell him where to go. No way he was gonna follow that guy anywhere, ever again.

He would have to avoid all the usual things that made meditation more difficult. Things that he'd learned over the last few months. He now knew that things like caffeine, alcohol or rich foods somehow seemed to affect his concentration. They made him fidgety and unfocused. Other things like water, fruit or vegetables seemed to have the opposite effect, making him more relaxed and better able to concentrate. Jack would probably know why. He must ask him sometime.

Today though he had to put the horrors of last night behind him and try and keep his mind on the day's paperwork. He shivered slightly and tried to pull himself together, looking around the bus to see if he recognised anybody. No - the faces were unfamiliar. Bored businessmen in dull suits reading the morning papers and harassed mothers with folded pushchairs trying to keep boisterous toddlers under control. For some reason he found himself studying their faces closely. The faraway expressions, the furrowed brows, the world-weary wrinkles and the taut muscles. He wondered if any of these people had ever discovered what the real world was like.

The inner world.

Real? What was he on about? God - he really must be losing it.

For a moment he felt the urge to tell them what they were missing. He wanted to tell them that there were other worlds, other dimensions out there - beyond the experience of the daily grind. And for a moment he wanted to help them in the same way that Jack had helped him, and to release them from the confines of dull routine - help them discover that there really was an alternative to the turgid prison of everyday consciousness. Then they too could join him in the amazing places that he had discovered beyond the boundaries of so-called 'normality'.

The ting of the bell interrupted Adam's reverie. It was his stop. Nah - no point...people didn't want to listen. They would just assume he was another spaced-out hippy on an acid trip (*Jesus! A few months ago, that's exactly what he was!*) People didn't want to hear about all that airy-fairy stuff these days. They wanted to stay in their cosy little boring semis' grumbling about the price of fuel and groceries.

He jumped down on to the pavement, turned his coat collar up against a brisk morning breeze and blew into his hands to warm them up. Nah - he never wanted to be like these dull people. Petty, conformist and boring. Life was too short. The real answers to everything lie within his grasp. All he needed now was the willpower and the dedication to follow it through to the end.

Whatever that meant.

So, tonight, he resolved, he would try and make sense of the nightmare. Rationalise it in some way.

And then defeat it.

Up ahead, the offices of the Gazette beckoned. He glanced at his watch. Fifteen minutes late. Not a good start for a new job. He'd better grovel convincingly to the boss. Something, he reflected, that he'd learned to be pretty good at.

Adam was impatient to start meditating again as soon as he got home from the Gazette but knew he would have to bide his time. What was that old adage about the best way to cure a hangover was to have another drink? Hair of the dog an' all that. There was no way he wanted another encounter with 'Bride of Frankenstein' or mad-eyed bulls again. And no more metaphysical pub crawls with Tom and his weird mates - that was for sure. This time he would either make contact with Shera or return straight away. Simple as that.

The evening seemed to drag. Carol couldn't be bothered to cook so had rustled up beans on toast instead.

The two of them sat facing each other across the small kitchen table. She poured Adam a cup of tea and pushed the cup and saucer over to him.

"Good day at the paper?"

Adam wondered why she never referred to it as the Gazette.

"Yeah. Okay I suppose".

"Have they still got you filing and making tea or are they training you to do anything else?" she asked with genuine interest.

"Bits 'n pieces" said Adam noncommittally, sipping his tea.

"Researching any juicy stories yet?"

"Nothin' much. Council business. Local events. That sort of stuff. Y'know".

Carol nodded. She knew when he wasn't in the mood to talk. Probably wanted to get back to his room and shut the door again until the morning. It wasn't natural.

Sometime after clearing away the tea things, she settled down with a newspaper in front of the TV. Adam waited until she was settled before leaving the lounge. He stopped momentarily. Aware that he ought to say something.

"I might go out with the boys' tomorrow night" he said conversationally, "We might go to the pictures. There's a good film on."

"Okay. Don't be home too late. And don't get drunk either."

"At the pictures? As I recall, there wasn't a bar there last time I went."

Carol threw a settee cushion at him across the room.

"You know what I mean."

Adam smiled, shrugged and closed the lounge door gently.

Before turning to go up the stairs to his bedroom he took a step over to the front door and ran his hand over the smooth panelled wood, half expecting to feel two gaping splintered holes but knowing, of course, that the door would be completely unblemished.

Sometime later, when the curtains had been shut, an incense stick had been lit and the door secured, Adam waited for the swirling mists to settle before mentally called Shera. This time he was determined to remain calm and focused. It didn't take long.

'Hello Adam, I'm here'.

Adam breathed a sigh of relief. Thank God. He wasn't in the mood to meet Tom and his friends again in a hurry.

'It was really easy getting here tonight Shera - I must be getting better at this meditation thing. Sometimes it takes such enormous concentration, then other times, like tonight it's - POW! - straight through.'

'That's good to hear Adam. You are indeed becoming very proficient.'

'There's something I need to ask you Shera. It's about a nightmare I had last night - if you can call it a nightmare. I was trying to meditate but I couldn't concentrate at all. I think I fell asleep but when I woke up a lot of strange things happened to me, and I got very scared. The scariest bit was not knowing whether I was actually awake - or dreaming that I was awake. It felt like reality, but something wasn't right...'

'Sometimes the boundaries between worlds are very thin Adam.'

'Well, they were certainly scary-thin on this occasion. I was attacked by this...this creature. I don't know why it wanted to kill me, but it did. It bloody killed me. It was like this huge bull-thing but standing on its back legs. Why does it always have to be a bull, Shera? It gored me right through with its horns. I remember screaming out in pain and thought I was dead until I came around a few hours later. I lost all sense of time too. It was the worst nightmare I've ever had - and believe me, I've had a few in my time. The pain was so real. What does it all mean Shera?'

'I am aware of the dream. I witnessed your suffering. Remember that I am the one who watches you.'

'You saw it all? What's going on then? There must be some explanation?'

'Everything has an explanation. There is a reason for the dream. You don't need to ask me to explain it because you already know the answer. The reason for the dream

and its meaning is in your own head. It has always been there. The answer to your question is already known to you, you just need to learn how to access it. Then you will understand.'

'I wish you wouldn't talk in riddles. How can I find it? Is it some sort of memory? Where do I look for an answer?'

'Yes, it is a memory. A very deep one. It is an important memory, and you should try to find it - it will explain many things about your life.'

'Can't you just tell me what it all means?'

'I could - but that will not help you to understand the deeper reasons for such dreams. It is something you need to locate and resolve yourself.'

'You're sounding just like Jack now. He more or less told me the same thing. Alright. Tell me what I have to do then.'

'You must face up to your fear. Everyone has to face their fears in order to remove them for good - because once you understand the reasons for your fear then you destroy its potency. You must analyse the reasons for your fear and then all will become clear.'

'Can I do that now?'

'No. Return to your body and rest. You must be mentally prepared before you face up to your fears. It can be a disturbing experience. But it has to be done sooner or later.'

'Will you be a witness to this um...experience?'

'Yes. I will be at your side Adam. As always.'

'In that case I'm prepared to go through with it. Oh...there was one other thing too - the last couple of times I've tried to contact you I didn't succeed. Some guy called Tom found me and led to me to a weird place with loads of kids just hanging out in a sort of bar.'

'I am aware of that too Adam, I was watching you.'

Adam felt his face redden. Shera must have seen everything that happened with Lammy then.

'You were? How come I didn't see you?'

'You have free will Adam. That's what being human is all about. It's about choice. I watch you and I care for you, but I cannot stop your own free will. If you wanted to see me enough then you would have seen me. Tom was offering you new experiences and it was up to you whether or not you chose to follow him. On that occasion you were more intrigued by Tom's offer to show you new exciting things than waiting for me. That is normal. It's a failing we all have to face called temptation.'

'By 'exciting things' you're referring to that girl - Lamia - that monster, aren't you?'

'Both Lamia and Tom are just manifestations of those who are trapped in the Interference layer as you call it Adam. The same as your other new-found friends. These are individuals who have passed over to the other side but who have not yet transitioned into the higher realms. They have chosen to remain in the 'Interference Layer' while they work through their own issues and karma. It is best that you avoid everyone that you meet in this layer. When the time is right, they will ascend. The monster that Lamia became was created by yourself though. Didn't Tom tell you that you could get anything you wanted in that place? Well now you know that there is always a price to pay. It's a powerful lesson. You have to decide what it is that you really want. I also recall that Tom promised you easy money?'

'Yeah - I'd forgotten about that.'

'And the following day someone at your work gave you money.'

Adam frowned, 'You mean the tenner Gavin gave me? No - that wasn't easy money - I made a bet with Gavin that's all.'

'And you really think there was no connection? If you had asked for more money from Tom, you would have received more.'

Adam considered Shera's words carefully. Somewhere from deep inside him a strange feeling started to unfurl. And with it came a realisation that pieces of a bizarre jigsaw were starting to slot into place. When he communicated again it was slow and precise.

'I don't want temptation any more Shera. Not ever. Not even if I can turn away from it more easily now that I'm more experienced. I want knowledge instead. I want to be able to understand what's going on in my life. Make sense of it all.'

'Then I will help you to do just that Adam. If that is your true desire. I will help you to do that next time we meet.'

'You will really help me to find whatever it is I'm looking for? Even if I don't even know myself.'

'If that is your heart's desire Adam. Yes. I will take you home.'

Adam wanted to ask Shera what he meant by using the word 'home' again, but then thought better of it. No doubt all would become clear in time.

'Thanks' was all he managed to mumble, feeling it to be a wholly inadequate response to the portentous nature of the offer.

At first it felt like a momentary sense of dizziness. Like when you jump up suddenly after sitting down for a long time and your body needs to quickly adjust to a new position. It was those little bones in the inner ear that did it - the ones that kept a sense of balance and orientation - so you didn't constantly fall over.

But this time it was more than dizziness. There were bright lights too. So bright that you needed to keep your eyes closed to stop them from blinding you.

It was the pain that was the worst though. Pain that started with a dull ache that grew in intensity until it felt like someone was hitting you over the head with a hammer inside a boxing glove.

'Damn' Marie swore, instantly recognising all the classic symptoms of another migraine coming on.

It was something she was used to. 'It's in the family' her mother had remarked matter-of-factly when she was young, 'Your grandmother suffered migraines all her life and it's been just the same for me.'

Thankfully it wasn't too regular an occurrence. Two or three times a year at most, but when it hit, it came back with a vengeance. It was always worse when it happened somewhere inconvenient like a shopping centre or at a social event.

At least today it was at home.

Marie's mother, Julie, noted the change in her daughter sympathetically and encouraged her to lie down on the settee and close her eyes until the worst of it was over. She turned off the radio and gently closed the lounge door. "Nothing you can do but rest" she said knowingly, "It will ease off in a while. Tell me if you need any pain killers."

Marie just nodded, kicked off her shoes and slumped onto the settee with a deep sigh, right hand shielding her eyes. She wondered if the migraine had been self-inflicted. After all she'd spent most of the last hour fretting and biting her nails thinking about the most irritating man on the planet. Adam Sinclair.

She might have known he'd forget to ring. Two weeks they'd agreed and then he'd get in touch again.

Only he hadn't.

'So why should I care?' she'd reasoned with herself earlier, 'We're not exactly going out together for heaven's sake. So, what does it matter?'

Annoyingly, frustratingly - it mattered. For some crazy reason it mattered.

Maybe it was something to do with the past. All those memories and stuff. Her mind had drifted back to those first days after they had first met and how she'd been so drawn towards him. She had been fascinated by those deep mysterious eyes behind an unruly mop of long hair. The sense that he was somehow different from the rest of the boys in her class though she could never work out why. And then they had fallen in love, and it had seemed so natural, and so much more than all those other ephemeral boy-girl flings that schooldays were all about. In those days they had been inseparable. They'd go for long walks in the country and talk about anything and everything, sharing their hopes and dreams, their insecurities and even their nightmares.

It was up on Greenwood hill, that magical place up on the South Downs overlooking the sea, that they had laid down together holding hands in the soft grass and Adam had really opened up. He'd talked about the day his father had died in a tragic car accident and left him feeling so numb inside - wondering why God had chosen to spare him and not his father on that fateful day. He'd talked about weird feelings that sometimes came over him - certain smells or phrases that inexplicably made him shudder and terrifying dreams about a big black bull that for some unfathomable reason always wanted to kill him.

And she had listened to every word, not mocking or patronising him, but hanging on to every syllable and trying to work out what exactly was going on in this strange young man's head. She'd thought back to those early days when Adam wanted to be 'one of the lads'. Experimenting with soft drugs and masking his insecurities by becoming the ringleader - the troublemaker at school. The more she'd begged him to stop the worse he became. Soon he was the one that the rest of the boys all looked up to. The extrovert practical joker who would always go that one step further in the quest 'for a laugh'. The chain smoker who'd play truant and never pay attention in lessons; the 'rough diamond' always at the heart of any trouble.

And she'd watched despairingly while his life became more and more of a mess, pleading with him at first then screaming at him in anger because of his pig-headed indifference. God only knows why she'd put up with him for so long.

...And God only knows why nearly two years later she still cared about him.

The migraine was getting worse. Maybe she ought to try those pain killers after all. Rationally, the migraine was nothing to do with Adam - it was just 'one of those things.'

So why - *irrationally* - did she so much want to blame him for it?

And why the hell couldn't he just pick up the phone to see how she was?

The film had been good. Adam had been feeling really relaxed and in top form. Some of his witty asides in the cinema had made Steve and Danny almost choke on their popcorn. It was like having the 'old' Adam back again. The whole evening had been a gas and after a quick pint at the King's Head Adam felt ready for a good night's sleep. He said goodnight to Carol then climbed into bed and thumbed idly through a couple of pop magazines yawning away, eyes growing heavy, gradually slipping towards slumber.

He thought about meditating but was really far too tired for the concentration necessary. The next meditation would need his full attention. It needed careful preparation and no alcohol. If he was going to follow Shera to wherever he might be led it was going to demand a strong and lengthy period of intense focus. It would have to wait until tomorrow.

Within seconds of laying his head on the pillow Adam was asleep. He was feeling good. Positive. Excited.

He slipped from consciousness into sleep easily and soon his breathing was deep and slow.

It was sometime later that something started to happen.

'Probably another weird dream', he rationalised momentarily. But then again it felt more than dreamlike. More like reality.

It started with a sensation of movement. Slow at first then quickening and more pronounced than before. A definite gathering of speed with the subtlest sensations of wind rushing past - like the exhilaration of suddenly accelerating in an open top car. And then a sudden swerve to the right then sharply up to the left. Now it felt more like one of those white-knuckled 'big dipper' fairground rides, yet this time there was no fear - only exhilaration.

Hey - this was fun...

The colours, at first fairground gaudy, were changing too. A deep intense blue was shimmering slightly and other, more subtle colours, were permeating in. The colours began to swirl around each other and blend into many different hues that were perfectly co-ordinated and mesmerising to watch. New colours were forming that Adam had never seen before and for which there were no words to describe. The swirling and blending became hypnotic, psychedelic and extraordinarily beautiful. For a moment it took Adam back to that night in the forest and the projections onto the white cliffs of the South Downs. But this was much more amazing. This was a natural 'high' that needed no exotic substances to enhance it.

Up, up, up - quickly down - then up, up, up again. A roller coast ride without the car or the tracks. The incredible feeling of the adrenaline rush without the presence of a physical body - stunning!

And then the movement levelled out. The up and down ride was stopping and a 'round and round' ride was beginning to start. Slow at first, and then picking up speed, the 'ride' continued round and round - faster and faster yet there was no giddiness. An enchanted, magical ride through a protean landscape of bewildering colours and forms. This was undoubtedly the most exhilarating sensation Adam had ever experienced.

And now the ride was both up and down and round and round all at the same time and then weaving in and out in graceful never-ending loop-de-loops. There was music too. Beautiful ethereal music that sounded like a choir of a thousand perfectly pitched voices in unison. Total exquisite harmony. Tunes that he had never heard before and yet he somehow knew and remembered in the depths of his psyche. Ancient and timeless.

...Up down - Round and round - In and out - Dip and dive - Fantastic! Amazing!

'I never want this ride to stop' thought Adam 'This is just the most incredible feeling in the world it's like...'

Like what?

And then a very distant memory suddenly flooded into his mind of another dance from another time where the colours had swirled around him just as fast and just as unpredictably. It was some kind of dance accompanied by drums and flutes and chanting in an ancient stone temple - and people were sobbing.

And there were other memories of dances with darker more scary edges to them where the music had been different still. Harsher - louder - sometimes discordant and yet equally as powerful. A crowd of thousands of festival goers swaying together in the night. And somehow the weird dances were tinged with sadness, a sadness that...

...broke the spell instantaneously.

The beautiful rhythmic stone temple dance was over and so too was the psychedelic crazy-hippy festival trip dance. The movement stopped. The music stopped. The colours faded. The magic gone. It had been so beautiful. So intense.

Adam opened his eyes and saw the angles and shapes of his bedroom gradually fall into gloomy focus again. It was all over. He wondered what had awoken him. The bedside alarm clock showed 3.16 and the house was in silence and darkness. Why did he have to wake up? It hadn't been a nightmare this time. Quite the contrary. The antithesis of the experience with the bull from hell.

Whether it was another dream or whether it had been an involuntary meditation Adam couldn't be sure. But he was sure of one thing.

Whatever it was it had affected him deeply. It was the most beautiful sensation he had ever experienced in his entire life. And now emotions that he was trying desperately to control could no longer be restrained.

For the first time since he could remember, he couldn't help but cry tears of unashamed joy.

Adam paced the room impatiently waiting until the door slammed. It was the day after that most amazing mental roller-coaster ride experience, but he needed the fix again desperately. It was like how he used to need a joint to chill out. Now he needed meditation like a drug. Couldn't get through the day without it. And now that Carol had gone to bingo for the evening he could indulge. Get the buzz again.

It didn't take long. Seemed like moments really but then he was getting pretty adept these days.

Strange though.

Strange because there was definitely something weird going on recently. It was like he was living in some sort of permanent semi dream-world.

Used to be, that there was a clear definition between being awake, asleep or meditating but now all the boundaries were starting to blur, and 'reality' was becoming a vague 'concept' rather than the certainty it used to be. Reality was becoming a series of events that could be happening in a dream, in deep meditation or something else. It was like being permanently drunk but without the hangover. It was addictive and intoxicating and filled with all kinds of images and experiences.

And the weirdest thing of all - *the really spooky bit* - was that it no longer mattered which 'state' he was in. Like a junkie on a hallucinogenic good trip, it just felt bloody good so why bother with meaningless labels like 'real' or 'unreal', 'conscious' or 'unconscious' anymore?

Now it was the *experience* that mattered and not the context. Like the experience two nights ago for instance. Was it just a dream? Or had he gone to sleep and involuntarily slipped into a meditative state but not actually been aware of any transition? It didn't matter anymore. The thing that mattered was that it had without doubt been the most delicious and ecstatic experience of his entire life. As though all the senses had conspired together to give him a maximum dosage of sensory overload. Total colours to feast the eyes, total harmony in the ears, total textures, total feelings, total experience. Indescribable beauty that there was simply no words or labels for.

Adam forced himself out of the self-indulgent daydreaming because, pleasant though it was, it created a barrier to slipping into the meditative state he was trying to achieve. This was going to be the big one, maybe even traversing the 'gate' for the first time, so he needed to be totally focused. He needed to find Shera. His guide to ultimate truth.

Adam pushed all thoughts aside so that he could concentrate on deep breathing. It was time to go within.

A few moments later something started to materialise from the shifting veils in the empty place.

It wasn't Shera.

Damn!

But then again it wasn't a 'person' at all.

It was a 'thing' that was being created in front of him, made out of nothing but wisps of cloud that were starting to coagulate together. The 'thing' that was materialising appeared to be some sort of three-dimensional cinema screen made of clouds. And the cloud-screen was now producing images. Some sort of cross? Yes - a wooden cross - a crucifix - yet somehow more symbolic than 'real'.

And now there was someone nailed on the cross with crimson pouring from outstretched palms and feet, someone wearing a crown of thorns, a face drenched in sweat, contorted with pain. Adam's first reaction was one of shock. This was not what he had been expecting at all. He had no interest in religious iconography. What was this about? Where was Shera? Why hadn't he been waiting like before?

The image was fading now, changing into something else - a shifting eruption of frothy white clouds that were beginning to shape themselves into something more substantial.

It was a building.

There were people singing inside the building... something about the 'Almighty Lord'.

It was a Christian church.

A Church? - What the fuck was going on here? He didn't want - or need - any of this religious stuff...

Another image – no, *many images* - all moving around each other in conflated kaleidoscopic motion. An angry priest stabbing a finger at the air in front of him and shouting something unintelligible. A young woman screaming as flames licked at her feet while a crowd chanted 'Witch! Witch!' in unison. A man kneeling to take communion before an icon of the Virgin Mary. A clicking of Rosary beads and whispered confessions 'Forgive me Father for I have sinned...forgive me Father for I have sinned...forgive me...'

Then more and more images tumbled into view, each one clamouring to be noticed but each one just a mere fragment of something much larger, a cornucopia of visual metaphors devoid of any kind of reference point.

...A child crying as an angry Father told her she would burn in hell because of some trivial misdemeanour.

...The pure dulcet voice of a young choirboy echoing around an empty church. The tolling of a distant church bell, sombre and resonant. Monks chanting the 'Benedictus' somewhere within dimly lit stone corridors and then the yellowed pages of dusty tomes rustling as they turned by themselves. Strange words that echoed around stone walls. Words like 'Apostles', 'Israelites', 'Sadducees' 'Pharisees', 'Exodus' and 'Revelations'. The sounds of lugubrious weeping and demonic blaspheming.

Then there was the image of a knight wearing the distinctive white tunic and red cross of the Crusaders riding a powerful brown horse with massive hoofs. A French Cathar from the Cevennes hills slumping to the ground with a bloody sword through his chest and a smiling rather tubby man with a small white cap raising his hand to acknowledge a devoted and cheering crowd from a balcony at the Vatican. A Spanish Conquistador slaughtering a whole family of Peruvian Incas and stealing their few gold trinkets, then placing the gold carefully into his saddle bag beside a small leather-bound Bible.

Someone softly intoning the Lord's Prayer, kneeling alone in a dark musty church - a shaft of laser beamed sunlight filtering through a stained-glass window. Then there were groups of white robed Missionaries in a straw hut throwing crude pictures and ornate carvings onto a small bonfire and hanging little wooden crosses in their place while semi-naked natives looked on in passive bewilderment.

Adam felt physical discomfort. He tried to shake his head and lose the constant stream of images - but they refused to shift. Why was he being shown all this stuff? What was it all supposed to mean?

And then...before he could stop the weird picture show inside his head...

...there was carnage.

Vivid scenes flashed across the cloud-screen so fast that there was only an after-image left that burned into the retina and burned inside the head. Weird Californian sects that milked your money, then your mind, and finally your body. The Spanish Inquisition, the Holy wars. Arab killing Jew, Sikhs killing Hindus, Catholics killing Protestants, Muslims killing Christians, Communists killing Buddhists. Blood gushing and frothing from so many open wounds that it spread out like a crimson river before him.

Unbearable inhumane scenes of death and suffering. Slaughter and sorrow.

Total slaughter and sorrow.

Religion?

God?

Salvation?

Hardly!

More a crazy, mixed-up phantasmagoria of iconic imagery, heavy with symbolism and less-than-subtle inferences that the overt promises of faith and blind obeisance were, in reality, no more than a flimsy façade hiding the cruel excesses of ugly ego-driven fanaticism and dogma.

The images softened and blurred.

Now there was an image of a little boy...a little boy that Adam immediately recognised as himself being cuffed around the ear by the school vicar because he didn't want to go to Sunday school and had openly said so. Then a little bit older in a classroom where the school vicar was teaching 'Religious Instruction'. The boy had put his hand up and dared to question something biblical and now he was being marched down the corridor to the headmaster's study where a cane was being taken down from the wall. His simple childlike question labelled as 'blasphemy!'.

And then trickling slowly down unblemished soft skin there was a little boy's tears.

Just a little boy's tears.

It took a few minutes for Adam to compose himself. He'd nearly lost it and been hurled back into the dark solidity of a physical bedroom again, but, somehow, he had managed to retain the focus, still his heartbeats and regain the calm detachment necessary to stay in the metaphysical.

He was puzzled by the series of images that he had just witnessed - movie films of multi-faith iconography and disturbing scenes of intolerance, fanaticism and persecution. But what did it all mean? Why was he being shown all this stuff?

The more he forcibly relaxed though, the more the clouds around him dispersed and finally they gave way to the serenity of the calming 'blue field' again.

He felt sure that Shera was somehow behind these images. He had asked Shera to show him the way to go beyond the 'blue' and the 'Interference' levels to the 'gate' and perhaps this what Shera was doing. Shera wanted to impart some information, and this was the method he had chosen.

'Okay Shera' said Adam smugly 'I can't see you - but I know you are here. I'm ready to learn more. Take me to the gate and lead me to whatever it is I need to see.'

It took only a moment for the shimmering blue field to start moving. It started to swirl slowly like a viscous fluid in a whirlpool. Various shades of blue were being whisked clockwise until the hues began to intermingle and create a dark blue swirling tunnel-like corridor in the centre that was drawing Adam inward. The spinning blue whirlpool - a sort of funnel now - soon engulfed him and a floating sensation, that was not at all unpleasant, sucked him deeper and deeper into the intoxicating hypnotic centre, eventually depositing him at what looked like a very ordinary set of household stairs. Ordinary except that the top of the stairs was hidden from view by a soft vaporous mist. Adam knew there was no choice but to climb the stairs, so he started to climb, step by cautious step. He expected to arrive at some sort of landing after a short climb but infuriatingly the stairs just carried on and on. After a hundred steps or so Adam's legs started feeling weary. What was going on here? This didn't make sense. It was when he made the decision to give up, turn around and descend that the steps ended abruptly before a very ordinary household door. Adam stared at the door for what seemed like minutes and realised that he had been brought here to make a choice. Open the door or return the way he had come.

To return now would gain him nothing. He had been led to the door for a reason - and hopefully by Shera. It was presumably to learn something important. The realisation that he had to turn the handle and face whatever was inside was overwhelming. It had to be done. There was something in there he was meant to see.

He just prayed it wouldn't be a bull on two legs.

Simultaneously with Adam's decision that he would open the door the handle turned automatically, and the door opened slowly and silently as if ushering him in with the flourish of a bowing servant.

Adam stepped into the room and into the unknown, calmly and unafraid.

There was no need for fear. An atmosphere of overwhelming peace and calmness pervaded the room.

This place was safe.

The inside of the room was much dimmer than the stairs outside and it took a few moments for Adam's eyes to adjust to the subdued light. As his eyes became accustomed to the softer glow, he began to see that it was a fairly small, square room containing all sorts of inanimate 'things' - lots of seemingly random objects scattered around the floor.

He reached down and picked up the nearest object. It was a teddy bear, with one loose leg and some stuffing hanging out of one ragged ear. Adam was just about to toss it aside when a strange sensation overpowered him.

It was the smell, a familiar comforting smell that he had not smelled for an awful long time. A prescience that he could not articulate.

It was the bear.

He looked at it more closely and gasped in surprise. It was his teddy bear. At least it had been. It was the bear that had lain beside him in his cot since the day he had been born until he was about five years old when he had tragically lost it on a shopping trip and had been inconsolable for weeks. Benny - yes that was the bear's name - Benny.

But how could it be *here*? Where had it been for all these years?

He laid it down gently then reached for another object. It was a toy - a wooden train covered in yellow paint - paint that he now remembered pinching from his dad's garage as a toddler to paint his favourite toy - a train that had been mislaid many years ago.

There was more. Raggy the cross-eyed clown doll, his favourite jigsaw puzzle of a space rocket, a bag of marbles, a toy gun, a book about red Indians and a jack-in-the-box. They were all his own long lost, and now mostly forgotten, childhood toys.

Adam shook his head and grinned. This was weird - but it was also great. It was like meeting some dear and treasured friends again after being separated for many years. He picked up the toys, one by one, and re-examined them, smelling them and running his hands over their individual textures - rekindling treasured old memories.

And over there in one corner of the room lay the coloured box.

Adam reached over and sat down hardly believing his eyes. It was the old 'slide viewer' that Mum and Dad had given him on his tenth birthday - just before dad died - along with a dozen, coloured slides of sports cars and dinosaurs.

Adam picked up the viewer and flicked a small switch on the side. Amazing - it still lit up like it used to after all these years!

He fumbled in the box and pulled out the old slides eager to get another look at those old dinosaur pictures.

He slid the first one into the viewing slot and heard it click into position.

As he lifted the viewer to his eyes however, the image caused him to recoil.

These weren't the pictures of sports cars or dinosaurs that he was expecting. These were photographs of something else.

They were images of himself...

Photographs that he was sure had never been taken!

The first was when he was about ten years old, sitting at a school desk laughing at something. Then the picture faded, and another photo took its place...he was a little bit older now, twelve perhaps, climbing over a wall scrumping for apples.

And then somehow - inexplicably - there were hundreds more photos in quick succession, and he didn't need the viewer anymore because the photos were now projected onto the wall in front of him in stark and terrible colours. The pictures were changing every two seconds or so as though controlled by some maverick zoetrope unable to turn itself off. Each isolated image a moment frozen in time, a moving tableau of his life.

Holiday snapshots with his parents, Susie - his first ever girlfriend, his grandparents, his first racing bike, his mates at the pub, parties, leaning on the wall outside a nightclub, his first cigarette, more parties. Marie, dancing with a bunch of crazy girls, Christmas dinner, holidays with his mates, riding a motorbike, smoking a joint in a friend's back garden, rock music, concerts, drinking whisky straight from the bottle, larking around with his old schoolmates, lying drunk in a field somewhere, acne, strippers, loud music, psychedelic flashing lights, girls, dirty back streets, dirty magazines, coloured tablets, cans of beer, vomiting in a gutter, lying in a hospital bed.

Lying on a mortuary slab!

Christ - what was this?

Adam jerked himself to his feet dropping the slide viewer from his hand as the slide show abruptly ended and the room plunged back into darkness, his heart pounding against his rib cage.

What the fuck was that about? - A cameo of his life? Pictures that were never taken - and a mortuary slab with his naked lifeless body on it staring at the ceiling. What was that supposed to mean?

Was someone trying to scare him?

They had bloody succeeded.

Adam licked dry lips as the walls began to ripple and fold into themselves until all he could see was an expanse of shimmering blueness that was rapidly fading to a uniform black.

...And then he opened his eyes.

He was sitting in his bedroom facing the wall, his legs a little cramped and his palms and forehead cold and damp.

It was over. Probably the longest meditation so far and this time much more - what was the word? Realistic? Tactile? Tangible? Yeah - all of those things and more!

And now he was left with a strange feeling that something extremely significant had been imparted to him - like an important secret delivered by a close friend in a hushed whisper. Something important that he ought to understand - must understand - even if it was something unpalatable.

Something that he *knew* he had to deal with.

Urgently.

"Hangover is it then boyo?"

"Uh?"

"I said, hangover, is it? You've been sitting there staring into space for about twenty minutes."

"Oh...sorry Gavin. No... it's not a hangover, actually. I'm just feeling pretty washed out today."

"That'll be too much shagging then."

"I wish."

Adam rubbed his temples and yawned. It was obvious his mind wasn't on the job today and it showed. Fortunately, Mr Stanley T. Morgan was locked away inside his office and it was only Gavin that had spotted Adam daydreaming the morning away.

"So - what is it then if it's not drinking or shagging that has reduced you to this state of pathetic inactivity?" asked Gavin playfully, "You haven't done anything stupid like taking up sport have you? Do I have to warn the Cardiff rugby club that they're in for some trouble?"

Adam laughed. He liked Gavin's humour.

"Nah - nothing like that. Maybe one day though..."

"Well, spill the beans then...it's got to be more interesting than the article on the local Women's Institute fund raising activities that I'm editing."

"I'll make the tea" said Adam, "Maybe it'll wake me up. Then I might tell you if it will shut you up."

"Grand idea boyo. You'll go far. All the way to the filing cabinet I shouldn't wonder."

Adam waved two fingers at the sub-editor and then carried two cups over to the office kitchen. He plugged in the kettle, rinsed the cups, and sighed deeply as he leant back against the kitchen wall.

'Well, it's like this Gavin me ole' Welsh mate' Adam said to himself, as if rehearsing a speech, 'I'm knackered because I'm finding it fucking hard to distinguish between reality and non-reality anymore. I'm living in a strange twilight world where dreams fade in and out of my head and I'm meditating so much that all the boundaries between what I used to believe in and understand and the world of fantasy have completely crumbled away. Half the time I don't know if I'm awake, asleep, meditating or somewhere in-between. I'm bloody confused and there's no-one I can even turn to or explain what the hell I'm going through because if I did then they would lock me up in an asylum. Well, no-one, that is except a metaphysical inner guide called Shera and an old guy with a limp that likes tending roses. So, you see Gavin, it's no wonder that I'm sitting at my desk staring into space like someone who's lost the plot because, boyo, that's exactly what has happened...'

The kettle whistled, and Adam poured two cups of tea carrying them back to the sub-editor's desk.

"Tea at last" said Gavin taking a sip of the steaming brew, "Now life may return to these weary limbs... or even to your weary brain Adam. Better, are we? Ready to face the dizzy heights of journalism again?"

"Yeah. I guess so."

"Good. Well, why don't you have a go at finishing this article while I catch up with your filing backlog? And don't say I never cared, eh?"

"Thanks Gavin. You're a star."

"Of course I am. Now...what were you saying about feeling washed out?"

"A feeble excuse mate" Adam shrugged, "You were probably right the first time. Too much drinkin' n' shaggin.'"

"Jack? It's me. Adam."

It was eight in the morning and Adam needed to be on his way to work. He prayed that Jack would be up and awake. Mercifully, the phone had been answered after only three rings.

"Adam, how good to hear from you. It must be a few weeks since..."

"I need to see you."

The phone remained silent for a few moments before Jack said, "What's happened?"

"A lot. More than I can explain."

"Try. I'm listening."

"Can't I come over and see you?"

"You're always welcome - you know that. Trouble is I have to go away for two days. My sister's house in Devon. Chance to see Ellie's grave you know. I try and get down there once a year. I have to catch a train in less than an hour."

Adam paced up and down the hallway holding the phone. For a moment he almost blurted that Jack could always visit his late wife's grave another day but stopped himself just in time. Even he wasn't that much of an insensitive bastard. It probably meant a lot to the old boy and the last thing he wanted was to cause offence.

"Oh," was all he managed to say.

"I'll be back on Monday" Jack continued, "You can come over then if you like. Lady's been missing you as well. Now tell me how you're getting on and what it is that's worrying you."

Adam sighed deeply then sat down on the stairs, looking around the banisters to make sure Carol was well out of earshot.

"I don't know where to start Jack...but you are the only person I can talk to. The only one who understands."

"Go on."

"It's the meditation. It's going well - maybe too well - and now I can't control it."

"What are you trying to control? You must just let it flow."

"I do. It's not that. I do let it flow. It's so easy now Jack. I can just relax and zap - I'm there."

"I wish I had your gift Adam," said Jack warmly.

"I'm beginning to wonder if it's a gift or a curse."

"That depends how you use it."

Adam waited for Jack to continue but Jack deliberately let the words hang in the air.

Adam breathed deeply knowing that Jack was encouraging him to talk by remaining silent.

"I think I've misused it," Adam confessed.

"I see" even toned, uncritical, "Do you want to tell me about it?"

"Not sure where to start. Shera's been great. Just like you said he would."

"You must always trust your inner guide."

"I do Jack. What's been happening is not Shera's fault. It's my own. I know this is gonna sound crazy - but I met some other er...people...when I was meditating. They seemed really friendly at first, but it turned into a bad experience."

"You met people other than your guide? That's incredible Adam. A lot of really experienced meditators can reach their inner guide but it's quite rare to meet other entities. I've read about that possibility of course and I know how potentially dangerous that can be. I warned you about negative influences..."

"I know...and like a fool I ignored the warning. Sorry Jack."

"As long as you have learned something valuable then there's no harm done. Be careful though Adam. Most inner world negative influences are fairly harmless, but occasionally you can get sucked in too far if you see what I mean. Then there can be real danger. To be honest I must confess that I suspected something like this might happen. In fact, I had a strange intuition that you were in danger a couple of weeks ago. I knew you were in some sort of trouble on the subconscious level. Anyway, tell me about it. I've got a few minutes before I have to leave."

Adam went on to tell Jack about the ordeal with Lamia and the bull-monster and then the weird religious iconography and the toys. Jack listened intently, asking more details at various points. When Adam had finished, Jack's voice took on a graver tonality.

"I have to confess Adam I don't like the sound of that."

"But what does it all mean Jack? Do you think these things are just nightmares?"

"I think" he said, after a pause, "That I know some of the reasons behind those particular experiences, but I'm only guessing mind. If I'm right, then there are some significant implications...but not necessarily all negative ones."

"You're talking in riddles Jack. What do you mean?"

"Sorry Adam. Yes, I'm rather confused myself. I'll tell you what you must do. You must ask Shera. Ask him for a straight answer. Then let me know what he said. We'll meet again as soon as we can. I need to hear Shera's explanation first...see if it ties in with my own theories."

Adam glanced at his watch. It was nearly twenty-past eight. He'd only minutes to catch the bus into work and couldn't afford to be late again. He didn't want Jack to miss his train either.

"Thanks Jack. I'll try and reach Shera tonight like you suggest. There is still a lot of stuff I haven't told you yet. Some other weird stuff Shera's been showing me. And beautiful music and crazy, surreal, fairground rides. I can't explain it all now. I'll call again."

"Call me again on Monday."

"Okay. Will do. Thanks Jack...and...um...have a good weekend."

Adam bit his lip wondering if visiting the grave of your dead wife could be considered a 'good weekend'. Fortunately, Jack took the comment in the spirit it was intended.

Adam replaced the receiver, glanced in the hall mirror at the dark lines under his eyes and ran his hand through his thick unwashed hair cursing himself for not bothering to shower first. He also noticed, for the first time, a grainy coating on his chin. About time too. The day wasn't all bad. At least he should get served easier from now on.

Seconds later he was running down the street waving his hands at the approaching bus and silently praying it would stop and let him on board.

He'd completely lost track of what day it was.

Somehow it didn't seem to matter anymore. The working day at the Gazette was becoming easier now that he was accustomed to the formalities, and he was paying Carol housekeeping regularly which made her life easier. Work was just the day job however, comfortingly humdrum and something to fill the hours until five o'clock.

Now it was the nights that were important.

And tonight was no exception.

Adam sat with his back against the bedroom wall so that his spine was held straight and after a few deep exhalations began the slow descent into the subconscious.

Focus, focus, focus.

He breathed deeply a few times and deliberately let his eyelids feel heavy while at the same time ensuring that his mind remained laser-beam pinpointed. Now the counting backwards, the shoulders relaxing, the pulse slowing, letting the blueness that hovered on the periphery of vision creep slowly and insidiously from somewhere behind the eyes into the forefront of his consciousness.

Beautiful - and as comfortable as old carpet slippers - and yet this time he knew it would be different.

Different because this time he had a question, and if Jack was right then somewhere - *somehow* - he would get an answer.

It was Saturday evening. All over the country other 'normal' blokes of his age were out on the town getting pissed or trying to get laid, preferably both. And here he was stone cold sober, virtually clean as far as cigarettes or any other drugs were concerned, sitting in his bedroom - *again* - trying to get in touch with a world that most of the sane world didn't even know about - or even believe, existed.

There were times he even believed he was going crazy. The life he was leading was 'unnatural' - wasn't that the word his mother had used the other day - unnatural?

'Yeah - face facts Adam - they all think you're losing it pal. Marie, your best mates, your mother...'

Adam shook his head slightly as though the clamour of thoughts were a swarm of mosquitoes skimming around his head trying to find some bare skin to puncture. He needed to relax and focus again. Find Shera. Ask Shera for the answer.

Answer?

Shit - until yesterday he wasn't even sure of the bloody question!

And then, unexpectedly, it had come to him. One minute he was staring disinterestedly at something on the TV and next minute the thought just came into his head as if from nowhere. It was a very specific question that needed an answer.

As Adam became more relaxed the images that had been bothering him - and the *words* that had been bothering him - floated in and out of his consciousness like pieces of some ethereal, other-worldly jigsaw puzzle for which there was no picture available to refer to.

There were images of bulls, both real and stylised, beautiful women that turned into grotesque monsters, bloody battle scenes, ancient stone temples, strange smells and strange unfamiliar music, old toys, old pictures, things that made him shiver. And these images were mixed with words or phrases that should mean nothing to him but somehow, irritatingly they did – yet he wasn't sure why. These were things that didn't - or shouldn't - be part of his life but for some reason permeated it like a seeping poison, bubbling just beneath the surface, waiting for every chance to break through the thin barrier between reality and unreality. Waiting to disrupt everything he knew as 'normality' and contaminating his life with something he couldn't understand. Couldn't deal with.

Adam sighed inwardly. If he started to become despondent the concentration would be lost. And he needed to concentrate desperately. A few moments later he was through the smoky thin layers of perception that were now as recognisable to him as the very street he lived in and by the time Shera appeared, shining, smiling and benevolent as usual the words were already forming in Adam's mind. Words Jack had said which now seemed so long ago. Words that had not meant much at the time. Until now.

"What I'm saying Adam is nothing is what it seems in this life. Each and every one of us is an amalgam of all of our previous lives and the sum of all the experiences from those lives."

Why the hell hadn't he thought to ask Shera this question before?

Before Shera had even spoken a word of greeting Adam had framed the question and the words came easily and silently.

'Shera, I have an important question to ask you and it is this. Who was I before I was Adam Sinclair?'

Shera remained silent for a few moments as if pondering the question. Then he smiled wider than Adam had ever seen him smile before. His deep translucent eyes seemed to penetrate Adam's very soul.

'I wondered how long it would be before you asked me that question.'

'It's something I should have asked you a long time ago. I don't know why I didn't.'

'Perhaps because at that time you were not prepared to accept and face up to the truth of the answer.'

'Well, if that was the case, I'm certainly ready now Shera.'

'Are you sure? Such knowledge once imparted can never be dismissed, denied or forgotten.'

'Absolutely.'

'Then so be it.'

The blueness seeped in like a sea mist that enveloped both of them, deepening in hue as waking consciousness once more gave way to a much stronger sibling.

Deeper, deeper, deeper...

Blue, blue, blue...

Shera seemed to have disappeared from view, but the incandescent shades of blue seemed to be lifting Adam off his feet and transporting him through swirling corridors of indescribable shimmering beauty to somewhere new. Somewhere he had not been to before. It was somewhere out beyond the Interference layer to an undulating and vibrating terrain that he found slightly disorientating. Beneath his feet a warm layer of sand dusted his feet while above the horizon a jumble of fractal geometric shapes seemed to be jostling each other in a weird dance. They were spinning and morphing into other dazzling bejewelled shapes that he had no names for and no way of articulating. But the shapes were intoxicatingly beautiful, and he felt strangely safe and protected.

And then, as the blue desert-like landscape began to fade, came other colours and sounds - but this time there was something more - much more!

This time he could smell a whole world of deliciously exotic - sensual even - fragrances.

Spice? Sandalwood? Jasmine? It was something like that...

Reminded him of something...

His mind searched for labels, but labels were frustratingly insufficient. Flowers? Incense? Candles? Herbs? Wood smoke?

Yeah - all of these and more - wonderful aromas that were achingly familiar and filled him with a strong sense of nostalgia though he had no idea why.

Didn't he read somewhere that smells - more than any other sensation - invoke memories?

My God it was true.

He belonged to these smells. These smells belonged to him. They were in his blood and bones. They were in his head. They were central to his deepest and most treasured memories. They were part of *who he was.*

And – somehow - they came from a time long before the little boy with a teddy bear called Benny had appeared.

The sensations were so overwhelming that Adam was aware of losing concentration.

No - must concentrate - stay with it - breathe deep - focus.

'Find out where the smells come from before you lose it'

He relaxed deliberately until equilibrium returned.

Good - that's better!

Opening his inner eyes Adam took in the scene before him and recoiled slightly as the unfamiliar slowly started to become more vivid. Where the hell was this place?

He was a child again and yet felt the awareness of a deep-rooted and profound knowledge already rooted within his young mind.

Yes - that was it - he was a child but a very special child. A child with almond shaped eyes that possessed and projected an unquestionable confidence and self-assured poise that was obviously revered by those around him. It seemed to be a confidence borne of intuition and faith rather than from academic pursuits and yet he was somehow the more respected for it.

But who was this child and where was this place? This was not so easy to ascertain.

The child was olive-skinned and Asiatic rather than European. His clothes were - inexplicably - not unfamiliar and consisted of a pale-yellow robe like affair - probably just one piece of material that wrapped loosely around the body. He resided in a large airy room built from some soft red sandstone - not bricks as such - a cave or temple perhaps?

A number of artefacts lay around the room but nothing Adam recognised from his own experience.

There was some crude furniture - could be a large seat or even a bed and a sort of pedestal, maybe even an altar, with a carved wooden bowl full of a potpourri of dried flowers beside a small candle - probably the origin of those exquisite fragrances. There were other olive-skinned people in the room too, but most of them were fairly indistinguishable from one another and quite obviously completely oblivious to Adam's 'astral' presence.

There was only one figure that immediately drew his attention. Tending a small fire was a young and very beautiful woman, probably in her mid-twenties, who roused within him a deep and painful longing.

There was no question that this was the child's mother - *his mother*!

His mother? But that couldn't possibly be...Carol was his...?

For a moment Adam nearly let the image slip, so intense and overwhelming was the burst of emotion within him. He held his concentration with difficulty. This time he could not afford to let the image go. In his mind he could hear his own lips frame the words "Mother..."

She was gazing at him now with the proud expression that only Mothers can bestow upon their sons and he – the boy - was looking up to her with dark wisdom-filled eyes that were both deep and respectful.

And yet, behind the wisdom there was a profound sadness, almost as if the aura of joy had been prematurely snuffed out like a rogue candle and replaced with an unwanted air of sadness.

Adam knew instinctively that this boy - *himself* - was dying, and the tragedy of his imminent death was eminently more tragic due to the innate hidden abilities that were clearly beginning to flourish within him.

His life was somehow a special gift to those around him and the gift was being withdrawn before it had even had a chance to manifest its true potential. His mother was obviously deeply saddened by the knowledge that she was shortly to lose a very special son and the community around her was also sad to lose someone that, for some reason, the holy men had a special name for. They called the boy "He who walks in the shadows."

Adam knew all of this instinctively. The boy was him. He was the boy. He was the one that the ancient wise ones also called 'The Stone' - the solid, unshakeable receptacle of concealed and deep-seated spiritual wisdom. But this time the stone was flawed, and now the stone was slowly cracking as life slowly drained away, invaded by an illness that not even the most learned sages and holy men could prevent.

As consciousness returned, and the image faded, Adam could feel his heart pounding. There was a weird feeling deep in his gut and a cacophony of voices in his head that finally coalesced into a single urgent whisper in his ear that said: "But what does this all mean?

And before the question had even reached his lips, he already knew the answer - it was so obvious really.

He and the boy were one and the same - and always had been.

And that realisation was truly mind blowing.

He, Adam Sinclair, was quite simply the reincarnation of the Indian 'Boy-God' who carried within him the seeds of a deep- rooted knowledge passed from generation to generation - a 'special' type of person that could move effortlessly between the multi-layered realms of consciousness. He had possessed a skill highly respected by the community in which he had lived - a skill that had lain buried and dormant deep within his psyche until now. A soothsayer, mystic, guru, seer, wizard - call it what you will - someone who could see and know things that others could never discern. This is what Jack had come to realise intuitively and this is what Shera had always known.

"Gramps reckons it's cos he 'knows things'"

Yeah, even dear old and confused Gramps could sense it.

It all made sense now. Everything made sense.

Everything – except perhaps the bull nightmares...

Adam jerked physically as conscious awareness flooded back into his cramped sweating body.

It was over.

He lay there panting and breathing fast. Head full of tumbling after-images, colours and sounds.

He felt thoroughly drained and reached over to the bedside cabinet for a tumbler of cool water, drinking it down in one long gulp, surprised at how much his hand was shaking.

'Christ' he whispered to himself, not sure whether the booming in his head and chest were due to pain or to pleasure. Maybe it was a little of both. He looked around the bedroom taking it all in. The wall posters, vinyl LPs over the floor, childhood books and toys, pop magazines and jumble of clothes that should have been hung in the wardrobe weeks ago. Up until this moment these things all defined who he was. They were his history. His past, his security, his very personality.

Now that was no longer the case. Now he was no longer just Adam Sinclair, an only child, twenty years old and working for the Gazette. Now he was something much more than all this. Now he was somebody that he would have to get to know and understand all over again - like meeting a long-lost twin brother. Now it was time to grow up, take responsibility and do just as Jack had told him. It was time to take off the mask and look in the mirror.

...If the rest of his life was to have any meaning whatsoever.

'Christ,' he said again almost inaudibly and then buried his face in both hands until warm salty liquid began to pour through his fingers and drip with a small plishing sound onto the bedroom carpet.

"**B**loody 'ell - Adam Sinclair! You do exist after all!" Adam gave an exaggerated bow then straightened up and punched Steve Lacey playfully on the shoulder.

"Hi Steve, you old tosser. How's things?"

It was a week later, and Adam had only just recovered from the shock of the last meditation. He'd spent most of Sunday walking around like a zombie trying to come to terms with his new-found knowledge. Wanting to talk to someone - *tell someone* - but too freaked out to find the right words. Jack would understand of course, but Adam couldn't keep on intruding into his life every time something happened. This needed some serious reflection first. On Monday, God only knows how he managed to get through the day. He couldn't actually remember what the hell he'd actually been doing at work except that Gavin had told him to 'wake up boyo - you're daydreamin' again' on several occasions.

Tuesday had been a better day. He'd even dragged himself off to the local library in the lunch hour and borrowed two books on the subject of reincarnation, carefully concealing them in a supermarket plastic bag before anyone could see the titles. He had almost finished reading the first one last night curled up on the sofa, oblivious to the frivolous chat show his mother was watching on TV. He'd also completely forgotten to phone Jack to ask how his weekend in Devon went.

The sound of Steve's voice bought him back to the present and the monotonous background hubbub in The Anchor public house.

"So where have you been hiding then? No one's seen or heard from you for ages."

"Oh y' know, here n' there. I've been pretty busy at work - the Gazette. I've just finished for the day. Thought I'd pop in for a pint. You?"

"Nah. Not working yet. Still signing on. Can't be bothered with the nine to five yet though. I'm doing some odd jobs though for some beer money."

"Good. You can buy me a pint then."

Adam leaned against the bar and looked around the room searching for the usual faces. Mick was playing pool with some bird he didn't recognise but he had caught his eye and nodded briefly. No sign of Danny though. There were a few other regulars that Adam recognised but had never actually spoken to. The old guy with the red nose that always sat in the same place, smoking a pipe and drinking stout was still in his usual place, as well as the twat in a suit with the loudmouth, who spent every evening trying to chat up the barmaids. The years passed, but life in The Anchor seemed to remain in the same depressing time warp.

Steve passed Adam's pint along the bar spilling some beer in the process. The bored barmaid used it as an excuse to walk away from the loudmouth and mop up the spillage.

"Cheers Steve."

"Yeah cheers. Should be you buying the beer now Adam seein' as you're the only one with a proper job."

Adam raised his pint in acknowledgement. "Yeah well at least I earn my money and not scrounge it off the state" he said mockingly, "I'm a taxpayer now mate. Anyway, if you're lucky I might get the next round in. So - where's Danny tonight then? Don't tell me he's in love or something."

Steve took a deep swig of beer, wiped his arm across his face and belched. "Nah - stupid sod has gone and got caught dealing. He was buyin' some dope in town centre to sell on - y'know Danny - thought he could make a few bob. 'Easy money' he reckoned - but it was a set up. The pigs took him down the station and are taking him to court for possession. Now his old man's gone nuts about it and won't let him outa the house."

"You're kidding! The bloody idiot. I thought he had more sense than to start dealing. That's a fool's game."

"Yeah, well he was gonna put some aside for you Adam. Your favourite - Moroccan."

"Yeah?" Adam bit his lip thoughtfully for a moment, "He should'na done that. He really should'na done that."

Steve shrugged, "I think he was too pissed at the time to even notice it was a set up. Do you reckon the police will ask him to name names? Y'know...ask him who else is into smokin' and tokin'. My ole' man would go crazy if he found out - so would yours..."

Steve stopped short, suddenly realising what he'd said "Jeez I'm sorry Adam. I didn't mean to..."

Adam waved it aside. "Forget it" he said "It's okay. No really. It's okay. Look...I...I can't be doing with all this hassle. Tell Danny not to be so bloody stupid. I don't want him sticking his neck out for me or any other idiots. Christ, if the Gazette found out about it, I'd be outa the door like there was a missile up my arse. My chances of getting to be an editor would be...well...like *never...*"

Steve stared at Adam with a frown "You kiddin' me?"

"Huh?"

"I can't believe you Adam. Sometimes you do my fuckin' 'ed in."

"What are you on about?"

"You!" said Steve, eyes flashing angrily, "I don't know what's got into you lately, but you've changed man. You used to be a real laugh, Adam. I remember when you used to drink whisky for lunch and smoke about four joints at the same time. Wearing 'em like fangs. Don't you remember when we used to go downtown, nick some beer, get stoned listening to Hawkwind and then look for some old tarts to chat up just for a gas? Look at you now man! Fuckin' white shirt and jacket like you're some cool reporter or something. You're only a soddin' tea boy. Now Danny might do time for trying to get you some smokes and all you care about is your bloody job. I can't believe you. You've never been the same since you got wasted at Reading - d'ya know that?"

Adam stared at Steve in disbelief. Did he really mean all that shit? Other people had heard the outburst and a lot of eyes were watching nervously. Mick had put down his pool cue and stood watching, arms folded. Adam looked at Steve's torn jeans and black T-shirt then at his own black shoes, trousers, crisp white shirt and jacket. His face reddened.

"Yeah, I do know that" he said softly "I'm sorry mate."

Steve visibly relaxed.

"Yeah, well I'm sorry too" he said, "Maybe I was out of order. People change..."

"You're right. People change. And I've changed. I realise that now. I've changed - and I can't go back Steve. I can't go back to what I used to be. It's too late."

Steve looked Adam in the eyes as though searching for something.

"What is it you've found out there Adam?" He said softly.

Adam let out a long breath and stared down at his shoes.

"It's not about 'out there'" he said tapping the side of his head, "It's what I've found in here."

"Do you want to talk about it?"

Adam considered the question.

"Nah. Not today. Maybe some other time. Look...I'll see you 'round, ok?"

Adam finished his pint then slowly walked out of the pub, aware of many eyes burning his back.

Mick joined Steve at the bar, removed a piece of chewing gum from his mouth then pressed it down into an ash tray.

"What's 'is problem?"

"Dunno" said Steve "But he's got really weird lately. Really weird. Maybe it's something to do with that old guy he's been seen hanging around with."

"Or maybe just because he's got a proper job now and earning some bread. Maybe it's gone to his head."

"Yeah" said Steve "Maybe it has. Anyway - who cares? Another game of pool then?"

Mick nodded and started to chalk up his cue. Steve lit a cigarette and stared at the pub door as though it might open again and Adam would return grinning, smoking a fag and laughing like he used to - because it was all just a big joke.

But Steve knew that this time Adam had not been joking. He also sensed that, sadly, it was probably the end of an era.

"See you around Adam" Steve whispered to himself, "And good luck mate."

Outside The Anchor public house Adam leaned his back against the wall, hands deep in his pockets and eyes closed. He groaned to himself before spotting a crumpled aluminium can on the pavement. He kicked it as hard as he could, sending it straight across a road and narrowly missing a passing car. The driver honked noisily and waved two fingers. Adam ignored it.

I can't go back Steve. I can't go back...

Adam glanced over his shoulder, through the smoke-stained windows of the pub and watched Mick and Steve playing pool. Two giggling girls at their elbows.

After a few moments his jaw tightened, and then he turned away, straightening his shoulders. Then he set off purposefully towards home.

There was something strange about the day right from the start. Not something tangible that Carol or anyone else might have noticed, but Adam knew. Sensed it.

He'd got up with the alarm as usual. Showered, put on his work clothes, had a leisurely breakfast and read the morning paper but all the time there was a nagging feeling that something was different.

Carol had made him some sandwiches to take to the office and gave him a peck on the cheek as he set off for the bus stop. The bus had arrived on time for a change, and he was soon pushing open the door to the Gazette and waving hello to the usual faces around the various desks in the main office.

At first, he thought the weird feeling was to do with the events at the Anchor the night before, but it was something more than that. It was more like the sense of something about to happen rather than something that had already happened. He knew that sometimes Marie could sense the proximity of a storm before it actually arrived due to being oversensitive to subtle changes in air pressure. If a big storm was forecast, she could even suffer a migraine. Now Adam sensed - no anticipated - that something important was going to happen though he hadn't a clue what. Perhaps it was something to do with his newly discovered alter ego. Maybe he was feeling weird all day just because of knowing so much more about his past life.

The feeling stayed with him all day and even into the early evening. He'd tried to watch the football on TV for a while, but the fleeting images became a blur and he rapidly lost interest, Carol had made a nice shepherd's pie for tea but even his appetite was less than usual. By the time the mantelpiece clock struck eight Adam knew what had to be done.

"I'm going up to my room for a while," he said casually.

Carol cocked an eyebrow, "Are you okay Adam?"

"Yeah. Fine. Why do you ask?"

"Oh nothing. You seem to be miles away that's all. Hardly touched your food."

"No - I'm fine. Really. Just not that hungry tonight. I'm going to play some music. Catch up on some reading and..."

"Meditating again?"

He shifted his eyes avoiding eye contact and shrugged. "Er...maybe...I'm not sure."

Carol frowned but decided not to say anything. Not now. Best leave him to it.

"Okay" she said airily, "I'm here if you need me."

Adam breathed a long sigh of relief. He wasn't in the mood for discussing anything at the moment. He climbed the stairs slowly, took off his suit and slipped into a pair of jeans and sweatshirt.

There was a pile of unstacked LP's littering the floor. He picked one up. It was Camel's "Snow Goose" - one of his favourites. Moments later the music blasted from the two speakers on the desk unit opposite the end of his bed. He sat on the bed propping himself up against the bedroom wall with a pillow and sat there looking out of the window at the darkening evening sky.

Some fifteen minutes or so later, even before the stylus had clicked noisily back into place Adam was breathing deeply, eyes closed and searching for whatever it was that was lurking in the depths of his being. It didn't take long to locate Shera.

'Hello Adam. It is good to see you again.'

'It's good to see you too Shera. I nearly lost it tonight. I was trying to rush into meditating. Getting too impatient I guess.'

'Meditation always requires patience.'

'Yeah. Jack's always telling me that. Anyhow I seem to have got through to you. The last couple of sessions were tough though. Scary.'

'But you learned from them.'

'Oh yeah. I learned from them all right. I learned heaps. Everything is starting to make sense at last. All my life I've felt sort of different from other people. I never knew why. Always felt there was something in my head - in my memories - that I couldn't explain. That Indian boy...the one who died...it was me wasn't it, Shera? Me in some sort of previous life.'

'Yes Adam. You and he are one and the same. You always have been. You always will be. You now know the reason why you are blessed with the ability to slip easily through the veils - 'meditation' as you call it. It is because you have always had 'the knowing' lying dormant within you. Waiting to be re-awakened.'

'The knowing?'

'The inner vision. The ability to see and know things others cannot. The ability to traverse the hidden realms and converse with others who are not bound to the physical world. Such gifts used to be recognised and revered. Long ago in the country you know as India those children who were born with the knowing were worshipped because of their wisdom and insight. When such a child died young it was a cause of much grief and sadness. And yet behind the grief at the loss of the physical child was the

certainty that the essence of the knower could never be extinguished. The eternal seed that can never be broken - The Stone - would always manifest itself again in another time and another place. You now know that you are 'The Stone' don't you Adam.'

'I don't know what to say or think Shera. This is too much to take in. Can I really be...this...um...The Stone? I'm just a regular guy. Adam Sinclair. I just don't feel that special. There are so many questions. Questions like why my whole life has been plagued with the same terrifying nightmares. What does it all mean?'

'It's hard for me to explain. Your physical world is very different from my world Adam. You have now discovered how many different layers of perception there are, but there are thousands more that even I have not yet experienced. Even those who have transitioned from the physical to the spiritual realms are still on their path to what some call 'God', some call the 'Source'. Essentially it is just the place we all know, and feel, is our true 'Home'.'

'But why have I always had these nightmares... these visions Shera? Has it got anything to do with me being 'The Stone'?'

'It is because a long time ago the infinite seed within you - your soul, consciousness - whatever you want to call it, led many others to seek wisdom and truth. You were an enlightened spiritual leader that many people followed, learned from and worshipped.'

'Go on.'

'What you must understand is that everyone has within them an affinity with other parts of the natural world and your affinity is with the creature you know as a bull.'

Adam scratched his head. Some of this stuff was making sense - but some not.

'But if I have some sort of affinity with bulls, then why do they want to hurt me? I don't get it.'

Shera was silent for a few moments. Adam sensed that his guide was trying to find the right words.

'Everything in existence lives in a state of duality. Black, white, good, bad. In the country where you were revered - India - the bull is both a very sacred creature and also a symbol of evil depending on the viewpoint of the perceiver. At that time, in that place, you represented the positive, sacred manifestation of the bull. The negative aspects of the bull therefore viewed you as a natural enemy. By attempting to overpower your influence the negative bull cults could seek to replace the sacred with the profane. In other words, their desire was for evil to triumph over good. And you, as spiritual leader of the positive bull cult, were the one thing standing in their way.'

'So - you're trying to tell me that I'm still on some ancient bull's hit list? It's still after my blood after all these years? Centuries?'

'Yes. But understand this. They fear you as much as you fear them. You are more powerful than you realise. You have the combined strength of all your previous incarnations residing within you. That makes you much stronger than you think.'

Adam sighed and shook his head. 'What am I supposed to do about all this Shera? I don't want to spend the rest of my life scared to fall asleep. Scared of some mad bull that wants to kill me to settle old scores.'

'There is only one thing to do Adam. You must face up to your deepest fears. Once you are no longer afraid of the negative side of your own psyche - the black bull as you call it - it will no longer have any hold over you. You will regain superiority over it and never be challenged again. Not in this lifetime.'

'So - you're telling me that the only way to break this cycle of torment is to actually meet this bull-thing face to face and have some sort of mental, sub-conscious showdown?'

'That is correct.'

Adam frowned, his mind in turmoil. There were still so many questions. So much he didn't understand. One thing was certain though. Having come this far there could be no turning back.

...And it sounded as though he had a very old score to settle and old wounds that needed to be healed.

'Shera' he said after a pause, 'Are you able to take me to wherever I can find this...this bull creature?'

'I can.'

'Good' said Adam gritting his teeth, 'I think you are absolutely right. I think the time has come to face up to my deepest fear.'

Shera nodded slowly.

'I knew you would come to that conclusion eventually' he said warmly. *'In fact, it is part of your destiny and all the answers that you seek will also come in time. But now is not the time to face that fear. You need more time to prepare for it so that you are invincible. Now that you have understood who you really are though, I can take you somewhere rather special - if you feel strong enough. Are you ready to learn more?'*

'Yes. As long as it's not going to be anything as heavy as mortuaries again.'

'This will be a much more enjoyable experience though it does require considerable courage from you'

Adam wondered what Shera was alluding to. No matter. If he was going to face up to his deepest and darkest fears very soon, then anything else was just a warm-up.

'I'm ready.'

'Then follow me.'

Shera started to move through the shifting vistas of blue that shimmered around them, and Adam followed effortlessly. Although 'time' was normally a meaningless concept in this environment on this occasion it felt as though quite a few minutes passed as Shera led Adam into a vortex of swirling colours. It reminded him of the old TV opening sequences of Doctor Who that he'd enjoyed as a kid - and more recently the LSD trips he'd been so into over the last couple of years. Weird.

And then all sense of movement stopped and there was another sense of 'place'. Without sufficient visual or spatial reference points to identify one location from another Adam found it very difficult to relate places to each other. But then again, normal space-time relationships did not seem to apply in Shera's world.

All he knew was that this new place emanated a sense of deep peace and tranquillity. His feet were enveloped into warm watery swirls that reminded him of walking in the surf on a tropical island and the 'walls' on three sides were an almost transparent silvery blue. Shera stood beside him, and they both faced the far wall which was conspicuous by the difference in colour. Unlike the silvery blue behind them and to their sides, the far 'wall' was glowing brilliant white that was so bright nothing was visible beyond it. For a moment Adam felt that he now knew what it must feel like to be a rabbit caught in the headlights.

'I need to leave you awhile' Shera said comfortingly, *'but you are safe here.'*

And then he was gone in an instant.

Adam accepted his disappearance without concern. There was no sense of fear in this place, and he knew that Shera would not be far away.

Anyway, he felt good. Calm, relaxed, intoxicated. There was something about this place - something about this moment - that was indeed rather special. His limbs started to tingle.

Then something made him jump. Nearly made him completely lose all concentration.

The dark shape of a man was walking purposefully out of the centre of the light and heading straight towards him.

At first the intensity of the light was so strong that Adam couldn't recognise any of the man's features. Under different circumstances the situation may have appeared threatening. But not here. Not now. Adam stood motionless overwhelmed by curiosity. Surely it wasn't Tom again?

The man stopped in front of Adam within touching distance and waited until Adam's eyes adjusted to the glare of the backlight.

It was then that Adam felt a deep jolt down his spine as though a sliver of iced lightning had seared through his body. His eyes widened - and he felt his jaw drop open. Every nerve ending in his entire body seemed to be alive and on maximum alert.

No - this just couldn't be.

Not this...

Not...

'Hello Son.'

'Dad?'

'It's been a long time. I've been waiting for you.'

The words wouldn't come. They struggled to break free from a throat so choked up with emotion that Adam could barely breathe. For a moment he almost lost the essential concentration needed to remain focused within his meditation - but this was too important to lose. If ever he needed the willpower to stay in the moment it was now.

'Is that really you dad?...But I thought...'

'That I was dead? I'm afraid that's true Adam, there's nothing I can do about that. But that doesn't matter anymore because in this place death doesn't matter. It's

irrelevant. It's so good to see you. You just don't know how much this moment means to me. Come here son...'

The figure held out his arms and Adam fell into them. He was half expecting to feel nothing but empty air - but the sense of solidity was very real. The figure was warm and tangible. Adam held on tight and felt a deep well of suppressed anguish rip through his body erupting in gushing sobs. His Father was crying too.

The tears could not be held back, and Adam let them flow until he felt that every last pain, frustration, anger and bitterness of the last ten years had been wrung from his eyes and erased from captivity in his heart.

He looked searchingly into his Father's eyes and his Father understood every question that needed to be answered.

'*I am so proud of you Adam.*'

'Proud?'

'*Yes proud. It's only one in a million people that can achieve what you have achieved - do you realise that?*

There are thousands of people praying and meditating all over the planet but very few have the ability to get this far. Do you know, I've been watching you growing up and I have witnessed all the things you have felt and experienced. I've been especially watching your progress ever since that night you went to Doctor Levinson's lecture. I've been willing you on every step of the way. I've watched your perseverance in overcoming all the odds and waiting for the day you would find your way back to me. And now you have done it. If only your mother realised what an amazing achievement this is. What an amazing person you are. We had no idea when you were born...'

'You saw all that?'

'*All of it. Jack knew you had it in you to find your way to me eventually. He's an incredible guy.*'

'Yeah, he is. I owe him a lot. I can't believe this is happening to me. I've missed you so much. Why did you have to die Dad? Why?'

'Leaving you and your mother behind was unbearable Adam. The dead grieve too you know for what they have lost. It was my own fault. I realise that now. I wanted the best for you and your mother. I was working silly hours to earn more money because I thought that was the answer. Not getting enough sleep, starting to drink too much then getting behind the car wheel when I was half asleep. We can only thank God that I didn't kill you too when I crashed. But it wasn't your time. You were too special.'

'I missed you so much dad...'

'And I missed you. Can you imagine how it felt to arrive in this place and to have to watch you grow up without being able to be there to help you through adolescence and all the rough times?'

'I've done some pretty stupid things. Things you wouldn't be proud of.'

'I know son - and a lot of it was my fault for not being there. But listen to me. This meeting will be exhausting your body and you will need to return soon so I want you to listen to me very carefully.'

'I'm listening.'

'I want you to know that I am always here for you, always watching over you like Shera. But unlike Shera I can't always be seen like this. This is a very special occasion, okay? Jack would understand what I'm saying - it's just that people like me that have passed over to the other side can't easily meet like this. Don't try to analyse what I mean by this - just accept it.'

'Okay.'

'So even if we don't meet again like this don't worry. I will always be there. Now listen to me, because what I want to say is very important. I want you to think carefully about everything that Jack has taught you because he has given you the tools to build a better and

more rewarding life than the mess I made of mine. God has given you a rare talent indeed that only re-manifests every few generations and you must use it to benefit everyone you meet who is distressed or has lost direction in life. You have a deep understanding of why things are so. You understand the true connectedness of all things and how the spiritual and the physical are intimately bound together. You must use this knowledge. You can give meaning to hundreds of sad or lonely people and when you do that it will give your life meaning too. Do you understand what I'm saying Adam?'

'Yes. I think so.'

'And another thing that you must know. Whether it seems right or wrong - it is your destiny to challenge the bull of your nightmares. You know that now. I want you to know that whatever happens I will be with you Adam. I will be right beside you and supporting you. Giving you courage and strength even if you can't see me.'

'You're fading away Dad...'

'Do you understand what I'm saying Adam?'

'Yes. Yes. I understand but you're fading away. Dad don't go yet. Don't go. I love you Dad...I...'

'Love you too Adam...always...'

Gone.

In an instant. Swirling clouds. Spinning colours. Nausea. Darkness.

And then awareness of writhing on bedclothes drenched in sweat. Breathing heavily. Red streaked eyes.

But smiling.

Oh yes.

Grinning from ear to ear.

Gavin Carter swung his legs onto the desk sending a bundle of papers onto the floor, lit a cigarette with his rather ostentatious and oversized gold cigarette lighter, and still managed to pick up the ringing phone all in one blur of movement.

"Gazette - Gavin speaking...oh...I see...hold on."

He swung his legs back down on to the floor where Adam was kneeling to pick up the dislodged filing and clamped his hand over the receiver.

"It's for you, boyo. A woman no less...girl even. Shall I tell her you're away investigating a hot story then?"

Adam ignored the remark and held out his hand. Gavin passed the phone over with a shrug.

"Adam Sinclair."

"Hello Adam Sinclair. Are you busy?"

His face flushed "No...well, yes, but...where are you?"

Shit! He'd promised to call Marie weeks ago.

"In reception of the Gazette. Downstairs. I wondered if you've got a moment?"

"Yeah. Sure. Look...hold on a sec - I'll be right down."

Adam passed the phone back to Gavin who was straightening his tie, "Ah - girlfriend is it?" he said knowingly with a grin, "Going to introduce me then?"

"Nope."

Gavin grimaced, "Scared she might prefer the debonair, dashing, sophisticated type then, are you?"

"Why?" frowned Adam, "Do you know someone like that then Gavin?"

"Cheeky bastard."

Adam walked out of the office, down the corridor and down the stairs to the reception area of the Newspaper.

Marie was standing there smiling. She was wearing a cream jacket and skirt and, unusually for her, a matching cream handbag. Her hair was tied back in a ponytail, and she was wearing black high heels. Adam's heart missed a beat.

"Bloody 'ell Marie. What's this then?"

"Do you like it?"

"Yeah. Great. It's just a bit of a shock that's all."

She laughed. "It's my interview gear. I had to come into town for an interview."

"Interview?"

"Trainee Manageress at the Supermarket."

"You're kidding."

"No kidding. It seemed to go well. They'll let me know in a few days. Thought I'd pop by as you haven't bothered to ring me for weeks."

Adam glanced nervously at the receptionist who was hanging on every word.

"Oh. Yeah. Sorry. I've been..."

"Busy. Yeah - I know. Anyway, what time do you finish? I'm going to Annie's coffee bar in a few minutes."

Adam glanced up at the Victorian clock above the reception desk with the yellowed face and faded roman numerals. It was four fifty-six. "About ten minutes."

"See you there in ten minutes then."

Marie fluttered her eyelashes making sure the receptionist noticed, then turned a little awkwardly on the high heels before pushing through the heavy glass doors back onto the street.

She smiled to herself.

Adam was still at the Gazette then! Miracles do happen. Longest job he'd ever managed to keep. Probably still skint though, so she'd probably have to pay the bill at Annie's. After all - he was probably still paying off the loan from when he took her to the Italian restaurant. Adam was Adam. Crazy but unique too...

Marie had barely taken the first sip of coffee when Adam appeared in the small coffee shop with the lace tablecloths and fake antiques. Gavin had told him that he may as well piss off early so that he didn't keep his true love waiting and that he could owe him a pint later as a 'thank you'. Adam thought it was a fair deal.

Adam pulled up a chair and ordered a tea with biscuits. They were alone apart from two old dears chatting animatedly about knitting or some such on a nearby table.

Marie looked up from her coffee and smiled at him sweetly, "You'll get fat if you eat too many biscuits you know."

"Good. I'm starving most of the time now that I'm working so hard."

"Do me a favour. You've always been allergic to hard work Adam."

"Ha ha. So...'Supermarket Manageress', eh? Good Money?"

"Not bad. Lots of prospects though. Sounds like interesting work. How's the Gazette?"

"Yeah. Good."

There was an awkward silence. The tea and biscuits arrived.

Marie waited until the waitress was out of earshot.

"I hope you didn't mind me disturbing you at work."

"No. 'Course not. As I said I've been meaning to ring you."

Marie gave him a disparaging look.

"Only you didn't..."

"No...well, sorry."

She sighed; the way Carol sighed when Adam tried to fob her off with some equally lame excuse.

Marie poured his tea and smiled at him over-sweetly.

"How's the meditation going then?"

Adam glanced over his shoulder at the two old ladies and dropped his voice a tone.

"Great thanks. Why do you ask?"

"Because I'm interested that's why. I wondered if you wanted to talk to me about it that's all."

"Yeah, well, it's going really well. You'd be amazed if you knew..."

"Go on. Knew what?" She was looking into his eyes with genuine interest. Adam felt uncomfortable.

"It's hard to explain."

"Try me."

It was Adam's turn to sigh. How the hell could he even begin to explain all the stuff going on inside his head?

"You look lovely" he said, changing the subject.

He meant it. She was gorgeous.

Marie rolled her eyes sensuously. "Typical man" she mumbled before taking a biscuit.

Adam stared at her a smile playing across his lips. Then he began to realise something.

He really did want to tell her.

He wanted to tell her about everything. About learning to meditate under Jack's guidance. About Shera - his own guardian angel. Shera who had shown him the reasons behind his own nightmares and the shadows from his own past. He wanted to tell her about his reunion with his father and about the need to face up to his own destiny if he were ever to find some sort of peace and harmony or resolution in his life. He wanted her to know about the strange and wonderful worlds that were hiding a mere hairs breadth away from everyone's conscious minds; worlds that most people did not have the barest conception of. He wanted to share it all with Marie. Make her part of everything he was going through. If only...

"Hello...?"

"Uh?"

"I said 'hello in there' - Adam you are miles away. Is everything all right? Your tea is getting cold."

Adam shook his head as though shaking off unwanted thoughts. He picked up his cup and sipped at the tea.

"Sorry Marie. Lots on my mind, that's all. Look... um...if you really want to know about meditation then why not come over one evening. Mum would love to see you. Come over for a meal. It's been ages since..."

Marie cocked an eyebrow at him, then relaxed.

"Okay. I'd like that. How do I know you won't forget though?"

"Trust me. I won't forget."

"Look I'd best be getting home. How about a night next week then? Unless..." fluttering her eyelashes, "...You can't wait that long."

Adam hesitated. There was one more thing that he really ought to do before anything else. Something potentially life changing. Then again, if it all went horribly wrong...

"What's today?"

"Wednesday dumb head."

"In that case let's make it this Saturday night. I'll get Carol to cook up something special."

"You sure?"

"Definite. Come over at seven."

Marie rose from her seat and leaned across the table. Adam caught the scent of perfume. He waited for the kiss.

It never came.

Instead, she whispered in his ear, her warm breath melting him inside.

"Saturday then" she whispered, lips brushing his ear lobe, "See you then."

"*This*" said the man in the tweed jacket, "is the most incredible thing I have ever heard in my entire life. Come on now Adam. Are you sure about all this? I'm not trying to suggest you are intentionally making things up - but you've already admitted that some of the acid trips were pretty weird too..."

Adam was mildly annoyed at the suggestion. "There's no connection whatsoever. Sure, I got fucked up a few times on acid, but I've not touched it since learning to meditate. I know the difference between an acid trip and meditation for chrissake..."

"Okay I'm sorry. But I needed to make sure. If you've not been tripping, then this is really really significant."

"It might be significant" scowled Adam, "but I'm also shit scared. What am I supposed to do about it?"

The man stood up and walked over to the window to stare out across the manicured lawns and large lily pond.

"It is a journey that you have no choice but to undertake."

"You make it sound like a holiday."

"I'm sorry. It won't be a holiday. It will require intense focus and concentration. Enormous preparation and sustained willpower..."

"You're frightenin' me..."

"Gentlemen!" interrupted Jack waving an old and rather tattered book in his hands, "Let's not disguise the truth about this. If we are going to move forward, then we all have to acknowledge what the ancients have taught us."

Adam looked up "Which is?"

"That the most frightening journey a person can ever take is the journey into themselves. Right David?"

"Right Jack."

It was all Jack's idea...

Adam had started to blabber down the phone about the meeting with the Indian boy and then his father. By the time he mentioned the potential showdown with the bull-man his voice was verging on the hysterical. Jack had stopped him in his tracks and said the time had come to seek professional advice.

A week later Jack and Adam found themselves in the rooftop study of Dr David Levinson who now sat in an expensive looking leather chair among a labyrinth of books and papers.

Adam held his head in his hands.

"I'm not sure about this Jack. In fact - if I'm totally honest - I'm bloody terrified. I'm just not sure I'm ready..."

Jack nodded and stroked his chin thoughtfully.

"I understand completely" he replied softly, "And I must confess that I'm out of my depth on this one Adam. I wish I could do or say something that could help you but this time I think it has to be Shera. Shallow meditation is one thing, deep meditation is something else. But this..."

"Jack's right" agreed Dr Levinson, returning to his seat behind a huge and cluttered desk, "Jack and I will do whatever we can from 'this side' if you get my drift. Once you are in deep meditation you must stay close to Shera and do exactly as he says. The other good news is that you will also have enormous support from other sources."

"Come again?"

"I'm talking about your father Adam. And the inner strength and experience of the Indian boy which is still there inside your subconscious. His latent energy still resides within you because it is carried through from life to life. You and he are one - and you are therefore much more powerful than you think."

"Yeah? But how can...?"

"Just trust me. You won't be alone. Careful preparation is the most important thing here."

"What sort of preparation?"

"Perhaps I can help on that point" said Jack, "I think what Doctor Levinson is referring to is making sure that body, mind and soul are all performing in unison and at optimum level when you face up to the bull-man."

"Go on."

"Okay. You need to arrange a time when you feel at your mentally strongest. Let's say one week from now. That means no alcohol or any other stimulants. No cigarettes, no negative thoughts, good quality drinking water etcetera."

"Fuck that."

"I'm deadly serious Adam. No rich foods. Good wholesome and healthy nutritious foods and drinks for a whole week. Surround yourself with things that are calming and positive. Don't watch any gory films. Don't get into any arguments. Avoid anything stressful. Meditate every night with a focus on developing all of your sub-conscious 'muscles'. Contact Shera if you need to - but no other entities! Don't attempt to go too deep in any one session but just make sure you are able to descend the layers required when the time comes. Shera can help with all this. Just stay calm and focused and keep giving yourself loads of positive affirmations."

"You what?"

"Keep telling yourself that you are 'invincible' and that the bull-man is powerless against you. Believe that with every fibre of your being because that is the truth."

"Anything else?"

"On the night of the...um...showdown" said Doctor Levinson, "Sit in your normal position, eat only a light meal during the day and drink only water. Before you start meditating do as Jack suggested. Surround your bedroom with as many positive things as possible. Things that make you feel good. Crystals, incense, candles, lucky charms etcetera. Make sure there is absolutely no chance of being disturbed. Then relax as deeply as possible before starting your normal routine."

"What if anything goes wrong?"

Jack and David exchanged glances.

"You must believe that nothing will go wrong - and it won't" said David softly, "Now let's make definite plans. When will you be ready Adam?"

It was Adam's turn to stand. He started to pace up and down the large study, floorboards creaking underfoot. He wandered over to the large picture window and looked out over the extensive and well-tended gardens. His mind though, was now concentrating on other things.

"Next Friday evening" he said at last. "Mum is out next Friday. I'll be alone. That will give me a week from now to get prepared. It will give me time to sort stuff out. Time to ask Shera things. I really don't want to have to do this...but I also know that I have to. So, I guess that's it then."

"Not quite" said Jack, "There is a couple more things - and this is very important - what time do you intend to start the big event?"

"Does it matter?"

"Possibly. Promise me that you will start precisely - and I mean precisely - at a specific time."

"Okay. I'll start at precisely 8.30 next Friday night."

"That's fine then."

Doctor Levinson raised a quizzical eyebrow at Jack who winked back at him.

"And the other thing?" asked Adam

"Ah yes" said Jack fumbling in the pocket of his raincoat.

He handed Adam a smooth pebble about two inches wide pressing it into his hand.

"What's this Jack?"

"I don't possess any golden feathers I'm afraid Adam. This is the best I can do. I picked it up from a stream bed on the last day of the war. I'd lost half a leg by then, so the war ended early for me. But on the day peace was declared I picked up this rather pretty stone from a local stream. It is a small symbol of good overcoming evil. I never meditate without it in my pocket. It's a mineral called green Aventurine."

"It's got good vibes then?"

Jack nodded, "Exceptionally so. It's yours now. After all, the man they know as 'The Stone' really ought to own a real sacred stone don't you think?"

"I'll take anything that might help Jack. It feels good in my hand."

"Aventurine is a form of quartz that is almost always an emerald-green colour flecked with gold and found in places that have high natural energy like India which you already have a connection with" said Jack enthusiastically, "It connects with your heart chakra and is a stone of healing and an exceptional tool for focusing the mind and energising the soul."

"Really? That's amazing!"

David nodded, adding, "It's a natural stone Adam, that supports decisive action, strong leadership qualities and encourages your inner strength to keep on going no matter what obstacles might seem to stand in the way. It also grants you space to heal old wounds which in your case is very important. From ancient times it has helped people to clear out old blockages that may have been holding them back. The energy of the stone will help you to find strength and courage when it comes to what you choose to let into your mind and what you need to let go of. Keep it in your hand when you meditate."

Adam slipped the pebble into his pocket, "Thanks David and thanks Jack. I really appreciate this."

Doctor Levinson stood up and grasped Adam firmly by the hand. His eyes looked deep into Adam's eyes.

"You really do have the power to defeat your deepest fears you know Adam" he said softly, "Your destiny is now in your own hands. Remember that you are the one they called 'The Stone'. You don't even know how powerful you can be if your heart is filled with enough courage."

Across the garden the wind picked up slightly and a flurry of leaves twisted and spiralled like a small whirlwind before being deposited onto the still surface of the garden pond. Clouds rolled across the sky tinged with grey underbellies like lumbering whales moving through a dark ocean. Somewhere on the horizon a storm was brewing.

"You did say seven o'clock, didn't you?"

"Yeah" said Adam, calling down the stairs, "She'll be here at seven. Marie's never late. Is the dinner all prepared?"

"Almost. What does Marie like to drink?"

"White wine. Medium sweet. Have you got any?"

"Of course," said Carol "One of us needs to do the shopping. What had you got planned? Beans on toast and a glass of water?"

"Very funny. But thanks anyway."

Adam finished drying his hair and splashing some more aftershave over the dark bristles coating his chin. He looked in the mirror again just to check that the newly emerged bristles were more 'sexy' than 'beardy' and nodded in satisfaction. Looking in the mirror was still a little unnerving. He was never sure whether he'd see the mad eyes of an enraged bull staring over his shoulder - but mercifully, tonight, all he was looking into was the reflection of his own eyes.

Well almost...

The deep, dark, liquid pools that stared back at him started to shimmer slightly as though the mirror was fogging over for just a second or two. And in those almost imperceptibly brief moments he suddenly caught his breath because he could no longer see his own reflection. The face that was staring back at him was not his own. It was that of a brown-skinned child with almond-shaped eyes from another distant time that were staring back at him with warmth and encouragement. Adam leapt back from the mirror in shock as his own reflection instantly reappeared.

What was that about? Why was he bloody hallucinating for God's sake?

Either that or he was going completely mad...

The doorbell interrupted his reverie. He slipped on a clean black shirt while Carol unlocked the front door.

"Marie. How lovely to see you!"

"Thanks Mrs Sinclair."

"I told you before. It's Carol. Now let me take your coat. Glass of wine?"

"Thanks Carol. Adam remembered to tell you that I was coming over then?"

Carol rolled her eyes, "He remembered this morning and then got in a panic. Nothing I'm not used to. Anyway, I'm delighted to see you again and it's so nice to have you over for dinner. Come and sit down and tell me all about your new job. Adam's just finishing in the shower, he'll be down in a moment."

Adam stood at the top of the stairs listening to his mother and his ex-girlfriend chatting away like old friends.

Ex?

Maybe it was time to re-kindle what they used to have. Get back to normal. Start going out again properly.

...Or maybe it should wait until a few days' time, when other matters were finally dealt with.

Unless by then he was either dead or consigned to a lunatic asylum that is...

Adam walked downstairs and kissed both Carol and Marie on the cheek. They both looked at him quizzically.

"Ouch. You're a bit stubbly." said Carol.

"Hairy beast more like," laughed Marie.

"Hi Marie. Mum's cooked up one of her specials tonight. You're gonna love it."

"I've been looking forward to it. How's the Gazette?"

"Okay, I guess. It's just an office like any other really. The supermarket?"

"Busy."

Adam glanced at Carol. It was a clear message.

"I'll...er...go and get everything ready then" said Carol, "Dinner in five minutes."

She left the room.

"Good to see you, Marie."

"You too. How are...things...?"

Adam raised an eyebrow.

"You know. Meditation. Still going well?"

Adam put a finger to his lips.

"Shhh. Keep your voice down. Yeah, all okay thanks. I'll tell you all about it sometime."

"Great. I'd like that."

"Thanks for coming over" smiled Adam, "I've missed seeing you recently. There's been a lot to deal with. Stuff to sort out."

"Yeah. I bumped into some of your dozy mates. They said they hadn't seen much of you and when they did you were acting weird."

"Well, that's because they don't understand..."

"Don't understand what?"

"Nothing. Not important. Look, I was thinking maybe we should..."

"Should what?"

Adam opened his mouth, trying to find the courage to say what was in his head.

That he wanted her back. That she looked stunning. That he really wanted to take her in his arms and...

"Dinner's ready" said Carol, "Come on now take a seat you two. Let's drink to the future. Whatever it may hold."

Carol raised her glass.

"The future" echoed Marie looking dreamily into Adam's eyes. She took a sip of wine and fluttered her eyelashes at him.

Adam raised his glass.

"The future" said Adam, "And here's to the two most wonderful women in the world."

This was the big one.

It was more than instinct. More than intuition. It was an inner sense of certainty that Adam's whole life had been leading up to this single moment and for a single purpose. Now the time had come to face up to his destiny.

He tried to console himself that he'd done everything possible to prepare for this moment - *as well as anyone could prepare for this type of situation* - laying off alcohol, stimulants, drugs, cigarettes - in fact, impurities of any kind, so that his concentration would be as acute and focused as possible.

Jack and Shera had been as helpful and instructive as possible, but even they knew, with barely concealed trepidation, that this was essentially down to Adam alone. The hidden laws of nature, immutable and unfathomable since the dawn of time, could not and would not be broken.

Which meant that any help they could provide to Adam would be well intentioned but probably minimal...

Adam made the final checks to his plan. Carol was out for the whole evening, and he'd locked the front door and even bolted it. He'd removed the phone off the hook and made sure all electrical appliances were turned off too.

He'd thought about meditating in Carol's bedroom as it was larger, but soon realised that familiarity and ritual were so much part of the process that any changes to routine might be detrimental - so it would be his own room as usual.

Although it was still early evening, he closed the curtains and tidied away everything that seemed to be just lying around the bed or the floor; books, records, clothes and even old toys kept merely because they were relics of the past. There were certain things, though, that he wanted to place around the small bedroom deliberately - for no other reason than they made him feel good - lucky charms of a sort and perhaps on this occasion something more. Talismans imbued with positive energy perhaps. Anything that might give him added inner strength. On his bedside cabinet he laid out the Indian neck beads he'd purchased at the ethnic stall at Reading Festival. Beside them he laid a 'lucky' fossil ammonite he'd found in an abandoned quarry as a young child, the cigarette lighter Marie had given him on his seventeenth birthday and most importantly of all an old brass telescope dad had given him for Christmas when he was nine. It was the one they used to share when looking at the planets together on crystal clear chilly winter evenings. Dad was always keen to point out the names of the major constellations in the night sky. He remembered how dad had pointed out the distinctive shape of Taurus, Adam's own birth sign, as well as how to recognise all the other configurations of stars that made up the signs of the zodiac.

When everything was in its right place Adam went to the bathroom for a few moments and splashed a few drops of cold water on his face. Then he returned to his room, climbed up on to the bed, leaned back against the wall and glanced over at the alarm clock. Friday evening. 8.25pm.

He felt ready to start but then remembered that Jack had asked him not to meditate until 8.30pm precisely.

Strange really - Jack had never mentioned anything about the timing of meditation before - but Adam knew the old man well enough to obey without question. There would be a reason.

Adam used the remaining time to relax each of his muscles in turn, from head to toe, feeling tensions gradually dissipating, particularly around his neck and shoulders. He noticed a quickening of his heartbeat and a rather tight feeling deep inside his abdomen. Not surprising really, he reflected, in view of what he was about to attempt, but such things had to be dealt with before he slipped into the meditative state. With a concentrated effort Adam relaxed his stomach muscles and consciously slowed his heartbeat down to a steady rhythm. Good - that was better.

Now he felt as ready as he ever would be. Now there could be no going back. Adam put his hand into his pocket and closed his fist around the soft surface of the Aventurine pebble Jack had given him. Good. Made him feel closer to the old man.

Shutting his eyes Adam began to breathe deeply and started to let the last fleeting thoughts disappear into the ether. He thought for a moment about Marie and then Carol. He thought about Steve, Mick and Danny and Gavin at the Gazette. Ordinary people leading ordinary lives. What the hell would they make of all this? No point in even dwelling on such thoughts. He was way past 'ordinary life' now. Within a minute or so the darkness before him started to move and blend with other shifting colours and shapes that after a while began to transform themselves from the dull cloudscapes of the 'Empty Place' into the creamy wispy clouds that presaged the arrival of the deep blue that Adam now thought of as 'home'.

The journey that paradoxically he was always pre-destined to make, had now begun.

Now there could be no going back.

Jack Harland bent down and rolled back the old lounge carpet exposing the wooden trapdoor beneath. He grasped the inset metal hand ring then pulled it open with a single yank. He'd remembered to feed Lady, who by now would be licking her paws contentedly before venturing out of the small kitchen via the cat flap to explore the overgrown environs of the back garden, so there would be no disturbances.

He fumbled in the half-light for the light switch, found it, and flooded the underground cellar with light. He walked down the rickety old stairs and brushed away the new cobwebs that had appeared since his last visit to the cellar two weeks before, when he'd fancied sampling a particular vintage of Montrachet.

Everything was in its right place. The rough whitewashed walls, the old table at the far end with a hundred or so candles, the wax frozen in various stages of being extinguished and a solitary box of matches. At the other end of the cellar resided a large selection of dusty wine bottles, all racked and labelled, the labels yellowed and curling. In the centre of the cellar a large old leather armchair, the leather cracked, mottled and faded, faced the table full of candles.

Jack pulled the wooden trapdoor shut and then went over to the table to select a large tallow candle, taller than the rest, its soft wick pristine and unblemished. He placed it in the centre of the table and lit it with a match. Once the flame had ceased flickering Jack flicked off the light switch and the harsh electric light from the single dusty bulb hanging from the ceiling disappeared leaving only the soft warm glow from the single candle.

It was cooler in the cellar than upstairs in the lounge. Good for wine, but not for old soldiers with a crippled leg.

There was an old tartan picnic blanket lying folded over the arm of the chair. Jack put his walking stick down beside the armchair then sat down with a sigh and pulled the blanket over his body from knees to neck. He felt good. Calm, warm and cosy. Just what he needed in view of what might be ahead.

Unlike Adam, who had learned instinctively the secrets of meditation in no time at all, it had taken Jack Harland some thirty years of dedicated concentration to get this far. Not that he begrudged Adam his extraordinary success - on the contrary - there were very good reasons why Adam should have achieved so much. The same reasons, Jack reflected, that on this night might place the unsuspecting lad in mortal danger. Jack pulled an old pocket watch from his waistcoat pocket and squinted at the time; the hands of the watch barely discernible in the dim candlelight. 8.29pm. Good. Not a moment to lose.

Jack took a few deep breaths and focused all his attention on the candle flame across the room. Everyone needed to find their own way through the gateway. Jack's way required candlelight. For him there was no other way.

The procedure was always the same for Jack. Habitual and precise. Yet tonight he knew it would be very different. Sure, he'd soon be encountering what Adam liked to call the 'empty place' and then hopefully he too could immerse himself into the awe-inspiring translucent blue that would draw him seductively into a strange inner world too beautiful to describe.

But beyond the blue and the interference level? Now that was different. That was a place Jack had rarely ventured into. It demanded a concentration deeper than Jack could normally sustain and he had only pushed himself that hard on a few occasions. Tonight though, he must push himself harder than ever before.

Even if it killed him.

Jack started to breathe shallower, his body barely moving. His focus on the candle flame started to blur until his eyelids slowly closed and he started the inner descent.

'I'm on my way Adam' he whispered softly, 'I'm on my way.'

'Shera?'
   '*I am here Adam.*'
   'I'm ready.'
   '*Are you absolutely sure? I must warn you that this could be very dangerous. For us both.*'
   'It's something I have to do Shera. We both know that.'
   There was a pause, then Shera said:
   '*So be it. Follow me.*'
   Adam followed effortlessly. There was no way of knowing precisely where exactly he was being led to, but then it hardly mattered. Location, time and level of 'reality' were all superfluous now. The seeds of this encounter began centuries ago and had been fermenting below the surface of reality like a malignant cancer waiting, with infinite patience, to manifest. Things that had been influencing his life, his actions, his very persona, had always been irrevocably connected to something evil and intangible that he had only ever perceived during recurring nightmares and visions. And all this time - throughout his whole childhood and into his late teens he had been powerless to do anything to stop this malevolent influence.
   Until now.
   Now it was make or break time. There could be no going back.

It seemed to take a long time before Shera stopped moving. There were fleeting glimpses of different colours, shapes and even landscapes to the right and left as though travelling on a high-speed train through rapidly changing scenery. And then at last Shera came to a halt somewhere strange and unfamiliar. It was also distinctly oppressive.

It was like nowhere else Adam had ever visited in real life or in the spiritual realms but reminded him of films he'd seen of tropical rainforests. There seemed to be a canopy of very tall trees blocking out most of the natural light, leaving the mushy ground, rich in decaying vegetation beneath his feet, dappled in various shades of light and dark. The verdant undergrowth concealed more than it revealed and shadows constantly flickered between twisted tree trunks and giant tropical ferns. Twigs crackled as unseen things moved in the depths of the jungle. It was the heat though, which made the air seem so oppressive and Adam could already feel a film of sweat coating his forehead.

'Where are we?' he whispered to Shera sensing that in this place even the trees might have ears.

'*Another layer*' said Shera off-handedly, as though it was unimportant.

Adam took an instant dislike to the surroundings. Rainforests are supposed to be full of life and vibrancy - but not this place. This forest was dark, gloomy, foreboding and reeked of something evil. For the first time Adam could sense Shera's unease too. Not surprising really.

'Where now?'

'*There are some rock formations ahead. There's a large cave. I can sense his presence there.*'

His?

Adam felt his physical heart beating faster though he also felt disassociated from it, as though it were the booming of distant thunder.

'Does that mean he - the bull-man - can sense our presence too?'

'Yes, he can sense your presence, Adam. He knows you are here. I don't think he can sense me though. I'm at a different vibrational rate from you remember.'

'Great' thought Adam, 'So much for the sense of surprise. If he already knows I'm here, then there's no point creeping along through the undergrowth. I may as well just announce my arrival.'

Shera read his thoughts immediately.

'You are right Adam. The more confidence you display the more his power is weakened. The more you defy him the stronger you will become. If you fear him though, his strength will overpower you. There must be no fear.'

Adam stopped and took a deep breath. He was scared. No denying it. And this was merely the prelude to something much more terrifying. Right now, he'd much rather be out with his boring mates in the boring Anchor sinking a boring pint. Anything but this. This was a nightmare that he wanted desperately to end but one that paradoxically, he had to endure if there was to be any hope of salvation.

A grim determination took hold of him. How dare this - this bull-thing - interfere with his life. How dare it intrude into his dreams and cause him so many distressing nightmares. How dare it taunt him so relentlessly over so many years?

How dare it!

Adam pushed through the undergrowth sweeping branches aside and treading down briars and clinging sticky things. After a few yards the greenery gave way to an open clearing where a huge grey featureless rock face loomed sheer above him, stretching away to the right and left with no end in sight.

And there at the foot of the rock face was the black hole, a huge repugnant yawning and toothless mouth from which hot foul air emanated in a visible heat haze and from which no light escaped.

Adam stood before the cave opening feeling like a helpless fly in front of the gaping mouth of a predator, half expecting a long sticky tongue to lash out from the darkness and curl around his feeble body sucking him into the innards. He shuddered at the thought. Bravery was not part of his make-up.

Again, he wanted desperately to turn back, rise up into the beautiful safe blueness and make his way back to the sanctuary of his body. But he knew that this time there must be no going back until the matter was resolved once and for all.

Shera seemed reluctant to enter the cave for some reason but signalled to Adam that he should go on. Adam didn't question Shera's judgement. There was no point. If anything happened to Adam, then it happened to Shera too. There was no point in being a guardian angel if there was nothing to guard. They both knew that.

Adam waited for a moment for his eyes to become accustomed to the cave's darkness then mentally prepared himself for whatever might be waiting inside. He was scared - *God he was scared* - but he was also angry, and the anger that was welling up inside him was also giving him strength and a focus that was driving him forward.

Within moments the black maw had swallowed him up and all the daylight in the forest was gone. He was in complete darkness, a gravelly wet feel to the cavern floor and warm humid dampness coating the uneven walls and roof.

He must have walked for a good hundred yards, gently downhill, before the small passageway finally opened out into a much larger chamber. There was some sort of light in the centre of the chamber - no, not a light - it was a crackling fire. The light from the flames lit up the whole underground cavern. It reminded Adam of a dusty circus ring with a fire at the centre and a huge domed roof above. It was still dark, dank, gloomy and oppressive but at least the general shape of the domed cavern could be discerned.

He waited at the threshold of the chamber letting his eyes become accustomed to the flickering shadows dancing around the damp black walls.

Maybe he should have thought of some sort of 'plan', some strategy for dealing with the situation?

Too late now.

All he would have to rely on were his own wits and strength of will.

Something moved on the far side of the fire. It was difficult to see anything clearly as the shape seemed pressed up against the far wall directly opposite Adam, the fire midway between them. It was something large, very dark and disturbingly familiar.

For a moment Adam stood rooted to the spot holding his breath and watching the shape beyond the fire moving slowly. It seemed to be moving away from the back wall now, moving towards the centre of the chamber. Towards the fire.

As it got nearer the glow from the fire gave the shape more defined edges and curves. It was tall; around seven feet in height and stood on two legs and it seemed to be wearing something resembling a long black fur covered cloak that fell from shoulders to floor disguising any upper limbs. There was a sickening sweet smell emanating from somewhere. Could be from the damp chamber walls, or even the animal skin coat. A smell as rancid and as evocative as faded perfume. It made Adam want to retch.

As the figure leaned forward towards the fire Adam let out a small gasp.

Something glowed in the flickering firelight. It was two long, thick, curved and ivory-white horns protruding from the head.

And then a voice suddenly boomed through the domed cavern making his heart jump as the sound echoed and bounced around the cavern walls.

'*Adam Sinclair*' the voice rasped, '*Well, well…How nice of you to drop in.*'

Adam stood trembling, terrified of the monstrous figure before him and even more shocked when it spoke in a voice seething with vehemence and hatred. Even in this mortified state he knew that real bulls can't talk. Was this deep meditation turning into another surreal nightmare? It was difficult to tell. Nothing made much sense anymore.

Although his throat felt dry and parched Adam was determined to stand his ground. This was not the time to reveal his inner nervousness. His words, when he found voice, surprised him in their hard-edged coolness.

'I don't know who you are, or what you are, but I came here to tell you that you don't frighten me anymore. I want you to stay out of my life forever.'

The bull figure seemed to shuffle from foot to foot, the fire a natural barrier separating them and making it difficult to see clearly.

'Do you now?' came the reply, each word hissed like a snake.

Adam was in this too deep now. He'd come too far. He knew that he had to start acting a whole lot tougher than he felt or risk losing everything.

'You never thought I could track you down, did you?' he continued, taunting the bull-thing, "Never thought I'd actually come after you. Well, let me tell you - you are wrong. You might have scared me when I was younger and weaker but that's all over now. D'you understand?'

The horns moved sideways slightly, crackling firelight reflected along their smooth curvature. It was as though the creature had inclined its head to listen.

When it spoke again it was in a mocking, chastising tone.

'My, My, brave, aren't we? Brave, but very, very foolish.'

Adam squinted over the fire, trying to get a better look at the animal figure opposite. The darkness of the cavern combined with the jumping yellow flames made everything look like flickering shadows. He could just about make out the whites of the creature's eyes. Memories of being gored through and pinned to a wooden door came flooding back and made him feel sick.

Adam spoke again, his voice almost cracking and betraying his fear.

'Tell me something. Why are you doing this to me?'

The horns rose up again pointing to the roof of the cavern.

'Because' hissed the voice, *'You are the one they call 'the Stone', the one who walks in the shadows between two worlds, you know that now don't you? You know there's something rather special about you don't you Adam Sinclair?'*

Adam licked his lips 'What of it? What does that matter to you?'

The bull thing snarled. The anger in the voice barely contained. *'Why does it matter? Don't you understand anything you fool? Because fate decrees that only one of us can exert influence in the worlds we inhabit – that's why. Don't you see that we cannot co-exist without one of us being the strong and one the weak? That's why it is your turn to die again. I thought killing you the last time you tried to suppress me would have taught you a lesson.'*

'When I was the Indian boy?' said Adam more bravely than he felt, 'You don't get rid of me that easily a second time I'm afraid.' A far-off voice spoke softly in Adam's ears:

'Take off your mask Adam - and find out who you really are...'

The bull's rage suddenly erupted into action. A flailing upper limb shot out from under the fur cloak and swept aside the upper part of the fire so that flaming branches were scattered and tossed all around the circular clearing. Adam had half expected the thing to come at him around the side of the fire but not through the middle of it. Blazing stumps of crackling wood came to rest all around the chamber, lighting up dark recesses; yellow sparks hanging in the stale air and spinning to the ground like dancing fireflies.

For a brief moment, Adam felt frozen to the spot but as the bull-thing approached directly through the remains of the fire he moved himself backwards into the darkness fumbling around for a rock or something - anything - to defend himself. He cursed himself for not having the forethought to bring a weapon.

The bull-thing strode confidently through the glowing embers of the broken fire and stopped when only a metre or so separated them. It clearly wanted to savour its moment of triumph before driving its sabre-sharp horns through Adam's soft body tissue for the second time.

'I should have killed you long ago' it said, spitting out each vitriolic word through gritted teeth, *'But killing you twice will give me immense pleasure...'*

Adam stared at the thing standing before him in shock and disbelief. He could see much more clearly now. It was not a bull at all. It was a dark-skinned man wearing some kind of cloak of rancid animal fur tied around the shoulders and dragging on the floor. He was wearing a huge mask or even possibly the hollowed-out skull of a real bull because the horns were real enough. The figure looked like one of those pictures of Siberian Shaman he'd seen in a book once, trying to take on the persona of an animal.

The realisation that this nightmare creature was more 'human' than animal and not a real bull or some kind of demon from hell made Adam suddenly feel a whole lot stronger. It was just a tall man, wearing some kind of bull's skull. He could feel the anger pumping adrenalin into his veins. He reached down to the floor of the cave and his hand fixed onto the cool end of a blazing stump of wood. He held it up defensively in front of him, brandishing it like a sword.

If the bull-man was scared he didn't show it. Instead, he lowered his horns and bellowed deeply.

...And then launched himself directly at Adam with a roar of pure evil.

Adam stepped sideways and gripped the stump with both hands swinging it like a baseball bat at the oncoming horns. The stump connected and there was a sickening crunching sound as the whole skull mask flew off the bull man's head and fell heavily to the floor.

The bull-man stopped abruptly, howling with pain and rage. Without the mask on he appeared much smaller. Less sinister. Although breathing heavily and sweating profusely Adam was heartened by seeing the loss of the mask.

It was man-to-man now.

The hatred in the man's eyes was venomous. He stepped back and found a similar blazing stump, raising it from the ground as though drawing a sabre from a sheath.

'*You shouldn't have done that*' he screamed at Adam, '*Not if you wanted a quick painless death.*'

He sprang across the small space between them and swung the flaming branch with surprising strength. It took Adam's stump clean out of his hands sending it spiralling across the cave, sparks flying everywhere before crashing to the damp and uneven cavern floor. Adam stepped back but it was too dark to be sure of his footing. Something made him stumble and fall backwards spreadeagled in the dust.

Shit!

A second later and the bull-man stood over him looking into his eyes. He raised the burning stump up over his head with both hands like an axe, slowly, licking his spittle-covered lips in anticipation.

'No...' Adam wailed, unable to move, defenceless now.

'*It's all over Adam Sinclair*' said the bull-man, '*Did you really think you could hurt me? I've killed you before and I'll kill you again. It's all over.*'

The bull-man swung the flaming stump over his head with a force hard enough to kill and all Adam could do was hold up one hand feebly in front of his face.

So - this was the end then? After all this effort he had failed. The evil bull-thing had proved the stronger and was about to preserve his rule for another century or more. Now he, Adam, would know what real death feels like.

But the bone-crunching sound of impact never happened.

Instead, something - *someone* - invisibly pushed the bull-man violently sideways sending him crashing into a pile of rocks and dropping the crackling yellow log harmlessly to the ground. Adam didn't need any further encouragement to jump to his feet and pick up a fist-sized boulder.

'*Now's your chance Adam!*' a disembodied voice said, '*That's done me in I'm afraid. If I were a younger man...*'

'Jack!' Adam yelled into the darkness almost crying with relief. 'Thank God. Where...?'

It was too late. Jack - in whatever form he'd employed to get to this place - was gone again and the bull man was also back on his feet howling with rage. Adam aimed the boulder like a cricket ball and threw it as hard as he could. It hit the man's shoulder with a crack that made him scream.

Surely now....?

But the bull-man was not finished yet. Instead, he seemed to have unnatural reserves of strength. Adam was mentally and physically shot to pieces.

'*I should have killed you once and for all in the car crash*' *the bull-man swore, foaming at the mouth and spitting blood*, '*It was very careless of me.*'

Adam wiped the sweat out of his eyes with a torn sleeve. His mouth fell open and his eyes narrowed. An icy coldness flooded through his veins.

When he spoke, he could barely frame the words.

'The car crash? You...you...killed my father?'

The bull man stared into Adam's eyes with an evil grimace and held up his hands to simulate strangulation.

'*It should have been you both you know. Somehow you survived. But you don't get that lucky twice. Ready to join him now?*'

He rushed at Adam again with a blood-curdling yell, head butting him in the stomach and sending him badly winded to the ground again. While Adam clutched his stomach the bull-man took a few paces back and then started to run fast towards him, launching himself off the ground in order to crush him with the weight of his own body before strangling the life blood out of him with his bare hands.

At least that was his plan...

Adam had fallen beside the bull skull. Although still lying prostrate in the dust, he managed to yank the mask off the ground with all his strength, twenty years of suppressed anger giving him new reserves of stamina. He held the bone mask firmly against his chest turning its horns upwards and outwards as he did so.

...Which meant the bull-man didn't stand a chance.

The centuries' old personification of evil was already in the air by the time his wide eyes realised what Adam had done. Adam braced himself for the impact and winced as the upturned horns drove deep into the bull-man's body, the mask sandwiched between them.

Blood poured over Adam's face and arms, and he wriggled from under the prone body. Even now the bull-man kicked and screamed, the mask horns firmly impaled in his chest.

The bull-man tried to stand up but started to stumble, blood pouring from his skewered chest. Adam raised a foot and kicked the bull-man backwards so that he fell clumsily onto the glowing embers of the fire in the centre of the cave. He screamed as the embers burnt into the already torn flesh of his back.

'That's for ruining my life' Adam screamed at him, blood and sweat streaking his whole body. A new sense of strength and power now surging through his veins.

The bull-man grinned at him - a pained crazed sickly grin, blood trickling from the side of his mouth. He tried to push the mask away to release the horns from his gored chest. Tried to lift himself off the fire. Adam stared in utter disbelief. Was this thing indestructible? Christ - was there no way to end this?

Adam once again felt raw anger welling up inside him. With a yell he pulled himself to his feet then ran towards the writhing figure and leapt into the air 'And this...' he screamed as both feet came crashing down on the back of the mask, 'This one is for my dad...'

For a moment flames, blood and bones all came together in a jumbled mush, swimming before Adam's eyes and making him lose orientation.

He thought he felt the impact, thought he saw the bull man's sardonic grin turn to horror, but couldn't be sure because he was suddenly spinning like a skydiver through spirals and kaleidoscopic fragments of colour. He felt sick to the pit of his stomach, nauseated, disorientated and very weak.

Before closing his eyes to blot out the confusion and pain he heard a voice very clear in his ear.

It was Shera.

'It's over Adam' Shera said softly and firmly, *'At last, it's all over.'*

PART FOUR

"Oh seeker, know the true nature of your soul
and identify yourself with it completely.
Dedicate your life to the service of
humankind and uplift them to divinity."

Yajur Veda – Ancient Hindu text

The images came before the coldness.

So, this was it then? The final frontier and all that? He'd always wondered what death would feel like - really feel like.

Didn't they always say that a drowning man sees his whole life pass before his eyes? This must be it then - all the images flooding into his head jostling for attention.

Most of the images were nothing new. The same old mind-movies he'd seen so many times before. Images of the car crash again, standing at his father's graveside, nightmares about terrifying bull-creatures from the depths of the unconscious, images of beatings-up, hospital beds and hangovers.

Not all the images were painful though.

There were scenes of lying in the grass with Marie overwhelmed by teenage adoration and lust. Childhood summer days when dad was still alive. Crying with laughter when fooling around with his mates, an old man called Jack raising a glass of fine wine in salutation and images of a smiling angel-being called Shera with outstretched arm offering a burnished golden feather for him to reach out and take.

There were other images too that were more confusing. Images from other lifetimes and perhaps even other dimensions, other worlds, or other layers of consciousness.

Crumbling old temples and caves with strange carvings on the walls and lots of chanting, unfamiliar foreign faces, half- remembered colours and smells, lights dancing in the clearings within forests of ancient trees and old parchments written in languages he could not understand. These were images that he felt he *ought* to recognise though they somehow remained frustratingly elusive - images that a little dark-skinned boy from another age would definitely recognise.

And then there were even hazier images of times long ago when strange beings of light fought archaic battles in the cosmos and of strange but beautiful landscapes that witnessed meetings of angelic beings with pristine white wings and shining swords. These were somehow both places and 'non-places' that existed on different vibrational frequencies – accessible only through deep-seated memories rekindled by focused meditations that reached out into the hidden recesses of the timeless soul.

Then after all the images began to fade came the coldness. A bone-weary coldness that sapped all energy and strength leaving a craving for warmth, solitude, and peace.

'And yet to some...just a few...it is the ultimate goal, the new beginning, the realisation of all ambition and the most sought-after prize of all...'

Today though, death was not to be.

Today death would be taking another soul to its final resting place. Adam, fate and karma had decided, still had far too much left to do. Somewhere out in the depths of the hazy borders of reality someone had decreed Adam's destiny was still unfinished.

He opened his eyes slowly and shivered slowly becoming aware of his surroundings.

He was lying naked on the bedroom floor. The bedclothes were strewn haphazardly around the room and all the contents of his desk lay scattered across the carpet. For some reason the bedroom window had been left wide open and he was covered in goose bumps, though a film of warm dampness coated his forehead and upper lip.

He tried to stand up and found himself stumbling and having to use the wall to support himself.

A fresh breeze caught the bedroom curtains and made them billow. He quickly wrapped a sheet around his shivering body. Outside the sun was starting to probe skinny yellow fingers through a frothing of marbled cloud.

Morning.

Adam ran a trembling hand through his greasy dishevelled hair and looked into the bedroom mirror.

The dark shading under both eyes were no surprise. It only took a moment or two before the horrors of the night before came back to him in all its graphic and gory detail. Little wonder he looked so drained. He stared at his reflection searching his own eyes for answers. Searching for anything.

The answer was there all the time of course.

In his own eyes, just as Jack had always predicted.

There, just behind the reflection and almost imperceptible, two shadows had always lurked. Two shadows as intertwined and inseparable as Jekyll and Hyde.

Today though the reflection was subtly different. So subtle it was barely distinguishable.

This time there was no shadow.

Which meant that this time Adam knew one thing for certain.

The bull-man was dead.

It was a few hours later; after the longest and most incredible meditation ever. He still felt emotionally drained and a bit feverish, but he had promised to phone Jack.

It was a surreal phone call and Adam apologised to Jack for the state he was in. As ever, Jack waved aside the apology and told Adam to take some time out to relax. It was Saturday morning and Adam needed time to fully recover. He suggested that Adam should come over on Monday evening, after work. There was a lot to talk about but now it was time to rest.

At least, reflected Jack, the lad sounded in good spirits.

For Adam, the weirdest thing was thanking Jack for his life-saving appearance in the bull-man's cave. Thanking him over something as mundane and conventional as a house telephone for coming to his aid in another parallel universe of the inner psyche seemed even more bizarre than the event itself.

To Adam's astonishment, Jack had modestly remarked that 'it was nothing', shrugging it off as casually as if he had intervened in a bar brawl, but adding that it had been fascinating for him to penetrate another layer of the meditative realms for the first time, after so many years standing nervously at the threshold. For Jack, a lifetime of meditative discipline had enabled him to summon up sufficient courage, when the need arose most, to finally bring him his just rewards.

The rest of the weekend was just a blur. Adam had fallen asleep on the living room couch in the early afternoon and slept soundly until 5pm, something he had never done before. The sleep was deep and undisturbed, and he awoke feeling both refreshed and hungry. Although he knew the lads would all be in The Anchor that evening, maybe followed by a bit of night clubbing, there was no way he wanted to join them. Maybe next weekend...

Or maybe never...

Instead, he had relaxed with Carol just watching TV - or more accurately being aware of a TV droning in the background. His mind was still racing with strange and bizarre images, and he still felt emotionally drained.

On the Sunday he decided to give his bedroom a thorough overhaul and clean-up and Carol had made a fantastic Sunday roast. He went to bed early after ironing a crisp blue shirt ready for work next morning. Again, he slept soundly although his head was still full of strange dreams. Dreams of a small boy with olive skin and almond shaped eyes instructing his elders in spiritual wisdom and the art of meditation in a far-off land. "*Watch,*" the young boy had said after casting a small pebble into a pond, "*See how the pond creates these beautiful circular ripples. Each ripple is a different layer that starts from the centre. You are the centre - and each layer emanates from you. Some layers are physical, the nearest ones to the centre. But the outer ripples are layers of other places beyond the body. Places that exist in other timeframes. These are wonderful places that you can discover when you meditate...*"

And the tribal elders had listened in wonder and bowed before this extraordinary child who had knowledge of things way beyond his years.

The following Monday evening, as he walked from the High Street, leaving the office behind him, Adam mulled over the events of the day.

Most days at the Gazette were more straightforward now - and over the last few weeks Gavin had gradually given him more and more responsibility; the odd fact-gathering mission here, the odd low-key interview there. Adam felt he had risen to each challenge well. Even on the days when he'd turned up late feeling like shit after a night out on the beer. Other nights it was the concentration from sustained meditation that left him weary next day - not that he'd ever admit to such a thing though. Not to anyone.

He must have done something right though, because this morning the seldom seen, and always aloof, Stanley T. Morgan had actually emerged from his office and called Gavin over just as Gavin was about to explain to Adam the fineries of reporting on a local domestic dispute that had hit the Courts. Gavin and Mr Morgan had remained in the room, door closed, for about ten minutes before Gavin emerged, straightening his garish red tie with the image of the national Welsh Dragon and winking at Adam.

"What was that about?" Adam had asked, nodding towards the small office door.

"You always were a nosey sod, Adam Sinclair. It was about you actually."

"Oh yeah...what's that then?"

"Sacked for being caught in possession of a stupid haircut" replied Gavin triumphantly.

Adam's initial shocked expression remained fixed until he realised it was one of Gavin's feeble attempts at humour.

"Ha Ha" Adam said laconically.

"Actually" said Gavin, sitting down again at his cluttered desk, and with a more serious expression, "It's good news boyo. Old Mildew Morgan, as I affectionately call him, quite likes some of those articles you and I have been putting together. You know - the articles that demonstrate my sparkling wit and command of the English language."

"The one's where I change your dodgy words to sensible ones you mean?"

"Detail Adam...mere detail...well anyway - the long and the short of it is he wants to put you on an editor's training course. You know...brush up your loose edges a bit."

"Yeah?"

"Yeah. And it also means a small wage increase. It means you can afford to go out and get pissed more often. My God Adam - this means the old buffoon actually likes you. I'd be seriously worried if I were you."

Adam had poked out his tongue at the sub-editor, copying one of Marie's rather endearing traits.

It was good news though and gave him a huge morale boost. He couldn't wait to let Mum know. Let her know that her 'useless son' was finally making the grade.

There was something else too, he mused, crossing the road that led to Jack's place. Dad would be proud of him too. Very proud. He stopped in his tracks for a moment, glanced over his shoulder at the empty street then looked up into the grey - blue streaked November evening sky. Life was, at last, beginning to take a turn for the better.

"Not bad eh dad?" he said softly, "Editor's training course. I'm gonna be a real editor someday."

Moments later he was standing at Jack's front door, knocking loudly.

Jack opened the door widely and smiled warmly, crystal blue eyes twinkling brightly; the welcome, as always, genuine and uninhibited. One hand gripped the gnarled wooden walking stick, the other outstretched towards Adam. Adam took his hand and shook it while the fat tabby left Jack's feet to curl herself around Adam's leg, purring softly.

"Told you she missed you" chuckled Jack, "Come on in then. We have lots to talk about. Tea? Or something a little more special?"

"Tea will do for starters thanks. It's good to see you again Jack."

"And you too Adam."

Jack locked and bolted the front door and waved his stick towards the lounge, "Take a seat then. I want to hear about everything. Everything that's happened, everything that Shera's told you or shown you. Everything."

Adam settled into the corner of Jack's ancient threadbare settee knowing that the old man always preferred the tatty armchair. Jack disappeared off to the kitchen for a few moments returning with a pot of tea and two cups.

He put them down on a small coffee table and then put his walking stick down beside the chair. Lady jumped up to settle beside him on the thick threadbare arms.

Jack reached across to the mantelpiece and rummaged around until his hand found a spectacles case. He flipped it open and took out a pair of specs which he perched on the end of his nose.

"Never seen you wear specs before Jack..."

Jack smiled. "My eyesight's not too bad for my age actually, but I do find it easier to write these days if I'm wearing them."

"Write? What are you going to write?"

"I'm taking notes of course" said Jack waving a biro and a writing pad, "You're the teacher now Adam. You've been to places I can't get to for love nor money. Now, start from the beginning...remind me about all the things you told me on the phone for a start."

"What? Things like you saving my life?"

Jack waved his hand in the air, "It was nothing. It took all of my strength and concentration just to shove that foul bull-man aside for a few moments. It was you that did what had to be done, Adam. Your own courage made you stronger. It's little wonder that you have been suffering tormented dreams all these years - that 'thing' was exuding evil. Now that you have defeated it once and for all I'm sure you'll sleep easier from now on."

"You really think so? I've been worrying about something Shera said - about the bull-man and how our destinies have been interwoven over the centuries and all that stuff. How can I be sure he's really dead? You know - like forever..."

Jack lowered his eyes, "No-one can answer that one hundred per cent. Not even Shera. What I can promise you is that if he's not dead then he's not going to bother you again for a very long time. Not in your lifetime that's for sure. Or even your next lifetime. His strength has been damaged irreparably."

"Do you know that for sure?"

"I know so - and so do you in your heart."

"But it's all thanks to you Jack. You got to me when I needed you most. Somehow you found me in that place and saved my life. When it really mattered you came through."

"Well, it just goes to show there's a bit of life left in the old dog yet" said Jack with a wink, "Anyway... you have a lot to tell me. I'll open a bottle soon and then we can drink a toast to the end of an era. And the start of a new one too."

Adam leaned back and shut his eyes as he tried to recall all the details again. Many of the experiences seemed to blend into each other. The things he had learned while meditating, were more like impressions, or feelings, rather than anything that could be explained in the physical world of tangible objects. It wasn't that the inner world was any less real - it was just as Jack had described - *'a different sort of reality'*. Most of Shera's wisdom was somehow transmitted directly from mind to mind and trying to put that knowledge into ordinary everyday words was virtually impossible. He did his best to try and explain, and Jack sat patiently and listened, scribbling away on his note paper, rarely interrupting unless to probe on a particular point of interest.

Adam surprised himself with just how much he was able to recall. When he reached the part about the fight with the bull-man - Jack removed his specs and leaned forward in his chair hanging on to every single word.

"This is truly amazing material Adam."

"Material?"

"Sorry. Sounds a bit clinical, doesn't it? Let me put it another way. Upstairs in my spare room - my study - I have shelves and shelves of books on meditation and similar subjects. I have devoted my life to studying every facet of this intriguing, captivating subject but never in my wildest dreams did I think I would be privileged to meet someone like you."

Adam blushed, "Give over Jack..."

"No. I'm absolutely serious. We all have our guardian angels Adam; every single one of us that walks on this Earth. But Shera knows that you are a very special person indeed, because you carry within your soul something unbelievably precious that is passed down through the centuries only to unique individuals. You might have lived your whole life through without even realising it. Fortunately, you have found your special key...your..."

Jack searched for the words.

"Golden Feather?" suggested Adam.

"Exactly. You have grasped the Golden Feather and followed it. Now it has led you to find not only your deepest inner self, but it has also allowed you to come to terms with the things that have held you back for so many years. You know what it is I'm talking about don't you Adam? The one thing that has bubbled away inside you for so many years, burning away at your insides, making you rebellious, arrogant, anti-everything that conforms, cynical even..."

"You're talking about the death of my father, aren't you?"

Jack nodded slowly, watching every expression that crossed Adam's face, watching the deep sorrow, the defiantly held back tears. Adam looked away self-consciously. His silence acknowledging his acceptance of everything Jack had said.

Jack leaned across and laid a hand on Adam's shoulder.

"Am I right?" He almost whispered.

Adam nodded slowly and sighed, "Yeah Jack. You're right. I've been a complete arsehole to everyone. I can see it all now."

The two men sat staring at each other in silence for a few moments. Jack poured the tea and passed a cup over to Adam waiting while the lad regained his composure.

"It's not just about the death of your father though Adam. It's more than that. The unconscious influence of your alter ego, manifested symbolically and super-physically by the bull has pulled you in different directions all your life too."

"Alter what?"

"It doesn't matter. Forget it. What you need to do now Adam is to integrate everything you have learned into a framework that you could call a 'philosophy of life' or similar - a kind of model of reality that you can live with - and live by."

"A kind of code of behaviour?"

"Yes. Exactly. But remember - and this is very important - most of us live in ignorance of the true meaning of life and we can therefore be excused when we don't always behave in accordance with the rules. But once we *know* the rules of the game, or know why we are really here, then there is no excuse. We have to either live by the cosmic rules, or consciously reject them...and the consequences of rejection can only lead to betrayal of ourselves as individuals, which in turn leads to a spiral of depression and despair. In short, it is better never to know than to know and reject."

"I think I understand what you're saying. So how can I be sure that what I've learned is the real truth?"

Jack sipped from his teacup then scratched his head. "Well, let's think. Truth...reality...call it what you will, *has* to be slightly different for each of us because of our individual karmic needs and circumstances, but these differences are essentially superficial. The important thing to grasp though is this - at the root, truth is consistent across all cultures and races. You told me that Shera showed you a lot of religious images associated with bloodshed?"

"Loads."

"Well, I think he was probably trying to show you that religious intolerance and bigotry are the opposite of the core meaning that underlies all religious experience - the search for the spiritual - which, when found, is the antithesis of violence. Meditation can only lead to the one consistent truth in the end - so you have no need to doubt the messages you are receiving. It is quite acceptable for you to interpret your experiences in a different way to say, an Australian aborigine, but ultimately you will always both come to the same conclusions. I hope this is making sense."

"Yeah. It is. And I accept what you're saying - that at some deep level there is a common link."

"That's right. So, you must try and crystallize your thoughts into some sort of rule book that you can live by. Rules for living a meaningful and fulfilled life."

Adam considered the question. What had this whole Meditation thing actually led to? What had he learned? What was his 'philosophy of life' now that Shera had led him into so many new experiences? And what did it all mean anyway?

"What is important is your own feelings" Jack continued, "The inner conviction that you understand why things are so, and not what anyone else thinks. We all have our own 'realities' and that is how it should be. My reality is not the same as yours - but if we have followed the same or similar path, it should be damn close nevertheless."

"You're right Jack...I'm comfortable with it now. At first it was very difficult but now I understand."

"Good. But this is thirsty work Adam. Now that you have finished your tea you must join me in a glass of wine. This is a time to celebrate."

Jack hobbled out of the room and was gone for a few moments returning with a two wine glasses and a dusty bottle. He opened a desk drawer and took out a rather ornate silver corkscrew and twisted it into the cork. It came out with a satisfying pop and Jack filled the two glasses passing one of them over to Adam.

"I'm not really into wine" Adam smirked, "More of a beer man actually."

"We can soon change that" laughed Jack raising the glass and chinking it against Adam's before returning to his armchair. Jack held the crystal cut glass up to the light and studied the crimson-black nectar as it swirled in the glass. He smiled at Adam. "You can't rush wine" he said softly, "It matures at its own pace and the less you interfere with it the better it matures - sometimes it can take many years to lose its effervescence of youth, but it is always worth waiting for. One day it reaches the perfect balance of depth, acidity, colour and aroma and then..." Jack took a deep mouth full and savoured the taste, "And then is the time to open the bottle and enjoy. Wasn't it Horace in the Epistles who said, 'Wine brings to light the hidden secrets of the soul'?"

Adam shrugged and shook his head in awe. Jack was extraordinarily good at finding succinct analogies that put everything into perspective. Adam sipped the wine. It tasted good. Velvety smooth but with a satisfying taste that was a revelation. He'd not really tried 'decent' wine before. Only pub plonk.

"So" continued Jack breaking his reverie, "What have you really learned from all this then Adam?"

Adam shifted his gaze to Jack's open fire where the logs sizzled and glowed, oozing warmth and sending yellow tongues of flame shimmering up the chimney like ascending angelic sprites.

He needed to choose his words carefully.

"I think the starting point was the realisation that reincarnation is an indisputable fact and not just a weird notion put forward by eastern religions - that came as quite a shock - a *big* shock. It took me some time to come to terms with it because my natural inclination is to deny the possibility completely..."

Jack nodded and signalled Adam to continue in his own time.

"So, once that key fact was established, a lot of other things started falling into place that had always puzzled me before. Not just the 'deja-vu' type of experiences but more deep-rooted stuff about our individual personalities and our interactions with other people - about the real nature and healing energy of love and about war, intolerance and other stuff. The awareness of the truth of reincarnation is mind blowing enough but it makes you wonder *why* it should be that way. You know...why should God, or nature or whatever, decide to create the concept in the first place? What's the point of it? What value is there in living many lives? And the more you delve into it the more obvious the answers become until in the end you realise it has to be that way, and anything else just wouldn't make sense - it would all be pointless. Every incarnation is a learning experience. A path from ignorance to enlightenment. A soul journey."

Jack's eyes opened wide in shock.

"My word, Adam. You really have grown up. Your level of spiritual maturity is blossoming at an incredible rate now. You have probably also come to understand that all the religions in the world have the same grain of truth at their core even if it's not obvious in their manifestation. That insight came to me quite late on in my own meditations even though I'm sure some hard-liners and radicals would dispute it. Reincarnation is a 'known' in all our hearts if not in our heads. Anyway, do go on. My pen is poised..."

Adam savoured another sip of the deep red wine.

"Meditation has also got me thinking more about things like God too. I can't quite work out why because I've never been the slightest bit interested in religion. For some reason it feels like you are closer to God when you are in deep meditation. Almost as if a physical body is a sort of barrier in the way. Does that make any sense to you?"

"It certainly does Adam and I think the way it works is like this. God - or whatever you want to call the divine centre and source of all things - can never really be described with our limited vocabulary, but all that needs to be understood is that we are all - *every single one of us* - part of God and he is part of us. This means that whenever we hurt another living person, we are really hurting ourselves *and God* simultaneously. I can't explain it any better than that - but I now know that this is the reality of things. Anyway, if God is the sum of all of us and dwells in a place - no - a *dimension* some would call 'heaven' - then it follows that in order to be a *pure* source of goodness, then all the component parts of heaven - that is us - *you and me* - have to be pure too. Quite simply heaven cannot ever be contaminated, or it would no longer *be* heaven - it *has* to remain always in a state of total purity. That's why Shera showed you all those religious images. He wanted you to understand that it is the underlying meaning of religion that is important - not the fanatical adherence to some beliefs or creeds that leads to conflict with anyone who subscribes to a different point of view. I think it was Jonathan Swift who said that 'We have just enough religion to make us hate, but not enough to make us love one another.' And, at the end of the day, only unconditional love will save mankind from ignorant and self-induced annihilation."

"Yeah, I can see that now, Jack. Anyway - you were asking me what I've learned. Well one thing is this. I reckon we all have this thing called 'free will' yeah? It's what makes us human - it means that all our life we have to make choices. Sometimes we make good choices, sometimes we make bad choices, and our lives unfold as a consequence of those choices. But the crucial point is that we are all in a constant state of learning - all through our life - and we soon learn about cause and effect and learn to take more and more responsibility for our choices and decisions. Right?"

"Right" said Jack, "And gradually we learn to distinguish between what is morally right and what is morally wrong. We learn that to kill someone is bad and to be kind to someone is good. This is an important point and goes back to what I said earlier - that in a way if you kill someone you are killing a part of yourself and part of 'God' too. If you are kind to someone then you are also being kind to yourself, God, and all the other people that are in God too. And I don't mean the Christian god either. I mean the divine source of all - whatever name you choose to give it."

"That makes sense too Jack."

"Good. So, let's now follow the argument through to its logical conclusion. Let's bring in life and death to the equation. Take a person who spends his or her whole life making the *right* choices, that is to say, he or she actively chooses not to kill or cause harm to another person but to devote themselves to kindness and consideration. Okay; by making those right choices, then everything he or she does to serve and help their fellow man - and God - enhances their own individual quest for unconditional total purity. What happens when he or she dies? Quite simply he or she - *and I don't mean the physical body* - returns to the source from which they came. Then there is a simple test, and the test goes like this - 'Is this person pure enough to be re-absorbed into the whole or does he or she have to be rejected for being less than pure?' It's a simple question with only two possible answers - 'yes' or 'no'. If the answer is 'yes' then he - *or more precisely the essence of 'he' or 'she'*- achieves the ultimate objective of life - nirvana if you like - they are reabsorbed back into God, or whatever you want to call the spiritual centre of things, and back into the place where they originated from in the first place. Now take the other guy - the one who continually makes the wrong choices - and that can mean anything from a serial killer to a petty thief - it's a question of scale. When this guy dies, he fails the purity check so he cannot be reabsorbed - so what happens then? According to my beliefs, he needs to go back and re-learn all over again - in other words he has to re-live another life - go around the cycle once again and see if he can make better choices next time around. Now the really important point is this - we store in our minds, maybe not consciously but certainly unconsciously, *everything we have ever learned in all our previous lives.* That's why hypnosis can sometimes access the hidden parts of our memory with past-life regression exercises etcetera. Anyway, the whole point is this - the average person can go through the life-death cycle many times, but each time they learn a little bit more and add to their internal wisdom store of right and wrong. It's called 'karma' by the Hindus and brings in another concept called 'karmic debt'. This means that theoretically everyone should get back to source eventually - but it takes each of us all a different amount of time.

Logically then, this means that you can get a pretty good idea of where specific individuals are on this... um... 'path' or journey, by the way they actually live their lives. Those people that spend their lives contributing positively to society and loving others will break their life-death cycle much earlier than those with negative lifestyles. It's about learning the deep and true meanings of words like 'gratitude' and 'forgiveness'. It's about an inner 'knowing' that expressing gratitude for all the blessings life has bestowed upon you - and unconditionally forgiving everyone who has upset or wronged you - is liberating you from any karmic debt and setting you up for full enlightenment.

In a way, it's very close to Buddhist thinking - the notion that life is 'suffering' and nirvana - the ultimate goal - is to be 'one with God' - the source of everything. In other words, the goal is quite simply to break the cycle. Ultimate death is to go back to the beginning, to the root. To source.

So - back to your original point about the meaning of life. Okay, this is how I see it - the meaning of life is essentially quite simple. We are all born out of a pure and totally integrated starting point - the source of life, heaven or God - the terms are interchangeable - and our quest is to return to the same source. It doesn't matter at all what religion you call yourself or what cultural standards you follow. Nature has designed our learning environment on planet Earth and has given us the intelligence and free will to choose our own path - from birth to death. If we take actions that contribute to the well-being of the whole, that is humanity at large, then we make progress quickly. Alternatively, if we take actions that cause harm to the well-being of the whole then we progress slowly - probably hundreds of lifetimes - each one a small step closer. However, the ultimate goal for all individuals is the same.

That's the point of life and I'm totally convinced of it. If you think it through, it all falls into place - everything - *everything* - suddenly makes sense. Do you know Adam, all my life I've been really puzzled by certain things. Things like, why people like you and I should have these nightmares about bulls and suchlike and why we feel certain affinities with people or places. Now I realise that these are all subliminal connections to things that we have experienced in our previous lives."

Adam nodded slowly. The soporific effects of good wine, a warm fire and Jack's enthused monologue were making him deliciously relaxed but equally interested enough to want to hear every word.

Jack had now stood up and was limping up and down the lounge like an animated University lecturer. "...And because Adam, in your own previous life you had developed the gift of being able to slip into the meditative state much easier than most people, it made you a very special person to those around you at the time. Your natural gift would not have been shrugged off like it is today. In the past you would have commanded a lot of respect receiving much reverence as someone who could tread the path between two worlds, a soothsayer, mystic, oracle or whatever you might want to call it."

"They called me 'The Stone' according to Shera. It's taken me a long time to discover my roots."

"The upright 'stone' or megalith is the time-honoured symbol of strength, resilience and unshakeable truth in some ancient Indian mythologies" nodded Jack, "And even a small child that carries spiritual wisdom in his heart can be likened to a rock that stands firm against all that is wrong in the world. Did you know that most people live through their whole lifetime without ever discovering their true past? You are only twenty Adam. What you have achieved in just this last twelve months is staggering."

"You think so?"

"Indisputably."

"So - where to from here then Jack? What do I do with all this stuff in my head?"

Jack reached down to stroke Lady who had appeared around the door frame.

"As I said to you before Adam. I'm only your first guide. I can't take you any further than this. You have found your own inner guide now, and he is the one you need to ask about what to do with 'all this stuff'. Think about what you have just told me though. Now that you know who you really are what do you think you should do about it...*in this life?*"

Adam sat in silence for a few moments.

"I dunno Jack. I still don't have all the answers."

"And you never will have. That's how it should be. What you have learned though is how to ask the right questions. That's what is important."

Adam let Jack's words sink in.

"In that case I think what I should do is to help others along the same path, I guess. Help them to find their way on their own spiritual journey. Just like dad told me to."

Jack raised his glass high into the air with one hand and slapped the other down onto the surface of his desk raising a small flurry of dust particles.

"I'll drink to that Adam. Just grant me one favour though..."

"What's that?"

"Pop by once in a while, and let an old soldier know how you're getting on eh? Keep an old chap happy."

Adam smiled. "Sure Jack."

Adam held out his hand and Jack shook it warmly.
"Look after yourself Adam. You are very special."
"You too Jack."
They stared at each other for a few moments, simultaneously draining their glasses and then both started to laugh spontaneously.

Adam waited calmly for Shera to appear.

This time it had been virtually instantaneous. The transition into the correct mental state of relaxed but focused calm, the traversing of the cloudscapes of the empty place and then slipping through the veil into deepest awe-inspiring blueness. Knowing instinctively that Shera would be there waiting, as always. Each time it became easier and easier, but never boring. No - never ever boring. It never could be.

'Hello Adam.'

'Hi Shera. It's good to see you. I wanted to say thank you. Thank you for taking me to face up to the bull-man - I know now that you were right. It was something inside of me that had to be resolved.'

'I wish I could have done more than just lead you to where he was waiting. My own destiny prevented me from getting involved in any other way. Thanks to you Adam he is defeated now. You have no idea how much that means for us both.'

'Well, I guess it means no more bull nightmares for starters" said Adam, "And I can get on with my life now, without all that inner turmoil inside my head. There were times I really thought I was going crazy. There's one thing I need to ask you though – something that doesn't make sense.'

'You may ask.'

'It's about the bull-man Shera. You said he's been defeated. Does that mean he really is dead? Remember the time he attacked me at night and ran me through? I really thought I was dead but next morning I woke up normally because it was not a physical event. It was all inside my head. Does that mean that when I killed the bull-man in the cave that he is not really dead either?'

'I can understand your confusion Adam and I will try to explain to the best of my ability – but forgive me if the explanation is difficult to grasp. Do you remember what the bull-man said to you as you stood face to face over the fire in the cavern?'

Adam cast his mind back to the incident and frowned in concentration. 'Something about not being able to co-exist without one of us being stronger and one weaker...'

'Exactly correct. The bull-man was acknowledging that since time immemorial you and he have co-existed as closely as night and day. In your terms you are both two sides of the same coin and always will be. All of us have a light and a dark side – it is part of natural law – but as I have said before Adam, you are very special, and your positive aspects are mirrored by the negative aspects of the entity that manifests itself in your mind as the bull-man.'

'But is he dead? I still don't get it'

'He is defeated to the extent that his power has been diminished to a fraction of what it was. He will not bother you again for the rest of your lifetime and you have nothing more to fear from him. It is just as Jack said. That night when he attacked you was through your dreams only - and not in the meditative realms. That is why you came to no physical harm. He was strong enough to manipulate your dreams but not strong enough to attack you in the meditative realm. He was saving all his mental energies for the showdown in the cave. Because you

ultimately defeated him in a specific layer of the inner realms he will not recover for hundreds of your years.'

'So - he's not actually dead then?'

'Dead is not a word that makes sense in this context Adam. You and he are bound together for always, but you have nothing further to fear from him. As I said before - he is defeated. You still have much to learn.'

'I realise that now Shera. I'm just relieved that it's over. There's another thing I need to thank you for too. And that's for taking me to see my dad.'

'I am glad you met him at last. I think it was right for both of you to meet. For many people it is not the right thing to do but I knew you would benefit from meeting your father again. He is a good man.'

Adam mentally noted Shera's use of the present tense. In this place it made sense. It made Adam smile.

'I needed to meet him. There was a big hole left in my life when he died. Now that I've met him again, I can still miss him but not in the same way as I used to. I feel more...'

'...At peace with yourself.'

'Yeah' said Adam, 'You're right. At peace.'

'You have come a long way since we first met Adam. You have learned much that you can take back with you.

Not so long ago you might have misused the skills you have learned. But now I think you will apply them more wisely.'

'I'll do my best Shera. I can promise you that. But I still feel that this is only the beginning of the journey. Jack led me to you, and you have led me into new worlds that I never even dreamed of. There must be so many more things to learn in this place.'

'You are right Adam. Follow me.'

Shera turned sideways and moved off into the shimmering liquid blue and Adam followed. Moments later the blueness parted in the middle like huge satin curtains and Adam seemed to be standing on a mountain ledge looking down upon a vast landscape that stretched away into the hazy distance. Shera stood beside him, and they admired the beauty of the pastoral wonderland in awe. Rolling green hills and sparkling silver streams, clumps of leafy woodland buzzing with life and dazzling blue lakes. Adam was enchanted.

'It's beautiful Shera, what is this place?'

'The place has no name because everyone sees a different place. It is somewhere you have created in your own mind'.

'It's not real?'

'Oh, it's real enough Adam. It's a whole new world waiting to be explored and it will take you a lifetime to explore it, maybe many lifetimes. Every path will take you to a new destination and every destination will bring you new experiences. In this landscape past, present and future are irrelevant because they are all seamlessly connected as you will one day discover. You will meet people here who have moved on from their earthly lives, people who are yet to be born and others who exist only in this place. This place has no beginning, no end and no limitations. It is everywhere - and it is nowhere. Don't you see that every single man or woman has the inherent potential within them to find this special place just as you have done? Yes, it takes a little effort and a little concentration, and few have the ability to achieve it as quickly as you. It takes some patience. Sadly, many who do possess the ability are not even aware of it and even less aware of those who watch over them as I have watched over you. There are no barriers in life that deep meditation cannot penetrate. Ultimate freedom lies within. You know that now.'

'Yeah Shera, I know that now.'

'And now it's up to you Adam. Now that I have shown you this place you will always be able to find it again. It

*is part of my own destiny that I should bring you here
and show you the path that will take you on the next part
of your soul's journey. You are, I think, nearly ready to
embark on this voyage of discovery.'*

'I think so too Shera. But not today. I need to make
some changes in my material life first. Clear away
some debris that's been distracting me for too long.
Sort out some unfinished business. Make a few
apologies. Start afresh.'

'I understand.'

'Can I go back now?'

'As you wish.'

'Oh...before I go there's something else, I've been
meaning to ask you.'

'You know you can ask me anything.'

'The Indian boy...what was his name?'

Shera was unusually silent for a few moments.
Adam sensed the question was causing some
difficulty. Eventually the answer came.

'His name was Shera.'

Adam frowned. His mind raced with the
implications of Shera's revelation. 'I don't get it...the
boy and I are one and the same...and I'm still alive...
but you...you're...? How can that be? That's like
saying you and I are one and the same too...as well as
the bull-man. Are you saying we are all connected?
Me, you, the bull-man? The Indian boy? We are all
one?'

Shera's silence spoke volumes. For the first time he
reached out and laid a hand on Adam's shoulder. A
warm tingling sensation emanated through Adam's
entire body. After a few moments Shera spoke again.

*'One day you will understand Adam. There is plenty of
time to understand these things.'*

The sylvian and arcadian landscape faded and
blueness returned in an instant. Adam breathed
deeply a few times then slowly opened his eyes and

stretched his limbs. The bedroom was in darkness as usual, the small, scented candle still burning in its holder, the soft tick of the bedside alarm the only sound breaking the silence. It was 10.32pm.

He stood up a little shakily and moved towards the door, something making him stop and look in the mirror once again.

This time there were no shadows. Nothing furtively hiding behind his own brown eyes. The bull-man really was gone.

Adam stared at his own reflection for a few moments, as though recognizing his own features for the first time. He looked deep into his own eyes as though searching for something elusive and they stared back at him. Two dark liquid pools that he had known since childhood. Or thought he had.

And today they looked much the same as they always had done, just maybe a little clearer, a little brighter. He turned away self-consciously and opened the bedroom door. Mum would be home from the bingo in a minute. He needed to see her. Give her a hug. Let her know how much she really meant to him.

And then tell her that tomorrow life was going to be very different because he'd decided it was time to forgive dad for dying when he was just ten years old.

It was time to move on.

Carol Sinclair knew something wasn't right as soon as she opened her eyes on that particular Saturday morning.

Adam, who never surfaced from the depths of his bedcovers until midday at weekends, was standing beside her bed with a cup of steaming coffee and a slice of toast. Even more startling was the fact he was showered, fresh-faced and wearing a new pair of jeans and smart casual white shirt. She had glanced over at the alarm clock just to check that she wasn't going mad and then sat up in bed, propping up the pillows and frowning at her son quizzically.

"Am I still dreaming or are you sickening for something?" she asked amidst a long yawn.

Adam handed her the coffee and put the plate down on the bedside cabinet.

"Neither" he said with a smile, "Morning mother! Thought you'd like a surprise - that's all."

"Hmm" she said suspiciously, "And what are you wearing? I've never seen those clothes before. The fleas won't like them you know. They much prefer the rarely washed and stained variety that you usually wear."

Adam ignored the sarcasm. "I bought them in town yesterday" said Adam doing a twirl, "So what do you think?"

Carol rubbed the sleep out of her eyes and frowned again, "Adam you never buy new clothes...you only like jeans with more patches and holes than material."

"Yeah...well...I decided to get a new pair. I've been saving up some money."

"There, I knew it...you are sickening for something."

That was only the start. Later that morning, while Adam was downstairs - (whistling to himself for chrissake!) she peeked into his bedroom for any lurking dirty washing and did a double take. The room had been transformed as though a fairy with a magic wand had cast a spell to put everything in its proper place. The bed was made, the bookshelves dusted with books neatly stacked, the floor cleared of jumbled records and dirty washing. In fact, the whole space had been converted into something closely resembling a bedroom.

Over lunch, still in a state of shock, Carol was amazed to find Adam communicating in English rather than in the usual series of grunts she'd become accustomed to. Talking about the latest news stories he was writing at the Gazette and ideas for the future. Most surprising of all, though, was when he casually suggested that it was about time that they (meaning the two of them) had a holiday. A few days break away from the humdrum. Somewhere hot and sunny. Maybe that cottage in Cornwall that dad had taken them to during an idyllic summer so long ago.

Carol had listened to all this in speechless silence. In some ways Adam was right. They had not been on holiday together for years and maybe a short break would do them both good. God knows she needed a break herself. It would be good to get away with her one son. Get to know him again like she did when he was small.

"Let's do it" she'd said, "I'll pick up some holiday brochures next time I'm shopping."

"Great" said Adam, "I'll pay my own way."

"Great" echoed his mother, "You're an editor now, so can I get that in writing?"

Later that afternoon, around 5pm when weekend TV was at its lowest ebb, Carol had wandered into the kitchen to make a sandwich and a cup of tea to find Adam scrabbling around in the 'odds and ends' cupboard and fishing out a pair of binoculars belonging to her late husband.

"It's a bit soon to start packing already" she observed.

Adam laughed "No. I'm not packing. It's for tomorrow."

"Oh yes. What's happening tomorrow then?"

Adam rubbed the dust off the lenses with a piece of tissue from the box on the kitchen worktop.

"I'm catching the bus over to Greenwood hill" he replied.

"Whatever for?" Carol asked suspiciously - Adam hadn't been out to the hill for ages although she knew the place was somehow rather special to him. Well, her too, come to think of it. They'd picnicked there as a family when Adam was young. Enjoying the magnificent scenery. The chalk cliffs, rolling green hills and invigorating sea breezes.

Adam and his dad had flown colourful kites from the top of the hill - and in the Winter they'd sledged down the gentle slopes together falling in a heap into the virgin snowdrifts in the hollows. Back in those days when...

Adam's voice bought her back to the moment.

"Because there's bound to be an amazing late afternoon sunset. I just need to get out in the fresh air for a while. It's a good place to sit and think. Watch the boats out at sea. You know..."

Carol stood with hands on hips, one eyebrow raised. "There's definitely something strange about you today, Adam. All that meditation hasn't fried your brain, has it? If it has, then do me a favour, eh? Go do some more! I've never seen your room so tidy."

Adam rolled his eyes. "I'm taking a break from meditating" he said seriously, "I've been overdoing it as you've probably noticed. I'll go back it soon... but right now I'm taking a holiday from that too."

"Well, that's probably not a bad thing" Carol concurred, "I was worried it might be an obsession the way you've been lately."

"You're right mum. It was an obsession."

"So - what's changed?"

Adam smiled and looked into his mother's eyes.

"Me" he said simply.

Adam climbed the last few feet to the summit of the grassy knoll known as Greenwood Hill, then flopped down to catch his breath and gaze out across the cliff tops of the South Downs and out to sea. The sea breeze ruffled his hair and caused his new white shirt to billow a little. He didn't care. It felt good. The whole world felt good today as though the fresh sea air was blowing away lots of old cobwebs and old long-forgotten things. Today was a day for throwing out the past and welcoming in whatever tomorrow had to bring. Although Adam had sat on this same hill many times before, today it somehow felt and looked different. The images were sharper, the smells of the sea were much more acute and the calls of the gulls much clearer. Everything was more - *vibrant?* Yeah, that was the word he was looking for.

He pulled up a blade of grass and held it between his teeth while watching the sun melting to molten gold on the horizon. Another hour and it would be gone. He could wait an hour. It would be worth it. He picked up dad's old binoculars and scoured the horizon for any old fishing boats.

As usual the boats were there. Fishing boats that had ploughed these waters for hundreds of years. Grandfathers, fathers and sons, born into sea-faring traditions and customs had been working these waters and riding the waves beneath the towering white cliffs and old smugglers bays day after day, year after year. Old boats and new boats – all chasing the ever-elusive cod, mackerel, herring, pollack and many other fruits of the sea. Fish stocks were dwindling nowadays of course, and the abundant catches of yesteryear were now mere folk-stories. The life of a fisherman was hard, and the French trawlers were constantly encroaching on British waters engendering battles both on the sea and in the courts. The ultimate losers though, would be the fish. One day, sometime in the future, the great traditional dish of 'fish and chips' would be consigned to history when the sea was barren due to the relentless quest for unbridled profit.

But today, Adam decided, was not the day to dwell on life's issues and problems. Today felt like a new dawn and the beginning of a new era. There was a new clarity in his thinking, a deeper understanding of the underlying cycles of time and space and a deeper understanding of what 'life' really means in the broadest of contexts. There was a warm feeling permeating through Adam's body as sensual as a perfect scented bath. Adam instinctively sensed feelings of gratitude and forgiveness welling up from somewhere deep in his heart – just as Jack had predicted so definitively. Gratitude for what he had experienced and learned over the last incredible twelve months of his life, along with a strange but profound sense of forgiveness. For the first time in his life, Adam was suddenly free of the feeling of resentment he had always felt about his dad departing from his life when he was ten years old. Dad was now fully forgiven. He also forgave Marie for walking away from him after the Reading incident and his mates for criticising his increasingly strange behaviour. He forgave all of them – as well as all the annoying people he had been employed by and who had riled him in one way or another.

But the hardest thing was learning to forgive himself for being such a stupid arsehole for so many years and driving his poor mother to despair. Adam knew that until he could find the courage within to genuinely forgive himself for all his wrongdoings those memories would continue to haunt him. So today was the day he needed to mentally review and cast off all those non-productive old memories. He decided to let each negative memory manifest itself, right here and now, as translucent 'thought balloons' that could be released up into the sky, over the white cliffs of Greenwood Hill and then lost over the horizon forever.

He lay back on the grass, stared up at the sky and listened to the call of the gulls and the sound of waves crashing on the shore. Something in the universe was shifting - and, in small, almost imperceptible ways - he was shifting with it.

Carol had been running a bath when the phone rang, and she only just heard it. She switched off the taps and walked down the stairs picking up the receiver from the small table in the hallway.

"Mrs Sinclair? Carol?"

"Yes?"

"It's Marie Cunningham"

"Marie! Hi, how are you? What's that? No - he's not here at the moment. Actually, he's been acting very strange lately - have you noticed?"

"Well to be honest yes I have" said Marie, "He's changed a lot recently. More like the Adam I used to know. He's doing well at his new job I hear".

"Yes. He's actually enjoying going to work for the first time in his life. Maybe he's finally growing up and becoming more mature".

"Well, I hope he doesn't mature too quickly" said Marie, "I like his spirit. Anyway, I wanted to see him. Do you know where I might find him?"

"Oh Yes" said Carol, "I can tell you exactly where to find him..."

The Anchor public house was full to bursting point. A teenage rock band had been booked and all the regulars were now joined by local rock aficionados hoping to hear some loud raucous noise whether doled out by semi-pro musicians or fumbling wannabees. As it turned out the 'Fumbling Wannabees' might have been a good name for the young band who were strong on attitude and aggressive screaming lyrics, but sadly weak on musicianship. No matter. The crowd were out for a good time regardless of the competence of "The Forgotten", whose prophetic choice of name would ensure their short duration and subsequent demise.

Steve, Danny and Mick were at their usual table, but hemmed in by the throng of newcomers swinging their long hair to the blast of major chords that were shaking the room and making conversation barely audible.

"You still working at the scrap yard?" yelled Steve into Mick's ear.

"Nah mate" said Mick, shaking his head, "Got the boot, didn't I? I'm signin' on t'morrer"

"Don't blame you..." said Steve, "I'm still signed on. Might as well. Bugger all jobs in this place".

"Anyone seen Adam recently?" asked Danny.

The three lads exchanged glances.

"I saw him in town across the street a few days ago" said Steve, "He was going into the Gazette office all dressed up in a nice white shirt and tie and a smart suit."

"I dunno what 'is problem is", said Mick, "Not much of a life is it? Working in a bloody boring office when he could have been having some fun with his mates. Normally he'd be here heckling the band..."

"Well, dat sounds loike the old Adam we used to know" observed Danny, "Before he abandoned his mates and started wearin' a fockin' suit".

They all gave assenting nods.

"It's a shame" said Steve, "Adam has always been my best mate and I miss his company. Something's got into him, and I don't know what it is. It's not girls and I don't even think it's his new job. Nah - it's something else..."

"Well sod 'im I say" said Mick, "He's missing out on a few pints with his mates and a bloody good band. It's his loss".

Steve raised a quizzical eyebrow. "Good band?" he echoed, "You must be fuckin' tone deaf Mick. The band are shite".

They all laughed.

"It's my round" said Mick, "Can anyone lend me a tenner?"

"Adam?"

The voice startled him. He turned around, shocked that someone might know his name out here in the fields.

"Marie!"

"Hello Adam. Guess I was the last person you expected to see."

Adam stared back gawping like a fish, "What are you doing here?"

"I came to find you."

"How did you get here? I mean how did you know where I was?"

She shrugged. "It wasn't that difficult. I just phoned Carol and she told me where to find you. So...how are you?"

"I'm fine."

They stared at each other for a few moments before he looked away feeling awkward.

Marie sat down and looked out over the sea. "It's a beautiful view from here...do you remember when we used to...? ...Well anyway...what are you doing up here all alone?"

"Nothing - Just sitting and thinking. Watching the sun going down."

"Mind if I join you?"

"No - of course not... I'm just surprised to see you. In fact, you're right. You were the last person I expected to see."

Marie looked Adam straight in the eyes "Why? It wasn't that long ago I came over for dinner."

Adam stared at her and smiled "Sorry Marie. It's just that a lot has happened since then. I'll tell you about it sometime."

"Why not now?"

"Because..."

"Because I'm a woman and I cramp your style?"

"Er, yeah. Exactly."

"Adam" she said sweetly, "Sometimes you can be the most infuriating man on this planet d'you know that?"

"Yeah - I do know that. To be honest I'm amazed that you put up with me. I thought at one time you never wanted to see me ever again."

Marie smiled. "That's true. Must have changed my mind then. It's a woman's prerogative you know."

Adam removed the grass from his mouth "So why did you come to find me then?"

Marie sat down beside him and followed his gaze out to sea. She sighed deeply "I came to find out if all the rumours I've heard are true..."

"Oh yeah? What sort of rumours?"

"Rumours that mister bad guy had turned into mister not-so-bad-guy."

"That's bullshit."

"I see...so you're still doing drugs then?"

"Nope. Kicked the drugs. And the cigarettes. Don't need 'em anymore."

Marie nodded knowingly.

"Beer?"

"Give me a break..."

"Hmm, well that's good to hear anyway. So - tell me...what does Adam Sinclair do with himself these days? Still hanging around sleazy bars with the same old sleazy mates?"

"Yeah. Sometimes..."

Marie looked searchingly into Adam's eyes. His discomfort was not just down to the scrutiny. There were other feelings too. Feelings he had forgotten about.

"You've changed Adam."

"Yeah? What's that supposed to mean?"

Marie tossed back her hair and turned her head to look out to sea.

"I think you know what I mean. Your mates have noticed it too. You've been withdrawn and unsociable - 'on another planet' as Danny put it. Where have you been Adam - if you don't mind me asking?"

He smiled. "You always were a nosey cow."

Marie poked her tongue out and Adam laughed. "It's good to see you again Marie. I've missed you."

"I've missed you too - you old sod. God knows why though - you're still a pain in the arse."

"I know. Always was. Probably always will be. So... as you have made such an effort to track me down, I guess I owe you..."

"Yes - you do owe me. An apology, a diamond necklace, a weekend in the Seychelles. Yeah, any of those will do fine..."

Adam laughed out loud.

"Well maybe I could take you out to a film or something?"

"Hm...I think I'll go for the 'or something.'"

She looked gorgeous. Adam had forgotten how much he used to...

Used to...?

He reached over and gently pulled her head towards him, kissing her softly on the lips. She responded by moving closer to him and pushed him back onto the grass, so she could lie across him and kiss him more fully. When she drew back with a smile, he lay there catching his breath, heart pounding.

"Marie...I..."

Marie put a finger to his lips.

"Don't say anything Adam. This doesn't need words. I love you. That's all that matters right now. Maybe both of us need a new beginning huh?"

Adam nodded. It was time to tell her the truth. "I love you too Marie. I always have done. You know that."

She blushed deeply "Adam can I ask you something?"

"Of course. Anything."

"Will you teach me to meditate?"

He was taken aback by the question and for just a small moment wondered if she was mocking him. But one look deep into her liquid green eyes found only total sincerity. It took a moment for him to find his voice. "Yeah. Yeah. I can show you...if that's what you really want."

She nodded "That's what I really want. Promise?"

"Promise."

Tears were burning behind his eyes. Burning partly because he now realised what he had so nearly lost, and partly because he suddenly understood something that had been bugging him for a long time.

Behind words there is energy and behind that energy are meanings. Behind meanings there is truth. Behind truth there is love. And love manifests itself in shades of deepest blue. He knew that now.

And, at the end of the day, he reflected, that is all that really matters.

On the horizon the hazy twilight break between sea and sky was no longer visible. Blue cloudless sky met deep blue ocean seamlessly, merging indistinguishably into a single wholeness.

About the Author

After a successful career as a Senior Executive in the Finance industry Joe then enjoyed a second career as an 'International Management Consultant' working all over the world at Board level in some of the world's leading Companies solving corporate problems throughout the eighties and nineties.

From 2014 - 2018 Joe worked closely with eminent philosopher, scientist and writer Ervin Laszlo as the Managing Director of the 'Laszlo Institute of New Paradigm Research' (L-INPR) in Tuscany, Italy - a conference centre and think-tank which brings together world experts in the fields of holistic and alternative health, consciousness, spirituality, immortality, sustainability and world issues.

In 2016 Joe was invited to join 'Eternea', the US based organisation founded by the 6th man-on-the-moon, Astronaut Edgar Mitchell. Eternea is an organisation focused on research into Consciousness, Reincarnation, Immortality and World Issues.

In 2018 Joe was also appointed UK Director of the "World Sustainable Development Forum" (WSDF-UK) which is focused on meeting the targets of the 'Sustainable Development Goals' (SDG's) and the 'Paris Agreement' on climate change. He also works as an Ambassador for the 'Earth Protectors' organisation.

Joe is an established professional Writer and Conference Speaker with over 3000 articles published to date in leading magazines as well as the author and editor of a number of books. In addition to his work as a Spiritual Mentor he is also a fully qualified Life Coach, Hypnotherapist and Energy Healer.

Printed in Great Britain
by Amazon